DANGEROUS DESIRE . . .

"Before you say a word," he told her, *"I want another kiss."*

There wasn't time for her to protest, nor did she want to. She again felt passion stir within her as their lips touched. She'd never known the thrill of genuine love, the hungry desire to kiss and be kissed, the need to love and be loved. His hands were moving in a slow, caressing fashion down her back, then back to her shoulders. He pulled her close to him, in a powerful embrace . . .

Leisure Books by Dorothy Daniels

NICOLA

MONTE CARLO

Dorothy Daniels

LEISURE BOOKS   NEW YORK CITY

A LEISURE BOOK

Published by

Nordon Publications, Inc.
Two Park Avenue
New York, N.Y. 10016

One

Lydia Bradley had no idea where they were going for dinner until the hansom pulled up in front of the six-story building at Fifth Avenue and 44th Street. At first she thought, somewhat wildly, that they might be headed for Sherry's, just across the street, but found her escort instead indicating the imposing structure that houses Delmonico's, the greatest and most elegant of New York City restaurants.

Bryant Drury had warned her to dress well, so she had worn her best—and only—dinner gown, bought back home in Lyttonville. It was a year old, but still in the fashion of 1891—a sea-foam green silk trimmed with white lace and large clusters of pink roses that were held in place by satin bows. A costly extravagance at the time, since she had no idea when she purchased it if she'd ever have an opportunity to wear it. She had further indulged herself with green silk gloves, stockings and matching satin slippers. When she regarded herself in the mirror before Drury called for her, she no longer had regrets about her prodigality. She smiled saucily at her reflection, noting that her fair skin shone with a faint glow of excitement, brought on by the thought of her evening out with a dashing newspaper man.

Drury's sophisticated dress and the cosmopolitan manner in which he helped her down from the cab, paid the driver and took her arm to lead her into the ornate interior of this famous restaurant made Lydia feel less than secure. But she held her head high, remembering she was Paul Bradley's daughter.

5

"Mr. Drury, sir!" The maitre d' rushed forward solic- itously, hovering over him, and Lydia was amused to see that because he was well-known, the management consid- ered it important to lavish attention on this gentleman whose presence in the restaurant gave it added prestige. While he and Drury discussed the champagne vintage, she let her eyes drift casually about the room, scanning the splendidly dressed, poised clientele, recognizing several from having seen them before at charitable or political gatherings in the last six months. There was a senator, a well-known legis- lator, and a judge now under indictment for accepting a bribe but looking as imperious as if he were sitting on the bench. There were beautiful women, too, among them one whom Drury later pointed out to be a noted, high-priced courtesan, sitting with a prominent attorney. For a twenty- year-old cub reporter, it was a world of glamour, fame and a hundred stories.

Drury finally selected a champagne, and turned his at- tention fully to Lydia. He had chosen to sit opposite her at a small table—almost too small, in Lydia's opinion, since it was well concealed by palms and afforded an intimacy she felt was not in keeping with the evening. It did not occur to her that it had been prearranged with the maitre d'. If it had, she would have been on her guard. Now she was only aware that she was following her father's advice not to look askance at someone who might be important to her career, as long as everything was proper and above board. Bryant Drury was a famous reporter who worked on the same newspaper as she and she was well aware that he could help her attain a measure of success she might oth- erwise have to strive years for. The fact that he was also a handsome and apparently charming man was furthermore not lost on her, and she was flattered he had invited her to dinner.

She told herself that the choice of such a private table held no ulterior meaning. At any rate, she had a view of other diners and they, if they wished to crane their necks a little, could observe her. She smiled wryly at herself. Did she really flatter herself that any of them would bother in a room filled with the wealthy, the famous and the notorious? Her resolve to make the most of the evening, to enjoy it to the full, again surfaced. A merry smile lit up her face as she glanced covertly at her escort.

Drury was a globe-trotting reporter, she knew, with entry to palaces, embassies, the far-flung homes of the great and the rich of the world. His stories were always exciting if somewhat flamboyant, a fact that only seemed to increase his popularity.

She decided that he looked the part of an adventurous man, for he was tall and slim, as handsome and clean-shaven as a Gibson man, with the masculinity that clever artist bestowed on his drawings. There was a suave air about Bryant Drury that matched his good looks. But Lydia wasn't sure she could trust him, even though she all but worshipped him for his skill and success in his profession, as his dark eyes, deep-set, seemed to probe hers too deeply now that they were seated opposite one another. She felt herself draw back with a slight inward shock, then chided herself for momentarily imagining that he expected repayment for having given her an evening in his company. Lydia forced the thought from her mind and returned the smile he was bestowing on her.

"I've already said you look charming," he said. "I withdraw the compliment." He paused, then drawled, "Exquisite would be a better word. You're the most beautiful young lady in this room."

Lydia raised an eyebrow, unconsciously arch. "Hardly that, Mr. Drury, but thank you for the gracious compliment."

"It's the truth," he replied easily. "All eyes turned as you entered. I hope you approve of my choice." He indicated the richly furnished setting.

"Indeed I do," she replied. "New York is still a whole new world for me. And I'm not yet accustomed to being a part of high society."

"Surely it's not the first time you've been among people

such as these," he disputed. "And I'd hardly term many of them high society. Quite the opposite, my dear."

She laughed. "I suspected as much. But it is the first time I've been fêted so grandly. Things are naturally on a much smaller scale back home. I've attended some large affairs here, but only in my role as reporter—and a minor one at that."

Drury paused as the waiter arrived with the champagne and filled their crystal goblets, placing the bottle in a silver cooler near at hand. His eyes studied her all the while, disconcerting her almost to the point of causing her to blush. She was glad when he finally spoke. "Not minor for long, Lydia. I predict great things for you."

"Do you mean that, Mr. Drury?" She was touched by his encouragement.

"Yes. When it comes to my work or any discussion of it as it concerns me or my opinion of another reporter, I'm always completely honest."

He waited for her comment. When she made none, he continued in smooth, velvety tones. "I predict you're going to become one of the best female reporters in the business. The opportunity you have is unequaled, you know. There've only been a few females in this line. Until I met you, I wasn't even sure there should be, but you've convinced me that you have the talent, the kind of inquisitiveness needed for the job, and the nerve. That's rare in a woman."

"Thank you again, Mr. Drury," Lydia said, somewhat taken aback at the condescension she sensed underlay his last words. But her dryness was lost on him.

"You also have something else perhaps more important going for you," he went on. "Your beauty. Your fair skin, blond hair and blue eyes will take you a long way. You have tremendous appeal, Lydia Bradley. Your mother must be quite lovely."

"She was," Lydia corrected him. "She died two years ago, six months after my father passed away."

"I'm sorry." Drury looked down at his drink, his voice sincere. "But it does give you free rein, Lydia, with responsibilities only to yourself. Why not take advantage of that? Perhaps you consider that cruel—my suggestion that you take advantage of the death of your parents?"

"No. I think I understand, Mr. Drury. You're simply suggesting I pursue my ambitions wholeheartedly now."

"For God's sake, make it *Bryant*. I thought we were friends."

Lydia looked at him directly, trying to read the character of this man. He seemed genuine, but. . . . She decided to keep the conversation to business. "You've helped me more than you realize by bringing me here where I'll gain confidence among important people . . . Bryant."

"That's the general idea. Clever of you to have grasped my purpose."

"I hope one day I'll be as clever as you," she said smoothly. "When will you be off on another of your trips abroad?"

Drury leaned back in his chair and sipped his champagne before speaking. "I don't know. Things are fairly quiet all over the world these days. Not a single good war going on, though there may be several brewing. I intend to investigate that soon." He smiled slowly. "Meanwhile you and I should make the best of our friendship. I intend to see you often, if you don't object."

Lydia answered with that smile her father had called her Mona Lisa look. It came unbidden to her face when her thoughts were in a quandary.

Suddenly Drury reached for her hand and held it between his own. Once again, his eyes looked deeply into hers and once again she felt a certainty that he would not expect the evening to end with dinner. She was about to withdraw her hand when the waiter arrived to take their order. Bryant freed her and sat back.

After more champagne was poured, he ordered a chateaubriand rare, as Lydia had given him permission to order for both of them. She was pleased at his choice. They drank the champagne, enjoying Oysters Rockefeller for an appetizer, which seemed like an entire meal to her, although she soon realized each course was served in leisurely fashion unless otherwise requested.

The beef, surrounded by a half dozen attractively arranged vegetables, arrived and was carved in style. Lydia would have preferred a lighter entrée at this point, but bravely made her way through most of it, finding it delicious. After they'd finished dinner and sipped Napoleon brandy while Drury smoked an expensive cigar, his leg touched hers lightly. Quite by accident, she thought, until a repetition made it evident that it was intentional.

Though she made no verbal protest, her features could not help but reveal her displeasure. He desisted at once, a slightly amused look on his face, but gave no other evidence she had scorned his attempt to make the dinner a more intimate affair. Lydia found herself blushing, feeling more naive than she had yet felt in New York.

"Tell me, Lydia, do you live alone?" Drury asked after a long silence, his manner one of friendly interest only.

"Yes. I don't have any family here . . . and not many friends yet."

"On your salary it must be a challenge to make ends meet."

"It is, but I'm resourceful. One day it won't be as difficult, for I intend to become highly-paid and well-known. I'm afraid I'm terribly ambitious," she laughed.

"Of course you are. In the meantime—and please don't be offended by this—you could—ah—come and live at my place. It's very large and comfortable . . . a hotel suite. No housework. . . ."

She looked at him in astonishment over the rim of the brandy inhaler. It took her a moment to be certain she had heard him correctly. Then she carefully set down her glass as she addressed him. "Mr. Drury, I thought you were paying me this much attention because you believed I had the qualifications to make a fine reporter. I see now that your intentions were quite contrary to this. I no longer desire even the smallest shred of your time or advice. Nor do I wish you to take me home." She had stood up abruptly, and spoke louder than she intended, so that several couples turned to listen.

"Oh, come now, Lydia, do sit down." Drury's face had slightly reddened. "I was only testing you to see how far you'd go with your very evident ambitions. I was about to tell you that if you ever accepted an offer like the one I made, you wouldn't last as a reporter."

Her smile was contemptuous as she remained standing. "Mr. Drury, you're a persuasive man and I can see why you've become successful. You're also a fraud."

He leaned back and laughed. "Lydia, can you blame me for trying? I've helped countless girls in my time all over the world. You're the only one who ever spurned me. Congratulations."

She didn't join him in laughter. "I don't consider it a distinction. I shall no doubt meet many other lotharios in my work, but at least I'll be ready for them. A pity you wasted the evening. Such an *expensive* evening."

"Sit down." Drury's sharp tone startled her more than his order. She obeyed, puzzled but curious, for his attention was no longer on her. He was looking over her shoulder and across his face came a look of mixed anger and maliciousness.

"Turn your head casually," he told her, "as if you're looking about merely as a matter of curiosity. At a table to your left there's a matronly woman romancing with a boy not half her age."

Lydia didn't care for prying, but she knew it was a part of the profession she had chosen, so she obeyed him and found that what he said was quite true. The handsome woman, certainly fifty or so, was holding the hand of a young man across the table and there was a look of open adoration in her eyes.

"That," Bryant said, "is Mrs. Hallett. Helen Hallett, famous in society for her lavish and exclusive parties."

"I've heard of her," Lydia admitted.

"Her husband is Paul Hallett, a broker whom I hate and with good reason. He once threatened to knock my head

11

off because of a squib I wrote about him. And he's made it difficult for me to reach some of the more important men on Wall Street. Long ago I made up my mind to even the score if the occasion ever presented itself. His wife has now made that opportunity possible." Bryant's voice had become quite unpleasant and his face had changed dramatically.

"Because she's dining here with a younger man?"

"Don't be so damned naive, darling Lydia. Her husband is a man of great moral character and his wife is presumed to be the same. Can you imagine his rage in the morning when he reads the lead story in my column?"

"You actually mean to write that up?" Lydia made no pretense of her astonishment.

He gave a derisive laugh. "I've changed my mind about you. I don't think you'll ever make a good reporter." He opened his gold watch and, as he closed the cover, began to get up.

"Where are you going now?" she asked, no longer in awe of him. "To interview her?"

The contemptuous look on Drury's face told her he had no such intention. "I've got very little time to get this story in type for the morning edition. I'm leaving, Lydia. Don't worry about the check. I have a charge account here." His dark eyes surveyed her with a certain impudence. "Go home and think about what I said. It takes more than beauty to become a good reporter. Any time you want to take up my offer, just let me know. There are a lot of things I can teach you . . . and not all of them about newspaper work."

He paused to sign the dinner check and then he was off, moving quickly, looking about the room as if he were accustomed to dramatic exits, and expected an audience for them.

Lydia sat at the table, still whirling a bit at the suddenness of this, wavering between disgust and anger. She tried to appear nonchalant, as if this happened all the time between reporters. But she felt embarrassed over Drury's precipitous departure, for it could have been construed as the result of the argument between them that several people had over-heard moments earlier.

She sipped the rest of the brandy, though she didn't want it. She did turn slightly to look back at the table where Mrs. Hallett had been seated. She wasn't there, though the good-looking young man was. Apparently she had gone to the ladies' room.

She made a sudden decision, then arose slowly, grace-fully. She threaded her way between the tables, attracting male attention as she did so. The maitre d'hotel directed her to the ladies' room, where, seated at a long makeup table, Mrs. Hallett was powdering her nose.

She glanced at Lydia as she sat down. "If you don't mind, miss, please sit somewhere else."

Lydia was too startled to obey, though she did look about the powder room. She and Mrs. Hallett were the only occupants.

"I know you were addressing me," Lydia said. "But why would you say such a thing?"

"I don't care to sit near anyone who is in the company of that beastly Mr. Drury. Has he, by chance, asked you to question me? Oh, quite innocently, of course, but hoping you might get something for his despicable column!" The woman spoke into the mirror with surprising fury, avoiding Lydia's gaze.

"Mrs. Hallett, Mr. Drury does write a column, but he's also one of the most intelligent reporters in the country."

"I know that. I even agree that he is, but when he's in New York, he writes a column of trash that has too often insulted friends of mine. If I ever find the opportunity to make trouble for him, I shall most certainly do exactly that. I know several others, of both sexes, who will do the same. We're just waiting for him to slip and make a libelous statement."

Lydia held her breath for a moment. "Mr. Drury just left the restaurant, Mrs. Hallett. Yes, I know who you are. He identified you for me. Like you, I respect him as a reporter, but it ends there. Now may I share this bench with you?"

Mrs. Hallett turned to study Lydia intently for a moment. Satisfied, she said, "I believe you. Ordinarily I wouldn't trust anyone in his company, but you seem like a decent young lady. How do you happen to be with him?"

"We work on the same newspaper, Mrs. Hallett."

Her face clouded. "Perhaps I've made a mistake. . . ."

"No, you haven't. I share your opinion of his gossip column. I can also assure you that no one will ever again see me in his company."

"Good! It's about time someone gave him a hint as to what he really is. It must have shattered his ego. I told my brother about him."

"Your brother?" Lydia managed to keep her voice impersonal, though sudden horror enveloped her.

Mrs. Hallett's eyes softened. "He graduated from medical school this morning and we're celebrating. My husband had an important meeting tonight, so I'm doing the honors."

"I noticed him, of course." Lydia began to gather her things and stuff them in her evening bag. She had to get out of here quickly, but not so abruptly as to arouse Mrs. Hallett's suspicions.

"Most women do notice, my dear," she want on confidingly. "He's really a handsome man, but he's not as young as he seems to be. I was the first born, he the last, and somewhat late in our mother's life. He's going to be a very fine doctor."

"His good looks will help assure that." Lydia managed a smile as she stood up and extended her hand. "I'm pleased to have met you, Mrs. Hallett."

"And I you, my dear, though you didn't give your name."

"Miss Lydia Bradley. Good evening, Mrs. Hallett."

She left the powder room, moving in a leisurely manner, and returned to her table where her cloak was still draped over the back of the chair. As she passed Mrs. Hallett's table, she smiled at the young man.

"Congratulations, doctor," she said.

He seemed startled, but he arose and bowed. A waiter assisted Lydia with her cloak and she left the restaurant, her step still casual, although inwardly she was churning to get back to the newspaper office before Drury's story would reach the presses. Perhaps she could catch Drury before he handed in his story.

Outside she looked vainly for a hansom or any other means of transportation. She found none and began walking, constantly alert for an empty cab. Two blocks farther she found one and told the driver to use all speed in getting her to the newspaper office.

Once there, she ran into the building, disdained the new-fangled lift and ran up the stairs. Drury was not at his desk. She lifted her skirts and ran up another flight of stairs, not stopping until she rushed into the night editor's office without knocking.

Guy Spencer was at his post, conferring with a man whom she had seen only once in passing, but immediately recognized as George Morgan, the wealthy owner of the newspaper. Both men were beyond middle age and well accustomed to enterprising and excited reporters, so that neither was unduly alarmed at her breathlessness as she stood before them.

"What is it, Miss Bradley?" the editor asked.

"Drury . . . Bryant Drury . . . he's writing an article about Mrs. Hallett. You have to stop the story. Drury is making a big mistake," Lydia said between gasps.

"Sit down, Miss Bradley," Mr. Morgan urged. "Slow down and tell me about it." He glanced at the editor. "I take it this is the young lady you hired recently as a reporter?"

"Yes, Miss Lydia Bradley. She's been with us six months. Now, Lydia, tell us what this is about."

"I was dining with Mr. Drury at Delmonico's. . . ."

"I understand." The editor gave her a knowing nod. "He tried to get fresh."

"It's much more important than that, Mr. Spencer. He saw Mrs. Paul Hallett, the society matron, at a table just

15

behind ours. She was with a much younger man and holding hands with him across the table. Mr. Drury is going to print a gossip item about her indiscreet behavior in a public place."

"The fool!" Morgan said angrily. "The Halletts are too important for that nonsense."

"He didn't check the story," Lydia said. "I found Mrs. Hallett in the ladies' room and I learned the young man happens to be her younger brother who today graduated from medical school. The dinner was a celebration. She informed me her husband was unable to be with them. Mrs. Hallett will sue him and the newspaper if he prints that item. She despises Drury."

"My God," Spencer exclaimed. "That kind of thing could have terrible consequences. I've got to stop it." He picked up the telephone and shouted for the rewrite room. "Is Drury there?" he asked. "Already left? Listen carefully. He just wrote something for his column. Is it at the pressroom yet? Go down there. Personally. Kill that whole column of his. . . . Let the goddamn paper be late! It's a life-and-death matter. Do what you have to. Just *kill* that column!"

Spencer hung up and sighed in relief. "Another half hour and that story would have been on the streets. Miss Bradley," he eyed her gratefully, "we're indebted to you for your initiative."

"Drury's self-conceit is destroying his effectiveness as a reporter," Morgan mused thoughtfully. "This isn't the first time he neglected to check a story. Or am I wrong, Guy?"

"You're right, sir," Spencer said somberly. "A damn shame. Up until recently he was the best in the country."

"And so far," Morgan went on, "we've been lucky in killing his inaccuracies before they got into print. Thank God, we caught this one. We'd have had no defense. You probably saved the paper a good deal of money, Miss Bradley. Thank you."

"My thanks also, Lydia," Spencer said. Both men

seemed awed at the realization of the seriousness of the disaster Lydia had averted. She herself was still too concerned to do more than nod her appreciation.

"We won't forget what you did," Morgan added.

The phone rang as she stood up to leave. Spencer answered it. "Send him up," he said crisply. He replaced the phone. "Miss Bradley, please wait a few minutes. They caught Drury as he was leaving the building. I want you here to listen to his explanation."

"I'd rather not," Lydia began nervously.

"Don't worry about Drury," Morgan said. He retreated to a far corner of the room that was in near darkness.

Drury came in without knocking. He started when he saw Lydia there, and his eyes narrowed.

"Now listen," he said, immediately on the defensive, "don't believe this girl's story. I wasn't harassing her. She was trying to get me to have her put on a big assignment and she offered me favors—"

"Drury," Spencer cut in, "you wrote a squib for your column about Mrs. Hallett."

Drury looked surprised. "Sure I did. Caught her dead to rights."

"Miss Bradley talked to Mrs. Hallett and discovered she was not being unfaithful to her husband. The man she was with happens to be her brother. They were celebrating his graduation from medical school."

Drury turned pale. "Good God! I've got to stop. . . ."

"The story has been killed," Morgan said quietly, moving out of the shadows.

Drury's mouth opened to voice an angry response, but when he recognized Morgan, his tone changed.

"Mr. Morgan, I didn't notice you were here. I'm sorry about this. It was good of Miss Bradley to check the story. Though I'm sure she told you I sent her to do just that."

"Damn it, Drury," Morgan said, "you didn't ask anyone to check the story. You hate Hallett and you thought you saw a chance to embarrass him. You should thank Miss Bradley for warning us in time."

Drury turned to Lydia, still bluffing his way through it. "Lydia, why didn't you tell these gentlemen you were supposed to contact me if you got anything out of Mrs. Hallett?"

"Hold on, Drury," Morgan said in rapidly rising anger. "You did *not* ask Miss Bradley to check. Even if you had, you wrote the story and sent it to press without waiting for any word from her."

"I thought she found nothing and went home. . . ."

"Drury," Morgan said, "you're a liar. You were a fine reporter until your head swelled. You think everyone's afraid of you. I don't want you working for us any longer, even if you do have a famous by-line. In other words, sir, you're fired. Now get out of here."

Drury turned threateningly toward Lydia. "A good game you play. Pretending to seek my advice when, in fact, you were out to get me from the start. From the way things look, you're after my job."

"Mr. Drury," she said more calmly than she felt, "I likely saved you a great deal of money, for Mrs. Hallett would surely have sued you, and you didn't stand the slightest chance of winning the suit."

"She's right," Spencer agreed. "You ought to be thanking her. And get this, Drury, if I ever hear of you making any trouble for this young lady, you'll not only never again work on any newspaper, but on any publication in the world. Now get out! I don't want to see your face again."

Drury hesitated, his face contorted, then yanked down the brim of his black homburg and stalked out, slamming the door behind him. Lydia sat down slowly. She was pale and greatly concerned, for she knew her actions had led to his dismissal. She had also glimpsed his vindictive nature and feared that one day she might feel the full extent of his wrath.

"Don't be afraid of him, Lydia," Spencer said. "He'll probably destroy himself before he does you."

"I don't like to be the cause of anyone losing his job," she replied somberly.

"It was coming to that," Morgan said. "We've been watching him, hoping he'd change. But he thought he was above reproach."

"Yes," Spencer agreed. "Too much drinking, too many women and a growing carelessness with his stories. Word gets around. As for you, Lydia, you saved us and also Drury from disaster. We give a bonus for a good story. You deserve one for stopping a bad story. You'll find one hundred dollars extra in your next paycheck."

"Make that two hundred," Morgan said.

"Thank you, gentlemen. I'm very grateful." She arose, ready to leave the office, still feeling somewhat overwhelmed by all that had happened.

"Don't be in such a hurry to leave, Miss Bradley," Morgan said with a chuckle. "Please sit down and tell me about yourself. How old are you?"

"Twenty, sir."

"Do you live with your family?"

"My father, Paul Bradley, died some time ago, and my mother shortly after him. I have no one else—"

"Good God! Not *the* Paul Bradley, of the Lyttonville Herald? Of course we knew of him. He was a fine newspaper man," Morgan interjected.

"Yes, sir. He was the one who taught me all the journalism I know. He always encouraged me to pursue it. . . ."

"Why didn't you mention he was your father when we hired you?" Spencer asked.

"I didn't want to trade on his reputation," Lydia answered. "I want to make my own way."

"I see. Then, you have no obligations that would tie you down?" Morgan presently continued.

"None, sir," Lydia replied, more and more mystified at this kind of questioning.

"No . . . young man?"

"None, sir."

Morgan, a heavy-set man with a somewhat florid face, sat down and leaned back in the leather chair behind one of the two oversized desks. He studied Lydia so frankly she felt uncomfortable. Spencer was following this, but it was clear he didn't know what the publisher was aiming at.

"I play hunches," Morgan told them, grinning. "I've been criticized for it in the past, but I seem to have done pretty well. Guy, you recall that two weeks ago I returned from abroad."

"Yes, sir."

"I traveled around Europe extensively. One place attracted and interested me far more than any other. I'm referring to Monte Carlo. Know where that is, Miss Bradley? Or what it is?"

"I've heard of it, but I know nothing of it, sir."

"Good. Not many do. It's part of the Principality of Monaco, located on the French Riviera near Italy. It's a beautiful place, and has one of the finest climates to be found in the world. It's taken off, like a skyrocket. They've built a big casino and several hotels there, grander than anything all Europe has to offer. And the gambling is for stakes that would stagger you. All kinds of gambling. In just a short time I saw a king, an emperor, the kaiser—supposedly incognito—a large assortment of dukes, barons and earls. Diplomats, military people . . . crowds of more-than-ordinary citizens, mostly the very rich." He paused, offered Spencer a cigar and lit up one for himself. After a few speculative puffs, he added, "I never saw anything like it in my life."

"What are you getting at?" Guy Spencer asked, still thoroughly mystified.

"Miss Bradley," Morgan said, and his eyes fastened on her face, "how would you like to go to Monte Carlo? Live there as our permanent representative. With unlimited funds—though not for gambling. You'll have the best of everything, for there's no other way to treat Monte Carlo, especially if you're there on business for the paper."

"I . . . am to go to Monte Carlo?" Lydia asked incredulously.

"That's what I said."

"But . . . why me? I've only been with the paper a short time!"

"That's why I'm selecting you. Granted, I'm impressed with your family background. But your father's reputation has little to do with this decision. I did have Drury in mind, but when I saw the two of you in this room, I had a better idea. He's too jaded. A good reporter, but he wouldn't see Monte Carlo the way I want it seen. And that's by a young person, a pretty girl who will be experiencing Monte and what it represents for the first time in her life. I expect we'll get fresh, not tired, reports. Your stories will be influenced by the importance of the people you'll meet. You'll see the harbor for what it is, a beautiful place ringed with mountains and filled with yachts from every country in the world. You'll appreciate the sunrises and the sunsets. For you and me, Guy, sunsets and sunrises don't exist any more. We've seen too many of them. That's why I want Lydia to go. She's young, smart and impressionable. She'll see the sunrises."

"What an idea!" Spencer said, getting carried away by Morgan's eloquence. "Good Lord, for once I've heard something original. We'll feature everything Lydia sends back. With photos. She can arrange for them on Monte Carlo."

"I don't know what . . . to say. . . ." Lydia was still in a state of shock, and had sat down again, rigid with excitement.

"Just tell us when you can go. Day after tomorrow?"

"Mr. Morgan, I'm flattered by your confidence, but I've done so little actual reporting."

"If you'd done a great deal, I'd never have considered you. It was an idea that just came to me while I was firing Drury. Say you'll accept this assignment. You'll be well paid. If you show promise, after a month you'll get full salary for a foreign correspondent, in addition to your accommodations, which will be a suite of rooms in the best hotel. You have to be important to talk to important people. What's your answer?"

"What a fool I'd be to refuse, Mr. Morgan. Indeed, I'm so happy about this I could . . . no, I won't cry. I'll just say I'll do the very best I can."

"Good. Guy will make all the arrangements, passport, money, salary." He jabbed his cigar in the direction of Spencer. "Be generous, Guy. Lydia just saved us a small fortune. I'm looking forward to your success, my dear, more than any assignment I've ever given."

Tears almost sprang to Lydia's eyes despite her promise, for at that moment she was strongly reminded of her father. "I'll leave as quickly as preparations can be made," she declared.

"Good. Oh yes, you have to dress the part over there. You'll be the representative of this great and important newspaper, so you have to look as fashionable as anyone. Guy," he gestured, "include an allowance for clothing, perfumes, everything. You may buy your gowns here in New York, or stop in Paris on the way. I don't think Monte has many good shops yet. Everyone is too busy gambling to shop."

"Pardon me for asking, but how did you do, sir?" Spencer asked with a grin.

"It's not polite to ask such questions," Morgan laughed. "But I'll confess I parted with seven thousand dollars in twenty-three minutes. My wife kept track of the time. To say nothing of the money."

"My goodness!" Lydia exclaimed. "That's shocking."

Morgan's laugh grew louder. "See what I mean, Guy? She's wonderful. We'll get stories the like of which no newspaper ever published before. I can just about guarantee that they'll be the most read feature we print. *How awful,* she said. The man next to me lost ten thousand in one minute! He bet it all at one time and he was still betting when my wife dragged me away. He was some kind of sheik fellow, wearing a white robe and headdress. He also had four unnerving bodyguards."

"I'm not sure what to say, Mr. Morgan," Lydia spoke fervently, "other than I appreciate this opportunity you're giving me and I'll do my best to justify your faith—and my father's—in me.''

''I feel certain you won't let us down,'' Morgan said, looking pleased. ''Just keep your viewpoint fresh and original. You'll move among the rich and famous, many of them jaded. Write about them. Mix with everyone who frequents Monte. Learn about them in whatever way appeals to you.'' He turned to Spencer. ''I have a feeling this is going to increase circulation by thousands.''

''It's a fantastic and novel idea,'' Spencer replied. ''Report to this office in the morning, Lydia, and we'll go over the preparations to be made and get you a passport. We'll have to move fast.''

Lydia was trembling with excitement when she left the office and made her way downstairs. In her dazed state, it was a wonder she realized she had to clean out her desk—the desk she'd occupied for only a few months.

To her chagrin, Bryant Drury was at his desk, emptying the drawers and piling the contents on top. He paused, arose slowly and walked over to stand beside her. She rested her hands on the center drawer, already open, and looked up at him bravely.

His voice was tight with suppressed anger as he addressed her. ''I just want you to know that I won't forget what you did tonight. If I ever find the chance to get back at you—and don't think I won't look for one—I'll take it. Remember that, Lydia darling. Yes, you'll do all right, climbing over other bodies. It's the only way you'll ever make it as a reporter and for a small-town girl you've made a good start. To think I believed you were on the level.''

''I didn't use you,'' Lydia said. ''I saved the paper from being sued. I did you a favor.''

''You had me fired,'' Drury retorted. ''What did you get out of it?''

Lydia stood her ground, staring him down. ''I'm not going to quarrel with you, Mr. Drury. I'm sorry Mr. Morgan dismissed you, but from what I understand, this wasn't the first time you neglected to check facts before writing up news—if you can call it that.''

"Will you be writing my column?" he asked, ignoring her statement.

"No."

"Then what did you get out of it?" he repeated bluntly.

"A bonus," she said quietly.

"What else?"

"None of your business. Now please get away from my desk."

"Remember what I said." His voice was bleak. He strode back to his desk, picked up a carton that sat on the floor and filled it with his belongings. She wished she didn't have to witness what could only be a final humiliation for him. He lifted the box, used his hip to brace it and without a glance at Lydia, who still sat motionless, left the room.

A tremor of delayed fear hit Lydia as she searched for a paper bag in the bottom drawer, sufficiently large for her needs. Though she had stood up to Drury, she knew the threat he'd made wasn't an idle one. He was a bad enemy, one to whom the taste of defeat was the taste of gall. Once he learned that she'd been given a plum of an assignment that might well have been his, he'd be a worse one. That was why she had sat motionless until he left the office, so that he wouldn't see her emptying her desk and ask her where she was going. Yes, she feared him, after seeing him in action tonight. He was as ruthless as he was unethical, a man who would stop at nothing to get revenge. Though she had been given the chance of a lifetime tonight, she had also made a formidable adversary.

Two

Lydia couldn't believe she was aboard a luxury ship only three days after George Morgan had given her the assignment, enthusiastically endorsed by Guy Spencer. It was Spencer who brought her to the ship and escorted her to her tastefully furnished cabin. On a table was a huge bouquet of roses sent by Mr. Morgan, plus a large basket of fruit.

The card on the latter revealed it had come from Spencer. "I really don't feel I merit all this good luck and attention," Lydia told him. "And my gratitude seems inadequate."

"Just send us some good stories," he said, "and we'll continue to show our appreciation."

"It doesn't seem as if I've been given an assignment," she protested. "This is more like having been in a contest and winning first prize—a Mediterranean vacation."

He laughed. "Just keep that viewpoint and your stories will have a wholesomeness that will so intrigue the readers, circulation will be boosted beyond our greatest hopes."

"*That's* quite an assignment," Lydia said worriedly.

"One you'll meet," he replied matter-of-factly. He reached for her gloved hand and held it between his. "I'm sorry I have to rush. I'd like to take you on a tour of the ship, but you'll meet plenty of passengers who'll do that. It's part of the fun."

She went back on deck with him and watched as he descended the gangplank. On the dock he stood with the others who had come to bid their friends and relatives bon voyage as the ship pulled away from the pier. When it did, the din sounded like bedlam. The cries of farewell from those departing, mingled with those on the dock, was almost drowned out by the constant blowing of the ship's whistles.

Lydia continued to wave, even after the night editor's face became a blur in the crowd. As the passengers moved away from the rail, eager to begin the journey, a wave of loneliness overcame her, such as she'd felt after the death of her parents. Monte Carlo seemed like it would be a long way from home.

She decided to find the salon and have a cup of tea to bolster her spirits. A steward directed her and she stepped into a circular room, thickly carpeted and fragrant with the scent of roses artfully arranged in glass vases on long tables set on either side of the wide, arched entranceway.

She chose a table near the door and to one side of the room where a large window gave her a view of the deck. The tables were small, round, marble-topped and dressed with dainty lace doilies on which chinaware settings had already been placed. A small vase of roses adorned the center. As soon as she was seated, a waiter brought her a silver pot of tea and a dish of petits fours covered with icings of every color. She ignored the little cakes, but sipped her tea and studied the other passengers. They varied in age from the very young to the elderly, but she appeared to be the only passenger who sat alone. She was just about to get up when a slender, dark-haired lady approached her table and asked if the other chair was occupied. She was dressed entirely in black, even to the gossamer veil covering her face. When she lifted it and let it rest on top of her hat, Lydia saw that she was attractive, and probably in her mid-thirties.

She flashed Lydia a grateful smile when her reply was negative.

"Then may I join you?" she asked.

"Please do," Lydia replied, returning the smile.

After she was seated, she said, "My name is Madame

Yvonne Dannay. May I ask yours, mademoiselle? Since I see no ring on your finger, I assume I address you correctly?''

"You do," Lydia assured her. "I'm Miss Lydia Bradley."

Madame Dannay ordered her tea, then turned her attention back to Lydia. "Are you traveling alone?"

"Yes." Lydia liked the directness of the woman. She also liked the flashing brown eyes that were as warm as the smile that seemed to perpetually touch her mouth.

"Then you won't mind my joining you. I also am traveling alone. I took a holiday in the States in the hope that it would ease the pain of my recent bereavement . . . my husband died six months ago."

"I'm very sorry," Lydia said.

"*Merci*, mademoiselle," she replied. "I try to be cheerful, but sometimes my efforts are misunderstood by the opposite sex. I wish no romantic attachments at present."

"That is understandable, madame," Lydia said.

"Please—call me Yvonne. I think we may be friends. At least, I hope so. Now—please tell me about yourself."

Lydia did so, her forlornness already forgotten. Her new friend sipped her tea and listened intently as Lydia related her reason for being on the ship.

"How exciting! A woman reporter," Yvonne exclaimed. "Will you spend some time in my beloved Paris?"

"Only enough to purchase a wardrobe," Lydia replied.

"That, too, is exciting for a woman, especially one as young as you. I wish I were going to be in Paris so I could accompany you—if you would allow me."

"I'd be very happy to have you with me," Lydia replied.

"I am going to Germany, however, to spend a holiday with my brother. He is a doctor. It is still too painful for me to return to my home north of Paris. You see, I was married only six months when I received word my husband had been killed in a train accident. However, I can tell you about Paris. I will tell you nothing of Monte Carlo."

Lydia looked chagrined. "Why not?"

"You told me your editor wants a fresh viewpoint. So you must discover everything for yourself. I will say only that it is beautiful, enchanting, exciting and yes, even shocking. But, oh so gay. At least, for the French. We like gaiety, beauty, a little bit of naughtiness, and yes—even intrigue, and there is plenty of that in Monte. All kinds. Now that is enough of Monte. Do you speak French?"

"No, but I brought some books to study while we're sailing."

"I will help you with the books and I will also converse with you. You'll find that you will absorb the language much faster that way."

"You speak English without a trace of an accent," Lydia observed.

"I was raised in a convent and we were taught several languages, among them English. It was always my favorite."

"I'll certainly appreciate your help."

"We will start tomorrow. What is your cabin number?"

"One fifty."

"Good. Mine is one sixty. I will meet you on deck tomorrow. We will stretch out on a chair, inhale the sea air and begin with *Je suis, tu es, it est, elle est. Nous avons, vous avez, ils ou elles sont.* Do you know what that means?"

Lydia laughed. "I haven't the faintest idea."

"It happens to be the conjugation of the verb *to be*. Before the voyage is ended, I'll have you conversing with me as if you were a born Frenchwoman." Her eyes sparkled merrily.

"You have far more confidence in me than I have in myself."

"We shall see. I shall also see to it that you make the most of the days on board ship. You are young and pretty and there will be many young gentlemen who will seek out your company."

"What if I prefer to learn French?" Lydia asked with a smile.

"You will learn that, too," Yvonne said. "But who

knows, we may find a Frenchman who will not be too amorous. However, I admit moonlight on board ship does strange things to all of us."

"I want to build a career as a newspaper woman." Lydia spoke with quiet firmness. "I'll let nothing interfere with it."

The Frenchwoman laughed. "Spoken like a true American. I have found in your country that the women are becoming quite independent. I like that spirit and I wish you luck, my dear. Now, will you dine with me tonight? If so, I shall seek out the purser and have him seat us at the same table throughout the voyage. Of course, I suspect you will be asked to dine at the captain's table."

"Goodness," Lydia exclaimed. "Do you think so?"

Yvonne's eyes flashed mischievously. "I would not question it once he discovers you. At present I must go to my cabin to rest awhile, as I am tired. Too much running about. Americans never rest. Fortunately, tonight we do not dress for dinner."

Lydia and Yvonne walked back to their cabins with Lydia insisting Yvonne come in long enough to take some of the fruit Guy Spencer had given her. She knew she'd never be able to consume it by herself. Yvonne thanked her graciously and departed.

To Lydia's surprise, but not to Yvonne's, they were both seated at the captain's table for the remainder of the voyage. In addition to this, Lydia spent the days with Yvonne learning the meaning of French words and phrases and how to pronounce them. Fortunately, she had a rhythmic ear and in two days had acquired a limited vocabulary of everyday phrases and sentences and was able to voice them with little trace of an accent.

Nights she dressed in her only gown and after dinner, when Yvonne insisted they go to the salon, they sipped a liqueur and watched the dancers. From time to time, male passengers approached and asked them to dance. Yvonne always refused, and if a potential partner approached Lydia whom Yvonne felt was not suitable, she spoke up quickly, giving a logical reason for Lydia's not being able to accept.

So much was she enjoying it that Lydia wished the voyage would never end. But the last evening came, an evening on which she danced with one of the ship's officers and at his suggestion, took a walk with him around the deck, bathed in bright moonlight. He flirted with her outrageously while the strains of a Strauss waltz drifted out from the salon, and before she knew what was happening, he had caught her in his arms and danced her into a secluded corner. His hands rested lightly on her waist.

"You are enchanting," he said. "The most enchanting American I have ever encountered."

"And you have encountered many," Lydia laughingly replied.

Though she liked what he had said, she wasn't taken in by it. Nonetheless, she wasn't offended either. She felt young and alive and he was handsome, suave and pleased to be in her company.

His head lowered and his lips touched hers. She stepped back, and he made no attempt to force his attentions further.

"I will escort you back to your chaperone," he said, disappointed.

"She's not my chaperone, only a dear friend," Lydia said. "A very understanding one."

"A pity I won't see you again."

Lydia smiled. They'd reached the door of the salon. "Good-bye, monsieur."

"*Au 'voir* is better since we may meet again."

Lydia's face was flushed when she rejoined Yvonne, who regarded the young woman tolerantly. "So you had your little flirtation."

"Oh," Lydia shrugged self-consciously, "it was just a brief kiss."

"A pleasant moment to file away in your mental diary. One day it will slip out and touch your mouth with a smile. He was attracted by your innocence. Come—we must retire. Tomorrow is your big day."

Lydia wanted to dispute that, saying every day had been

a stupendous one. Tomorrow she would be alone. Just as alone as she'd been when Guy Spencer had bade her adieu. She smiled, noting she was already thinking in French.

Much to her surprise, though she arose early the next morning, she had no time to be lonely. She checked into the Hotel de Ville, feeling overwhelmed by the luxury and femininity of the room and adjoining bath. She took time to bathe leisurely, luxuriating in the perfumed soap that sat in a white porcelain dish with a gilt mermaid stretched full length on one side. Then she dressed quickly, wearing a simple suit and a sailor hat, and set forth on her mission to the House of Worth, located on the Rue de la Paix. It was the most prestigious, made so by the imperiousness of its owner. Mr. Morgan, true to his word, had informed her that he'd made certain arrangements and that she was to go there immediately after her arrival. When she finally saw the shop across the street, she approached it somewhat hesitantly, quite awed by its elegant facade.

Luxurious carriages of every make and description were leaving and pulling up before the establishment, and Lydia wished she were not arriving on foot. A doorman in a brown uniform assisted the ladies in and out of these carriages, while Lydia admired the parade of beauties with their colorful little parasols and beautifully decorated hats. They were dressed rather formally for midday, and she herself suffered in comparison.

The doorman didn't deign to notice Lydia as she headed for the entrance. She wasn't surprised. Probably no one came to Worth's except in a carriage, and dressed in the height of fashion.

However, once he was assured she was about to enter the establishment, he did hold the door open for her. Inside, a dark-haired man in a high collar, a narrow, black bow tie and a custom-designed tuxedo stood his ground as she approached him. He surveyed her critically, and she saw censure in his eyes, no doubt caused by the modest dress she'd bought before she left.

31

"I wish to see some gowns," she said in English, not quite sure enough of her French. She only hoped he could understand her.

"*Oui*," he replied, but didn't bow as she expected. His voice was rather embarrassed as he added, "Mademoiselle understands, of course, that this a most . . . ah . . . *expensive* fashion salon."

"Everyone knows that," she replied calmly. "I have a letter . . . *une lettre*." Lydia opened her handbag and produced the sealed envelope that Mr. Morgan had given her. The store manager opened it, and his already uplifted eyebrow raised higher as he read. Then he folded the letter, placed it in his pocket and hurriedly executed an elaborate bow.

"Forgive me, Mademoiselle Bradley, I did not realize. . . . It is my pleasure indeed to welcome you to Worth's. Your every need will be taken care of, as the gentleman has requested. Whatever you wish, you have but to name it." His hands gestured expansively toward the salons. "Now—please allow me to escort you to one of our private rooms. It is better there . . . you do not have to be in the company of some of our patrons." His voice lowered. "They are demimondaines, you know, so many of them. But naturally, we deal with them because men of great wealth send them."

Lydia wondered what was in the letter, but she soon had reason to guess quite accurately. She was brought to a salon decorated in a pale rose shade. Everything in it was bathed in a pink glow, even the Aubusson rug. She was seated in a large, velvet-upholstered chair beside a table of black onyx, while the manager clapped his hands once and a tray was immediately set on the table. It held a sparkling crystal glass and a decanter, which, when opened, filled the nearby air with the sweetness of very old, very rare and expensive sherry.

"Now!" The manager clapped his hands twice. This time a woman with white hair, fashionably arranged, and wearing a tea gown of pink chiffon with matching satin slippers, entered and smiled graciously. Lydia thought she looked like a Dresden figurine, rather ageless and still beautiful. She was introduced as Madame Renaud.

"Mademoiselle," the woman began in charmingly accented English, "it is arranged that our mannequins will display for you only the best of what we have. Also there are fabrics, divine ones, from which you may select gowns to be made especially for you. And there will be lingerie, *très fine*, mademoiselle, everything you need except for gloves, shoes and handbags. We have arranged a private showing of these for you in another salon. But first, may we have the honor of providing you *le diner*? It can be served here while you examine our gowns."

"Thank you," Lydia said, smiling, "I've already had my noon meal."

"Ah. Then there will be tea at four. Now, shall we begin?" She turned and beckoned toward a doorway, her voice a command. *"Commencez!"*

Lydia wondered how long they expected her to stay, and how many gowns she would be allowed to buy. Four o'clock seemed quite a long time away.

It wasn't to prove so. The mannequins began parading before her a few minutes later. They showed one gown after another until Lydia was dizzy with the wonder of them, and the hours ticked by. At first she was inclined to select everything as it was shown, but she was discouraged in this by Madame Renaud, who informed her that there were even better gowns yet to be modeled, perhaps more suited to her, and that the *chère* mademoiselle must not select until she had seen everything, *"toutes les robes!"*

Tea was served, with tiny sandwiches, small cakes and more of the exquisite sherry. An inhaler of brandy followed, until Lydia felt mellow enough to buy the entire showing. She selected two gowns, but the parade of fashions continued and she was finally told by the petite Madame Renaud, most discreetly of course, that there was no limit to what she could buy.

Lydia decided on six more evening gowns, each one a

marvel of design, then moved on to the daytime dresses, walking dresses, morning dresses, tea gowns, negligées, capes and cloaks. After that, she was shown hats, shoes, handbags, gloves, fans and stockings in a nearby salon. It was like a dream—coming true while she dreamed it. The fabrics ranged from delicate chiffons, crisp taffetas, crêpes and shimmering velvets to soft lawns, linens, bengalines and wool.

"Everything," she was told, "will be delivered *au plus vite*—very quickly—to your suite at Monte Carlo."

"How soon?" Lydia asked, knowing each garment would be made to order.

"Ah," the little saleswoman gave an eloquent Gallic shrug, "for you, mademoiselle, three weeks. That will be day and night work for us."

"In the meantime," Lydia said worriedly, "what will I do for clothes? I brought only a few things. My employer wished me to be as elegant as anyone holidaying in Monte Carlo."

"For that, we have the solution," Madame Renaud said with a smile. "I shall send for some gowns that you must try on, *immédiatement*! It will give us a most excellent opportunity to see which styles become you. Let us have hope you are as slender as our manneguins. If so, you may have the dresses for a pittance. We shall work . . . ah, *comme les chiens*, to deliver your order in one week. If one of these gowns fits, it will not be a problem that you are absent for the fitting. Your measurements will do for us nicely. And the mannequin who models the gowns that fit, she will serve in your stead."

After four gowns were tried on, one finally fit. Lydia breathed a sigh of relief. So did Madame Renaud.

"*Bon!*" she exclaimed with enthusiasm. "We can outfit you with one of each kind of garment until your selections are completed and delivered."

Lydia breathed a sigh of relief. "Thank goodness." She knew that her confidence would get a needed boost, certain she was beautifully dressed. She left the salon feeling far more sure of herself than when she had entered.

The next day she boarded the overnight train for Monte Carlo, after making inquiries for directions at her Paris hotel. She spent the time en route studying French, hoping to become more proficient.

Many hours later, and after a fitful sleep, she changed trains at Nice for the now short remainder of her journey. As they swept into Monaco in the early morning, she gazed spellbound at the unexpected grandeur of the setting. She had known, from Mr. Morgan's description, that it would be beautiful, but she had not expected it to be spectacular.

Against the backdrop of the Alps, the densely clustered hills and headland looked south to the sparkling Mediterranean. The old town of Monaco jutted out on a rock face into the sea, forming the southwestern arm that embraced the Port of Monaco. On the other side was Monte Carlo. Lydia caught a glimpse of formal gardens surrounding what could only be the Place du Casino, described in a little booklet she had purchased as so ornate that at one time it had been dubbed "The Wedding Cake." She was enchanted with the red-and-green-studded mosaic domes. The opera house, she knew, adjoined it on one side. If its twin turrets were any indication of the interior, it would be as embellished as a bejewelled dowager.

In the distance was now visible the palace, a structure described as having one hundred and eighty rooms. It was there that the current ruler of Monaco lived. Lydia leaned back from the train window. The entire picture was to her an awesome sight and she was wondering if she could ever muster sufficient poise to mingle with the society that must dominate this gambling city, described as "the playground of the wealthy."

When she alighted from the train, she selected a brougham from a line of them and the driver helped her onto the rather high seat. She had an idea the ladies who used these carriages liked to be seen. Her destination was the Hotel de Paris, a two-storey building said to be the oldest hotel on Monte Carlo and by far the most opulent, rivaled only by the newer Grand. She wondered what to expect there. Certainly Mr. Morgan hadn't spared any expense so far.

The carriage passed many restaurants on the way, and all manner of shops, mostly very expensive. Now and then, at the end of a street, Lydia glimpsed the shimmering harbor, the bluest water she had ever seen. It was crowded with boats of all descriptions, though yachts predominated, most of them very large and suggesting well-to-do owners. In the other direction was the gray-pink granite mountain range towering high above the town. She'd managed to pry a little information out of Yvonne Dannay and learned that they shielded Monaco from the chilling north winds and that this was what made Monte Carlo such a popular winter resort.

At the Hotel de Paris, she found the luxury of the lobby equal to that of the hotel she had checked into so briefly in Paris. Myriad Persian rugs were scattered on pink marble floors, and square pillars of the same marble graced the vast room, along with many strategically placed palms that almost concealed small groupings of furniture. A great number of people were in the lobby, seated on soft sofas, but their voices were muted by the plush decor. And the air was fragrant with the scent of flowers arranged on tables in vases of every size.

Some of the walls and pillars were paneled with glittering mirrors, offering a glimpse of oneself in passing, and reflecting back the green plants, the polished pink stone, and innumerable overstuffed sofas and rattan rockers with plump cusions. Lydia was quite dazzled by such elegance.

At the hotel desk, amid the splendor of this immense lobby, she was greeted by a trim, well-dressed clerk with the same skepticism that the manager of Worth's had first exhibited. It was evident one either had to be known or have excellent connections to be fully accepted here.

"I have a reservation." To her surprise, she spoke with quiet confidence. "My name is Lydia Bradley and the reservation was made by the New York Star-Press.''

"Mademoiselle Bradley!" the clerk exclaimed. "Of course, we were expecting you." He tapped a bell on the desk. "Suite 221 for mademoiselle," he told the bellhop who appeared. "She will be along later." He turned back to Lydia with a deferential air. Mademoiselle, we are sincerely honored to have a representative of the American press with us as a permanent guest. I assure you we shall do all in our power to see that you are comfortable and well protected. Of course, we did not expect such a beautiful and . . . ah . . . young reporter, but that makes our welcome even more pleasant.''

"Thank you," Lydia said, amused at the clerk's ingratiating air. "I would like to go to my suite now. The journey was rather uncomfortable, not only because of the heat, but my car was filled with cinders from the train.''

"*Oui*, mademoiselle, those trains! You will dine with us, I trust?''

"Yes, indeed. I am told the food is superb." She smiled, pleased with her growing air of self-confidence.

"Ah, yes, it is better than the Grand has to offer, even if they did bring in a famous Parisian chef. We have one coming here, too, mademoiselle. You will also notice we have electric lights and a lift. *Oui*, we are quite, quite modern. I pray you will reflect this in your writings.''

"I will indeed," Lydia told him. She was already thinking that a rivalry in French chefs might make an interesting little story.

The clerk summoned another bellhop to the small lift that creaked its way up the one flight. She entered a two-room suite where a maid of no more than eighteen, dressed in a crisp, black bombazine dress, with a dainty white apron and cap was already unpacking her luggage. Lydia tipped the bellhop, who left quietly, closing the door behind him.

"Is there something mademoiselle desires?" the maid asked politely when she had completed her task.

"Just a bath," Lydia replied.

"Does mademoiselle wish me to draw it?''

"No, thank you. I can manage."

The little French maid curtsied and left. Lydia turned her attention to the suite. Both the living and bedroom were furnished with delicate white-and-gold appointments. The legs of the tables, chairs, dresser and dressing table were so delicate they looked incapable of supporting any weight, yet their very elegance belied that. Fringed satin lampshades added to the splendor. The walls were covered with blue silk printed with tiny stars, and this color was picked up in the blue of the rug. Other walls were paneled with gilt. The theme of gold and blue was carried throughout the dainty French furniture with its gold accents and the pale blue satin upholstery. And the bird of paradise embroidered on the white silk spread lent an exotic air to the bedroom.

She turned and noticed that on the wall of each room alongside the door was row of buttons; slipped into a metal slot alongside each button was a narrow strip of paper designating the duty of the employee who would be summoned at a push of the button. Lydia exclaimed in delight at the thought of being so pampered.

She knew at once that her first article would concern her impression of Monte Carlo. There was so much to write about. She remembered the mimosa, orange and lemon trees in full bloom as she rode to her hotel, the air heavy with their perfume. Half-planning her first descriptions in her head, she stepped into the bathroom and saw a stack of towels and washcloths facing a wall that was entirely mirrored. She couldn't wait to stand in her bare feet, curling her toes in the softness of the thick rug that would absorb moisture easily.

She returned to the bedroom. Propped against the bureau mirror was a sealed envelope bearing the imprint of the Place du Casino. It was an invitation to attend, whenever she wished, so that she might become accustomed to the surroundings. It occurred to her that she didn't know anything about gambling, and the thought made her more and more uneasy. So much so that she wondered if Mr. Morgan had made a mistake in sending her here.

A feeling of disloyalty made her set aside these doubts. After all, Mr. Morgan prided himself on his good judgment. She must start having faith in herself.

Lydia's morning arrival gave her plenty of time to rest, bathe, and then examine the limited wardrobe she'd brought from Worth's. To begin with, she reveled in the large, ornate bathroom and bathed leisurely. She was tying the belt of her cotton robe when she heard a knock on the door. She returned to the parlor and admitted the maid who had unpacked for her. She was slim, petite—no more than five feet in height—and pretty, with a ready smile, flashing dark brown eyes and curly hair only partly hidden by her crisp lace cap.

Her smile was bright, now, and her curtsy graceful. "If mademoiselle wishes, I am to help her dress for dinner."

Lydia returned the smile. "Is it customary?"

"*Oui*, mademoiselle. And since I already unpack for you, I know where everything is."

Lydia found this intriguing. "Do you always unpack for guests?"

"*Oui*. It is a rule of the hotel."

"I see. I never heard of that being done before except by special request."

"Mademoiselle, it is not that the hotel is curious what the guests bring. It is to search for guns or poison."

"Guns or poison?" Lydia asked in alarm.

"*Oui*. There are those who . . . shall we say, suffer bad luck and lose everything they have. They will go into the gardens and weep, perhaps. Then . . . zoof . . . they blow their brains out. Always in the gardens so they die amid beauty, it seems. And good for us, too. When they do it in their rooms, there is a mess—except for those who take poison."

"Good heavens," Lydia said, suddenly aware that newsworthy stories were developing wherever she turned. She switched to French, thanking the girl for the informaton, and asked her her name.

"Angelina, mademoiselle. *Vous parlez français*," she added in surprise.

"Whenever possible, though I'm just learning the language."

"You speak well."

"I must speak it a lot better," Lydia said slowly, her mind turning to thoughts of what to wear.

"I will help you if you wish," Angelina offered eagerly.

Lydia found the young girl's enthusiasm contagious. "Thank you. That's very kind of you."

Angelina beamed.

"I think we shall become good friends," Lydia added. "And I'll be grateful if you'll speak to me occasionally in French."

"I speak English very well, but I still sound French, while you have only a little accent in French," Angelina continued, a question in her voice. "Why?"

"I was fortunate to have a French lady tutor me on board ship."

Angelina nodded somberly. "You have learned quick. Now we must see what you will wear tonight. May I help you select?"

"Please do," Lydia said. "It shouldn't take long, because I didn't bring much. My wardrobe will come from Paris in about a week, I hope."

"*Bon*. But for now, with the accessories you brought, we have no trouble making it seem like your wardrobe is very large."

Lydia paused and looked the girl directly in the eye.

"Before we make the selection, I wish you to tell me more about having to search the guests' belongings for guns or poison. I think you're making that up."

Angelina laughed. "It is so, mademoiselle. We don't do it. I am teasing you. You see, that is the rumor that goes around. People like to believe it so when they come for the first time, we say the lie. It is like—intrigue." She gave a dainty shrug of her shoulders. "They love it. They think they have a secret."

40

"I didn't think people would bring guns or poison," Lydia said, pleased she hadn't been taken in by the tale.

"Ah, but some do," Angelina said seriously. "Some people lose that which they cannot afford. They can't go back because to begin with, they stole the money—from their employer most likely. And some take a desperate gamble. They need money. What they have is their own, but it isn't too much. When they finish, they have nothing. So they do what I told you. Go out to the garden. . . ."

Lydia grimaced and held up a hand. "No need to go on. I believe you."

"Thank you, mademoiselle. Now we shall turn our attention to your choice of gown."

In the next half hour Lydia discovered that Angelina had a silvery, merry little laugh that came and went like quicksilver. In her low-pitched voice, speaking clearly and not too quickly, she moved in and out of the closet with the garments, commenting on each one in French and touching the part of the gown to which she referred. When Lydia looked puzzled, Angelina, with her bell-like laugh, translated the French into English. Lydia began to feel she'd master the language in no time.

Angelina was as enchanted with the gowns as Lydia was pleased with her new maid. Since there were only two evening outfits, they decided on the pale blue chiffon. She was tired of the one she had brought and worn aboard ship, her old green satin from home. Besides, the blue chiffon from Worth's complimented Lydia's fairness and her slender form in a startling way.

She could scarcely believe her eyes when she finally stood before the full-length mirror, balanced on brass lion's feet between two windows. The beauty of the gown lay in its very simplicity. The skirt consisted of layers of chiffon graduated in length until they reached the floor, so that, with Lydia's slightest movement, the fabric seemed to come alive. The bodice was cleverly draped and edged with delicate iridescent beading. Angelina had dressed Lydia's hair with a mass of curls on the crown, letting the back hang loose in soft curls that rested on each shoulder. Her long gloves, also purchased at Worth's, had the same beading as the bodice.

"You need no jewelry, mademoiselle," Angelina said, clapping her hands in approval. "No royal princess will look as regal as you tonight."

"Thanks to you," Lydia said, smiling at Angelina's reflection.

"If I did not have such excellent material to work with, I could not make this miracle. I am certain you will be asked to dine with the Baron Maxfried Hetzler."

"Who in the world is he?" Lydia asked, twirling her skirt.

"Oh, the baron is a nice old man," Angelina confided. "He will tell you he is cousin to the emperor Franz Josef of Austria, and yes, it is true. But he is poor, he lives on some sort of pension that only lets him gamble a few francs a week. He is harmless and he asks all young women, especially pretty ones, to dine with him. I do not know how he manages to live in this expensive hotel. A small room, perhaps by arrangement with the Austrian government. You will learn much for your newspaper from him, mademoiselle. Also, I think the casino management arranged for him to escort you."

Lydia looked surprised. "How did you know I'm with a newspaper?"

"We have to know. We are well-trained to help the guests should they need it. I do not know how I can help a famous reporter, but if I can, I will. And the baron will also help as well as be amusing."

"Thank you. I'll remember. But I must confess I'm not famous," she laughed.

"You will be, mademoiselle," Angelina predicted loyally. "There are so many stories here, mademoiselle. The more favorable ones you write, the more the hotel and the casino will like it. Even now the casino pays *Le Figaro*, the Paris newspaper, twenty-five francs a week to be mentioned somewhere in the paper every day, if only to tell of the beautiful weather."

"Angelina," Lydia said decisively. "I want you to come to me with any little stories or anecdotes you hear or learn about or observe from now on. I'll arrange to pay you for them. You'll be most helpful if you'll do this."

"*Oui*, but I do not seek money. It will be my pleasure."

"We'll see about the money. Now let's make sure I don't disappoint the baron. Imagine, a month ago nobody knew who I was and tonight I'm dining with a baron at Monte Carlo." She laughed. "And I don't even know him yet."

"He is delightful company for an unattached lady, and very, very safe," Angelina explained as she left.

Although Lydia was somewhat amused by the unaccustomed spate of attention, she was also pleased that she was to have a male companion for dinner. It had worried her to be dining alone. Nevertheless, when the baron knocked and identified himself soon after, she felt a secret relief that he was old enough to be her father. He was a balding, pudgy little man with an infectious smile above a neat goatee, dressed in beautifully tailored evening clothes. His blue eyes regarded her with interest and mild good humor.

"Mademoiselle Lydia Bradley," he said formally, in a deep bass voice and with a slight bow of his head, "I am Baron Maxfried Hetzler. I have come to welcome you to Monte Carlo and express the hope that you will be my dinner companion."

"That is most kind of you, Baron Hetzler," Lydia said graciously, "and I'm honored, but I must tell you that it's unusual for an American lady to accept an invitation from a gentleman unknown to her—even though he is a member of royalty."

His eyes sparkled merrily. "Ach . . . you flatter me, mademoiselle, and I confess it pleases me. However, you may be assured that I am beyond the age of romance and wish only the pleasure of your company." His voice lowered confidentially. "Of course, mademoiselle, to make it quite decorous, separate checks would be advisable. Or—since I am well acquainted with Monte and can give you a great deal of information, plus many stories with which you could entertain your readers—you might well

43

"A pleasure, Baron," Lydia said, scarcely able to contain her laughter. "I appreciate your thoughtfulness and look forward to an evening that will be most informative."

"To be sure, fräulein."

As they descended in the lift, he told her, "You may be interested to know that I am also cousin to the emperor Franz Josef. He comes here and stays in this hotel with—ah—his mistress. His wife does not like Monte so she remains at Nice or Cap Martin."

"With her paramours?" Lydia asked, surprised at such abrupt confidences but questioning him with the directness of a reporter.

"*Ja*—it is a scandal, but done away from Vienna so at least they are considerate of their subjects. If you are ready . . . I have a table waiting." He offered Lydia his arm.

She wasn't certain whether or not the heads turning her way were simply looking in admiration at the handsome pair they presented, or knew that she represented the Press, but if so, no one objected, for she was met with smiles and nods. She suspected the latter, and that an American reporter carried some prestige here.

She permitted the baron to order and he did so with skill, producing as a first course a salad composed of small bits of seafood and a great quantity of caviar. The main course was a roast of beef, served amid vegetables contrived to make the platter look like a flower garden. Dessert was a chocolate mousse, the likes of which she had never tasted in her lifetime and wondered if she ever would again, for its creamy perfection was such that she thought it not to be repeated. Throughout the meal, they drank champagne. It seemed to be the favorite beverage in this hotel and downed far faster than the decanters of water.

The baron kept up a steady flow of trivial talk, which was interesting, though too inconsequential to be used in filing a story. Lydia had hoped for more, because in the morning she planned to send her first cable. She prayed that it might be something at least fairly sensational.

"Tell me," she asked, "why you choose to remain in Monte Carlo all this time, Baron? Why have you not returned to Vienna where you certainly must be a man of some importance, being related, however distantly, to the emperor."

"That is a sad story, mademoiselle. I might be of some importance, if the emperor accepted me. However, he does not. It seems my mother irritated him so she was forbidden to his court and when she died, his petty dislike of the family was passed on to me. Most unfortunate. Anyway, I have grown to like Monte. I like the people, the food, the excitement, the gambling. And I especially like the mild climate. Have you found it exciting here, fräulein?"

"I haven't been here long enough to know where to look for it, Baron."

"Excitement is everywhere, especially in the casino. There you can see a wealthy man reduced to poverty in a few hours, or find joy in watching a poor man grow rich. Yet if you play, stay away from *chemin de fer*. It is not a game where you can win. Not much, anyway."

"What of roulette?" she asked.

"The most popular game, fräulein. Strictly a game of chance. It is nothing like reading the cards, memorizing numbers . . . you put down your money and—*voilá*—it is gone." He snapped his fingers and looked infinitely sad.

"I have nothing to gamble with," she confided. "My orders are *not* to gamble."

"Then you have a wise employer, fräulein. But if you like, we can go into the casino and observe. I would show you how to play the wheel, but alas, I am temporarily embarrassed. My stipend does not arrive for two more days."

Lydia said generously, seeing her chance, "Baron, if you search your memory and give me some kind of a story I can use, I'll pay for our dinner and even give you a few francs for the wheel. I can charge this to my expense account."

"I am saved," he said with a happy flourish of his hand,

his face lighting up with a beatific smile. "I have so many stories to tell, I shall be on a pension forever. You have saved my life. . . ."

He stopped talking abruptly and began looking about the room, which had grown unusually noisy. Something seemed to have happened. Guests were chattering excitedly, and a few left their half-eaten dinners to hurry toward the exit.

"What's going on?" Lydia asked.

The baron stood up and bowed. "I shall find out. Pardon me a moment, fräulein."

He strode over to someone he apparently knew, listened a few moments and returned hurriedly. He didn't sit down, but stood behind Lydia's chair to assist her in arising.

"There is no time to lose. You can sign the check later. Come along, this you cannot afford to miss."

Lydia stood up and turned to face him. "Can't you tell me what's going on?"

"There is a man . . . in the casino." The baron's voice held a deep undercurrent of excitement. "He has broken two wheels and it looks as if he is going to break the bank. No one has ever done this before. It is a great thing to happen."

"You're right. It's something I want to see," she agreed.

He placed her cape on her shoulders and they made their way from the restaurant and along a sidewalk well-filled with people hurrying to the casino. The word had spread rapidly. As they entered the ornate building, Lydia had little time to examine it, though she was aware of silk brocades, rich leathers and soft lighting.

The activity was now concentrated on a table around which a hundred or more people were pressed. The voice of the croupier sounded as monotonous as ever, but the chattering of the onlookers was not quiet.

The baron managed to edge a way through the crowd until they stood almost at the side of a rather poorly dressed man with a scruffy beard. The only impressive thing about him was the mound of counters before him.

The croupier called for bets, spun the wheel, tossed the

ivory ball and the chattering magically ceased. All that could be heard was the hoarse breathing of those who watched, and the clicking of the spinning ball.

There was a great sigh as the ball came to a stop. The croupier's rake pushed the counters toward the man who held the spotlight.

"Baron Hetzler, can you find out who he is? How much he's won?" Lydia asked. "Here is where you can earn some of that pension you were talking about."

"Trust me," the baron said. "I will find out, but not until the play stops."

"How long has he been playing?" Lydia asked a matronly looking woman at her side.

"Since early evening, my dear. He has lost but two or three times. His luck is phenomenal—I think he has won perhaps a quarter of a million francs so far. Two tables could not pay and he was brought to this one. It has to stop soon or the entire bank of Monte Carlo will be broken!"

"Would that mean Monte Carlo would go bankrupt?" she asked innocently.

The woman stared at her. "My dear child, they can provide another bank quickly enough, but this is not something that happens often. Not in a lifetime for most."

The baron had left her and was quietly circulating, asking questions, peering with that suave manner of his into the faces of those he buttonholed. Lydia thought he seemed to be getting answers, too.

The croupier said something in a voice that was as calm as his attitude, and the gambler called for a bucket into which to place his chips. A black cloth, like a pall, was drawn over the wheel.

"He has broken another table!" the woman beside Lydia exclaimed in awe.

Lydia moved away from the table, swept along with the crowd. The gambler was on his way to another table, followed closely by what looked to be anxious casino executives. The baron took Lydia aside and called to a waitress to bring drinks.

He announced importantly, "His name is Charles de Ville

Wells and such a run of luck has never before been seen here. No matter what he plays . . . *manque, passe, pair, impair, rouge, noir* . . . he wins five times out of six *and* he keeps doubling his bets. It's uncanny and thrilling. Ach, that I would have such good fortune!''

"Explain to me, please, how he does it," Lydia demanded.

"That is what everyone is asking. They think he has a system, one never tried before or even heard of. If he has one it is most successful, as you can see."

"How long will this go on?"

"Until he chooses to stop or . . . he breaks the bank. It has never been done before."

Lydia's eyes were alight with a reporter's excitement at a good story in the offing. "Baron, stay with this. Keep track of everything. See if you can talk to Mr. Wells or someone close to him. Find out all you can. I'll be back later. I have to send a cable even if the story isn't finished," she told him crisply.

Lydia left him just as the crowd around the new table was making a sound like a long, low moan. She didn't know if that meant the player had won or lost, but she was more concerned now with filing the first part of the story, for she sensed it was a sensational one. This was the break she had hoped for.

Her heart pounded as she was stopped short near the exit of the casino by two suave men in evening dress.

"Mademoiselle, would it be convenient for you to come with us?" one of them asked.

"Only," she said, somewhat nervously, "if you tell me why I should."

"We cannot say, but it would be most advisable for you to accompany us," the taller of the two pointed out.

"And to your advantage," the other added.

She looked at the stolid expressions on their faces, at the cold, uncompromising look in their eyes, and decided it might be wise to obey them.

She was promptly taken to the rear of the casino where

48

a heavy, polished wooden door was opened and the men stood aside as she entered a large and opulent office. Two men, also in evening dress, who'd been pacing the room as she entered, paused to regard her. The door was quietly closed behind her.

"Mademoiselle Bradley," a plump, somewhat distraught man said as he seized her hand and bowed to kiss the back of it. Lydia was beyond surprise, though this was the first time this had ever happened to her. She was too filled with the excitement of the Wells story, and the realization that these were casino officials. From their somber expressions it was obvious they were filled with concern.

"May I ask, gentlemen, why you have detained me?"

"Detained? Ah, *non,* mademoiselle. We only wish to ask a favor of you."

"I'm in a hurry," she said. "Please be brief."

"To be sure. We ask that you do not embellish this story of a man who wins too much. Naturally you must report it, but not in a sensational manner, if it pleases you." Sweat beaded the forehead of the rotund manager, and he mopped it with a large handkerchief.

"The only way to please my editor is to tell it as it happens," Lydia said bluntly.

"Mademoiselle," the second man implored earnestly, "this winner is running on astounding good luck and he may keep playing for days. If he breaks us, it will not be to our advantage if the story—"

"On the contrary," Lydia interrupted him, suddenly inspired by an idea, "it will make Monte Carlo famous. If he breaks the bank . . . I think that is what you call it . . . the whole world will be interested. If he takes days to do it, even to finally lose, the suspense will still be great. I can keep the story going until all over the world people will wonder if he is to win or lose. If he wins, there are millions who will be convinced it can be done and they will come to Monte in droves. You will lose money now, if he breaks you, but the final result will be worth a thousand times what this will cost you."

The two men looked at one another, and then at the vision in blue chiffon that was Lydia, a woman with the power to influence their futures. "*Mon Dieu*, she is right!" the manager exclaimed. "Of course . . . of course . . . we have thought only of losing."

"You will see that the story gets to your newspaper, mademoiselle?" the other asked eagerly now, actually managing a smile.

"I guarantee it, and papers all over the world will pick it up. This could be something very great for Monte. May I go now—to write my cable and send it off in the morning?"

"You write the cable," she was told, "and when you are finished, you will find the cable office open. It will relay the story at once. There is no time to lose."

Lydia hurried back to the hotel to find the lobby all but deserted. Using the stairs, not the lift, to reach her floor, she promptly locked herself in and sat down at the small desk to collect herself for a few moments before beginning to write. She called upon all she had learned about reporting, even recalling the advice Bryant Drury had given her. The story must be brief, but still contain detailed information and the elements of suspense and excitement. She must also remember space and the cost of cables. Rewriters at the *Star-Press* could embellish if need be. She discarded the first two attempts, but the third one flowed smoothly.

THE MAN WHO BROKE THE BANK AT MONTE CARLO

Today a small, quiet, unobtrusive man named Charles de Ville Wells, a British inventor—or so he claims—has broken the bank at Monte Carlo. Three roulette tables were covered with a black cloth when Mr. Wells won almost every bet in the sum of twenty thousand British pounds—and he is not through yet. If he has a system, no one has determined what it is. If his luck holds and he breaks the rest of the tables, he will have won perhaps fifty thousand pounds. Mr. Wells is by no means a flamboyant player. He is quiet, doubling his bets with no show of emotion or excitement. It is said he is not a professional gambler, but only a man with a phenomenal run of luck. If his good fortune holds, he may walk out of here with nearly a million American dollars. More tomorrow after he resumes playing.

Finished, she hurried downstairs to the desk, asked where the cable office was and set off on foot, despite the lateness of the hour. The office was open, though the sign on the door proclaimed it closed at six. An operator was waiting to take her copy and began to send it immediately.

She remained there until he had finished and handed back her copy. Perhaps she would have it framed one day, she thought, if it achieved what she hoped it would. On her return, she didn't stop at the casino. She was exhausted and left it to the baron to develop anything further, though she doubted it would be much, for people were streaming out of the casino by now. The play must be over for the night.

She prepared for bed, then stared wide-eyed at the ceiling, convinced she would never sleep. But the next thing she knew, it was nine in the morning, and Angelina was tapping softly on the parlor door.

Three

"There is great excitement, mademoiselle," Angelina whispered. "And the baron has been pacing the hall waiting for you to arise."

"I overslept," Lydia said, yawning, and with a trace of self-annoyance. "Last night held too much excitement for my first day. Has the play in the casino resumed?"

"Ah, no—not until this evening, I imagine. But everyone waits for it to begin. Such luck this man has, I have never seen the likes of it."

"I suppose it's all everyone is talking about," Lydia said sleepily.

"Indeed, yes. So much commotion, mademoiselle. I have ordered breakfast to be served in your parlor."

Lydia spoke as she headed for the bathroom. "Please make it for two and invite the baron. I'll bathe and dress quickly."

She received the baron in a morning gown of dove-colored taffeta. He in turn looked quite elegant in gray trousers with a matching vest piped in red, topped by a short black coat beneath which was revealed a blue scarf, substituting for a cravat. He carried a gray top hat, which he placed on a nearby table as he sat down to enjoy a breakfast of eggs, ham and hot croissants. Lydia sensed he was delighted to get a free meal, but she felt it was money well spent.

"I spoke with the man Wells last evening," he told her. "No one saw me as far as I know. I asked him for his system and he told me, very honestly I am convinced, that he has no real system other than this: he plays, then lets the stakes double and redouble for three plays; then he begins again, win or lose. When he loses, he stops for a time and then resumes. So he wins big and loses little. A phenomenal man. I would go mad with stakes that high and the risks increasing against every play.''

''Who is he? Where is he from? What do you know about him? I need all the information I can get.'' Lydia hurled her questions at him between the excellent croissants and coffee.

''He is a very ordinary man. I will find out where he comes from, his family background, and what he does for a living. I can promise you this information this afternoon, Fräulein Bradley. You see, I am drinking with him today,'' he added smugly.

''Do you have money to pay for the drinks?'' She smiled at his feigned embarrassment. ''Why do I bother to ask! How much?''

''Perhaps a thousand francs.''

''Here are five hundred,'' she said. ''You can get very drunk on that much, but don't. Get me a lucid story with facts. We'll talk later about the other five hundred francs.''

''I will see you at supper, fräulein, if you will do me the honor.''

''Early, then,'' she said, knowing she'd have to pay for it. ''I want to get the story on the wire quickly.''

At noon she received a complimentary cablegram from Guy Spencer of the *Star-Press,* ordering her to keep on top of the story and to send whatever she found out as soon as possible. It seemed that her hunch that everyone would be interested, had proven correct.

On the third day the house declared itself broke. Charles de Ville Wells had broken the bank at Monte Carlo and through Lydia's stories, one following another, the events had reached the world. Other reporters would be here soon, she knew, but it was over now and she had been the one to tell it first.

Mr. Wells, who seemed to be a rather shy man—or a most suspicious one—desired no interviews. But the baron was up to that. By prearrangement with him, Lydia entered the café one day soon after, and was beckoned by the baron to a secluded table where he sat with Wells.

"Ah, my dear cousin," the baron said, standing as he greeted her. "Please sit with us. You will have a small sherry, of course." He summoned the waiter and gave the order, playing his part to the hilt. Now she was able to see Mr. Wells at close range, she was astonished that he looked even less impressive than she had thought. He was bald, his black beard was sorely in need of a trim and he spoke with a heavy cockney accent. Moreover, he seemed to be a very evasive man, one who would lie easily. Lydia made up her mind to send cablegrams to London to ferret out some facts about this lucky man's past.

"I have no system," he told her. "I bet my money, I watch and wait, and I win."

"May I ask how much you began with?"

"Four hundred pounds, miss."

"And how much did you win?" she asked guilelessly.

"Such questions are not asked by true gamblers," the baron said, his smile apologetic. Then he added, "But, monsieur, she is only a young girl who knows nothing about roulette."

"I won forty thousand pounds."

"He broke the bank six times," the baron said in hushed, reverent tones. "He placed six tables in mourning. Ach, imagine!"

"What will you do with all this money?" Lydia asked, her eyes widening in wonderment that was only partially faked.

"I'm an inventor, miss. I guess I'll do some inventing now that I have money enough to take care of myself." As the waiter returned, he added with a harsh smile, "You pay for the drinks, Baron. I don't pay for drinks."

With that rude statement, he left them and all but ran out of the café to avoid being stopped and questioned by curious onlookers. The baron sipped his brandy and smiled conspiratorially at Lydia over the rim of the glass.

"Am I earning my money, little cousin?"

"You are, indeed, Baron Hetzler. What do you think of the man?"

"Not much. He sounds to me as if he'd gladly strip a man of his shirt if he was foolish enough to take his advice. But . . . he won fair and square. There is no doubt of that."

"Do you think he'll lose it all?" Lydia asked.

"In confidence, he told me he's going to slip out of Monte tonight. That will add to your story. You see—and you cannot blame him—he's made all he wants to. Such good fortune as to balloon four hundred pounds into forty thousand pounds! If only luck like that would come to me," he sighed.

"It has in small part," she smiled. "I'll give you a thousand francs and more if you discover anything else. Not only about Wells, but anyone who comes here."

"In other words, you are hiring me." He spoke with quiet assurance.

"At an undecided salary, Baron. So far, you have been a great help. Now, excuse me so I can write the finish of this story and get it off to New York."

Lydia's personal interview with Wells proved to be sensational. Other reporters, arriving after the event, filed stories, but hers was firsthand and more detailed. She learned that a song had been written about the incident and was already one of the most popular to date. Everyone was humming "The Man Who Broke the Bank at Monte Carlo."

Her idea of following up Wells in England also proved productive, although she had no exclusive on that. British newspapers ran him down and learned that he truly was an inventor, but one regarded as somewhat shady in his dealings, a side of him that was forgotten by the public in the glory of his phenomenal win. When the story was finally concluded, all of three weeks after it began, Lydia was the exhausted recipient of cablegrams from Morgan congratulating her and advising that her salary had been doubled.

She felt a quiet satisfaction. She'd come to Monte Carlo, an untried journalist knowing little about the place, and by the same run of luck that Wells had enjoyed, she'd come upon a story matching the best over a twenty-year period. She knew she had handled it well and that she was now a full-fledged foreign correspondent capable of handling any assignment. The first of her ambitions had been realized. Now she was aiming at becoming a name known all over the world. And she was certain the means to do it lay right here in Monte Carlo.

Because of all the favorable publicity, Lydia was given carte blanche by the casino and the hotel. Whatever Mademoiselle Bradley desired was hers. She had entry everywhere, except to some of the trysting places where emperors, dukes and barons kept their mistresses.

Lydia was also developing a keen sense that told her when something was going to happen. She visited the casino every night, quickly learned the fundamentals of roulette, *chemin de fer* and the very popular *trente et quarante*. She also acquired a knowledge of baccarat and its high stakes, but she played no tables, risked not a French sou, even though there were times when she was tempted.

This particular evening about five weeks after her arrival she watched a lanky young man, perhaps twenty-five, sweating at a roulette table while he lost again and again. She had discovered that such a steady series of losses often depressed a player to the extent that he became dangerous to himself. There'd been one suicide during the time she'd been here, but it had been well hushed up.

She walked over to stand behind the young man, who was now openly distraught. Lydia pretended to concentrate on the player next to him—a dowager who coolly surveyed every play through a lorgnette—but Lydia was watching as the young man finally threw in his last counters on *masque,* which meant he would win if the ball stopped in any of the slots from one to eighteen. She held her breath as the ball fell into zero, the table winning every counter on it. The young man arose and seemed to shake his long limbs in order to limber up after such a long session at the table. Then he walked casually out of the casino. Lydia saw him heading for one of the more secluded sections of the formal gardens.

She remembered Angelina's comment about suicides ending their lives in the gardens. Feeling far less casual than she appeared, she began to saunter after him, but when she lost him outdoors, she began to run, clutching her evening bag with one hand and holding up her gown with the other.

Rounding a dark corner in a rush, she found the young man seated on a concrete wall surrounding one of the smaller gardens. There was a pistol on his lap. As she neared him, he looked up and started to raise the gun, not at her, but at himself.

Terrified that he would pull the trigger, Lydia dropped her evening bag and called out, "Please, monsieur!" She reached for the arm that held the gun, and tried to make him drop it. He struggled with her, but rather weakly, as if he were in a state of nervous exhaustion. Nevertheless, she was afraid of the gun. What if it went off accidentally? Though she might be the one to stop the bullet, she dared not let go.

"Let go of me, mademoiselle!" he exclaimed angrily.

"No," she retorted, "I won't let go until you drop the gun!"

"I'm going to finish what I came out here to do," he said tightly. "Release me!"

"No!" she exclaimed.

"Very well," he said, his tone one of disgust. "If you get hurt, don't blame me." He struggled grimly to throw her off.

Lydia knew she couldn't maintain her hold, and also that once she let go, he'd kill himself. There was only one thing left for her to do. She opened her mouth and screamed loudly, feeling weak and dizzy. Apparently the would-be suicide was also, for he stumbled. The movement forced her to loosen her hold and she went hurtling to one side and fell backward into a bed of flowers. This broke her fall and shook her up, but she was none the worse for wear. A metallic clink echoed as what she hoped was the gun fell on the stone walk. In the struggle, the young man had also fallen, landing on his stomach with his arms bent and held against his body. His elbows knocked the wind out of him and for a moment he lay still.

"Are you hurt?" she asked, not thinking the question incongruous despite what he intended to do.

"No, dammit," he exclaimed angrily, once he caught his breath.

Lydia was sitting up, looking at him still lying prone. If the situation weren't so serious, she'd laugh. As it was, she could see his mind was still bent on self-destruction.

"Have you got my gun?" he asked. He turned on his side and slowly, painfully, raised himself to a sitting position.

Before she could answer, running footsteps approached, slowed and stopped. She saw another man bend down and retrieve what she hoped was the gun rather than her evening bag, also lost in the scuffle.

The steps resumed and a stranger peered down at them both. It was so dark she couldn't make out his features, but she had an impression of an angry scowl and dark, flashing eyes.

"What the hell's going on here?" he demanded.

"None of your business," the lanky young man, seated beside Lydia, replied.

"You could be right," was the sarcastic reply, "unless this gun belongs to one of you."

"It's mine," the young man held out his hand for it.

"Don't give it to him," Lydia exclaimed in horror. "He tried to kill himself."

"Because of you?"

Lydia's tone stiffened in response to his gruffness. "No. Over losses while gambling," she retorted. She tried to get up, lost her balance and sat down again in the bed of flowers.

"Here. Let me help you." He extended a hand to her. She was about to reach for it when the man beside her made a lunge for the gun held loosely in the stranger's other hand. Lydia rolled out of the way. The man holding the gun slipped it into the pocket of his tuxedo and threw a punch at the would-be suicide. The fist connected and he dropped back onto the flower bed, to lie there motionless, obviously dazed.

The stranger addressed Lydia again. "Give me your hands."

She obeyed and he pulled her none too gently to her feet. "Why did you let him gamble to the point where he was going to do this foolish thing?"

"I don't even know his name," she said indignantly. "I was just watching him in the casino. He lost everything and seemed quite distraught. Because I'd heard stories of suicides, when he walked briskly from the gaming room I followed him out here."

"How did you end up in the flower bed?" he asked, his tone now almost one of amusement. "Both of you."

"I tried to keep him from killing himself," she replied, making no attempt to hide her irritation. "I gripped his arm to prevent him from lifting the gun. He stumbled and threw me aside, but he fell himself."

"You were as foolish as he," came the cool reply. "He might have shot you instead of himself."

"He's still lying motionless," Lydia said, now openly angry. "Perhaps you accomplished what he failed to do."

"He's not dead, if that's what you're thinking." He bent down, gripped the young man by the arm and hauled him to his feet. The man staggered a little, still dazed by the force of the blow.

The stranger addressed him. "A word of advice, young man. If you can't afford to lose, stay away from Monte Carlo. From any gambling resort for that matter."

"Thank you for telling me what I already happen to know," the young man said self-righteously. "If you'll give me back my gun, I'll finish what I started before this lady interfered, which she had no right to do."

Lydia expostulated, "Killing yourself won't solve anything!"

The tall man who had intervened patted the gun still in his pocket. "You heard what the lady said. If you haven't enough money to get home, see the manager and he'll advance you a train ticket. I'll keep the damn gun and pay you a hundred francs for it."

He opened a well-filled wallet and removed the promised bills. The young gambler accepted them with a resentful nod and moved away toward the street. Then the stranger picked up Lydia's evening bag and handed it to her.

"Now you have tomorrow's headline story," he said.

"How dare you!" she exploded. "What do you think I am? And who are you? Not that it matters except you seem to know me." She sat down on a stone bench, feeling shocked and drained suddenly.

"Everybody in Monte Carlo knows Miss Bradley of the *Star-Press*. But I'm warning you, if you write about this story and include me, I'll sue your newspaper and deny it ever happened."

He now took Lydia's arm and urged her to her feet, moving in the direction of the casino where there was more light. "Let me have a look at you," he said. "Do you always go out of your way to stop stray bullets? Aren't you afraid of ruining such a lovely . . . gown?"

"Are you always so hardhearted and rude?" Lydia countered.

In the gaslight before the casino she took a long breath, and tried to will the embarrassed flush from her face. She was looking up at him from a distance of about two feet, into dark gray eyes that regarded her with sardonic amusement. His jaw was square, clean-cut and clean-shaven, his chin aggressive and his mouth finely sculpted, with slightly grim lines. He was almost a foot taller than she, a broad-shouldered man, elegantly dressed and completely poised as he coolly surveyed her. A lock of his unruly dark hair had fallen down on his brow, the only vulnerable detail about him. He brushed it back with his hand in an impatient gesture.

"Well," he asked mockingly, "do I pass inspection?"

"Yes, though I'm surprised," Lydia replied. "From the callous manner with which you handled that young man, I thought you'd be quite ugly."

"I can be," he said, eyeing her as if cataloguing every contour of her face.

She stepped back and broke into a small nervous laugh. "I don't doubt it, but I didn't mean to be rude—just because you were."

"On the contrary, I thought I handled the situation very well," he said coolly, watching her. "Especially when I assumed that your honor was at stake when I came upon the scene."

Lydia said hotly, "As I already told you, I saw the young man in the casino. I've been here long enough to recognize a loser who can't stand up under it. So I followed him, hoping to talk him out of what he was about to do. That's all."

"Bravo, Miss Bradley. But they're not hard to spot, so don't flatter yourself you made a clever deduction."

"Are you always so insolent?"

"When young ladies might get themselves shot—yes." He paused, then continued in crisp tones. "My name is Jeffrey Marcus. I'm an engineer engaged to study Monaco, including the Monte Carlo section, to see what measures must be taken to prevent the whole site from eventually sliding into the harbor. My company sent me to assess the situation."

"You're an American, then," she guessed.

"Yes, and since you're one also, let's take a walk. The night was made for it." He suddenly took her hand and gently kissed the back of it, holding it moments longer than etiquette required.

Lydia blushed. She didn't know how to respond to such total self-assurance. "I agree that the night is beautiful. However, I'd like to be sure that my escort would assume a . . . gentlemanly manner. You're not exactly . . . correct, are you, Mr. Marcus?"

He looked down into her eyes, his expression unreadable.

"Please forgive me. I'll be honored, Miss Bradley, if you'll accompany me on a stroll through the gardens, or wherever you might wish to go. My motive is simple—you interest me."

"You're certainly direct," Lydia said, her astonishment completely unfeigned.

"When you're ferreting out a story in your role of reporter, I imagine you are, too," he pointed out. "But if being honest is being direct, I'm the most direct person you'll ever meet."

Lydia smiled, despite herself. "It's good to be with an American, Mr. Marcus. I'll take that stroll with you."

He took her arm and guided her along paths that were obviously familiar to him. Eventually they reached a spot overlooking the harbor. Without a word, he bent, placed his hands on her waist and lifted her, setting her down gently on a large round rock. Then he stepped up beside her, took the gun from his pocket, held it between thumb and forefinger and let it drop into the water. His momentary preoccupation with what he was doing gave her a chance to study him. When he turned and caught her eye, she said in confusion, "Do you gamble, Mr. Marcus?"

His reply was a deep, brief laugh.

"Well, do you?" she persisted.

"I came here some time ago. The first time I entered the casino I made up my mind that I'd put twenty American dollars on the red. If I won, I'd stay. I lost. I walked out and I've never bet since. And you?"

"I'm under orders never to bet. I don't believe I would, anyway."

"That sort of gambling never appealed to me," he said.

"How did you know who I am?" she asked, changing the subject.

"I move around quite a lot," he replied, looking out to sea.

"Perhaps you know I came here knowing absolutely nothing about Monte," she explained. "I think my publisher and editor sent me with the thought that I might provide them with stories written from the viewpoint of a novice. That might have been true when I arrived, but I learned quickly. Otherwise, I'd never have guessed that young man was going to kill himself.''

''Why not do that story? It's just another side of this rock of splendor and money—the dark side. There have been suicides here. Quite a few of them, but not as many as some ragtag newspapers would have you believe. It's a subject worth going into. I'm sure you can do it without preaching.''

''Thanks. I'll think about it. I wish I knew more about that young man.''

He turned and looked at her, then said slowly, ''He's from London, a clerk who saved his money and hoped to make a killing. He'll be back. He'll get another job and save again so he can return here once more. Or he may try Cannes . . . anyplace that a spinning wheel determines whether you get rich or die poor. You can find out who he is at his hotel.''

''You're a cynical man, Mr. Marcus.''

''Of course I am. And you'll be cynical, too, very soon if you're not already.''

''I don't agree. I doubt I ever will be. It's not in my nature,'' she protested.

He simply laughed in reply. ''May I buy you a drink? At the hotel, not the casino. It's less . . . distracting.''

''I'd be delighted,'' she said, ignoring the slight hesitation of his last words, and the intent look he gave her.

They walked back along the harborfront toward the hotel. At a corner table there, which he asked for, they ordered bourbon and soda and began to reminisce about New York.

Lydia wanted to like him. For one thing, he breathed of America and made her yearn for home. He seemed sincere as they talked on and on, but she grew increasingly puzzled. Although she probed with all her reporter's skill, he skirted any questions that were even remotely personal, and this after his comment about getting acquainted. He mentioned nothing about his family, his ambitions or how successful he had been in his work here. In fact, he asked most of the questions. Almost without realizing it, Lydia had soon told him the story of Bryant Drury and how she came to get the assignment to Monte Carlo. Not until later did it occur to her that he was far more skilled at getting information than she.

"Your Mr. Morgan made a good choice," he said. "I read your story about Wells and the way he broke the bank. It was very good. You did no embellishing, yet kept it suspenseful and exciting."

"It was just one of those strokes of good fortune that seem to come too infrequently," she said modestly. "But it did serve to establish me, and I have an assignment here permanently now. Though I don't intend to stay forever."

"Still, we'll likely see one another," he said. "I'm often at the casino or the hotel with business acquaintances. Perhaps we might have dinner one evening, if you wish?"

She smiled. "Yes, perhaps we might, Mr. Marcus."

"Jeff, please. In order that I may call you Lydia."

Lydia gave a rueful shake of her head. "You're the boldest man I've ever known."

"Worse than your friend Drury?" he challenged.

"He's not my friend. And that was different."

"I'm sure your little triumph didn't endear you to him. I'm also certain he got fresh with you. His kind usually do." He looked at her speculatively.

"That doesn't concern you . . . Mr. Marcus," she added pointedly.

He raised his eyebrows as if he disagreed, but said nothing.

"Besides," Lydia rushed on, "he was fired because of me."

"He deserved it."

"Yes, but I didn't like to be the cause of it."

"The devil with Drury. Let's talk about you, *Miss Bradley*."

"No, let's talk about you," Lydia countered. "You succeeded in getting my life's history, although I had no intention of telling you as much about myself as I did. Now it's your turn to be revealing."

"I'm not all that interesting, I assure you. But I'm delighted you were sent here."

"You never even saw me before tonight," Lydia scoffed.

"Oh, but I did, Miss Bradley, several times, in fact. And I thought you quite charming, even at a distance. And much more so tonight."

Lydia attempted to look him firmly in the eye. "It's quite a line you have."

He leaned across the table and the amused drawl crept into his voice again. "You needn't be so priggish."

"I'm not priggish," Lydia retorted.

"What would you call it, then?" he demanded.

"I'm irritated," she replied, looking deliberately away from him.

"Obviously," he said, relaxing and settling back in his chair. "How can I make you believe I'm sincere, Miss Bradley? Would you prefer me to deny that you are . . . utterly charming?" He went on calmly. "Your naivete is refreshing, especially here. You were walking around the casino tonight with your mouth open."

"I think I always will," Lydia replied, laughing now. "It's a wonderland. The grand marble foyer, the silk wall coverings edged with every kind of passementerie. And I've never seen so much gilt paneling. Plus the palatial splendor of the gaming rooms!"

He regarded her with interest. "Have you dined at Le Privé?"

"No. Is that one of the restaurants in the casino?"

"Yes. I think you'll find it enchanting. It's a long, narrow room—something like an Orient Express dining car. It has banquette seats, gentle lighting and the most delicious food."

"I'll dine there," she said. "With the baron."

"No. With me," he corrected. "Please. I'm not being rude now. We're Americans, we're lonely so far from home and I think we'd get along splendidly."

65

"But, Mr. Marcus," she replied archly, "I'm not lonely. Monte is too exciting a place ever to be lonely. Yet perhaps I'll dine with you, if you promise not to be rude."

"I shall make it a point not to be," he said. His eyes regarded her, his expression amused.

"What are you laughing at now?" she asked, frowning.

"Most women would have catered to my male ego by telling me they were as lonely as I."

She scoffed at this. "I don't believe you're lonely. And I repeat—I know I'm not. If you wish to take me to dinner under those conditions, I'll be happy to accept your invitation."

He executed a hint of a bow from where he sat. "And there's also the Opera House. You'll find that unbelievably beautiful, the jewel of Monte. And below the casino—have you been to Le Cabaret? Besides dinner, there's dancing, plus an exciting show."

Lydia's eyes widened with heightened interest. "How can I possibly work it all in?"

"I'll find ways for you," he replied, watching her with an enigmatic look in his gray eyes.

"Now you're flirting with me," Lydia said, sobering.

"No, I just think our interests might be similar. I think it's worth finding out."

"You know, of course, I'm here to ferret out stories," she said seriously.

"They'll come to you," he replied, his smile once again one of amusement.

"What I'm saying is that my career comes first. I just felt you should know that. I want no romantic entanglements."

"As you wish," he replied, his manner suddenly brusque. "It so happens that I'm not looking for romance, either. Nonetheless, I'd like to indulge a whim of mine. I'd rather be with you and watch your face registering constant surprise and wonderment, than be with some of the other ladies who come here every winter."

"I can tell you're a sophisticate and I appreciate your willingness to be my escort."

"Just until the novelty wears off," he said lightly, maintaining the tone Lydia had adopted. "As you say, no entanglements."

"Exactly, Mr. Marcus." She looked pleased.

"Make it Jeff, please," he urged. "It's easy to say."

Lydia relented. "Very well, Jeff."

He exhaled audibly. "I never had to work so hard before to persuade a lady to let me take her out. Did your baron have to work as hard?"

"Don't call him my baron. I happen to like the man. He's like a kind uncle and he's been a great help to me. I won't tolerate any belittling talk about him."

"I'm sorry." His grin was sardonic. "You really do have a temper, don't you? But I think the baron's a fine old gent, even if he is completely broke, with a title that doesn't mean a thing. I'm glad you've given him a break, but don't be too generous. He'll only gamble it away. It's a compulsion with him."

"I'll handle the baron as I see fit. And now I must call it an evening. I have to write the story of this poor fellow who tried to kill himself. Please excuse me, Mr. Marcus."

She stood up abruptly, only to feel him grip her arm. "Jeff, remember?"

She managed a thin smile, knowing he would not release her arm unless she complied. "Good night, *Jeff*."

He resumed his seat at the table, signaling a waiter to bring another drink, and she felt his eyes follow her as she went directly to the lift. Once in her suite, she sat down and rested her head in her hands, exhausted. She didn't know what to conclude about Jeffrey Marcus. He was unlike anyone she'd ever known, but then, she realized, she'd never known many men. He'd been insufferably rude, but had managed to intrigue her as no one ever had before, while at the same time exasperating her.

She sat at her desk and wrote the story, beginning with her observation of the young man, and her noticing his growing nervousness as his losses mounted until he had nothing left. She related how she had followed him and prevented him from taking his own life, including Jeff in the article, but under a fictitious name. Afterward, she luxuriated in a relaxing bath to ease the pain in the muscles of her arms and shoulders.

Once she had climbed between the scented sheets of her bed, she reviewed the events of the evening and laughed aloud. Though it could have ended tragically, it had a humorous aspect to it. She turned on her side and settled down for sleep, a sleep long in coming, for a strong-featured face with penetrating gray eyes kept intruding into her consciousness. Jeffrey Marcus was personable, she admitted, with a way of convincing her he was in earnest, when he wasn't making her angry. But there was also a secretiveness about him that troubled her. He'd been adamant about her keeping him out of the story he knew she'd write.

With a start, she realized she was cultivating suspicion and cynicism. She wondered if it was a trait all reporters acquired as they grew in their profession, a learned tendency to disbelieve or to accept with reservations any information they uncovered about anything or anybody until it was thoroughly checked. Yet it was a characteristic every good newspaperman—or woman—must have.

It also occurred to her that Jeff had succeeded in prying from her the story of her life and he'd done it so cleverly she hadn't realized until he referred again to Bryant Drury. Also, Jeff had stated he'd watched her in the casino. She wasn't so naive that she believed he'd done so merely because he was interested in her. He was too sophisticated for that. And when she'd asked him to tell her about himself, he'd skillfully avoided doing so.

She worried the thought until gradually sleep claimed her.

Four

The wardrobe Lydia had selected at Worth's had arrived only three days beyond the three-week period she had been promised, so she was well-outfitted by now. A fact that not only pleased her but delighted Angelina, who, with a certain proprietorial air, stated that mademoiselle must be the most fashionably dressed lady in Monte Carlo. When Lydia pointed out that such a thing was not expected of a reporter, that she was neither a millionairess nor a member of royalty with endless jewels at her fingertips, Angelina brushed her arguments aside.

"We will see, mademoiselle." Angelina spoke with the air of a conspirator. "We will see."

Lydia had to agree that the young girl had a knack for knowing what jewelry to wear, when to substitute a silk flower for a gem, when to wear no jewelry at all.

Tonight as Lydia prepared to descend to dinner, Angelina chose the nile green taffeta gown that complemented Lydia's luxuriant blond hair and petal-soft skin. It had a lace overskirt that seemed to enhance the shimmering effect of the taffeta, the bodice was cut low and edged with small bunches of silk violets and the off-the-shoulder bouffant sleeves had a small bouquet of the same flower pressed into their fullness. Angelina swore no member of royalty could have looked more beautiful. Lydia expressed her thanks, wondering wryly if she would have carried more prestige with Angelina had she been a member of royalty.

The baron arrived and blew an enthusiastic kiss in the air when he saw her. "If I were a young man, I would get on my knees and kiss the toes of your slippers. All eyes will be on you tonight, fräulein."

"If so," she said graciously, "it will be only because I am escorted by a member of royalty who commands great respect here."

He beamed. "You are most kind. Especially since I am certain you must be aware—yes, I remember telling you—that I am *persona non grata* with Emperor Franz Josef."

"His Majesty has done me a favor, then." She spoke with sincerity. "Because you have been, in large part, responsible for my success."

"After such a compliment, we shall dine at the Café de Paris, the best restaurant in Monte Carlo," the baron declared.

"I'm already looking forward to it, Baron."

The restaurant was almost filled when they entered, for the baron had insisted on a late arrival.

"So that more people will see us," he explained. "It is not fashionable to be early—anyone who appears on time for any function is said to be a peasant."

Lydia noticed that the baron, for all his impoverishment, was given special consideration. After all, he still had a title and was related to the emperor of Austria—even if he wasn't accepted by Franz Josef's court. So long as he paid the bills, the Monte Carlo restaurants favored him. Tonight they were provided with a table in the center of the large dining room, where they could be observed on all sides. Lydia felt a bit conspicuous at first, but that feeling soon left. Women at nearby tables acknowledged her presence by bowing their heads slightly, while their escorts were not averse to admiring her in a more open way.

"I'm beginning to like all this attention," she said. "It may not be the best thing for me, Baron, because one day I'll be called away from Monte and I'll miss it too much."

"Ah, but you will have the memories. They are very

important, especially when you reach my . . . ah . . . age. But I did not ask you to accompany me for that reason alone.''

"Perhaps you were in need of a good meal," she suggested in mock seriousness.

"That, too," he admitted freely. "Will you permit me to order?"

"I wouldn't think of denying you the pleasure. The newspaper accounting office may, but not I."

"Good. Afterward we will get down to the business of providing you with a story. I have something special, well worth the cost of this dinner, even though it is going to be considerable," he promised.

He called the waiter captain, and ordered Chateau Y'chem champagne and a decanter of fine brandy, which he mixed with his champagne. Lydia refused this concoction. There was an elaborate seafood appetizer, enough for four people, a specialty of the café, and the price on the menu made her hope the home office wouldn't warn against future expenditures like this, or chide her for extravagance.

The baron ordered pheasant. Not one serving, but the entire bird, festooned with its feathers. To Lydia the sight of it was less than appetizing, but she persevered. There were also vegetables, exotic ones for the fall season. Dessert was a frozen concoction of ice cream, and a mousse completely covered with a sauce Lydia couldn't identify, but which was pleasing to the palate. The baron then ordered liqueurs, selecting only the most expensive. The baron, she could see, when he didn't have to pick up the check, ordered from the price side of the menu.

He finally leaned back replete, and lit a cigar taken from the tray proffered by a pretty girl. The baron, of course, had grasped a half dozen. Yes, he was a confirmed sponger, Lydia thought, but so artful at the task that she was amused rather than annoyed.

"And now," the baron said, "down to business. I can tell you more about Monsieur Wells, who left with perhaps a quarter of a million dollars. After his serious gambling was over and he had broken the bank, he found himself with a few counters of his original stake—I judge perhaps two hundred pounds. He gambled them quite recklessly at *trente et quarante* and he left the table with six thousand more pounds. That man cannot lose, it seems."

"Thank you for the information," Lydia said. "I've been assigned to do a special story on him."

"So I suspected; you might find this a help." He handed her a photograph of Wells.

She studied it, then looked up at the baron with an expression of delight. "How in the world did you get this?"

"I didn't. A friend of mine took the picture. Monsieur Wells did not even know it was taken."

"I can almost tell that by the expression on his face. This is excellent work on your part. But who is this photographer?"

"A woman. Not one of great fashion, or even beauty, but still—a woman, and talented in the art of taking photographs. She has a camera that uses the newfangled film instead of plates. A small camera. It looks like a little box and she can conceal it rather well when she wants to. She lives for picture-taking—and for me," he added.

Lydia suppressed a smile. "*L'amour?*" she asked.

The baron smiled blandly. "That would be a gallant way of putting it. But, to be more truthful, I can tell you that she is a woman in need of a man from time to time. I happen to please her."

"I see. Can you get her to work for me? I'll pay for every photograph, ordered by me or not."

"She will be delighted. In fact, I have already closed the deal. You will pay whatever the picture is worth. Now, this picture of Wells is worth more than the cost of this dinner, however extravagant it is."

The baron waited for her to agree, but Lydia's mind was still on the photographer. "I will talk to her tomorrow. I have to cable my newspaper for permission, of course, but I have no doubt it will be granted. I'm certain your friend will find the arrangement most rewarding."

72

"She will not disappoint you. Now—shall we visit the casino? You are certain to find material for a story there every night. If you will kindly fold your napkin and place five hundred francs inside it. Then slip it closer to me. . . ."

"Five hundred?" she asked automatically, for it was far more than the amount of the check.

"Tips," he explained. "The maitre d', the waiter, the captain—"

"And Baron Hetzler?"

"But of course," he replied with polished assurance.

"Let's go to the casino," Lydia's smile was one of quiet resignation, "before you think of something else to buy here."

As they walked the short distance to the casino, the baron revealed he had more information for her.

"There will be a certain German general, an important staff officer close to the kaiser, at the tables. He comes twice a year. He will lose. He bets heavily and has yet to win a sou. Always he becomes very angry, for losing is not in accordance with his way of life. He is supposed never to lose. Yet he does, without fail. There might be a story there for you, mainly because the kaiser sends the man to play new systems that he cannot use himself for fear of losing prestige. It is remarkable to see how this general loses his temper as well as the kaiser's money."

Just as the baron had described, the general was already at one of the roulette tables with a dwindling stack of high-priced counters before him. Lydia discovered him to be a thick-set Prussian officer, partly bald, with heavy jowls and a considerable paunch. He had a stern expression on his face, which had gone somewhat florid in a rage that threatened to boil over at any moment.

"I don't exactly know why," Lydia said impishly, "but I'd like to see him lose."

"Some day," the baron said, "the kaiser will come. It is said he looks for a system and this man tries them out. When the kaiser thinks he has the right one, he is coming—to boast of the invincibility of the Prussian to beat any odds. And he will lose, too." His tone was fatalistic.

They moved to stand behind the general, who soon reached a stage of near apoplexy. He wasn't alone. Seated next to him was a younger man, perhaps forty, with a strange pasty skin, small eyes and an ugly look on his thin face. He was losing too, at about half the rate of the general, but he was taking his losses even harder.

"*Messieurs, faites vos jeux! Les jeux sont faits? Rien ne va plus!*" the croupier announced blandly. The wheel began to spin. He tossed the ivory ball and it clicked noisily as it ran around the wheel, stopping on zero. The croupier's rake cleaned the table.

The man beside the general suddenly leaped up. Behind him an elderly man had been watching, fascinated at the play. The gambler said, "Damn you, don't stand behind me. I don't want people standing behind me!"

"I meant no harm . . ." the elderly man protested indignantly.

The player pushed him hard enough that he staggered back to collide with another table, almost upsetting it. Then the pasty-faced man resumed his chair, growling under his breath.

"He's certainly a poor loser," Lydia observed.

"I have seen his kind many times," the baron confided. "He grows that angry because the money he is losing is probably not his, and he will have to replace it. Perhaps he is an absconder, or a plain thief. A man so worried at what will happen if he loses his bankroll that he grows impossible. He will make trouble all evening unless he recoups his losses, and he won't. They never do. There is bad luck connected with those who steal money to gamble with."

Lydia and the baron moved a little closer to further observe the play. The general won—not a large sum, but enough to relieve his tension. The other player lost again, heavily. He pushed most of his bankroll onto the table in what seemed to be a last desperate effort. He lost. The baron quickly took Lydia's arm, urging her away from the table.

The loser got up slowly and surveyed those who had been watching the game. "I hope you all had a good time," he said loudly and belligerently. "I also hope you lose as I did."

He began to turn away, but suddenly seemed to recognize Lydia. In three long steps he reached her and thrust his pale face close to hers as he spoke. "And you, will you make capital of this?"

"I don't know what you're talking about," she said calmly.

"You're the American reporter, are you not? You came here to get stories on all of us, winners and losers. Don't deny it. You prefer losers because they make better stories. Well, if you print my losses and my name, I assure you I will gladly separate your head from your shoulders."

He strode away before she could express her indignation. "Who is he?" she asked.

The baron left her for a moment, approached a man wearing the casino officer's uniform, talked a moment and then returned.

"He is an Englishman named Osgood Trencher. He's been here two days, gambling and losing all the time. That's all I can tell you, because Trencher has been very reticent at the tables."

Lydia's anger was still aroused. "I'm going to print the story—he's a spoilsport—and I'm going to use his name."

"Would you care for his picture—for say, two hundred francs?" the baron asked immediately.

"How could you get it now?"

"Look to your left. That woman, the rather stout one with graying hair and a perfectly plain face. Her body—well, it's not so bad when you get used to it. Her name is Regina LeFond. A native of Monaco."

"I see her. She doesn't look as if she belongs here."

"She gets around. Now, notice the large handbag she carries. In that handbag is a camera, one you've probably never seen before."

"In *that* handbag?" Lydia asked. "It doesn't seem large enough for any camera I've ever seen."

"She has two cameras, actually. She explained this to me."

"Two cameras?"

"Yes. One is a smaller version of the Carlton bellows camera, and she uses that for portraiture and landscape work. But she's also carrying another type of camera."

"Another one?"

"Yes, one you have not seen, nor have many others. It's a tiny masterpiece called the Kombi, a specially designed, custom-made camera that measures two inches by one and a half inches. The camera can easily be concealed in the palm of your hand."

"That's amazing."

"And what's more amazing are the kinds of pictures she has taken with it. She has shown some to me, and they are as sharp as any I have ever seen. If she can stand close enough and there is sufficient light, she can take anyone's picture without their knowing it. I am sure she has taken the picture of this crazy man. It is against the rules to photograph anything in the casino, but she manages."

"I'll guarantee two hundred francs," Lydia promised, "although my editor is going to wonder how I manage to spend so much money."

"He will say it's worth whatever you spend, fräulein. I have read some of your stories. They are very good. They make me want to read everything that is under the name of Lydia Bradley."

"I'm complimented, Baron Hetzler. Tell your friend to have the film developed and printed as quickly as possible."

"Tomorrow. She does her own developing and printing. I shall obtain the picture by morning, in time for you to make the first mail. It is a pity it cannot be sent like a cable is sent. But in a week's time it will be there."

"Thank you." Lydia said. "Now, let's see how the general is doing."

He was doing poorly, if the sweat that ran down his beefy face and soaked his stiff formal collar was any indication.

Yet he persisted as if this was a vital military campaign.

"I've had enough for this evening," Lydia finally said. "I'm going back to my hotel to write the story of Mr. Osgood Trencher, so that it can be ready to dispatch at the same time I mail the picture. Thank you again, Baron."

"I will see you tomorrow," the baron said. "You will please excuse me now."

He walked briskly to the side of the woman who had taken the snapshot, linked his arm under hers and escorted her in his usual regal manner from the casino. Lydia smiled ruefully; she had just lost her escort to another woman, though she could hardly begrudge her. No doubt this Regina LeFond with the camera was sharing living quarters with the baron, she realized. The authority with which he took possession of her indicated an intimate and even tender relationship, despite the baron's nonchalant way of referring to her.

Lydia returned to her suite to write the story of the ill-tempered loser, though she was careful to in no way accuse him of losing someone else's money. It was just a short, breezy article of interest to anyone who followed the adventures at Monte Carlo.

As she prepared for bed she found herself wondering what had happened to Jeffrey Marcus. He was a stranger, still, one whom she had found both reticent and mysterious. Yet she missed him and had been hoping he might contact her.

In the morning she received a batch of mail, including a letter from Mr. Morgan telling her that he was pleased with her stories and that they had assured him he'd made no mistake in assigning her to write about the gambling world.

You have already addicted a large number of people to your accounts of life among the reckless and the rich.

The story about Wells was superb and you provided us with a photo as well. You have indicated that your expenses are high, but we're getting worthwhile stories at a relatively

cheap price. Also, our circulation is growing at an aston-
ishing rate.

Don't spare yourself or hold back on what it costs to get
these stories. Just keep them coming. You'll be world-fa-
mous in six more months.

Lydia smiled with delight at Morgan's praise, and
stretched languidly before she began to prepare for the day.
More and more she was coming to recognize how many
stories awaited her on this bit of rock with its elegant hotels,
restaurants and gaudy casino. For one thing, she had never
before seen such a variety of people, from all parts of the
world. Many were drawn here with the hope of getting rich
overnight; others, with the hope of simply increasing their
fortunes. No one thought of losing. She opened up the
notebook full of possibilities that she had jotted down, and
began to study these and plan more human interest stories.

A messenger knocked at her door, interrupting her train
of thought. The sealed envelope he handed her contained
a picture of Osgood Trencher in an ugly mood. It had
definitely been taken last night, and was a good photograph.
The woman evidently knew her business. Lydia wrote a
brief letter to Guy Spencer, enclosed the photograph and
rang for a messenger to post it. In a week it would be
released, she hoped, enhancing her growing reputation.

Planning a morning of sunlight and exercise, she donned
a cerise walking dress, perched a small hat jauntily on her
head and selected a dainty parasol. She strolled leisurely
down to the harbor, greeted by almost everyone she met,
sometimes with nods and sometimes with brief conversations. It touched her to know she was held in high regard
by the residents as well as the vacationers at Monte.

She walked out along one of the docks, admiring the
expensive boats with their tall masts, gently bobbing in the
mildly flowing tide. The clear waters glistened in the bay,
as sapphire blue as the calm skies above her.

"If you're intending to jump in," a man's voice said
behind her, "it might be best if you put on a bathing suit."

"Jeff," she exclaimed happily as she turned about, his first name leaping spontaneously to her lips this time. "What a pleasant surprise. Where have you been keeping yourself?"

He strolled alongside her and smiled. "I had business in Cannes. But I found your newspaper there and read some of your recent articles. Not bad, although they're going to make you a few enemies if you don't watch out."

"I'm only reporting the truth," she retorted as they began walking back toward the casino, her cherry-colored gown matching his gray morning suit in elegance. "I don't want to hurt anyone. Although I must admit . . . there is one man . . . an Englishman who has been losing consistently, and getting so angry he causes trouble at his table. He pushes people, even insults them. He went so far as to threaten me because he thought I was planning to do a story on him. As a matter of fact, I did."

"Why would he be an interesting subject for a story?"

"Because the baron believes, and I agree, that this man is in such turmoil, and so downright nasty, that he must be losing someone else's money."

"In other words, an embezzler?"

"I don't know. I haven't named him as such. I've written only about his being such a bad loser."

"If he's run off with somebody's money, he likely hasn't given his real name. So he has no reason to make trouble if you use the name he's registered by."

Lydia stopped for a moment and said, with a smug twirl of her parasol, "I also sent a photograph of him."

Jeff whistled sharply. "Now he *will* have cause to resent you. That is, if he's absconded with someone else's money. You're living—or writing—dangerously, my dear."

"He'll likely be gone long before the picture is used," Lydia reasoned. "Anyway, he deserved to be labeled a spoilsport. He's rough and vindictive, a most unsportsmanlike player. You need only to observe him at the table to dislike him."

"We'll hope for the best. If he makes any more threats,

79

let me know. I'll do some threatening of my own." He took her arm protectively.

"That's good of you, Jeff, and I appreciate it. But I'm sure I can handle him if he gets out of line."

"I'm not," Jeff retorted bluntly.

Lydia regarded him with annoyance. "You really do think I can't take care of myself, don't you?"

"You weren't doing too well trying to stop that young fool from committing suicide," he drawled at her, his voice edged with anger as he recalled that night.

"I might have if you hadn't interfered," she snapped.

Jeff folded his arms across his chest and eyed her coldly. "You might also have ended up dead."

Her head tilted defiantly. "You see yourself as a knight-in-shining-armor, don't you?"

His brows raised quizzically. "And how do you see yourself? As an Amazon? You'd never qualify. For one thing," he teased, "you don't have the build."

Lydia twirled the parasol angrily now. "I could use stronger words to describe you."

His face relaxed in a smile. "Please don't. Let's call a truce."

"Not without your apologizing," Lydia said sternly.

"I don't know what I did to apologize for," he murmured.

"You make me feel stupid."

"Really?" he mocked. "An intelligent young lady like you?"

"Why do you poke fun at me?"

"I'm not really. Or if I am, it's because I like to see you angry. Your cheeks flame with color, your eyes shoot off sparks. You really need taming."

"You've started again," she said angrily.

He turned on the street and looked at her, tilting her face up at him with his hand tucked under her chin. "I'm sorry. I'll be good. I want nothing more than to cultivate your friendship, but I really suspect you like to quarrel with me."

"You started it by telling me I could have ended up dead," she said stubbornly.

His mouth opened to say something, then closed. When he spoke, his tone had softened. "I didn't mean to start an argument, Lydia. It just so happens what I said made sense. And since you want to become a successful journalist, you should place a higher value on your life."

"I do place a high value on all life! Even the life of that young man so filled with despair he was going to kill himself."

"I didn't hear him thank you for your efforts," he said angrily.

"Did he thank you for your generosity?" she retorted.

"Oh, dammit, Lydia, what are we quarreling about?"

"You seem to get angry at everything I say," she countered heatedly.

"I'm not angry at anything you say. But don't ask me to apologize for what I said, though I'll apologize for *how* I said it. Am I forgiven?"

She relented. "Very well. In a way, you're right. I'm sorry I got angry."

He firmly tucked her arm in his. "Then let's start anew. We'll do nothing to jeopardize our evening. You may call me any kind of lowlife you wish. Just be with me tonight."

Lydia gave a little sigh. "It won't be dull, anyway."

"Not with you," Jeff smiled. He bent suddenly, kissed her cheek, then studied her face, his gray eyes thoughtful. "I couldn't resist. Your cheeks are flaming, but they don't balance." He kissed her other cheek.

"You're absurd," Lydia said, hiding the sudden rush of pleasure she felt by speaking quickly. "But perhaps I'll consent to your dining with me at my hotel tonight.

Jeff's eyes twinkled above her parasol as he said, "That's very kind of you, Miss Bradley. We'll visit the casino afterwards and perhaps I'll get reckless and wager—well—maybe ten American dollars, just to make the evening exciting."

Back at her hotel, she gave him a farewell smile that he made her promise to be wearing when she greeted him in the evening. Lydia found herself continuing to smile long after he had left her, though she'd managed to conceal the reason from herself. She admitted only that Jeffrey Marcus was by turns infuriating and pleasant to be with. She just wished his explanation concerning his work was more convincing. Even when she had mentioned it at the pier, he seemed momentarily puzzled by her question. Could he be lying to her and if so, why? How could she find out more about him? She couldn't dismiss the feeling that he was in some manner hiding a few facts from her. Still, his charm did much to overcome that. She warned herself not to let his masculine appeal sway her judgment, reminding herself he could also be very rude.

She tried to put him out of her mind, still not an easy thing to do. But she had work to do. There were expenses to add up and plans to make for more interesting stories. None would ever rival that one about the man who broke the bank, because this likely would never happen again, Lydia knew. She'd been lucky in finding it waiting here for her when she arrived. She was more than thankful for this luck, too, for she knew, without boasting, that it had established her as an entertaining writer and reporter, one who handled unusual stories from an unusual place.

Supper was delightful; she enjoyed Jeff's company and his conversation, but at the end of the meal she still knew little about him. He seemed to be fairly well known at the hotel, but not by the wealthy patrons so much as by the waiters, captains and clerks, who all greeted him in friendly fashion. She wasn't surprised that his idea of a hearty supper was a thin consommé, a thick slice of beef, potato and an ordinary salad, without dessert, followed by innumerable cups of strong coffee. It was so American. The baron certainly outdid him, but of course, as Jeff had reminded her, the baron's money didn't pay for the meal.

In the casino Jeff placed his bet on the red and lost it. They wandered away from the table, smiling happily, neither of them as interested in gambling as they were in each other.

The baron arrived soon after they did and spent his time pointedly ignoring them, in an attempt to make it obvious that he was hurt that he had lost his favorite escort.

"He has all the nerve and arrogance of the aristocracy," Jeff observed, "but he's an honest man. A schemer and conniver, yet an honest man. He admits he has no money and has to live by his wits with a meager income from his government. He also admits he's *persona non grata* with his emperor. I can't help but like him, despite the contemptible looks he's been giving me tonight, because of you."

"Oh, come now, Jeff," Lydia scoffed. "How could he possibly dislike you because of me any more than you could dislike him because of me?"

"Simple," Jeff said. "I'm a danger to his fatherly interest in you. If he were younger, I'm sure he'd challenge me to a duel."

Lydia laughed. "Not so long as I'm around to pick up the checks. However, in fairness, he earns his money. He's been a great help to me."

"He's a leech," Jeff said matter-of-factly. "And I'll admit I'm jealous of the old duffer. I resent every moment you spend in his company, just as he resents my being with you."

"Why are you jealous of him?"

Jeff eyed her with one eyebrow raised, his tone mock-serious, "Of course, how stupid of me. No romantic entanglements."

"So you can stop talking nonsense," Lydia said sternly. "Tell me about yourself."

"That would be talking nonsense."

"All right. I'll ask you a question. Do you like Monte Carlo?"

"Not particularly, though the climate is great. As for my job—I'm paid well."

"For doing what?" she asked innocently.

Though his smile seemed careless, Lydia felt that inwardly he was on guard. "Aren't you being overly curious? I already told you—I'm an engineer, here to study ways to prevent the place from sliding into the sea."

"This is solid rock, Jeff."

"Then I'm lying," he said caustically.

"I didn't say that."

"My dear, your face betrays you. As for Monte—solid rock decays over the ages. My work is so monotonous I don't like talking about it because then I realize what a bore it is. So please take my word for it."

"I will if I ever see you out measuring rock faces."

"I work with my brains," he countered. "I don't have to even leave my office. But we're getting testy again. Notice how we can't seem to be together for any length of time without starting an argument?"

Lydia smiled acquiescence. "I'm sorry. I *was* being rather disagreeable. I do like you, Jeff, even though I find you something of a mystery."

"Ah, but I like to intrigue you. I'd like to have you lying awake nights thinking about mysterious me."

"I can't take you seriously."

"Why the hell not?"

"You needn't get profane about it," she chided.

"I'm getting angry again."

"So am I. You profess jealousy, yet you implied you want no romantic attachments."

"You don't either," he pointed out.

"True," she admitted. "But I wouldn't be jealous if I saw you with an older woman."

"You'd have no right to be."

"You don't either," Lydia said heatedly. "Simply and honestly put, you're a distraction. You intrude in my thoughts when I'm writing my cablegrams." Her voice rose in exasperation. "To be completely frank, you're a dreadful annoyance."

"Good," he exclaimed, then abruptly changed the subject. "Let's go over to the baccarat section. That's where you can see money vanish as if in the hands of a magician."

"I don't know why I should, but there might be a story there."

They watched the play for a while, but soon tired of it

and left the casino to stroll along the lighted pathways between the formal gardens, enjoying the soft, warm air. Below, at the harbor, the glittering lights of the boats were seemingly strung in garlands like lights on a Christmas tree. The perfume from blossoms permeated the air and the sky was a canopy of stars . . . perfect evening for lovers. They moved along the paths, circling the formal gardens and topiaries. Once they encountered a pair of lovers locked in an amorous embrace. They beat a hasty retreat, even though the pair gave not the slightest notice of their presence.

When they were a discreet distance from the couple, Jeff said, "You can't blame them. Monte is a most romantic place."

"It is," Lydia agreed quietly. "It would be nice if I could write a story about a romance that blossomed in Monte Carlo."

He looked down at her with that bland expression she found so upsetting. "Who knows? One day you might. Certainly there's enough of it around."

"I don't mean liaisons," she said impatiently. "I mean a love that's innocent and beautiful."

"You mean an awakening," he teased.

"Exactly," she exclaimed. "Everyone loves a sort of Romeo-and-Juliet story, don't you think?"

"Oh, yes. Yes, indeed."

"Of course," she said thoughtfully, "that's difficult to find since young lovers wish to be by themselves."

"True," he agreed. "I suppose we could hold hands as we walked along. A sort of just-pretend game." His voice was mocking.

"Oh, don't be silly, Jeff." She laughed softly. "I'm not thinking of two practical people like us."

"I just thought if we held hands and breathed the per-fumed air. . . ."

"You're impossible!" she interrupted. Impetuously, she asked, "Have you ever been in love?"

"Not enough to ask someone to marry me."

"Then you haven't known real love."

"No. And I don't suppose I ever will."

"I hope *I* will one day."

"Have you forgotten your career?" he asked, with a sardonic lift of one eyebrow.

"Of course not," she said quickly. "But I don't see why a woman can't have a happy marriage and a career."

His tone was dry as he said, "I'm glad you put the marriage first. I'm not certain she could have both. Not a reporter anyway. You might get an assignment at the other end of the globe, and if your husband was unable to accompany you because of his work, you couldn't expect him to sit home and wait until you could return."

"Why not?"

"I know I wouldn't do it. Not for any woman."

"You're selfish," she accused.

"Very," he admitted.

"This foolish talk is getting us nowhere," Lydia said dispiritedly. "Besides, it's getting late. We'd better go back to the hotel."

"You wouldn't care to go down to the harbor?"

"No," she replied quickly. "I'm afraid we're about to quarrel again."

"Such a thought never entered my mind," he said blandly.

"It didn't mine, either," she almost snapped.

"Then why bring it up?" he asked.

"I don't know," she replied irritably. "I just want to go back."

"Did I say something to offend you?"

"No, Jeff." She smiled up at him. "I suppose I'm just being perverse. I'm not a very reasonable woman—"

She paused in confusion, for suddenly Jeff stopped in the middle of the path, faced her, took her in his arms and kissed her. Gently, and then more insistently. Finally he released his hold and looked solemnly at the astonished Lydia.

"There was a small response," he said judiciously. "Very small. Hardly noticeable, but still there. Perhaps I ought to try again?"

"Don't be absurd," she said in a rush. Before she could stop herself, she added, "But I'll be honest with you . . . I rather enjoyed it."

"Well enough to return it?" he asked, watching her lips.

"Jeffrey Marcus, you're very bold," she said, color flooding her face.

"And you're very exciting," he replied soberly, then covered her lisp with his. This time he drew her close. Her heart seemed to skip a beat as his lips became more demanding. The parasol fell from her hand and, forgetting all her earlier protestations, her arms moved slowly around his neck, until she felt the wild beat of his heart and knew hers was beating in unison. She felt as if she wanted to stay locked in his arms forever. Without breaking the kiss, he spoke her name over and over, until she was suddenly aware of a wondrous feeling completely alien to her.

"Jeff," she managed to speak finally. "Let me go. Please—let me go."

To her surprise, he did, though his arm still remained about her waist. She was glad because she wasn't certain she could support herself or even walk steadily.

His eyes were triumphant as they looked into hers. "I rather think you might enjoy a romantic entanglement, Lydia."

"I don't know," she replied, her voice as uneven as his. "I can't think."

"Why should you want to?" he demanded. "Are you afraid?"

"It isn't fear," she replied, her voice steadying as she attempted to reason with herself. "I have my work, I've made plans. I don't want to be sidetracked."

As he ignored her protests and made to kiss her again, she said hastily, "Oh, Jeff, please. I'm too shaken."

"I'm delighted to hear a lady reporter can be shaken," he said in his maddeningly bland tones again.

She looked up at him and, for the first time, let her eyes linger on his face, studying its every line. Had the kiss meant anything to him? His eyes told her nothing, and she was suddenly afraid that it had been only a pleasant interlude for him, one such as a sophisticated man like Jeffrey Marcus would be well used to. Had he been simply mocking her naivete?

He had made no move to draw her close again, and now he picked up her parasol, closed it and tucked her arm through his. She found herself concentrating on quelling the trembling in her limbs, the shiver of delight that went through her at his mere touch.

They returned to the hotel in silence, and she refused to allow him to accompany her inside. He caught her hand, raised it to his lips and kissed it lightly.

"Good night, Lydia. Sleep well."

"You too," she said, then turned and fled indoors. She was grateful for the dim light outside the entranceway, for she knew her face had flamed when his lips touched the back of her hand. Even now, her breathing was too fast and there was no reason for it except that something was happening to her that she hadn't wanted to happen. She hadn't thought about falling in love. She mustn't let herself. She had to fight it. Fight it? She chided herself quickly upon entering her suite, her smile bitter as she regarded her reflection in the mirror. No need for concern. Jeff had not once mentioned loving her, and he had clearly stated that he wanted no romantic attachments.

That, added to her own ambitions and Jeff's disapproval of a woman such as she—independent and bent on a career—made it a hopeless situation. She undressed quietly and spent a sleepless night tossing and turning. Not until dawn did she drift off.

Five

For a week, Monte Carlo seemed to quiet down remarkably. Lydia wondered if it was due to the fact that Jeff had once again gone off on some mysterious errand, not even informing her that he would be absent. She was hurt, even though she had no claim on him. She discovered with each passing day her suspicions regarding his secrecy grew less and less. Her growing attraction for him had taken precedence over whatever misgivings she'd had about him. However, from now on, she told herself, she must be on guard so that he wouldn't suspect her true feelings for him.

Still, she felt quite alone, for the baron had contracted a cold and preferred to remain in bed, no doubt well cared for by Regina, the photographer whose camera work enhanced some of Lydia's stories. Angelina was also absent, having gone to Paris on vacation.

Lydia paid regular visits to the casino where she was still accorded the same royal treatment. But no stories developed and the week became, for the first time since she had arrived, boring. As the days passed, her hurt at Jeff's prolonged absence changed to annoyance.

She spent her time planning future articles and writing letters to her editor and publisher, finding a quiet satisfaction in the replies that stated she was handling her assignment like a veteran. However, she kept in mind she was still a neophyte, an amateur with a long way to go. She realized that a good reporter on this kind of an assignment must make news, not just wait for it to develop. She thought she had done this rather well with the Englishman who had lost so consistently and displayed such a suspicious anger. While she had not yet seen the newspaper that carried the story, she knew his picture had been run along with the article about his phenomenal losses. Although she'd been careful not to insinuate that his actions were an indication that the money he lost was not his own, printing the story and the picture together inevitably brought out the truth. She read later that he had embezzled a large sum of money from his employer and had been the subject of a police search, which had never reached Monte. But now he would be arrested on sight.

She finished an interview with an elderly statesman from a small Balkan country, a man who was eager for any kind of publicity that might overcome his deplorable reputation at home. She was also able to write general-interest stories of such people, pseudo-royalty or genuine, for she found them fascinating. Her honest interest in them gave a freshness to her articles. She even managed to inject a subtle humor into her writing when one of her subjects was pompous. With every story, she was fast learning the tricks of her profession, although she was careful to write objectively. Even when she disliked the individual, this was never revealed in her interviews.

Yet, on this balmy evening, Lydia found little satisfaction with the progress she had made in her work since her arrival. Despite her annoyance with Jeff and the fact that she was more certain than ever that he was engaged in some kind of work other than geology, his absence depressed her. She would even have enjoyed the baron's company. He had a way of lifting her spirits, for he loved the little game they were playing and had been most helpful in ferreting out various types of characters.

She walked up the single flight of stairs to her floor, continued on down the corridor and unlocked her door. As she opened it there was a rush of sound behind her and someone shoved her hard, sending her reeling into her parlor. Before she could turn around or get her breath, she heard the door close. When she did turn, the room was too dark to see who had viciously assaulted her, though she was certain from the force that had been used that it was a man.

The figure was only a blurred shadow, dimly silhouetted by the window light, but when he spoke she recognized him at once and her fear mounted. The man who called himself Osgood Trencher faced her, and he was openly hostile. As he turned on the recently installed electric light and advanced slowly toward Lydia, she automatically moved back until a heavy table blocked any further retreat.

To make matters worse, she was sure he had been drinking, for his face was florid and his eyes bloodshot. Lydia was, in fact, astonished to see him, because she had believed he'd fled from Monte Carlo some time ago.

"I warned you," he said ominously.

"Keep away from me," she threw back at him. "You'll only get yourself in more trouble than you're in now."

"I couldn't be worse off," he snapped. "I'll get ten years when they find me now, and a few more won't matter for I'm finished, anyway. Thanks to you. Why didn't you leave me alone?"

Lydia looked about for some avenue of escape, but found none. He had locked the door and contemptuously thrown the key onto the chaise longue.

He moved closer. Lydia edged toward the end of the table, but if she managed to get around it, there was nowhere to go. Her only recourse she quickly realized was to try and talk him out of it—or fight him. And she had little faith in either method.

"I told you I'd get back at you if you printed the story about me. You did more than that. Somehow you got my picture and printed that, too. Now I haven't a chance, but before they get me, you're going to remember me well."

As he lunged at her, she darted around the end of the table, but he was after her so fast she was unable to raise a hand to defend herself. Then his hand slapped her across the face so hard that she staggered back to hit the wall. He slapped her again and a third time until her senses spun. He had blocked any chance of her moving away from him, and now he pressed her against the wall, using his body to hold her there. When he first turned on the light, she had seen only a raging anger on his face, but now, with his body tight against her, his face inches away, she saw that look change to lust. As his hands moved up and down her, she tried to scream, but no sound came. He saw her open mouth and clapped a hand across it. His hands manipulated her breast before drifting downward.

"If you so much as whimper," he rasped, "I'll wring your neck. Do you understand? You're too damned beautiful to kill. And I appreciate beauty. Now keep your mouth shut or I'll forget that."

He stepped back suddenly, putting about six feet of space between them. His eyes roved up and down her body and he drew a long breath.

"Take off your clothes," he ordered.

"You'll have to kill me first," she gasped.

"I may do that, but not before I have my way. Take off your clothes or I'll tear them off."

While he made known what he was really after, she glanced at a tall, cut glass vase on the table she'd circled. It was heavy enough to be a good weapon if she could get her hands on it.

"Do as I say," he commanded. "I'm not a patient man. I don't have much time."

"You'll spend the rest of your life in prison," she warned. "Your entire life. What you have in mind isn't worth that."

"To me it is because I'll have my revenge for what you did to me and at the same time get pleasure out of it. Take off your clothes! I'll not tell you again."

She suddenly discovered that her terrible, crippling fear had left her; she was cool, her brain searching for a way out. The vase presented the best method, but she had to get to it before he could stop her. Making a lunge for it wouldn't work. He was too close. Still, she was sure he hadn't considered that she would seize it as a weapon. He was far too engrossed in watching her, far too confident of himself.

She kicked off one shoe and bent to pick it up. He tensed, but didn't make a move. Slowly, she loosened the other and picked it up, inching forward each time just enough to be within range of seizing the vase. She slipped down one shoulder of her gown to reveal more skin and drew her arms behind her back to reach the buttons, her breasts straining against the front of her gown. He watched every move, his pupils dilating and his breathing loud and fast.

Suddenly she half turned, as if tugging at the buttons, and her right hand shot out to seize the vase. She raised it over her head.

He laughed. "Foxy, aren't you? Getting me all excited so you could grab that vase. What're you going to do with it? Hit me over the head? I can take that away from you easily. But if you happen to hit me with it, I'll kill you after I'm done with you. I don't care any more. Nothing scares me. I'm finished. . . ."

"They use a rope here," she said. "A rope around your neck."

He shuddered once and she knew she had reached him, but he was still intent upon satisfying his lust. He raised his arms to counter the blow she would try to inflict, but instead, she wheeled about and hurled the vase at the large window.

It crashed against it with a great noise, bound to attract anyone on the street below. At the same time she found her voice and screamed. Trencher's face blanched stark white. He hesitated a moment, but reason told him that before he could corner her again people would come to investigate. He mumbled a curse, picked up the key from the chaise, unlocked the door and rushed into the corridor.

Someone shouted, there was a sharp scuffle, the sound of a blow and a cry of pain. Lydia ran across the room and out into the corridor, where three men were engaged in a scuffle. Trencher was being roughly shoved against the wall face first by the taller of the two men in civilian clothes, his back to her. She saw her assailant's hands pulled behind him, and a uniformed Monte Carlo policeman running down the hall toward them. The man who had pinioned Trencher spun him around and shoved him at the waiting policeman, to be led off in handcuffs. Everything had happened so quickly that Lydia was still dazed as the other man turned toward her and approached with brisk strides.

"Jeff!" she cried out in amazement and relief. "Oh, Jeff!"

His arms enfolded her, and his grim face peered down into hers. "Are you hurt? Your face. . . ."

A sob escaped her, muffled against his suit coat, before she gasped, "He slapped me a few times, but otherwise he didn't hurt me." He pressed her tightly against him, holding her so that she was on tiptoe, her arms around his neck.

"He was going to rape you, wasn't he?" he said roughly.

"Yes," she whispered.

"Thank God I got here in time."

"I prayed someone would come! I threw a vase through the window to attract attention, and I screamed."

"We heard you, all right." He looked around as doors opened along the hall, and people eyed Lydia's torn clothing. "Too many guests poking their noses into the corridor."

She swayed and would have fainted, but Jeff caught her. Swiftly, he scooped her up into his arms and carried her into her suite. He eased her gently onto the settee, closed the door and sat down beside her, his hand covering hers. Lydia was still trying to combat the weakness in her knees and a tendency to shake all over.

"Tell me what happened," Jeff said, his voice tight.

Lydia swallowed once, and waited till she could speak. "He must have been hiding in the corridor. When I unlocked and opened the door, he rushed at me and pushed me into the room. He . . . he closed and locked the door before I even knew exactly who he was. Then he said I had ruined his life, that he had been recognized as an embezzler in England and that they were after him. He was going to punish me for what I'd written."

Lydia stared at the floor as she spoke, still in shock. Jeff's face whitened. "I notice you're not wearing shoes and your gown and hair are disarranged. . . ."

"He . . . he shoved me against the wall. I guess that was when he decided he wanted my body more than he wanted to hurt me. Then he ordered me to remove my clothes. I started to, but only so I could move about and reach for the vase. I intended to smash him with it, but I was afraid it wouldn't work, that he would prove too quick and too strong for me." She paled, then continued. "So I threw it at the window and screamed at the same time. After I had told him they hang murderers in Monaco. Do they?"

He managed to laugh, though it rang somewhat hollow. "You're a wonder, Lydia. I don't know if they hang murderers in Monaco."

"Well, it gave him something to think about, and he decided to get out while he had the chance." She slowed down, still shaken. "Has he been hiding in Monte all this time?"

"No doubt. The police were on the lookout for him, but he managed to stay out of sight. He's finished now—for good. They'll send him back to England along with the facts about what happened here tonight. That'll add a few years to the term he'll serve."

"Jeff," she asked with a slight frown, "you said the police have been after him all this time. How did you know that?"

His eyes avoided hers as he answered, "How? They told me. Just now, when I turned him over to the policeman."

"How did it happen that you were . . . right here? So close? And with a policeman?"

"It's just one of those things that happen, I guess. I'd just arrived back from Cannes where I had been attending conferences, and was on my way up here to see if you were in your suite. They'd assured me in the casino that you'd left some time ago. I didn't know what was going on until

I heard the crash of the breaking window and your scream, and then Trencher came flying out right into my arms. A passerby, one of the guests from an adjoining room perhaps, helped me hold him. The policeman must have been the one I saw in the lobby, chatting with the desk clerk. He rushed up here when he heard the ruckus.''

"So it was just . . . luck?" Lydia's eyes revealed her puzzlement.

"What else?" he asked in a mystified voice.

She sighed, still drained from her ordeal. "I don't know. It seems too coincidental."

"For God's sake, Lydia, are we going to fight about this, too?"

"Of course not." Her smile was apologetic. "I'm grateful beyond words, Jeff, that you're back."

"That's better."

"But you could have told me you'd be absent for several days, couldn't you?"

"I didn't know it myself until I got an urgent message to meet my superior in Cannes, a message I couldn't ignore. It came in the middle of the night. I'm sorry, Lydia, I just didn't think of leaving word." His eyes met hers, melting away her doubts.

"You're forgiven," she said, smiling. "Thank heaven you arrived when you did. It was wonderful to be saved by you."

A ghost of a smile played about Jeff's lips. "Don't give me credit I don't deserve. I grabbed Trencher, but you saved yourself by making enough commotion to scare him away. You're a very resourceful young lady."

Lydia sighed in quiet satisfaction. "Nevertheless, I'm awfully glad you're back."

"So am I," he replied soberly. "And I hope nothing like this happens again."

"With Trencher locked up, I'll be in no danger."

"In the kind of work you're in, there's always the chance someone isn't going to like what you write and perhaps try to harm you," he cautioned her. "Most of the people who come to Monte are rich, sophisticated and intelligent. Yet Monte draws another element, too, one that can be dangerous: the reckless and the unpredictable.''

Lydia laughed softly. ''To think that earlier today I was bored and lonely. That's why I came up to my suite.''

''Where's the baron?'' Jeff asked.

''He has a cold. I've been alone for days—it seems like eons. I didn't even have an exciting story, but I certainly have one now.''

Jeff stood up, amazed at what she'd said. ''You're going to follow this up with a story? After you've almost been raped by that madman?''

''Of course. Not about what he tried to do to me, though I intend to intimate what his intentions were. But the story itself will be how my article resulted in the arrest of a wanted criminal. Good heavens, Jeff, I'm a newspaper reporter. And I want to show my readers that my stories aren't all silly, light-hearted adventures of Monte Carlo and the people who come here.''

Jeff's expression hardened as Lydia rushed on. ''A story is a story and this is a good one. It follows up what I already wrote about the wretched man. Readers like to know what happens to the subjects of my stories, and it's a rare instance when I can tell them. You'll have to excuse me, Jeff. Thank you again, but I must get this on the wires tomorrow morning.''

He nodded. ''Business first, eh? Career above all else? Well, it's the way to success, I grant you. Funny . . . you don't seem the type.''

''I am the type. I want to become a famous reporter, Jeff, the first world-renowned woman correspondent. I want to prove that I can make something of myself and by my own efforts. My father believed I could do it and so did Mr. Morgan. And I'll never have a chance like this again.''

At the door Jeff looked down at her, still unsmiling, then nodded a cold farewell, as if they were suddenly strangers. After he'd closed the door softly she locked it, strode directly to the desk and removed paper from a drawer, dipped her pen in the sterling silver inkwell, touched the tip of it against the side of the inkwell so that any excess ink would run off, then set it down. Suddenly all her bravado crumbled. She covered her face with her hands and began to cry softly. The reaction to the terrifying episode she had experienced set in, causing her to shake violently. At the same time, she started to sob. She ran into the bedroom and buried her head in the pillow, hoping to muffle the sound.

Long after the sobs had faded and the shaking stopped, she lay there. If only she were in Jeff's arms, safe and comforted. But she had sent him away, on the verge of one of their arguments. She shut her eyes in an attempt to blot out the memory of Osgood Trencher's face. But she still saw it, twisted in lines of lust and hate, haunting her. In her whole lifetime she'd never known such fear.

When calmness finally returned to her, she bathed her face in cool water, donned an embroidered silk negligée and returned to her desk, focusing her thoughts on Jeff in an effort to compose herself. How easy it would be for her to open her heart to him, she reflected. He was everything a woman could desire in a man. A normal woman, that is. She, Lydia, was too ambitious to be content with marriage and a family.

Did the anger and concern he'd shown at what had happened to her today mean that he cared deeply for her? She doubted that it did. Any good man, she knew, would react similarly, wanting to protect a woman whose honor was threatened.

Jeff had been upset, even angry, when he left. What he didn't know was that it hadn't been easy for her to send him away. His presence had comforted her, but it had also disturbed her. In her vulnerable state it would have been hard to resist him if he had made overtures.

She reminded herself that he was mysterious, that he was not to be trusted. He had gone off without leaving even a note, and she couldn't believe that he was that forgetful. More likely, he didn't think it mattered. But even if he did love her, he wasn't being honest with her. At least, she didn't think so. And since she didn't completely trust him, she shouldn't really let thoughts of him occupy her mind. She gave a firm nod of her head, as if to convince herself of that.

This determination made, she discovered her nerves had settled down enough that she could resort to pen and paper again, writing the story of Trencher's revenge and its outcome. Now her readers would realize that being a foreign correspondent wasn't all roses and caviar.

When it was finished, she sat back and read it aloud.

This is a follow-up to the story of Osgood Trencher, the man who behaved in an obnoxious manner in the casino to compensate for his losses. This reporter sent a picture of him that was printed some time ago in the paper. As a result of that picture, the police of England identified him as Osgood Trencher, who stole money from his employer and gambled it away here in Monte Carlo.

Last night, at the Hotel de Paris, he hid on the floor where this reporter maintains a suite and forced his way into her apartment when she opened the door. He started to abuse her physically and tried to force his attentions on her, but she managed to grab a heavy glass dish and toss it through the window, screaming to attract attention.

The commotion frightened Mr. Trencher and he ran out of the suite into the arms of a man who held him until a Monte Carlo policeman arrived and apprehended Trencher, moments later. Your reporter was assured that the culprit will receive an added sentence to the one he'll get for theft of money from his employer.

In the morning she again overslept. She cabled her story rather late, and then sought out the baron to see if he was recovering from his bout with a cold. He was not in his room and hadn't been for the past two or three nights, the desk clerk told her.

Lydia looked up the address of Regina LeFond, intending to walk there. It was a half mile away from the gambling center, but she enjoyed strolling in the fresh air. She soon discovered that Regina occupied a four-room apartment, more of a flat, in one of the older buildings erected when the casino was first built and striving hard to gain fame.

Regina was, as the baron had put it, a plain-looking woman, husky, with wide, square shoulders and a face crisscrossed with many fine wrinkles from too much sun. A too-prominent nose, a wide mouth and rather small, bright eyes were set in that plain face Lydia had observed at the casino.

But she was affable and friendly. "*Oui*," she told Lydia, "the baron is here. His cold is better, but I have insisted he remain in bed for another day or two. He will be glad to see you, mademoiselle."

"I like being called Lydia by my friends, and I feel you're already one," she responded. "Thanks again for the photographs. They were excellent and I put them to good use."

"Ah, it is my ambition to become a good photographer," Regina said modestly. "Come this way . . . the baron has heard us talking and knows you are here. Any moment he will begin yelling his head off at being neglected."

"The baron surely is in need of someone like you, Regina." Lydia spoke softly this time.

"And I," she said with a big smile, "am even more in need of him. He sees me as a woman and my lack of beauty is no bar to his affections. *Oui*, he sleeps here often. It is good for both of us. You are not shocked by this, Lydia?"

"Not in the least," she answered. "Let's see how he's getting along."

The baron, between wheezes and sneezes, welcomed her heartily. She thought some of his symptoms may have been put on for her benefit, but she didn't mind that. As soon as she sat down by his bed he made her tell him about Trencher. He'd already heard of the incident, but insisted on the details, snorting in contempt of such a man and murmuring his gratefulness at the way it had ended.

"I shall be up and around tomorrow," he said. "I would be up now, but Regina will not have it."

"Regina is right, Baron. You must be very careful."

"At my age," he added with a groan. Then he brightened. "Regina, show Lydia your newest camera. I have never seen anything like it before. And it should serve you well, Lydia, if you are in need of pictures taken secretly."

Regina, in the kitchen, provided delightfully strong coffee and a brioche before proudly showing Lydia her two cameras. One was a folding version of the Carlton bellows camera, a rather large instrument but a fine camera for portraiture work. The other was a Kombi, two inches by one and a half inches; hardly room for a lens, let alone the roll of miniature film. There were few of these around, Regina added. She had been very lucky to get one.

"I can conceal this camera in the palm of my hand—fortunately for this business, a very big hand," Regina said. "I do my own developing and printing and while these pictures are small, I know how to enlarge them to a rather good size. The roll of film takes twenty-five pictures, which doesn't force me to change film all the time as the old plates used to. With this Kombi I can take a series of pictures, but of course, the light must be good."

"If I have need of pictures," Lydia said, preparing to leave, "you can be assured I'll let you know, and the price I pay will be substantial. The one you took of Trencher was responsible for his being recognized in London as an absconder. It did most in bringing the man to the justice he deserves. And I can well imagine it was likely the first time secret photography was responsible for such an identification. Thank you again, and take care of the baron. He's a charming gentleman and indispensable to my work."

"And to me," Regina added frankly. "He will be well soon. All he needs is the same care you would give a rather difficult baby. But when he is well, he is really a very nice little man."

Lydia ate her noonday meal alone at the hotel, giving her time to think about several stories she wanted to write. She finally selected one about the history of this rocky point, realizing little had been known about this once obscure principality until her story of the man who broke the bank had been released. The knowledge that it was her work brought modest pleasure and satisfaction. It was a long step in the direction she'd set for herself. She decided she would get the history of Monte written up now, and on the wire in the morning.

There was a woman who frequented the casino every afternoon and evening, always wearing a long black gown fitted snugly to her somewhat ample frame. Her hair was black, drawn back and enhanced by a large black ribbon. She was haughty, austere, and gave the impression of being not only wealthy but someone of great importance. The only article of jewelry she wore complemented her black dress—a sterling silver chain from which hung a square piece enameled in white, the background for a two-carat diamond. This itself was sufficient for her to gain attention. Lydia had noticed that she held herself aloof, but nevertheless made her living in a strange way.

In playing routlette, counters were placed by a number of people, sometimes one player's counters piled upon another's. This woman, who said she was the archduchess from a Bavarian province and called herself the Archduchess Sophie Ziegler, made excellent use of her apparent wealth, breeding and importance. She would place a counter or two on the table atop someone else's similar bet and, when there was a win, she would grandly sweep all the counters on that bet, claiming they were hers. As the counters were the same color and size, there wasn't much the other winner or winners could do about it, especially since they were invariably overwhelmed by her imperiousness and the speed with which she whisked the counters off the table.

The dealers and croupiers all knew her and let her have her way without protesting any of the plays. Of course, she never tried to cheat the table or she'd have been banished long ago. What she did do was add considerable color to the festivities at this kind of casino. She never overdid her take and always acted with supreme dignity.

She might make a good story, except for the fact that she had declined to be interviewed or even to talk about her real identity; it was commonly supposed that the one she lived under was false. But there was no way of telling without checking her antecedents, and Lydia doubted the story was worth that much investigation.

She studied the woman carefully all that afternoon and evening. She won, perhaps, a few francs and stole about three times that number, leaving a few players angry, but more of them only amused and unwilling to argue with her. Part of her ploy was to make certain the stakes were not high enough to be the cause of controversy or worth reporting to the authorities. Yet, when added up, they provided her with a rather good living. Perhaps, Lydia thought, her success was owing to the large diamond resting on her ample bosom—anyone who could afford a stone like that wasn't apt to lie and cheat to gain a paltry sum. But was the diamond real?

She did write a two-part article on the woman and was tempted to ask Regina to take photographs of her in secrecy, but decided against it. The archduchess wasn't hurting anyone; no one had registered a complaint about her idiosyncrasy.

Once again, Lydia spent the evening alone for Jeff had not put in an appearance, and the baron was still enjoying his indisposition. Of course, she was well enough known that she didn't lack for someone to talk to, but she was growing more and more aware of the fact that Jeff kept intruding into her thoughts. She found it highly disconcerting.

She walked home alone, this time remembering how she had been trapped and warning herself to be on guard. She knew Trencher had been taken out of Monte Carlo with an armed guard that afternoon, so she had nothing to fear from him. Still, the memory was there and strong enough that she unlocked her door with some apprehension. The room was dark, but even before she entered it she was aware that someone was waiting for her—an unannounced visitor who had managed to gain entrance without her permission.

The fear returned with a rush. Before she stepped over the threshold, she said shrilly, "Who is it? Who's in here?"

"Lydia," a familiar voice came out of the gloom, "come on in. What're you afraid of? Here, I'll turn on the light."

"Drury!" she exclaimed in fresh dismay as the light illumined the intruder. "Bryant Drury! How did you get into my room?"

"My dear Lydia, have you forgotten that a good reporter can go anywhere he likes if he has the gumption to do so? And carries a set of skeleton keys that can open any locked door in this old building? You're looking well and just as enticing. And you're most successful, of course. Congratulations," he said sarcastically.

"What do you want?" she asked, her voice somewhat harsh. Remembering his behavior the last time she'd been with him, she didn't trust him for a moment.

"Want? Why, nothing, my dear. I just thought I'd pay you a courtesy call." His voice was cool, almost friendly but not quite. "I haven't forgotten you cost me my job," he added.

"That was due to your own carelessness, Drury," she reminded him.

"I well remember that in your opinion you saved my neck, for if that crazy story I wrote had hit the streets, I'd have been reduced to the status of a beggar after the civil action was over. Or that is how *your* theory goes."

Lydia made no comment, feeling none was needed.

"Drury, if we're going to talk, it won't be in my room behind a closed door. However, I'll go down to the lobby with you and we can talk there."

"Still a prude," he said mockingly. "You should have been a schoolteacher."

"Now, see here—" Lydia began, irritated by his manner.

"Oh, hell," Bryant broke in, "I don't blame you. Sure, we'll go to the lobby. Who knows? Something might happen down there that'll give you a story."

Lydia ignored the dig and gave him a sidelong glance

as they made their descent in the lift. He was as handsome as ever, yet there was, in some way, a change. Keeping her features noncommittal, she tried to analyze what it was. Was it that she was no longer in awe of him, due to the fact that they were in the same field and she had now proven herself? She sensed there was something else. His usual cocksure manner was still evident, only now it seemed more marked. Certainly the fact that he'd been dismissed from the *Star-Press* hadn't destroyed his ego. The latter seemed, if anything, to be more pronounced.

"May I ask what you're doing in this part of the world?" she asked, her tone casual, after they seated themselves at a small table and ordered drinks.

He smiled. "I might try to improve my image by saying I couldn't get you off my mind and that I came here just to see you. But that wouldn't be the truth. I'm here because I intend to write a book on Monte Carlo."

"You're not assigned here?"

"I had a devil of a time trying to get a job after what happened," he said with a degree of bitterness. "That man whose wife I almost maligned heard about the incident and was responsible for my being blacklisted. So I decided to cash in on my reputation, which is intact up to now, I hope, and write a book that might sell because of ny name. Notorious or not, I'm still well known."

"I hope your book will be a great success," she murmured politely.

"I'm sure it will. After reading your pieces I can see there are a million stories in this place. However, I doubt that I'll interfere with your work in any way. Whatever I write about, I'll find out about for myself. There's room for both of us on Monte . . . or so I hope."

Inwardly, Lydia felt relief. His words seemed mild compared to those of that night in the newspaper office after he'd been fired. "That means you don't hold a grudge for what happened. I mean—you were terribly angry with me, even though you know I saved both you and the paper from a civil suit."

It was almost as if he read her mind, for the smile that crossed his mouth was cold. "Certainly I hold a grudge. I was at the top. You pulled the rug out from under me."

"I did you a favor," Lydia protested.

"Like hell you did."

"I did, Drury. And you know it. You should have checked the identity of the young man with Mrs. Hallett. But you were too intent on getting your revenge. You must really hate her husband."

"If I didn't before, I do now," he said. "As for you, you're a deceitful wench. You like playing innocent, too, don't you. A little difficult to believe when you're wearing gowns that must have cost a small fortune. Someone must be footing the bill."

"They're expensive," she retorted, "but all are paid for by the paper. I have to dress the part if I'm going to mix with the patrons."

"And I suppose you consider yourself a little princess." His smile now mocked her.

"No. I'm a hard-working reporter," she replied angrily. "I hope one day I'll reach the top of my profession."

"Hardly likely for a woman," he scoffed.

"I was hoping we could be cordial," she said. "I can see now you sought me out only to let me know you were here, hoping your presence would upset me. You might as well know it hasn't. I merely do not trust you."

"That goes for both of us. Shall we agree to be civil when we meet?"

"Of course we will, unless you pull some rotten stunt, which I know you're perfectly capable of doing. Thank you for the sherry and this illuminating conversation. I'm not enthused by it, but I'm grateful that we know where we stand."

"Thank you." He arose and bowed briefly.

"One thing more," she said. "If you go into my suite again without permission, I shall report you to the police who are, I assure you, no respecter of fame and most severe in punishing wrongdoers."

She was shaking again as she went to the lift, stopping to look around just before she entered the car. Drury gave her a mocking smile and another bow.

Despite her brave words, she was still afraid of him. Trencher had placed a great physical terror upon her, but Drury brought something else, even worse. It was subtle, a promise of trouble, ever-present and ready to strike. He was a dangerous man, a clever man and a vindictive one. She was certain of this.

Whatever he did to her would be done cleverly. He'd never overstep, but whatever plan he had in mind regarding her would be destructive. She wondered if all this good fortune that had come her way was now about to be reversed.

For two consecutive nights she went to bed troubled and frightened. Drury's presence in Monte made her unsure of herself; she wondered if she could stand up to this man and whatever he planned for her.

Lying awake, she thought of telling Jeff about Drury's presence but decided against it for the time being. It was like asking for help against a shadowy menace, for Drury would never be specific in what he wanted of her, or what he would do. In time, Jeff would know because she was sure the two men would meet. Jeff wasn't a fool . . . he'd see how it was between her and Drury. She was, she thought, fortunate in having Jeff on her side, even if they did argue constantly, and he was secretive about his comings and goings.

She had to admit that she needed him.

Six

Lydia's regular column was now being printed by several other newspapers, although still strictly controlled by George Morgan's publication. During dull weeks, she continued to expand her stories on the history of Monte Carlo—how it had grown from an unknown, poor, and almost barren spot of rock into the most famous of all gambling palaces and high-society resorts. How it had nineteen hotels, an opera house, sumptuous villas, modern apartment houses, banks and elegant shops. How its restaurants vied with one another to provide the most delectable and exotic foods, prepared by world-renowned chefs.

She wrote about the comings and goings of the rich and the famous, able now to set up interviews with people she'd have once been awed by. She described the yachts, many of them now motorized and worth millions. She filled her columns and articles with anecdotes, most of them humorous and all of them colorful.

Asked by Guy Spencer to stress the exciting and glamorous aspect of Monte, she avoided writing about the pawnbrokers, the voracious money lenders, and the cheap labor employed by the most successful enterprises. Respecting the needs of the paper, she never again mentioned the suicides, of which there were surprisingly few. She did write a prolonged article about a story that had appeared in a Parisian newspaper, saying that well behind the gaudy casino was a secret cemetery where the suicides were buried.

She refuted this with figures and statements from the authorities, finally filling the Paris newspaper story so full of holes that it became ridiculous.

When this refutation appeared in print, the management sent her an enormous bouquet of roses and orange blossoms, and she soon became as well treated as the wealthiest and freest gamblers. As her publisher and editor had prophesied, her youth, inexperience and naivete had made her writings spectacularly successful. Lydia realized very well that this naivete had worn somewhat thin by now, and she had to restrain herself in the writing of some stories. She wished that she could reveal the seamier side of Monte, too, "the dark side" as Jeff described it. But the *Star-Press* had asked for glamour.

The winter season was beginning, the hotels were jammed, there was a waiting line in all the restaurants unless one was influential or a big gambler who threw money around. The new British-owned-and-built Hotel Metropole was worth a series of articles. Lydia found herself riding high among the rich and famous. The baron had fully recovered by now and once again accompanied her to many of the functions her work made it necessary for her to attend. He provided a few more stories, but was rapidly running out of them. Regina provided photographs and had even opened a studio, which was doing well. And with the new season, Angelina had returned.

Drury seemed to come and go, sometimes staying in Monte Carlo for three or four weeks and then vanishing for an equal amount of time. Lydia maintained no contact with him other than a brief nod when they encountered one another in the casino or restaurants, as they invariably did. Each time she saw him she felt prickles of apprehension and didn't know why, because there didn't seem to be much he could do to harm her. Yet, aware of his vindictive nature, she sensed he'd find a way. She was even tempted to see that he was banned, which she knew she could do, but quickly gave up this idea as petty, unfair and quite possibly dangerous.

If Drury had told the truth about writing a book, he didn't

spend much time on it. Lydia was aware that he gambled, but not excessively, and now and then squired a young female visitor to the tables. He seemed to have plenty of money, but there was a possibility that he'd saved and invested his earnings for he had once been the most highly paid reporter in New York.

Jeff's long absences provided the most anguish, and the plainly evident lack of results in the kind of work he claimed to be doing. Despite her mixed feelings, she hoped that with the new season beginning, she might see more of him. She was still worried about the unfriendly note on which they had last parted.

Opening night of the new season would be a gaudy, lively and expensive affair. Lydia had kept in touch with The House of Worth and made several purchases successfully without going to Paris. For this occasion, she had ordered a special gown and had been assured it would be different from anything else.

Lydia exclaimed in delight when it arrived. She lifted from its wrappings a very pale lavender satin gown bordered with black fur. Bead embroidery in an iris design ascended each side of the skirt almost to the waistline, and fur shoulder straps completed the square décolleté. The short puffed sleeves of dotted mousseline de soie were visible under a ruffle of satin beaded in the same design as on the graceful skirt, also trimmed with fur, which fell in godet pleats. Angelina decided against any hair ornament. Instead, she looped Lydia's hair at the back, extending it to the top of her head in a second loop. The effect was similar to the sculptured head of a ballet dancer, complementing Lydia's pretty profile. Her long silk gloves in a matching shade of lavender, and a black lace fan, which had arrived in its own box nestling in tissue paper, would complete her costume.

Angelina clapped her hands in delight as Lydia held the creation up before her and viewed it in the mirror.

"It will be the most beautiful gown at the dinner, mademoiselle," she exclaimed. "Come, let us make you ready. There is much to be done."

"I wonder how I did without you," Lydia said. "The new season is of importance to me mostly because it brought you back. Did you have a good summer?"

"In Paris, nothing is good in summer," she said with a shrug. "But one manages. And one does what one is told. I am back now and I will not put on a long face."

During the process of getting ready, they talked about the casino, the restaurants and the people. Lydia had actually begun to feel lonely, especially with Jeffrey gone so long, but Angelina furnished a confidential friendship she sorely needed.

"This prince, or whatever he is," she said, "who is giving the dinner. What's he like, Angelina? Or do you know?"

"Once," she said, "I took care of his wife, the one he brought. They say all these desert princes have several. If she was an example of the others, I pity the man. But he is very wealthy and he gambles heavily, almost always losing. This doesn't seem to make a particle of difference to him, perhaps because he is so rich. Why is it, mademoiselle, that those with much money are so reckless?"

"They can afford to be," Lydia replied with a laugh. "We work for ours and we spend it wisely. Most of us do anyway. The very rich have so much it doesn't mean a great deal. I suppose they get their pleasure from spending it. Recklessly, as you have said. What is the prince like?"

"Mademoiselle, a lowly one like me is not permitted to look up at His Highness. They are very haughty, these desert princes. I think this one is from Algeria, though I cannot be sure."

A bouquet of flowers arrived in a box while Lydia was getting dressed. Angelina accepted them and laid them aside in the parlor.

"Flowers, mademoiselle," she said. "I did not look at the card. There is no time. You must hurry—and I cannot stay with you. There is a guest—an old harridan but a heavy loser every time she comes. She insists I help her dress and she will be furious if I am much later."

"You may go," Lydia said. "I'm ready. Don't get into trouble because of me."

"I will pray that the evening is very successful for you." Angelina made a quick curtsy. "You will outshine every lady."

She left hurriedly. Lydia made a final study of herself in the mirror, felt satisfied and prepared to leave. The baron, she knew, would be in the lobby, probably fuming with impatience by now for Lydia was late. She turned to the box of flowers lying on a table in the parlor. In her anxiety and haste to leave, Angelina had neglected to open it and place the flowers in water. Beside a large bouquet of carnations, there was a lovely corsage of the cinnamon-scented flower.

Lydia glanced at the card. It bore only the imprint Prince Ali Jouhaud in raised letters. She realized the prince probably sent bouquets to anyone the casino operators suggested, and especially to an international reporter who might write favorably about him. In deference to his gracious gesture, however, she pinned the corsage of carnations at her waist. The bouquet she placed in a vase of water.

She couldn't resist one last glance in the mirror and she smiled slightly, wondering if this was the same shy, naive girl who only a few months ago had aspired only to be a good New York reporter. Now here she was, an honored guest at a gala event in Monte Carlo, hosted by a prince! She would consort with some of the most famous people of the world and many of the wealthiest ones.

The baron was fuming, but he was also dazzled at the sight of her as she emerged from the lift. He bowed and kissed the back of her hand in his usual courtly manner.

"Lovely," he said. "Absolutely beautiful. I only hope the prince does not add you to his harem."

"Good heavens!" Lydia said in astonishment. "Do you mean he has more than one wife?"

"I am not sure. These people do not talk much about themselves. They only spend money, which is entirely to my taste. He may have a dozen wives, fifty, a hundred.

112

Who cares? So long as his gold pieces are authentic."

"Very true, Baron. I must say that you look extravagantly grand this evening."

"*Merci,* mademoiselle. One would have to be what you say to have a lady such as you on his arm. I have a carriage waiting. Of course, you cannot walk to the casino and then to the Café de Paris."

The casino was a lively place this evening. The opening of a new season brought most of the regulars back, along with newcomers attracted by the gaudiness and the excitement.

The casino door was guarded by several uniformed men and no one without the proper credentials was allowed inside, at least for the time being. However, the baron and Lydia were well-known and promptly bowed into the lobby, crowded with people, all talking loudly in order to be heard above the voices of the others.

As Lydia, on the baron's arm, walked slowly through the crowd toward the casino, a young man, in evening dress as demanded by the casino on a night like this, suddenly broke from the group he was with and lunged at her. She was so startled she didn't even try to avoid him. He savagely pulled the carnations from her waist, almost tearing her gown in the process. Then he shredded the flowers to pieces, the petals falling at his feet.

"*Sacré bleu!*" he exclaimed. "Such a thing on a night like this!"

"What in the world are you talking about?" Lydia asked in growing anger. "What's the meaning of this? How dare you?"

"Carnations!" he cried out. "Carnations in the casino! Do you wish to bring misfortune on all of us by wearing carnations in here? Don't you know how we feel about those filthy flowers that smell like the grave?"

"I don't know what you mean, sir," she said.

The baron sighed. "I will take the blame. I did not notice the flowers against your personal beauty, mademoiselle, or I would have warned you. Carnations are bad luck in the casino. They bring nothing but loss to those who are even near the flowers.''

"Such nonsense!" Lydia exclaimed.

"Mademoiselle, it is not nonsense," the young Frenchman declared. "I may have saved you from losing all you had in the world. That is what carnations do."

Lydia realized she'd have to surrender to his fantastic belief because by now she knew everyone else around them in the casino was agreeing with the young man. She turned to the baron.

"Why then would the prince send me such a bouquet?"

"Are you certain he did? He must be familiar with this superstition."

"I read his name on the card, Baron."

"Ah, then, perhaps he does not know. It doesn't matter now that they have been destroyed. Shall we go into the casino proper and lose a few francs?"

The emotional young man bowed apologetically to Lydia. "It is my fault, mademoiselle, for being so rash and impulsive, but carnations scare me to death in here. I intend to win this night and that is why I became so alarmed."

"It's for me to apologize," Lydia said. "I should have known of this belief, but I confess that I've never heard of it before, so please forgive me."

Lydia and the baron then entered the gaming room, already crowded with men in evening dress and women exquisitely gowned, moving about graciously yet seeking open areas they might move into for the purpose of showing off their elaborate gowns and jewels. Lydia, her eyes and mind now well-trained, locked in her memory descriptions of these wonders, along with the names of the ladies who wore them. Those she did not recognize she would have identified for her later, either through the baron or the gentlemen who strolled casually around the premises, yet were actually employed to keep an eye on the guests merely for the purpose of protecting them and their jewels. At the same time, these men had to learn the names of the guests so that should there be an occasion for them to have any personal contact, it would be a decorous one.

At the crowded tables the baron, impulsive as always, placed a bet on the black, promptly lost it and Lydia pulled him away from the wheel before he became too immersed in the play. She knew she would have to assume responsibility for his losses.

"We'll come back later," she said. "There's no time now. People are already leaving for the café and the dinner."

"It's a bad thing when I would rather lose my money than eat the prince's dinner, of which you will find there are few better. But it is so. I would rather gamble than eat, and this has been my downfall."

"Weep later," Lydia said happily. "Our present objective is the café. Come along."

There were landaus waiting to transport everyone next door to the café, all generously provided by the prince. By now, Lydia was anxious to see what this man who seemed as rich as the famed Croesus looked like.

The main dining hall of the café had been transposed into a fairyland of flowers, paintings from the prince's palace and silken hangings. The table was glowing with orchids and a gold plated service; the finest china and Florentine and Venetian crystal in which wine would soon be served.

"Good heavens," Lydia whispered. "Is this real?"

"It is real and yet I would rather be gambling," the baron said. "But I promise to make the best of it."

"You'd better," Lydia laughed, making mental notes of the magnificence, "if you want to escort me again."

Places were, of course, assigned and Lydia sat between the baron and a young, quite handsome gentleman in evening dress. Someone tapped on a glass, everyone arose and the prince and princess made their entrance. Lydia had visualized a bearded, slim man in a gaudy uniform, with an austere, princely attitude. Instead, a rather roly-poly man of about sixty signaled genially for all to be seated. He wore evening dress like the others, but several rows of medals and a scarlet ribbon decorated his ample chest.

He made a brief, uninspired speech in fairly good English, added to it in fairly good French and then sat down. Waiters in burgundy-colored uniforms, wearing white gloves, began to serve now. Lydia thought there seemed to be a waiter for every two or three guests. She watched them do everything quietly, efficiently and with artful care so that there was no interruption in the guests' conversations.

Lydia was most impressed with the princess, she decided, who wore a gown that must have come from Paris and fabulous jewelry that she seemed comfortable in. She was young, not more than thirty, a lovely woman with a glowing skin, black hair and very dark eyes that were somewhat slanted, but not enough to be Oriental. Lydia had heard her beauty was breathtaking. Perhaps it might have been to her subjects in the desert, but there were women here even more expensively dressed and equally attractive. Although picturesque, the princess lent little else to the affair, speaking only sparingly and then with downcast eyes as if she feared her husband's wrath if she became too vivacious. Lydia felt a stir of sympathy for this woman.

She turned her attention to the food. The first course was an ample serving of fruits, many of which she was sure she'd never heard of before.

"Do not eat it all," the baron whispered. "There is a great deal more."

This course was followed by a hot soufflé with unmelted orange ice in the center. She wondered what miracle of cooking had accomplished this. It was followed by a fish course in a light curry sauce, and after that, a breast of chicken supported on a layer of paté de foie gras. Again the baron warned her to eat only part of each serving. She knew why when an entire bird stuffed with crayfish and truffles was placed before her along with an eye-opening array of colorful vegetables. And, finally, a work of art consisting of mandarin ice enclosed in a creamy meringue decorated with real violets, crystallized into small objects of great beauty and tasting beyond imagination, was set before the bedazzled eyes of each guest.

Wine was poured lavishly, a different one with each course, all vintage, all highly expensive.

The attractive, dark-haired man at Lydia's right had conversed politely on general, not very interesting, topics, but now he began talking about the food and how it was prepared.

"The prince brought with him four of his own chefs who likely produced much of what we've eaten. There can be no failures, because if such a thing happened—if, for instance, the soufflé fell—someone would have his ears chopped off."

"Do you really mean that?" Lydia asked in astonishment.

"My dear young lady, heads, ears, noses and hands are frequently cut off as penalties for the crime of gross failure."

"I can scarcely believe it, sir."

"It's true. I can verify that, for I'm the prince's equerry, the man in charge of his stables. He's a fancier of horseflesh and racing. We're quite close, so whatever I say is the truth, I assure you, mademoiselle."

"How interesting," she replied. "I'm Miss Lydia Bradley, a reporter for an American newspaper. Do you think the prince would allow me to interview him?"

"No, mademoiselle. No! For God's sake, don't approach him with such a request. He abhors publicity."

"It's odd he would, being a member of royalty, with endless wealth and prestige."

"There are certain things he is afraid you would ask." The man's fine-featured face was enigmatic.

"What sort of things?"

"You're a curious one, mademoiselle. But perhaps I am talking too much."

"I'm sorry," she said. "I shouldn't have asked so many questions. Forgive me."

"But of course, Mademoiselle Bradley. It is your business to ask questions. But not of the prince. He would stalk out of the casino or anywhere else if you did this," he assured her.

"I wouldn't approach him without an appointment, which it seems he wouldn't grant anyway. Thank you for the warning."

"I'm pleased you understand. It took me some time to get used to the man. You see, I'm French. Armand Martel, mademoiselle, at your service."

"Monsieur Martel," she acknowledged, bowing her head slightly.

"The ways of the desert people are strange to me, you see. There is, of course, much to be told, but I am sworn to silence."

"Then we'll talk about him no longer, sir," Lydia said. "I wouldn't wish to intrude in his secret life."

Martel chuckled briefly. "Secret life is the right expression, mademoiselle. You would be surprised."

His words intrigued her, hinting at a story to be uncovered, but Lydia said nothing more in an effort to be polite. But she was aware that he had dangled a temptation in front of her, then hastily withdrawn it.

Speeches followed dinner, some of them rather long and all greatly praising the prince, who inclined his head now and then, agreeing with the words spoken in his honor. Certainly it had been an excellent dinner, not to be bettered, leaving everyone feeling mellow. Even the speeches seemed for the most part interesting. Fortunately, the prince didn't let these affect him, for when he was called upon to close the festivities, he merely arose and spoke two words: "Let's gamble." Everyone applauded.

The prince had done or said nothing to offend her, but somehow Lydia didn't care for the man. She wondered if this was owing to the vague innuendoes of his equerry at the banquet table.

As there were not sufficient carriages to accommodate the exodus of so many people at one time and Lydia was not inclined to wait in line, she picked up her skirts and walked. The distance was short and her gown would not suffer. Besides, after so much food, she welcomed the exercise.

The casino seemed more crowded than ever, now that the festivities were over, and Lydia suspected that many not included in the prince's party had been admitted. After all, the casino couldn't be closed to others. There was money to be made.

The baron gravitated directly to the first table and, to his surprise and Lydia's astonishment, won thirty-six to one. He promptly forgot that his attentions should be directed at Lydia. The lure of the wheels and the excitement of finally winning made him oblivious to anyone or anything other than the action at the table.

Lydia was free to wander about, as was her custom, for it was the only way to find out who was present. Also, she was eager to observe whether the prince's presence altered the behavior of the guests or the employees.

For quite some time now she had no longer found it difficult to approach people and ask countless questions. She realized they understood this was her business. Those who did not wish to comply with her questions showed no animosity and Lydia gracefully withdrew, a considerable change from the way she worked when she first arrived. She'd learned many ways of approaching people now and of asking leading questions. Furthermore, she'd acquired a great deal of poise, self-assurance and skill.

The prince was gambling as she moved closer to his table. She saw he was losing and consequently not in a very good mood. A casino official whispered to him and he arose, moved his head to signal that his wife should follow him, and made his way upstairs to one of the private salons where heavy gambling was conducted. Here there were no limits set for those who did not wish to let it be known how much they lost—or won. Lydia had never violated the confidentiality these salons provided and she was not inclined to do so tonight.

Yet she realized more and more that the prince was an enormously good subject for a story. From what his French equerry had intimated, it would likely not be a lovely story about a Prince Charming. Yet the more she thought about it, the more she wished to do it.

There was, of course, but a single source of information and the man had not been inclined to enlighten her. She thought this unfortunate as she moved about the casino, stopping to chat or to compliment some guest on her gown, her mind still on the prince and a story concerning him. For some weeks now she knew her column and reports had been lacking in excitement. During the off-season there wasn't much exciting to write about, and she'd been forced to revert again to detailing the history of Monaco and the families who had created this empire of gambling amid spectacular scenery.

Suddenly she saw the man who had spoken to her at dinner standing alone in one corner of the room, holding a glass of champagne and looking thoroughly bored. Lydia threaded her way through the crowd toward him. When he saw her approach, his face lit up with pleasure.

She had made up her mind that if she could get him to talk, she would write the story of Prince Ali Jouhaud. If it was negative in approach, even a cruel story, she would still write it. Her readers needed something to stir their blood.

"Good evening again, Monsieur Martel," she said. "Don't you accompany the prince when he gambles in private?"

"He would not have it, mademoiselle. And neither would I, especially if he lost a great deal."

"He's not a good loser, then?"

"No indeed. It's not the money—the amount he loses—but the fact that he doesn't win. He isn't used to losing in anything, and it brings out a rage that falls upon anyone near him. I have deep sympathy for his wife when he loses."

"You don't sound as if you like the man very much," Lydia observed.

"It's not hard to dislike a man such as the prince," Martel said with a slightly bitter air. "Yet he pays me well, and so long as I see that his stables produce fine stock—racehorses that win—I am secure. But if it comes to a point where his horses do not win consistently enough to suit him, you can wager a great deal of money on the fact that when he looks for someone to blame and punish, I won't be there—I'll know when to get out—and fast."

Whether Martel knew it or not, he was again whetting Lydia's curiosity and her firm determination to write the story of this prince.

"May I get you a glass of champagne?" he asked.

"Well, yes, I would like one—and a chance to talk to you about Prince Ali Jouhaud," she said bluntly.

"To write about him, mademoiselle?" Martel asked warily.

"He should make an interesting topic, Monsieur Martel."

"Indeed he would, but I do not violate confidences, even if I am inclined to do so. Please—you must not tempt me." His eyes held a hint of hesitation.

"Very well. I promise not to ask any questions. Of course, if you wish to volunteer. . . ." She knew she had him hooked. He was filled with resentment of the prince, and despite his claim of loyalty, actually eager to talk. She had long since learned the symptoms of someone who hesitated and yet wished to tell her a story.

Martel summoned a passing waiter with a tray of glasses, placed his empty one on the tray and took two filled with champagne. Lydia thanked him and sipped her drink slowly, thoughtfully, wondering when he was going to talk. He, in turn, was quite silent, saying little as they moved about. She realized, before long, that he was steering her toward the exit. On the way he provided two more glasses of champagne as they strolled out into the summer air, so sweet and pure, filled with the perfume of flowers now in full bloom.

"Tell me," he asked, "what sort of story would you write about him?"

"The truth, monsieur. Always the truth."

"Good or bad? Favorable or unfavorable?"

"Of course."

"And you would keep your source of information a secret?"

"It could not be pried out of me for anything in the world."

Martel seemed to pause and then come to a decision. "We'll sit awhile on that bench just ahead of us. It's quiet there, and open enough that there can be no eavesdroppers. You'll listen, sympathetically, and not call me a scoundrel for what I have to say?"

"My word on it, monsieur."

He dusted off the bench with a handkerchief, sat down beside Lydia and seemed to think deeply. She wasn't quite sure if his reluctance signaled he would talk or decide not to talk at all. Suddenly, after a spell of this intense silence, he drained his glass and hurled it at one of the orange trees on the casino estate.

"I hate him!" His repressed anger finally exploded. "He looks so innocent, so full of joie de vivre. But he is a murderer, a lecher, a cheat and the cruelest man I have ever known."

"As bad as that?" Lydia found herself encouraging him.

"Worse. He is known to take a young girl to his bed and if she fails to satisfy his inhuman demands, he has her beaten while he watches. He has married more times than he can count and he keeps his women in haremlike conditions. They are allowed no freedom and find escape from his tyranny only by fighting among themselves, which amuses him very much. A thief has his hands removed . . . if he steals from the palace, he loses his arms. A woman who offends him is turned over to one of his prisons and circulated among the vilest criminals on earth. I tell you, there are times when I think he is a madman—until I watch him manipulate some poor soul and cheat him out of whatever he has. He takes great delight in this."

Lydia listened to him in horror. "But isn't any of this known except in his own country?"

"It's not even known there. You ask any of his subjects

and they will flatter him with praise and say he is the most honest and kind sovereign they ever knew. In fact, ask any of his retinue other than me, and they will know nothing or pretend to. I only know of his real nature because of what he did to my lovely sister, Françoise, who came to Algeria with me. She was completely broken. . . ."

"Monsieur Martel, would you object if I wrote this story?" Lydia asked him. "People should be warned against such a man."

He looked at her with an expression of terror. "It would be worth my life."

"You wouldn't be mentioned anywhere, not you or your sister. Nothing I write will be traced to you because very few people have seen us together. I'll leave you now, and if we meet in the casino, or anywhere else, I'll treat you as I would any casual acquaintanceship, begun at the prince's dinner."

"I don't know," he said slowly. "I detest the man and it would do my heart good, but then . . . the way he reacts to something like this. . . . There's no telling what he'll do."

"If you don't wish me to write this, you have only to say so and not one word will be published."

He bent his head and massaged his brow. Looking up, his expression harried, he finally burst out with, "It's best that the truth be told, better for everyone connected with this man, as you say. If his real nature is exposed, perhaps he'll soften in the years to come. And it is the only thing I can do to avenge my sister. So, I will tell you about him and you may tell the whole world what a scoundrel he is." He banged his fist into his open palm.

"I swear he will never know where the story came from, m'sieur," Lydia once more assured him.

"I believe you, Miss Bradley. Well, as I said, he treats his women abominably. He uses them only to satisfy his unusual sex desires. Then he abandons them to a life of disgrace. And his subjects in his desert kingdom are held in check, paid little, worked half to death. He taxes them as high as he dares. He owns everything—banks, business houses, even the small rug manufacturing places. His palace is worth millions and his people live in tents. I am in charge of his stables, as I told you. If he has a favorite horse that loses a race, he personally goes down to the stable and shoots the poor animal. I resent this mainly because it is unnecessary cruelty and because I devoted so much time to raise a good animal. Even the best thoroughbreds can't always win. However, if they don't win for the prince, they are dead horses.''

"The man seems unreal," Lydia commented, her pencil flying.

"I never thought of him that way, but it's true. For instance, he also raises birds. All kinds of game birds. Two times a year he holds shoots, bringing all his friends in for the sport. Birds are freed from their cages, sent aloft, and his friends try their luck in bringing them down. But when the prince shoots, a special flock is released, all of them with wings clipped enough that they fly slowly and cannot make evasive turns to avoid the guns. It is outright slaughter. It makes me sick every time I see it.''

"There can't be much more," Lydia exhaled deeply. "What kind of a man can he be? I have enough material. In a day or two the whole world will judge him. Thank you very much and be sure I'll never betray you.''

"My head will suddenly leave my body if you do," he said, grimacing.

"I'll go back to the casino now," Lydia suggested. "It would be best if you returned there only after some time, in case anyone noticed us leaving together.''

"The baron! You are in his company, and he is a noted tattletale.''

"I won't mention a word of it to him, or anyone else, Monsieur Martel. I'll write the story as soon as I get home and send it in the morning. I understand the prince is returning home tomorrow and that you'll go with him. Perhaps he'll never even hear of the story.''

"That's not likely, but as you say, there's nothing to

124

connect me with what you write. I'm not the only one who knows about him who might have spoken to you."

When Lydia entered the casino, she discovered the baron morosely standing at one table, his expression clearly showing that he had lost whatever he'd won, and more. He shook his head as she approached.

"I am the most wretched of gamblers," he confessed. "I don't know how to quit when I'm ahead. I had a small fortune for about fifteen minutes. Where have you been? I looked for you. Could you spare a small stake? It could be my lucky night."

She handed him a hundred franc note. "Thank you for lending me your arm on these occasions, Baron. I hope you win back your fortune. As for me, I'm very tired and I'm going directly back to the hotel and to bed."

"There are carriages at the door," he said. "I saw them when I went out for some air and to contemplate suicide."

"Good luck," she laughed. "If you win, take a long walk."

"Yes, and a very long walk if I lose," he declared. "Straight down to the ocean."

"If you don't lose too much, I'll settle your debt."

"I'm overwhelmed, my dear Lydia. I may not kill myself after all."

She smiled and patted his arm, knowing he meant none of this. She then took a carriage back to the hotel, went directly to her suite and slowly removed her gown while she pondered the story she had just been told. What should be her approach to it? She reflected that her readers needed something of a jolt.

She put on a silk robe, sat down at the desk and drew paper from the drawer. She removed the used pen, inserted a new one in the holder, dipped the pen in the inkwell and began to write. She rarely had difficulty in preparing a story, but this time she had so much information she had to decide what to use and what to discard.

She wrote a full description of the dinner, including the food, the decor, the wines and the guests. She described the princess—the one he brought with him, she made certain to say. After two hours on the story, rewriting some of it, she wished she'd had time to ask Martel more questions that came to mind. She had no doubt that what he had told her was the truth, for his great reluctance to talk, his repressed rage and fear, were more than enough proof. Still, she wished she could cross-check the story. But to do so would be to betray Martel, or at the very least put him in danger. This she dared not do. She wondered if he were having second thoughts now about what he'd done and would deny what he'd already told her, if she saw him again. She could take no chances—she had to get her story published at once.

When the article was finished, she read it over with considerable satisfaction. She hadn't been vindictive and her indignation wasn't too evident. To make certain she'd spelled the prince's name correctly, she looked for the card that came with the flowers. She'd dropped it on the table beside the vase of carnations, but it was no longer there. She looked everywhere and finally decided that Angelina must have returned and disposed of it. No matter. She was certain she had the name right.

Seven

In the morning Lydia dressed hastily and took a carriage to the cable office before breakfast. She arranged for an immediate transmission, then returned to the hotel and had a leisurely breakfast while she considered what sort of story she would search for today. With the new season, there were many fresh ideas to be followed up. One was to see what she could learn about certain Russian dukes and duchesses who seemed to be accompanied by larger entourages every year. Some brought as many as forty serfs along, and hired even more servants on arrival. She already knew the serfs slept in the hotel hallways outside the doors of those they were assigned to serve. No one seemed to think much about this, but Lydia saw in it another unusual story to enlighten the American reader on how others lived, especially royalty and their retinues.

At noon, as was his habit, the baron appeared, this time in a state of great excitement. She met him in the lobby and, of course, he was not averse to having luncheon with her.

"From your expression," she said, after they ordered their meal, "you must have won last night."

"On the contrary," he sighed deeply.

"Then what seems to excite you today?"

"I will tell you. It is a great thing. You should ask Regina to see if she can get a photo, though it will be worth her life if she is found out."

"Go on, Baron, tell me whom she should photograph."

"The kaiser."

"Really?" Lydia's interest now equaled his.

"He has sent his generals here every year with new systems to play and they have always lost. This time he is coming himself for he has a system worked out by a professor at the best German university. He is going to try and break the bank." The baron's voice barely hid his excitement.

"What university?" Lydia was already taking mental notes.

"Heidelberg, of course," he said impatiently. "I said the best. Certainly you have heard of it."

"Oh yes," Lydia said, smiling at his indignation. "It has quite a history of romance, duels and songs."

"It is a very prestigious institution," he said indignantly. "Scholarly."

"I know, Baron." Lydia made her tone properly apologetic. "But I was thinking of the much-touted romances, both the unsuccessful and the fulfilled. Now please tell me about the kaiser's visit."

"There is little to tell, other than that he is coming," the baron said, appeased by her explanation. "As you may well guess, I am not in his confidence."

"Since you are in mine, I'm pleased you brought me this information. It would be to Regina's advantage if she used that little camera of hers."

The baron pursed his lips thoughtfully. "It would be very risky."

Lydia fell in with his broad hint. "I know, and I expect to pay well for such a risk. Will you be my escort tonight? I want to get as close to the kaiser as possible."

"Have I ever failed you?" He grinned wickedly.

"Be here at seven," she said. "That will give us time to dine and be in the casino when he arrives."

"He is coming incognito," the baron confided. "He wants no one to know he is here unless he wins. So there is no royal entourage this time, and no royal reception.

Everything is to be very quiet, at his command."

Lydia's excitement was now tempered with annoyance. "He's a famous figure. He cannot escape publicity, even of an adverse kind. I'm beginning to tire of writing about the pomp granted these rulers, without any mention of what they're really like."

The baron shrugged. "They are men like everyone else. They do good sometimes, they have great responsibilities. If they transgress now and then, especially with a mistress or two, who can blame them? They need an outlet, being the same as most men. I do not censure them."

"I'm not restricting my criticism to that." Lydia retorted mildly. "I'm thinking of how they flaunt themselves over others. They are so often martinets who make their own rules and laws as they go along. In my country that's against what we believe. It does no harm to expose them for what they are."

The baron's eyebrows raised slightly. "Do you have anyone in mind?"

Lydia wasn't prepared to tell him about the prince, not yet. The cablegram must first reach the newspaper, and if there was any follow-up she would take care of that, too, before telling anyone.

"Baron," she asked, avoiding his question, "have you seen Bryant Drury about? The reporter I mentioned."

"Not in several days. He must have gone off somewhere, but I wouldn't know about that."

"Keep an eye on him when he's here," she requested. "I have a hunch there's something strange about his presence in Monaco. He acts as if he has a mission to perform, and though he claims he's writing a book on Monte Carlo, I'm not convinced."

"I will keep an eye out for him, fräulein. And I will try to arrange for Regina to be at the casino. My only fear is that the kaiser may not play at the open tables, but gamble in one of the private salons."

"Not if he wishes to retain his incognito, Baron. Anyone going to one of those salons has to be a famous, wealthy

129

or very influential person, so he would arouse the curiosity of everyone working in the casino or patronizing it. No, if the kaiser comes to gamble and wishes to keep his identity a secret, he'll gamble at the regular tables,'' Lydia reasoned.

"If he wins," the baron said with a chuckle, "his incognito will vanish like his money; if he does not win. I should be most discreet about all of this."

"We have to be careful these days," Lydia commented soberly. "My stories have been successful so far and other papers are taking note. That means other reporters have been drifting in. None stay long, for which I'm thankful, because they don't see the stories staring them in the face. But come they do, and I now have competition."

"Quite true," the baron agreed. He frowned and slowly pushed aside his appetizer of caviar and tiny biscuits. With head still bowed, he announced, "I would like to say something to you if you promise not to be offended."

"My dear Baron, how can I promise not to be offended when I've no idea what you are going to tell me?" Lydia asked.

"Yes . . . that is true. You speak of success. Of course, you have been very successful. Your stories are reprinted all over the world. Those you did on Wells, who broke the bank, were a stroke of good luck, though the way you handled them showed what promise you had even a few days after your arrival."

She grew apprehensive. "What is wrong, Baron?"

"I am old enough to be your father, Lydia. I know I'm nothing more than a man who lives off others and I chose you because you were new and inexperienced. However, the arrangement turned out to be something more than I expected. At least I earn some of the gratuities you grant me—in the form of many meals, gambling money and sometimes a little extra left over."

"Come to the point," she ordered tersely, guessing that what he had to say was not complimentary.

"You have grown too important for your own good," he said bluntly.

"What are you talking about? Explain yourself, Baron!"

"Your first success was due to your innocence, the un-jaundiced way you saw things. Lately you have grown too sophisticated, and it reflects in your stories and . . . in the way you go about getting them."

She leaned back and studied the baron's anxious expression, noting idly he'd let his side-whiskers grow too long. She didn't want to hear any more and yet she knew she must, for she had a well-rounded suspicion that what he was saying happened to be the truth.

"In other words, I'm now a selfish, demanding person and in my irresponsible hands are the reputations of many people. I no longer look for the small and different stories that abound here. I consider only the wealthy and famous for my articles. Am I correct, Baron?"

"In a way, yes. You are angry with me, I know, but I speak as a favorite uncle who thinks highly of you and wishes nothing but good for you."

"I'm not angry," she said. "I can take criticism, even from you. And I'm sorry I said that. Without you I'd never have reached the success I've had. Forgive me. Give me an example of where I've gone wrong."

"Remember, I am speaking of how you appear in my eyes," the baron said slowly, but with a little more confidence. "It may not apply where your editor and your readers are concerned, but . . . a week or so ago you wrote about a Hungarian diplomat with a reputation for being a great man. You wrote that he engaged a villa on Monte and installed not one, but three—shall we say, *les dames horizontal*. Three whores for the benefit and delight of certain people he was trying to impress."

"That was a legitimate story," she protested. "He was not deserving of the reputation he carried at home. Not after what he did here. His own people—who obviously support him with their taxes—have a right to know how he spends some of their money." Her voice was indignant as she recalled the diplomat's actions.

"My dear Lydia, by now you should realize that it is a way of life among people like that high-ranking Hungarian. In some ways you are still incredibly naive. There is no

131

suggestion that he employed the women for his own use, but only as a means of ingratiating himself with the people he was trying to impress and to gain business benefits for his country, not himself.''

''I still say it was wrong,'' she insisted. ''And if that is being naive, then I am.''

''Why should we argue about it, Lydia? I think now I was wrong in being candid, in telling you what I believed was happening to you. I beg of you, forget the whole thing. I have been wrong far more times in my life than I've been right.''

''It's harsh criticism,'' she said, keeping her tone moderate, for she believed she understood the baron's viewpoint. He was an elderly man, born to the aristocracy, even if he had been deprived of his birthright by an angry emperor. Naturally, he would be on the side of nobility. Also, it was possible she'd grown a bit too enthused about some of the stories she'd sent, though her editor and publisher had not commented so far, except to say they were highly pleased with her work.

''Would you say I have become someone who thrives on writing about facts that are no more than gossip?'' she asked.

''It is not an elegant way of putting it, but yes. I think it has become more gossip than fact.'' The baron sipped his wine, looking uncomfortable.

''Baron, I was given this assignment on Monte because I exposed that man Drury for trying to get a story published that was based on his particular brand of gossip. He assumed something that wasn't so. Don't sit there and tell me I'm guilty of the same thing!''

''I hate arguing with you. I hate arguments no matter whom they are with. Perhaps that's why I am what I am, a sponger, but I prefer that to—''

''Being a gossip?'' she interrupted.

''Well. . . .'' He gave a continental shrug of his shoulders.

''Is that what you mean?''

''Perhaps. I'm not sure what I mean any more. I wish

I'd kept my unfortunate mouth shut. I am no good at this."

Lydia went relentlessly on. "This morning I filed a cable about Prince Ali Jouhaud—who gave the banquet last evening. He is a vicious, ugly man who shoots his racehorses when they lose, who entertains his guests with bird shoots—a slaughter, because he has their wings partially clipped to impede their flight. He has disgraced girls who did not please him in his bedroom. He marries all the women he wishes and likely discards them as easily. He lives like Croesus while the people who support him live in tents. Don't you think a man like that should be revealed for what he is?"

"Jouhaud?" the baron said in disbelief, his expression astonished. "I never heard anything like that about him. And I know all the gossip and innuendoes—true and false—that circulate about these people."

"Well, you may read the story when it comes out. It will be an education. I obtained the facts from a secret source whose name I can't reveal. This person has come to a point where they can't abide the man and what he does. As a competent reporter, it's my duty to expose a man such as he. And believe me, Baron, *that* is not a story written by a naive girl from small-town Lyttonville. I consider myself a seasoned reporter. Gossip? Yes, I indulged in it. Mainly because during the off-season there wasn't too much to write about. If that offends you, please don't read my column. And be sure to forget that I obtained the information about the prince from anyone. I gave my word my source would never be revealed."

The baron half arose. "Would you like me to leave your table, fräulein?"

"Oh, sit down," she said impatiently. "Perhaps you're right about my quick success spoiling me. I didn't realize it. However, I thought I'd always been eminently fair in what I wrote. I felt I was being completely objective in my reporting."

"You did?" the baron had resumed his chair, but he was in no way placated.

"Yes," she replied seriously. "However, just in case

you're right—though not in every instance, I'm sure—''

The baron cut her off. "Even if I was right in one instance, it means. . . ." He held both hands, palms open, about a foot from either side of his head.

"Success has gone to my head." Lydia felt her face flood with color.

He nodded, but made no comment.

"I'd hate to believe that about me. I'd also hate to lose your friendship."

"Forgive me, Lydia," he said earnestly. He leaned forward and extended a hand to pat hers where it rested on the table. "I have hurt you. But if so, it is only because I have grown fond of you. I was pleased that you grasped the feeling of the casino so quickly. Your stories have been a delight. You really were like a child in the beginning—your enthusiasm—the freshness of your writing. Everything. Now you have grown sophisticated. I suppose it was bound to happen. Next you will become jaded. You will become bored. And why not? You would not wish to spend the rest of your life here." He paused, eyeing her carefully. "Or would you?"

"Of course not," she said vehemently.

"Good. I'm relieved." He sat back in his chair and managed a smile. "I'll say no more. I'm sorry, in a way, that I opened my mouth, but remember I did it only because you thought you were doing so well."

"I'll continue to do well—with or without you," Lydia affirmed. "But I want it to be with you. I value your friendship, Baron. I'll be the first to admit you've given me tremendous help. I never could have accomplished so much in such a short time if it weren't for you."

"That's true," he said, looking pleased. "However, we will call a truce. I'll criticize you whenever I feel there is need for it. If you do not agree, that is your privilege. If your head continues to grow, I fear I will have to bid you farewell. I could not bear to see you destroy yourself and, mark me, you will if you continue as you are."

She leaned over and kissed his cheek lightly. "Perhaps

your little lecture was just what I needed. Anyway, I'll think about it. Will you continue the friendship?"

"An excellent idea," he declared, "and we will now concentrate on the kaiser. He will be in the casino this evening. I will have Regina be present with her small camera in the hope she will be able to get a good picture of the man, a close one."

"Excellent," Lydia said. "Call for me at the usual time. Or earlier, if the kaiser grows impatient and begins to gamble before supper."

They finished their meal on a pleasant note, with no further reference to their brief disagreement. Lydia had been more impressed with the baron's criticism of her than he realized. She remembered how Drury had almost had a slanderous story published, one that was completely untrue. That she, too, could be guilty of such a thing sent waves of terror through her. There was no excuse for careless reporting or character assassination.

She thought of the article she had written and already cabled concerning Prince Ali Jouhaud. Of course, what she had learned came from a source very close to him, from a man who despised the prince largely because of the harm that had come to his sister, yet through force of circumstance—financial, no doubt—continued to work for him. The wise thing to do might be to seek him out and again question him as an additional check, nevertheless.

She entertained no doubts as to Armand Martel's genuineness, else he'd never have been able to attend the banquet. Guests were carefully selected and had to be identified at such affairs. Yet she began to wonder if the man had been a bit too vindictive. She remembered how he had refused to talk at first, professing loyalty. Yet when she sought him out a second time, after a few demurrals, she'd had no trouble gaining his confidence. Had he capitulated too easily?

She'd stated in a firm tone of voice to the baron that she had always been objective in her stories. He had just as firmly disagreed. Had she been objective in the story she'd just sent? Was there not a feeling of resentment against the prince, who pretended to be a kindly and noble man when really he was a despot? At least, that was what his equerry had stated. And what she had believed.

The prince was registered at the Metropole, so it was likely Martel also stayed there. After parting with the baron, who was going to arrange for Regina to be at the casino with her miniature camera, Lydia went straight to the Metropole. She wore a coral-colored walking dress, carried a little silk parasol as usual, and stopped twice on the way to talk to friends she'd made.

She had convinced herself she ought to take the baron's criticism, not lightly, but still with a grain of salt. Also on her mind was Drury, who continued to worry her. He had indicated he had come to Monte Carlo to stay, and yet he was around only part of the time. She wouldn't have been concerned if he was any other man, but Drury was angry at her, jealous of her status and success. He was a man who had, as a reporter, stopped at nothing to get his stories, and as an ex-reporter wouldn't be any less determined. He had sworn to get even and she believed he meant it.

She felt a sharp ache of loneliness, at the thought of Jeffrey. She was hurt by his many and continued absences, with no real explanations. His answers to her queries were brief and evasive. Why didn't she put him out of her life? The answer came easily. She cared for him—a great deal. Yet she wanted her career, also. She knew he was hurt by that, especially on their last parting after Osgood Trencher's attack on her, but she couldn't help it. Or could she? Had she always been selfish or was it something that came with her success?

Her mind was a jumble of complexities. Fear of Drury, irritation with the baron because he had questioned her integrity as a reporter, bewilderment at Jeffrey's actions. She even felt a twinge of anger directed at Prince Jouhaud and chided herself mentally for such foolishness. She hadn't even held a brief conversation with him. Armand Martel had told her such a thing would be impossible. He would know, wouldn't he? Or had she placed too great a stock in Martel, because of the sympathy he had aroused in her? If only Jeffrey were here, she could talk with him and benefit by his advice. She'd even repeat the baron's criticism of her today and ask if he agreed. If he did, she would know the baron had been right. If that was true, she certainly needed to take stock. But Jeffrey wasn't here and the problem she was now confronted with had to be faced and resolved by herself.

She reached the Metropole and secured an appointment with the assistant manager for later in the day. She didn't dare ask questions about Armand Martel other than in private. In no way did she want him connected with her story about the prince. She had given her word that he would not be named.

Returning to her suite she passed the open door and glimpsed Angelina inside, dusting a bureau. Angelina called out that she would be finished in a few minutes. Soon after, she arrived at Lydia's suite to help her select a gown for the evening.

"Inconspicuous is the word for this evening," Lydia specified. "I don't want to attract attention because tonight I have to watch a man gamble who doesn't want anyone to know he can lose—unless he wins."

"He must be very important," Angelina said with a smile. "Perhaps royalty? Perhaps—a kaiser?"

Lydia's brows arched in surprise. "How did you know?"

"We servants exchange information very often. It is known that the kaiser will stay at the Metropole, for he never stays at an old hotel when there is a new one close by. I have friends there and, as here, when royalty comes incognito even more preparations are in order than if there is an entourage. The royal secret must be protected by elaborate methods."

"That's interesting," Lydia said. "Angelina, when do you go off duty here?"

"After I have helped you, mademoiselle. I have two hours then before coming back to turn down beds and con-

137

sole the ladies who have lost at the tables.''

"Could you talk to your friends at the Metropole and ask about someone I'm sure checked out with the prince's party?"

"Yes, I could do so."

"The man's name is Martel. Armand Martel. He is the prince's equerry. I met him at the banquet. I wish to know more about him and where he might be now.''

"I can do that, of course."

"Thank you. Leave a note on the bureau in case I don't return until late.''

"There will be a note," Angelina promised. "Now it is almost time for you to prepare. Shall I draw your bath?''

The baron and Regina were both prepared for action. As Lydia, dressed in a comparatively plain silk gown of simple styling, entered the casino escorted by the baron, she observed Regina already there, moving about inconspicuously. No doubt the tiny camera was ready for business. Lydia left the baron and moved about at random, stopping to chat with casino officials or friends she'd made. The action at the table was considerable, for Monte Carlo was now crowded with visitors. Recognizing two reporters from minor newspapers, one from Nice, the other from Paris, she smothered the apprehension she felt because of their presence and even helped out the young man from Nice by showing him about.

The baron was again at the tables, but keeping an eye out for the arrival of the kaiser. It was beginning to grow a bit late and Lydia worried that somehow the kaiser had learned he was expected and therefore would not appear.

But half an hour later she spotted him as he entered with two bulky aides, not in uniform although they might as well have been wearing their boots, spiked helmets and medals. Each time the kaiser requested something of them, they promptly clicked their heels and threw back their shoulders. Besides this giveaway, there was the kaiser's physical appearance. He had a withered arm that he kept well concealed, but he appeared awkward when he used only one hand to manipulate his chips across the table. Then, too, there was that outrageous, upturned, waxed and pointed mustache that few other men dared to wear—or even wanted to.

Lydia hovered around the table while the play was going on. The betting was not heavy and the kaiser seemed to be testing out whatever system had been provided him.

Twice she saw Regina saunter close, raise an arm slightly and take her photographs in secret. Then, quite abruptly, the kaiser began to plunge. He had benefitted from several of his plays and was probably convinced he had the proper secret. In less than an hour he had gone through a fortune. As he progressively lost, his face grew redder and his manner almost offensive. He would shove aside anyone standing too close to him. Regina had been the victim of one of those shoves to one side, but she'd already got her close shot.

Finally the kaiser muttered something in German, made angry gestures to his aides and then stalked out of the casino. The German people had just lost a great deal of money. Lydia determined they would hear of it.

Once the kaiser left, there wasn't much going on from which Lydia could profit. She did talk to one casino official, however, who admitted the kaiser had come incognito.

"He's such a vain man that he wouldn't want it known he lost."

"I can see that," Lydia said, "but certainly a number of people recognized him. I know I did, with his crippled arm and his mustache, not to mention his flunkies who all but saluted whenever he looked their way."

The man grinned and agreed with her. "Of course he was recognized, but had he won he would have stepped on a soap box and screamed about his victory. In defeat he slinks away. Should there be gossip, he will swear he never came to Monte and that whoever looked like him was either an impostor or a double."

"I shouldn't let him get away with that," Lydia said.

"Please—it would be best if you wrote that it was an

impostor—for the sake of the casino. Who knows? Next year—he may come back with another system. We look forward to it."

"I shall abide by your suggestion," she promised, "to a certain extent, which will protect his claim of not having been here and your statement to me that he did not come. But it will also allow people to make up their own minds. Is that agreed?"

"I think you are going to hang him in a delicate sort of way, mademoiselle, but that is your business."

"My profession," she reminded him with a smile.

"Yes, I beg your pardon. Anyway, he is not very well liked here. Of course, what we have just said to one another never really happened. I have never conversed with you."

"Never. Thank you, monsieur." Their parting smiles were ironical.

Lydia returned to her suite, satisfied that she had her story—and with pictures. It would make an interesting and even humorous article, written in a tongue-in-cheek style and printed along with the photographs Regina had taken.

As Lydia slipped out of her dress and donned a negligée she saw the folded note propped up on the bureau. Angelina had kept her promise, but because Lydia wished nothing to interfere with the writing of the kaiser's story, she ignored it. On her return from the casino she had written the incident in her mind and wanted to get it on paper at once. She spent an hour describing a man who looked like the kaiser, had been taken for the kaiser, of course erroneously, and who had played a system that didn't work. She described his arrival, his playing, his anger and his inconsiderate treatment of others at the table. This would be headed up with a series of photos of the kaiser, labeled as that of an impostor—a statement no one would believe. Yet she told her story without actually accusing the kaiser of being there.

The beauty of all this lay in the fact that the reporters from Paris and Cannes would write only of someone impersonating the kaiser while losing a great deal of money. Her story would have the photos to refute everything she and they wrote. Pictures, she came to realize, were going to be of extreme importance in the life of a reporter.

Satisfied with the article, she placed it in a drawer until morning when she would deliver it to the cable office. Afterward she would obtain the photos from Regina and dispatch these by mail. Her story would be later than those printed in Europe, but the impact of hers would be many times greater. At least, that was her hope.

She recalled the note on the bureau, secured it and sat down at the desk again to read it. As she read, her face turned white and she drew a sharp, worried breath.

"Mademoiselle," Angelina wrote, "I have talked to everyone I know at the Metropole and not one has ever heard of this man Armand Martel. He was never registered there and the prince's entourage did not include anyone from France. Also, I learned that he does not, and never did, employ a person known as an equerry. The prince seems to be a very modest man. His only vice appears to be the spending of so much money on this once-a-year banquet at Monte, a vice everyone here enjoys. I shall keep asking."

Lydia came to her feet in a newborn fear. She had not checked the story with anyone else because it seemed so authentic. None of it was supposition on her part. She'd believed Martel, but now he didn't seem to exist, nor did the position in the prince's entourage exist either. Perhaps there was no sister—no Françoise Martel—either.

Lydia had no idea what this was about, but she knew she must somehow send a cablegram to her newspaper in New York to stop the story. It would wreck her reputation for accuracy and dependability, but that was a small price to pay if the article was wrong, or the result of some vicious prank on the part of Martel, who might wish in some way to get even with his employer. It occurred to her now that the story might have been deliberately planted to destroy her credibility.

She tried to make up her mind what to do. What if Angelina had been given wrong information? Martel might

141

be registered at some other hotel, though she remembered she hadn't seen him at the casino tonight. Yet she could take no chances. She knew the story could be delayed if she reached the newspaper in time, and that it could be printed after it had been verified. The main thing now was to stop the story, temporarily at least.

Lydia hastily changed into a street dress. Outside, she summoned a carriage. "Drive me to the casino and wait," she ordered. "I won't be long."

In the casino she looked for the night manager. He was nowhere to be seen.

"I must see Monsieur LeGrand," she told one of the lesser officials. "It's of great importance."

"*Oui*, mademoiselle, you will find him in his office," she was told.

She knew then that she wasn't thinking properly. She should have gone to the office first. Her anxiety was impeding her judgment and that could be dangerous. She did her best to quiet her jittery nerves as she hurried to the manager's office.

"But of course," the short, round official replied to her request. "We arranged long ago that the cable office would be open whenever you wished, no matter how late or how inconvenient for the man who runs it. The office is closed now, but I shall send a man to the operator's home at once and I assure you he will be there to meet you in less than an hour."

"Thank you very much," she said. "My gratitude will be expressed in everything I write about the casino."

She hurried outside and ordered the carriage driver to take her to the cable office. She arrived before the operator, so she had to sit in the carriage. Even with the blanket the driver provided she was cold, for the late night air from the sea was chilly.

All the while she berated herself for being so careless as to take the word of one informer about a story as important as this. Now, if only she could be lucky enough that the story was, somehow, held up in New York so she might rectify her carelessness. But she didn't have much hope.

She'd submitted little in the past week, and the office was quite liable to use the story promptly. If so, it would be on the newsstands now. If the information proved incorrect, and she now suspected it must be, it would be too late for anything except to resign and leave Monte as quickly as possible.

Where was Jeffrey? she asked herself. He was never around when she needed him and yet he had sworn to protect her and her interests. She was growing more and more certain he wasn't telling the truth about his work, about his being some sort of an engineer. If that was true, whatever his mission here might be, there would certainly be some evidence of it by now. To think of this rock sliding into the sea was as improbable as the sea rising to flood the casino!

And there was Bryant Drury to consider. Slowly, she began to wonder if he was behind this, if Armand Martel was not what he claimed to be and his stories of the prince's excesses and cruelties were lies. If so, this might well be Drury's way of getting his revenge. But, she reminded herself, she had no proof. She would have to investigate carefully before she pointed an accusing finger.

She had torn a handkerchief to shreds by the time the cable operator arrived, a long coat over his nightgown, and properly indignant for having been awakened at this time of night. He admitted Lydia to the office and turned on the swinging overhead light.

"Now, mademoiselle, how can I serve you?" he asked grumpily.

"You recall the long cable I gave you for transmission this morning?"

"*Oui*, I remember it well. It was very interesting, mademoiselle."

"Did you send it?"

"But of course! My orders are to send your cables before any others and to respond to you at any time of the day or night. As you can see now," he said pointedly.

"I appreciate your kindness, monsieur." Lydia tried to keep the impatience out of her voice in an effort to placate him. "Do you have the copy I gave you?"

He opened a drawer and removed the papers. "I do not ordinarily keep the originals, mademoiselle, but this one was so interesting I wished to read it at my leisure. When I send a cable, I do not really read it."

"Now I wish you to send another cable. Right now, while I stand here."

He activated his instruments, drew on a green eyeshade and looked up at her expectantly.

"This is to the editor of my paper. You have the cable address. Send this message: 'Kill prince story if possible. Urgent you do so. Will explain later. Please verify one way or another.'"

The operator had written the message as she spoke and now he began sending it. Meanwhile, Lydia opened her handbag, took out a French banknote of ample size and pressed this into the operator's hand.

"Thank you, monsieur. I also wish strictest confidentiality concerning what happened here tonight, even from the casino officials."

The operator glanced at the money. "We do not divulge a word of what we send, mademoiselle. Especially what we send for you. *Merci,* a thousand times, *merci.*"

She accommodated the operator further by having her carriage drive him home first. When she reached the security of her suite again, she sat down heavily and contemplated the uselessness of what she had just done. Of course the story had not been held up. At this very moment, they were reading it in New York. The Paris branch of the New York *Times* would have it as soon as it could be transmitted and then all Europe would have it, and so would the country ruled by Prince Ali Jouhaud. She would have no more than two or three days' grace before everything fell apart.

She didn't weep, she didn't curse her bad luck. Lydia knew she had only herself to blame for her carelessness. As the baron had suggested, she was now in the same category as Drury, a reporter who no longer checked a story to verify its authenticity before writing it.

Eight

Lydia awoke with a severe headache and sent for a quick remedy. It helped, but only partially. The remaining pain, she realized, came from anxiety and nothing else. She was grateful Angelina had not yet appeared. She needed time to think, for her brain had been too befuddled before she went to bed. Now, in the morning, when she was clear-headed, she could see no way out of her dilemma. In twenty-four hours she would be told she could no longer enter the casino. There would be nothing left to do but quietly board a train for Nice and then arrange passage home.

She thought again of Jeffrey and wished he were here, but she had no hope he'd arrive in time to be of any help. Offhand, she felt the damage she'd done to herself was irreparable. The baron had been right. The brief success she'd enjoyed had gone to her head. She wondered if Jeff, too, had noticed the change in her. If the baron had, certainly Jeff must have, even though he'd been in her company only briefly. She recalled that when they'd first met, she'd not been the slightest bit reticent in impressing him with the fact that her career came first. The thought filled her with further self-condemnation. She felt she deserved to be fired just as much as Bryant Drury, who'd become so obsessed with his own importance as to forget the ethics and rules of his profession. So had she, because she'd been too eager to get a story. So eager she had neglected to check the accuracy of what she had heard. No matter that Armand

Martel had stated he was an equerry of the prince, and had played upon her feminine sympathies with his story about a wronged sister. She should have made certain he spoke the truth. Also, because of what she'd learned about the prince, she had allowed herself to form a dislike for him instead of being completely objective. If she'd made the effort to check the information and found it to be true, she could have written the article without any embellishments or innuendoes. She'd done none of that. For such foolishness she deserved a quick return to anonymity. She was just as certain she'd be on the receiving end of ridicule from Bryant Drury. What's more, she told herself, she merited it.

At ten o'clock Angelina knocked softly, then entered. One look at Lydia's drawn features assured her something was wrong. "Mademoiselle, you have been crying!"

Lydia nodded. "I am afraid I have made a fool of myself, Angelina."

"How, mademoiselle?" Angelina's voice was sympathetic. "Perhaps I can help. You found my note?"

"It was your note that assured me I have completely lost my sense of values. I'm going to be fired. I'll never get another job on a newspaper, nor do I deserve one."

"Did I put something in the note that hurt you? If so, I must make amends. Please tell me how. . . ."

"You did nothing wrong, Angelina. I did. I wrote an article about Prince Ali Jouhaud. It was an unpleasant story, for it made the prince out to be a very cruel, vicious person. I received the information from the man who called himself Armand Martel."

"It is he you told me to get information about."

"Yes. The contents of your note assured me what I wrote was untrue. My error was in not checking the story before sending it to my paper. I'm certain it's been printed already. I'm expecting a cablegram from my editor at any moment telling me my services are no longer required. Once the prince gets word of the article, I'll be told to leave this hotel. Did you hear anything more about this man Martel?"

"No one seems to have heard of him. The name is unfamiliar." Her usually sparkling brown eyes darkened with concern.

"What puzzles me is if he's not what he claims to be, how did he obtain an invitation to the prince's banquet? I thought precautions were taken so no intruder could attend."

"*Oui*, that is true, but of course there are ways. There are always ways, mademoiselle. Is it that bad, what has happened?"

"It means the end of my career. It means I have to leave Monaco and never return. It's the end of everything. And all because I became careless and took the word of a stranger," Lydia said dully.

"I am so sorry." Angelina was on the verge of tears herself. "I shall try again to find this man Martel if you wish. But I must tell you, mademoiselle, I have also asked about the prince."

"Yes?" Lydia asked, knowing very well what Angelina was going to say.

"I have talked to hotel servants who attended him. He came with a very small party—six, I think, and three of them ladies who served the princess. The men were advisors to him, not servants. Also the prince is a good man with a great respect for the rights of others. He is kind, a true gentleman. So they have told me and, mademoiselle, I am sad for you because they speak the truth."

"I'm sure they do." Lydia spoke with certainty. "I've been duped by Martel. That man must be a consummate actor. Everything he told me is the reverse of the truth, yet I believed him. There's nothing I can do now but wait for the ax to fall."

"If there is anything I can do," Angelina said, "I will do it."

"Angelina, you did what I asked and I appreciate it. I doubt even prayers would do me any good."

"I will pray anyway, mademoiselle," Angelina said, then moved quickly into the bedroom to set it in order.

Lydia got up and paced the floor slowly, her features thoughtful as she considered her next step. First, there would have to be a public apology to the prince. Then she would send a letter of resignation to the newspaper, she hoped before she heard from them, informing her she'd been fired. She was aware her career was ended. No other publisher would henceforward trust anything she wrote. And she couldn't blame them. She'd destroyed herself and her future as a reporter.

A firm knock interrupted her dismal musings. Before she could reach the door, Angelina came dashing from the bedroom, brushed past her and opened it. The man from the cable office stood there with a message in his hand.

"Come in," Lydia said wearily, her hand automatically reaching for the fateful cablegram.

He entered slowly, uncertainly, and handed her the envelope.

"Please wait," she said. "There may be an answer."

She opened the envelope and read the message. She read it again, more slowly this time, for her senses began to swim. She wondered if she was losing her mind, if her brain hadn't absorbed the words correctly, or if she was conjuring up the dispatch as she would like it to be. The cablegram read:

WHAT MESSAGE? HAVE HAD NO COPY FROM YOU IN FOUR DAYS. WHAT IS GOING ON? SPENCER.

She looked at the operator. "You know what message is referred to, of course."

"Of a certainty, mademoiselle."

"What do you make of it?"

"I do not know. I have considered and I do not know."

"Are you certain you sent my cablegram? Perhaps you misplaced it."

"Mademoiselle, I sent it minutes after you handed it to me."

"But why wasn't it received in New York?"

148

"I do not know," The little man insisted.

"Is there any way it could have been stopped? Intercepted?" Lydia pressed.

"There is no way. It went, it was received, for it had to be received. There is no way it could not have been received. Of course, the New York office. . . ."

"They'd have no reason to intercept it. They don't even know me. There has to be some explanation."

"*Oui*, mademoiselle. And when you find it, please be good enough to let me know, for I shall not sleep nights worrying about it," the man assured her.

"Thank you," she said. "You've been very helpful."

"And you have been very kind. *Bonjour*, mademoiselle."

"What has happened?" Angelina asked. "I'm confused."

"So am I," Lydia exclaimed. "It's beyond comprehension. I sent an article about the prince by cablegram to my newspaper. The man who just left swears he sent it out. After reading your note last night regarding Armand Martel, I sent another cablegram to my editor telling him to kill the story. This cablegram I'm holding asks me what I'm talking about. Obviously he never received the article. Thank God for that, since I maligned Prince Ali Jouhaud. The character who must be masquerading under the name of Armand Martel and posing as the prince's equerry gave me an unsavory and untrue portrait of the prince. Without checking on Martel or the information, I sent the story to my newspaper. Fortunately—at least I hope that's it—the cablegram went astray. Whatever happened to it, it didn't reach my paper. I've been given a reprieve, Angelina, one I don't merit, but I'm grateful. I'll remember this for the rest of my life." She sank down on a chair, almost weak with relief.

"But what happened to the cablegram, mademoiselle?" Angelina asked.

"I don't know," Lydia said. "To lose it seems impossible."

"The man from the cable office? Was he telling you a lie?"

"I don't think so. He was as worried as I and at the moment, just as puzzled. I still don't know how that cablegram didn't reach its destination. But I thank God it didn't. Still, I must find out what this is about. It's a mystery, but I'm sure one that is solvable. It's up to me to uncover the clues that will lead to the culprit."

"How will you do that?"

"First, I'll handle the story on the kaiser. I know *that* one is accurate and truthful. I'll get photographs and talk to the baron. I'll talk to someone else, too. The man I half suspect of being responsible for this entire miserable business—Bryant Drury."

Two days later, as puzzled as ever, but genuinely relieved, Lydia learned from casino employees that Bryant Drury had been gambling again. She visited the casino every night as usual, keeping an eye out for him. This was her best chance of seeing him, for she had no idea where he lived. It was apparent he had been away for several days or he'd have been seen about the casino. Drury, as a handsome man, attracted the attention of most women employees. Lydia decided to strike up conversations with them and cleverly switch the conversation to talk of Drury; she learned he'd been gone for some time.

She had already dispatched the photographs of the kaiser, which had turned out very well indeed. There was going to be a good deal of chuckling around Monte Carlo when the article was published, though there'd be no chuckling at the kaiser's palace, even though the photographs were plainly labeled as those of an impostor.

Lydia had conducted a thorough search for the man she knew as Armand Martel through endless inquiries, but no one had heard of him. She hadn't been able, so far, to detemine how he had managed to get an invitation to the prince's ball or a seat next to her. The more she asked, the more obvious it was that she had been duped. Apparently the entire incident had been very carefully planned and carried out. With Osgood Trencher gone, Lydia knew of no enemies other than Bryant Drury. She suspected it was his work. Probably Martel was an old crony of Drury's, or a well-paid adventurer.

She entered the casino in the company of the baron who had also conducted an unsuccessful search for Martel. Drury, in evening dress, was seated at one of the tables with three pretty girls standing behind him, each vying for his attention. Lydia felt only pity for them. She hadn't forgotten she'd once been in awe of this man—before she discovered what sort of person he was.

She moved up behind him and, excusing herself, edged in front of the girls, ignoring the angry looks they directed at her. Then she bent down and whispered in Drury's ear, "Meet me in ten minutes in the west rose garden."

He looked up with an ingratiating smile that quickly faded when his eyes met Lydia's.

She said softly, "I'll have you barred from Monte if you're not there, and don't think I can't do it."

His eyes mocked hers as he made no attempt to arise. Instead, he turned his back to her, placed his bet and waited for the wheel to spin. Lydia rejoined the baron, who was eyeing Drury speculatively.

"I don't think he's going to pay any attention to you."

"He'll meet me, if for no other reason than to find out why I want to talk to him."

"Do you think it's safe to be with him? Do you wish me to remain close by?" he asked.

"I'd rather you didn't. I'm not afraid of him and, believe me, he's *going* to be afraid of me."

She waited five more minutes and then walked out of the casino and made her way to the rose garden. Lydia allotted Drury a few extra minutes, for if he was winning he'd find it hard to abandon the table.

He finally appeared, sauntering in an arrogant manner down the walk to the bench where Lydia had seated herself. A lighted cigarette hung from the corner of his mouth. He didn't sit down, but stared at her, anger evident in his narrowed eyes.

"One more trick like the one you just pulled," she said, her eyes flaming, "and I'll use all the influence I have to banish you from Monaco. Do you understand me, Mr. Drury?"

With studied insolence he dropped the cigarette close by her satin slippers and tramped on it. "I don't even know what you're talking about, my dear Miss Bradley."

"You know very well what I'm talking about. I'm warning you not to do it again."

"Look here, we might as well get this straight. I don't like you. You're attractive, yes. I find you desirable, yes. You're young, beautiful and inexperienced. But you're also an ambitious talebearer. I haven't been in Monaco for days. I've been in Paris assembling information on the family that started Monte. If I'm going to write a book about the place I have to know how it all began. I'm referring to the Blanc family, the Grimaldis. I don't know what happened to you. I hope it was bad, but I had nothing to do with it."

His manner seemed sincere, if biting, though Lydia knew how persuasive he could be. She replied, "When you see your friend Martel, tell him that if he shows his face here, I'll see to it his welcome will be less than warm."

"I don't know anybody named Martel," he insisted.

"You're a liar."

He sat down beside her. "Leaving aside our differences, I honestly don't know what happened and I swear I had nothing whatever to do with it. I never heard of a man named Martel. I've been very busy. I haven't even been here. If someone's been making trouble for you, it wasn't me. I'd like to, but I'd put that under the heading of pleasure and my work comes first. You are of no importance in my life." His voice became threatening. "Nevertheless, I'll get around to you some day. Just don't accuse me of something I know nothing about."

"Who has authorized you to do a book on Monte?" Lydia asked.

"None of your damned business," he said pleasantly.

"I'm not going to help you check up on me."

"You know I can."

"I know you've become a very important person here—not least in your own opinion. So go ahead and check on me. But don't expect me to help you."

"I don't. But I'm going to check on it. Thoroughly!"

As she arose and walked away from him, she heard him laugh and it grated on her nerves like the screech of a saw hitting a nail. The baron, standing in the background, made no attempt to stop her, knowing she was upset and that it was best for her to be by herself.

Once in her suite, seated at her desk, she shut out all thought of the unsatisfactory encounter with Drury and went to work on a story about the prince. This time it was the truth, verified through several sources, and it was an article that the prince would find extremely satisfactory. Lydia rewrote it twice, then read it slowly, pleased with the result. In fact, she felt it was the best thing she had done in some time. It had to be. Nothing less would atone for her carelessness. And nothing like it must happen again.

She picked up the article and started reading it aloud.

The name Prince Ali Jouhaud is little known outside the desert kingdom ruled by him. Yet it is revered by all his subjects because Prince Ali Jouhaud is known for his compassion and concern for his people. He is, at present, a guest in Monte Carlo.

Unknown to him, your reporter learned that in no other desert kingdom is a ruler as loved as he. He has sent many of his subjects to be educated in the United States, some of whom have become doctors. He has even sent young women to study nursing. And that is only a small part of his generosity.

She didn't read the rest of the article. There was no need. She was thoroughly satisfied with it, though still troubled as to how the erroneous one she had written became lost in transmission. Guy Spencer, in New York, had asked her again, by letter, about the meaning of her cablegram regarding a story to be killed. It had never been received, he repeated. She'd written back that it was all a mistake. To her, it was also an aggravating mystery, one that could have wrecked her career. Had that been the intention of whoever was behind it? She could think of no one but Drury who not only could think of such a thing, but would know how to carry it out. Yet she had no evidence to confront him with and he had maintained a steadfast denial of any knowledge of playing a dirty trick on her. He had stated merely that he disliked her, but still found her desirable. She colored angrily at the thought of it.

Had it been done merely to frighten her? If so, whoever was responsible had certainly accomplished his purpose. Yet it had served also to jar her out of that smug attitude she'd slipped into. She hadn't believed the baron when he'd expressed his disapproval of her articles. She'd even laughed at him. But she hadn't laughed once she'd read Angelina's note regarding the elusive or even nonexistent Armand Martel.

Was the cablegram operator being honest with her? Lydia could think of no reason for him not to be, since he seemed as troubled and bewildered by the lost cablegram as she. Yet how could a cablegram, which had been sent, get lost?

Angelina came in to turn down the bed and expressed her surprise at finding Lydia back so early.

"It was quiet at the casino," Lydia explained. "Besides, I need a rest and I'm going to bed early. Have you learned anything else about Martel?"

"If it were not you who asked me to inquire about him, I would say he did not exist. There is nothing, and in Monte, any servant knows all about everybody."

"There were servants at the banquet. Perhaps they. . . ."

"The prince hired them in Cannes, mademoiselle. They are not known here and there is no record of their names."

"I checked the registers of every hotel. If I hadn't talked to him at length, I'd also say he didn't exist."

"He must be a strange one," Angelina agreed. "Of course, there are villas and private homes. He could be someone's guest."

"But he would have been seen around the casino, or at

least in the theater. No one has seen him that I know of before or after he tricked me into believing him.'' Lydia paused. ''There's another young man I'm curious about. Do you know Jeffrey Marcus?''

''*Oui*, but only by sight. I have talked to people who do know him and it is said he is a very fine young man.''

Wishing she had thought to ask Angelina earlier, Lydia now probed, ''Do you know where he comes from? How long he's been here? What he does for a living?''

''Alas, mademoiselle, those questions I cannot answer. But I will keep my ears open.''

''He's not like this Martel man,'' Lydia said in some embarrassment. ''Jeffrey is a friend of mine. I'm fond of him, even though he puzzles me almost as much as Martel.''

''Then I shall be most discreet, of course,'' Angelina tactfully promised.

''Has there ever been any thought that part of the city might somehow slide into the sea?''

''*Non*, mademoiselle,'' Angelina answered with a laugh. ''This is solid rock. Nothing can move it. There was once an earthquake, and there was no sliding of anything into the sea then. It is impossible. I have spent several years here and never once have I heard such an idea.''

''I was just wondering,'' Lydia said. ''It was mentioned to me after my arrival and I didn't believe it either.''

''Would there be anything else, mademoiselle?''

''That's all. Thank you very much.''

''*Merci*, mademoiselle. If I can be of any further help, I am always here.''

Lydia sat at her desk, her blue eyes thoughtful, wondering again why Jeffrey insisted he was handling an engineering problem connected with the danger of a part of the city slipping into the harbor. Even she, ignorant of such things as rockslides, couldn't bring herself to believe such a slide could occur. Was Jeffrey using this as an exucse to cover up the real reason he was in Monaco? But if he lied, there must be a reason for it, she decided. Her censure melted as a wave of longing for him swept over her. She missed him. She had never before really missed anyone other than her parents. The feeling was alien to her, but still it was a pleasant sensation. She wondered if he missed her.

She retired rather early for Monte, but she was fatigued, and worried about the purpose behind Martel's treachery. Her fear of him even surpassed that which she felt for Drury. After what had happened, she believed Martel capable of any mischief. And, despite herself, she was inclined to believe Drury was telling the truth.

She awakened in mid-morning feeling rested and clear-headed. She decided to have her breakfast sent up, for she felt she deserved a lazy day. Since Angelina would be due about the same time as the breakfast tray was delivered, Lydia ordered croissants and extra coffee. They'd often made a ritual of this. It helped relieve Lydia's loneliness and she was always delighted with Angelina's little stories of the people who came to gamble. Besides the companionship, it gave Lydia a chance to have an easy conversation in French.

After breakfast Angelina drew Lydia's bath, but before the tub was filled they both heard shouting in the street below. Angelina turned off the water and hurried to a window overlooking the street, and in a moment Lydia joined her.

They were in time to witness the arrival of seven ornate carriages, each manned by a driver and at the rear a footman in satin knee breeches, white stockings, and powdered wigs atop which sat cocked hats worn sideways. Each man also wore a scarlet jacket and white gloves.

In the well-filled carriages were men, both young and middle-aged, every one of them shouting and waving. Most were in gaudy uniforms weighted down with medals.

"Who in the world. . . ?" Lydia began.

"See the reins in the driver's hands?" Angelina asked. "They are white. That means the passengers are of Russian nobility. In Russia only royalty can drive with white reins. It is an old law and well enforced."

"What are they yelling for?"

"They are considered the most exuberant visitors to come to Monte. Some say they are crazy. Others say they act like wild men. We servants shudder whenever they appear, but I am lucky because they always stay at the Hermitage, one of the new hotels. It is named after the Czar's favorite place in St. Petersburg, so any Russians who come to Monte always stay there."

Lydia was familiar with the Hermitage Hotel. The baron had once taken her into the lobby to let her see the romantic decor. In the center was the hotel's stained-glass-domed winter garden replete with potted palms and islands of rattan chairs, in intimate arrangements for cozy conversation. The sunlight screaming through its domed ceiling scattered rainbow-hued colors throughout the lobby, giving the place an enchanting air. Outside, wrought-iron balconies—delicate as black, lacy spiders' webs—stretched the length of the front of the hotel, serving to emphasize its size. The building was painted a pale banana yellow, a color, the baron had informed her, that was identical to that of the great Leningrad mansions, another reason it was favored by the Russians.

Her attention was distracted by the sound of explosions. She observed men in two of the carriages firing revolvers into the air. To her surprise, Monte police stood on the curb smiling and saluting, making no attempt to interfere with the horseplay that was going on.

"Do the Russian men always leave their wives behind?" Lydia asked.

"Always, if they can get away with it. These will be dukes and archdukes; possibly a grand duke. Their wives stay in Cannes or Nice and have their own kind of fun. Cannes has many young men and so has Nice. Gigolos."

"Do they act as uproariously as this at the casino?"

"*Non*. It would not be tolerated and they know this. They gamble recklessly and they don't care how much they lose. The casino, it is much richer by the time they leave. In the banquet halls and the restaurants—there is much wildness and destruction."

"Destruction of what?" Lydia asked, still staring with interest at the carriages below.

"Anything that can be destroyed with much noise.

Dishes, glassware, mirrors, especially anything that is breakable and makes a crash as it shatters.''

"They pay for what they destroy, I hope."

"Sometimes three, five, ten times what it is worth," Angelina told her. "It is said that in some places that they frequent, stores of inexpensive objects are kept until word of their coming reaches Monte and then the valuable items are removed, the cheap ones put in their place and, of course, anything broken is *always* valuable. They are crazy, these Russians. They are too reckless and too rich."

Lydia turned away from the window with a smile. "Well, I should certainly get a story out of them."

"A dozen stories, mademoiselle. A hundred stories. Each year it is always different, what they do. The destruction is usually the same, however. It is also said that wherever they stay, the chambermaids are raped and then paid enough to retire on. *Mais oui,* they are a crazy people."

After Angelina had tidied the rooms, Lydia sat down at the desk and wrote a series of short items for her column. She mentioned well-known guests, what the women wore, what parties were held. It was gossip, but handled in such a way that the copy was good and interesting. She had worked up a large following for these occasional columns that antagonized no one and augmented the longer and more serious articles.

She walked to the cable office with the dispatch. The operator, she found, was still agitated that his cablegram had been lost.

"Mademoiselle," he said, "I sent my own cablegram to New York and asked that they make certain there was no receipt of your message. They assured me on the day and the hour when I sent it that no cable was received from Monaco. It is a great puzzle and it still worries me."

"So long as the story doesn't turn up," Lydia said, "I won't worry. I suggest you follow my example. I received a letter from my New York office and they stated once again that no cablegram had been received. It will probably remain an unsolved mystery.''

Instead of returning immediately to the hotel, Lydia sauntered about in the warm sunshine, enjoying the climate and the beauty of the place, for each day she found something new to admire: There was history here, much of it never recorded. If Drury looked deeply enough, she reflected, he might write an excellent book about Monaco. That is, if he was writing one.

As she passed through the lobby of the hotel, a desk clerk called to her and handed her a cream-colored envelope.

"This came a few minutes ago, mademoiselle. Hand delivered.''

"Thank you,'' she said. Turning the envelope over, she saw the back of it was embossed with a crest such as nobility used. A Russian crest, she guessed. Opening it in the lobby she read the card inside.

It is commanded that Mademoiselle Lydia Bradley attend a banquet at eight this evening in honor of the birthday of His Highness the Grand Duke Dmitri, cousin of the czar. A carriage will call.

Lydia was delighted. It wasn't an invitation, but a royal command. She felt that if it was accompanied by an armed detail, she would have cheerfully gone. Little or nothing had ever been written about this Russian nobility who came to Monte, though she knew they had a reputation for glamour, boisterousness, self-indulgence and mischief-making.

She asked that Angelina be spared to help her dress. Angelina was doubtful, shaking her head as she laid out Lydia's things. "There is no telling what will happen with those crazy Russians,'' she warned.

"Angelina, at a formal banquet nothing serious is going to happen. They're gentlemen.''

"They are not,'' Angelina spoke with quiet emphasis. "They are devils.''

"Well, there will be other ladies present. I'll be safe enough. If it wasn't to be a formal affair, certainly they wouldn't have sent out these elaborate invitations.''

"I will pray for you," Angelina said seriously.

Lydia hugged her and laughed aloud. "You're a much greater worrier than I am. Worse, in fact. I tell you, I'll be all right. No matter what's been said about them, they're civilized. Besides, I'm an American."

"That won't stop them, mademoiselle. They are savages. They have no morals. Had they come to this hotel, I would have gone on a vacation until they left. I would not care to become the mother of a Russian baby."

Despite Angelina's doubts and warnings, Lydia decided to wear a gown that seemed both modest and daring. It was a black chiffon, with folds of filmy fabric fashioned in a flowing Grecian style. It made a striking contrast to her fair skin and gave her an ethereal look. Only beaded straps held the gown up and the same beaded effect edged the low décolletage. The fabric was attached to the beaded edge and though the voluminous folds made it seem modest as it touched the tips of her black satin slippers, when she moved it billowed, then clung to her figure, revealing every curve from her youthful breasts to her small waist, then outlining her slender hips. It even revealed her shapely legs without exposing an ankle.

"Mademoiselle," Angelina exclaimed worriedly, "you are taking a great risk."

"I wish I could take you with me," Lydia said calmly. "I would show you how self-sufficient I am. And how safe. I already told you I'm an American. They wouldn't dare lay a hand on me."

"You do not know these crazy Russians. They don't care about your nationality. To them, you are a beautiful flower, ripe for plucking."

"We shall see, Angelina. I'll tell you all about it tomorrow and then you'll laugh at your fears. So will I."

"I have a feeling neither one of us will be laughing. Now I dress your hair with curls on both your shoulders. They will help to cover your beautiful white skin and your bosom, so tempting to those wild devils. You should be wearing something that is high at the neck."

"Would that protect me from them?" Lydia asked archly.

"Particularly since you say they are savages."

"Nothing will protect you," Angelina said dismally. "And no words I speak will convince you it is reckless for you to attend."

"Do you forget I received a royal command to attend?" she rebuked her.

"As an American, do you feel you have to obey?" Angelina argued.

"Oh, come now, Angelina, stop fretting. I'm eager to go. This might be the greatest opportunity to come my way."

Angelina shrugged. "Whatever you say, mademoiselle. I hope you are right and that I am a silly fool, but I will continue to worry until I hear you were not torn apart."

After Lydia slipped on the long black silk gloves, Angelina handed her the black lace fan, then held the door open.

"You look rapturous, mademoiselle. May your evening be a happy one." Her doleful face belied her words.

"Thank you, Angelina. I'm sure it will be."

An ornate carriage awaited Lydia outside with a footman standing by the door, which he opened the moment she crossed the sidewalk. He was outfitted in a gaudy uniform and cocked hat. She felt very regal as she sat back on the satin upholstered cushion, wishing the ride was longer than the few minutes it took to get to the Hermitage, which was only a few minutes away.

Once there, she was received like royalty by the hotel staff and escorted to the banquet hall. This was one of the few times Lydia had ventured out alone, without the baron's company, for she hadn't dared let him know about the banquet or the command that she attend. Like Angelina, she suspected he would be filled with grave misgivings. Lydia told herself that she was of sterner stuff than either of those two and that she could handle the Russian nobility. Besides, alone she might be able to obtain a better story, for she intended to make a long article of this adventure—especially if she could elicit some information from the female guests.

The door to the banquet hall was closed and guarded by two stolid-looking serfs whose faces might have been made of stone. They merely opened the door for her, and she swept into a very large, very opulent room.

She didn't know much about this new hotel, and hadn't been in this particular banquet hall before. She found it graced with marble pillars and a painted ceiling from which hung eight lovely chandeliers. The walls were mostly mirrored, and where there was no glass, paneling of deep mahogany gleamed with polish. The rug was pale blue, very thick, and the center was ornamented with the royal seal of the Czar. She was amazed to realize they'd even brought the rug along.

Standing at stiff attention along the walls were more servants, also bewigged, gloved, and with knee breeches of white satin and coats of white serge, and wearing white bow ties. Each of those outfits would have provided food for a family of serfs for weeks, she thought.

Then she had no more time for thinking. At the long table, with considerable space between each setting, a dozen Russians arose as if by silent command. They were dressed completely in white, relieved only by a bright red trouser stripe and ribbons of various colors, no doubt depicting rank.

On the table was what appeared to be solid gold service and colorful china, gold embossed; the thinnest of crystal glassware; napkins and cloth of fine linen. Several elegant bouquets of flowers also decorated the table. On a sideboard, guarded by flunkies, rested an array of champagne and whiskey bottles in a quantity to render a party three times this size into a state of unconsciousness.

As she approached the table, she saw that the only vacant space was at the head of it, obviously meant for her. The men were silent until she stood at the table with a servant ready to assist her into her chair. Then the Russians gave wild Cossack yells, she presumed in her honor.

All those things impressed her, yet what impressed her most of all was the fact that she was the only female present.

Nine

Wondering why this was so, Lydia stood alone at the head of the table and regarded each of the uniformed men studying her blond beauty intently, their smiles depicting genuine satisfaction. All were young except the one at the foot of the table who was middle-aged and had a beard that was dyed and center-parted. She gave him a gracious nod, then addressed them, expressing her thanks for honoring her in such a fashion.

Obviously, not one of them either spoke or understood a word of English, for their smiles didn't change and their only reply was brief nods of acknowledgment. The middle-aged man raised his glass with one hand, used his other to touch his ample chest and said, "Dmitri." Then he bowed, clicked his heels, drank the toast and threw the glass at one of the marble pillars. Lydia started as the delicate crystal goblet broke into bits. This ritual accomplished, the man then proceeded to introduce the others, one by one.

"Vladimir . . . Nicholas . . . Georgi . . . Paul . . . Sergei . . . Gregor . . . Vassily . . . Boris . . . Anatoly . . . Victor."

As each name was mentioned that individual stood up, bowed to Lydia, drank his toast and threw his glass at either a pillar or the mirrored wall. Lydia no longer jumped at each crash. As the servants poured more champagne and left the empty bottles on the table, she wondered why they weren't removed, but not for long. When the toast had gone around the table, there were ear-jarring shouts of glee, after which the Russians picked up the empty bottles and threw them at the mirrored wall, causing it to shatter in several places and pieces of glass to fall and sliver into fragments. Through all of this, Lydia had remained standing. She was so astonished at this last act of open vandalism that she now sat down slowly, speechless in wonder at what was coming next. Only then did she notice that all eyes were upon her in a way that brought to mind Angelina's grave fears for her safety.

She managed to conceal the concern she felt with a polite smile. Nor did she reveal further anxiety at their continued boorish behavior, or at the absence of other female guests. But she was glad, for her fears were allayed, when a door opened and servants appeared, carrying trays of dishes of caviar and tiny rolls on which the Russians happily smeared the expensive fish eggs. Lydia was not averse to caviar, though there were things she liked better. She ate sparingly, waiting for what must be a sumptuous banquet to be served. However, when the servants left, she realized this was all the banquet consisted of—champagne and caviar. And every time a glass was emptied, it was hurled away to shatter and add to the debris. She began to think she had walked into a madhouse.

The men talked incessantly and rarely took their eyes off her. Then Dmitri, the middle-aged man with a red beard, produced a deck of cards. Lydia's bewilderment was replaced by dismay. She wondered if their idea of entertaining a guest was to play cards. Besides, she was hungry and no more food was forthcoming, though one bottle after another of champagne was emptied and the bottles still thrown at the mirrors, until half of them were shattered and the floor was littered with shards of glass.

Her uneasiness grew as each man drew a card amid uproarious laughter and loud talk. They were bordering on intoxication by now. She wondered if she should make some excuse and leave.

One man waved his card aloft. At once the others left the table, hoisted him on their shoulders and marched around the room while they sang wild Russian songs.

By now Lydia had had enough, as there seemed nothing she could do to put an end to this foolish boisterousness. She was growing more and more worried, for they were plainly beyond the state of acting like gentlemen. Inviting her to an affair like this was an insult. She wanted to get out, but she hesitated, telling herself that these were men of the Russian nobility and important persons, held in high esteem by Monte Carlo officials. It might not be wise to offend them. Yet she found their behavior increasingly offensive.

The man they lifted and marched around the room was thrown high and caught as he came down. The yelling was deafening. Once the man was on his feet again, more glasses were filled, drained and shattered. Champagne was poured for Lydia as well, but she disregarded the filled glass.

Once she stood up and tried to speak, but the levity kept right on and she wouldn't have been heard if she'd used a megaphone. So she sat down again, now thoroughly terrified and completely disgusted with these men.

She was about to make a dash for the door when the man who had obviously won something by the card draw was seized and pushed toward her. When she arose in sudden fear, she was seized by this man and embraced until his body was tight against hers. One of his hands lowered and he began to paw her.

She wrested herself free of his grasp and, when he came at her again, slapped him as hard as she could. That brought on laughter that rang in her ears like the vibration of a massive dinner gong. He seized her again, this time clutching the bodice of her gown and tearing it. His hand moved on, exploring other parts of her body.

She screamed and tried to get away, crying out in protest, but nothing stopped him. The man she'd slapped finally released her to the one who seemed to be the most important person here. She wondered if he was the Grand Duke Dmitri, cousin to the czar. Not that she cared. She was too concerned with her safety to worry about offending a member of the Russian nobility now.

He didn't touch her, but stood there smiling at her and speaking in Russian, which she didn't understand. He placed a hand on her shoulder in a fatherly sort of way and then, without warning, pulled down one shoulder of her gown. His hand delved beneath it to grasp her breast.

She was panic-stricken by now, for she realized that these men were about to physically attack her. She backed away again. The Russians gathered in a tight circle, apparently holding a brief conference. It enabled her to back into a corner close by one of the doors. As they conferred, she made a dash for it, but found it locked. Nobody even glanced her way.

Four of the Russians now marched to another door, unlocked it and filed out, closing it behind them. The others resorted to more champagne and caviar, smashing glass after glass. Then one of them seemed to have an idea. From under his white formal coat, he drew a revolver and began shooting at the chandeliers. Prisms crashed down. Three or four of the others decided this was an excellent game, produced guns and shot at the rest of the chandeliers. Lydia pressed back against the wall near the door.

"You're all crazy!" she shouted. "You're insane! Let me out of here!"

They laughed at her, presented her with elaborate bows and much clicking of heels. The room was, by now, a shambles. With every step they took, glass crunched underfoot.

The main double doors now opened wide, and the four who had been dispatched on some errand produced the object of the orders. They carried in a bed, fully made and held high over their heads. Lydia shuddered, and then made another dash for the door, only to have it closed in her face.

The grand duke approached her again. This time he backed her against a wall, pulled at her bodice with one hand and with the other dropped a fistful of gold coins into her bosom.

"Wait!" she cried out. "You're making a great mistake! I'm Lydia Bradley. I'm a reporter. Amerikanski! Do you understand? Amerikanski!"

"*Da!*" they chorused and began moving toward her en masse. She realized then that she was going to be raped, probably by each of them in sequence to the value of the cards they'd drawn. *She* was the object of their crazy lottery and there was nothing she could do about it except scream, though her cries wouldn't be heard, or if they were, disregarded. Everyone knew the Russians were only having a little fun that would be well paid for in due time. She'd been reckless in shrugging off Angelina's fears.

As the grand duke reached for her, she tried to evade him but failed. He lifted her in his arms and carried her to the bed. She was dropped on it, but scrambled to her feet before they closed in. Frantically she reached into her bosom and found some of the gold coins, and approached the grand duke and threw them in his face.

The grand duke gaped at her in astonishment. Then he stepped back and threw out his arms in a gesture of hopelessness. For a moment they were all quiet, seemingly confused, and Lydia felt a moment of hope. But they were under the influence of too much champagne to stop now. They began to converge on her.

Her heart hammered in her chest as someone banged on the door. They ignored it, but when it continued, one of the Russians, with an angry shout, went over and opened it. The baron came rushing in. He needed only one brief glance at Lydia, her torn gown that she was holding up and the bed that sat nearby, to know what was in store for her. He began to speak rapidly in Russian, accompanying his words with a great deal of hand-waving.

Gradually, he won their attention. It was the grand duke who now seemed astonished. The dialogue continued with the baron speaking in tones of righteous indignation, and the Russians listening to him, first arguing with him, but finally quieting, their manner attentive. Lydia, with barely perceptible movements, sidestepped behind the Russians

167

until she had a clear path to the door. The baron, facing her, had been watching her and knew what she was up to. Once again, he raised his voice, waved his arms and spoke with apparently eloquent fervor, for the anger evident in the Russians' faces at his intrusion slowly began to fade. Lydia took a deep breath and sprinted for the door.

She reached the lobby, ran past the few astonished on-lookers and continued running. She was still holding her gown up to cover her bosom. At the Hotel de Paris, concious that she didn't make a very attractive figure, she hurried around the edges of the lobby, drawing more astonished glances for the gown was torn in several places. But that was unimportant to her. All she wanted was to reach the safety of her own hotel, then the sanctuary of her suite.

With the door of the room safely closed and locked, she sank weakly onto one of the chairs until her wits cleared, the terror left her and she was able to slip out of the gown. Gold coins clattered onto the floor as she removed her corset. She regarded them with fresh revulsion and kicked them with the side of her slipper, sending them flying across the room until they hit the wall. She drew a bath, immersed herself in it and gradually her nervous trembling ceased.

When a knock sounded on the door, she recognized it as the baron's. She had a negligée over her nightdress and, after insisting he identify himself, let him in. He was too distraught to even greet her, though he directed an angry glance her way as he went directly to the sideboard where there was a tray on which sat decanters filled with a variety of spirits. On another tray were glasses of various sizes. He chose a brandy inhaler, poured a generous quantity of liquor into it, drank it in one gulp and then poured another.

Before he downed that, he asked in anger, ''Why did you go there? Don't you know what kind of people those Russians are?''

The bath had calmed Lydia, but she could scarcely repress sobs as the baron's wrath was directed at her recklessness. She was almost at the breaking point. Yet she knew his concern was genuine and she appreciated it, for if it hadn't been for his timely appearance, she wouldn't have escaped the mad Russians and their lascivious intentions.

"Baron, they sent me an invitation. I'll show it to you," she explained in an unusually shaky voice as she opened a drawer and removed the card. He glanced at it, threw it onto a table and emptied his glass.

"You might have consulted me, Fräulein Lydia. My job is to see that you are protected, but I cannot do this if you will not let me know where you are going."

"Baron, please sit down. Pour me a brandy, too, and another for yourself. Then tell me what in the world that was all about and why those crazy idiots thought they could disrobe and rape me. Don't they realize what would happen if they harmed me? They're not so savage or stupid that they'd do such a thing to an American journalist."

"Please, you are the one who is excited. I will sit down if you will sit down. And, yes, more brandy."

He poured two brandies and sat opposite Lydia, who told him, "They gave me enough champagne to get me drunk—but I had more sense than to touch it."

"That was the general idea—to get you drunk."

"Why? I'm as mystified now as I am angry."

"They thought you were—well, a prostitute."

"A what?" she exlaimed indignantly. "Do you realize what you are saying?"

"Calm down. It can be explained and, after all, you were not harmed."

"Not harmed? I was pawed by them! My gown is ruined. They insulted me by dumping gold coins down my bodice. You call that not being harmed? They were going to strip me. I know that now. I'd be their plaything for the evening and you say they didn't harm me?"

"I meant they did not fully succeed."

Lydia went pale. "That was thanks to you, my dear Baron. Tell me what brought you to that banquet hall? How did you know I was there?"

"I came to your suite. Angelina told me where you were."

"I thank God for Angelina, too," Lydia said. "Now, go on with your story. Why did they think I was a prostitute?"

"I can't answer that. I . . . never asked them. All I wanted to do was get you out of there. After you ran off, they were apologetic. They explained it was all a mistake."

"Some mistake!" Lydia gasped. "Five minutes later and I'd have been on that bed. Imagine it! They even carried in a bed! Of all things. . . ."

She stopped and began to laugh hysterically. The baron patted her hand, as the laughter dissolved into tears.

"In all my life I never heard of anything half as crazy." Lydia blurted out after a bit. "The whole evening was crazy. First, they sent me that invitation. I should have known better than to accept it without asking you. Even Angelina was skeptical and warned me, but I went because I wanted a story—I always want a story. They received me as if I were their czarina! They toasted me, gave me caviar. Caviar and champagne. That's what the banquet consisted of—caviar and champagne. I tell you, they're a mad bunch. But the bed! Carrying in the bed! And drawing lots for me. Honoring the one who won. And there I was, not really knowing what was going on until I saw the bed. They didn't understand anything I said. I didn't understand them. It was awful, Baron, and if it weren't so terrible it might even be funny. But if they'd managed to go through with it. . . ." She went white again, and stopped.

The baron said flatly, "I don't think it will strike me as funny for a few weeks. If ever."

"But imagine. The bed! Bringing it in scared the daylights out of me because I knew what they were up to by then."

"You have a story. That's what you went after." The baron downed his brandy and set the glass on a nearby table.

"Baron, I have a story, but how can I write it without involving myself? How can I write about the craziness of everything they did?"

"You'll find a way," the baron declared morosely.

"But I'd set the world laughing . . . or maybe crying in disgust. What am I going to do?"

"You are asking me? Who nearly went mad with anxiety before I got to the hotel?"

"Yes, there is a story, all right," Lydia said seriously. "An unusual story. The only thing is—the Russian serfs who would profit by it can't read. Those idiots must have smashed a hundred glasses, all of the finest crystal, and you know what that costs. They smashed most of the mirrors, too—they'll have to be replaced. Then they actually shot bullets at the chandeliers . . . those lovely chandeliers. The destruction was terrible."

"They will pay for it. More than pay for it."

"And where does all this money, wasted in such reckless fashion, come from? You know as well as I do. The Russian people are paying these bills. What do these dukes and grand dukes, and cousins to the czar care what they spend? It's always ground out of the hides of the Russian people. *That's* what I'm going to write about."

"The casino management will not like it," the baron reminded her. "Before those Russians leave, they will have spent a million rubles, or something approaching that."

"But they destroy beautiful things without any reason!"

"Before they go, much more will be destroyed. But then I tell you, my dear Lydia, that Monte is no ordinary place."

"Neither are many of the people who come here, I'm afraid."

"I suppose you will write the story anyway?" he asked.

"Yes, though it must be softened. What else can I do?"

"You are being very wise."

"I don't agree. I'm behaving as if I were born here and the place deserves my loyalty. It's not improving my integrity as a reporter, but I realize I must go along," she sighed.

"There are many other stories here," the baron comforted her.

"But not like the one that brings a girl innocently into

the hands of those circus clowns who carry a bed into the banquet hall. I'll tell you one thing, Baron, I've learned. If I have the slightest hesitancy about going somewhere, if I'm given the barest hint of possible trouble, I'll see you first. And I'm going to ask the head office to put you on the payroll. You'll be worth far more than anything they'll pay you."

"I think you are growing a bit giddy, Lydia. I never worked for anyone in my life," the baron said with dignity. "I'll be going now. You will feel better after a good sleep."

"Baron, I must thank you again," Lydia said softly, kissing his cheek.

"Oh, yes." He brushed her thanks aside with embarrassed gruffness, as he turned around near the door. "Be dressed by noon," he added.

"What's going on then?"

"The grand duke is coming to see you. Don't worry. I'll be here too, as interpreter."

Her face mirrored her shock. "If you aren't, he won't get into this suite," she said. "I wouldn't trust that man in a room filled with a thousand people. He'd probably bribe every one of them to go somewhere else. Good night, Baron."

Lydia was barely awake when Angelina arrived in the morning, anxious to hear about the banquet.

"Banquet?" Lydia scoffed. "It was more like an assignation. A dozen men and one woman. If you hadn't alerted the baron as to where I'd gone, I might not be here this morning. It was terrifying!"

"I warned you," Angelina said remindfully, then asked for the details.

Neither woman wasted time sitting down, once the breakfast table arrived. Angelina had her coffee and croissant while Lydia sipped coffee and related her frightening experience. Angelina listened wide-eyed, sometimes forgetting to eat the croissant she held close to her mouth.

"Truly," she said, "those Russians are crazy. But this . . . even for them is unheard of. Sending you an invitation. . . ."

"A royal command," Lydia corrected her. "You saw the card."

"Command, then. And to have such a thing happen. Do those imbeciles have no sense at all?"

"Not the ones I met," Lydia said grimly. "And you may be assured they haven't any morals. But I'll know better soon. The baron is bringing the Grand Duke Dmitri here at noon. To apologize, I suppose. I want to talk to him and get to the bottom of this. I want to know what made them think I was nothing more than a strumpet!"

"Sometimes," Angelina declared, "I am sure they think all women are alive only to provide Russian nobility with someone to debauch. They scare me to death."

"I can assure you I'll never knowingly be alone with one of them again. Not if I can help it—or unless I happen to have a gun in my handbag. Shooting down those beautiful chandeliers. . . . Just target practicing with them, though the chandeliers must cost thousands."

"You will write about this incident?"

"No. The baron advises me not to, and common sense tells me not to relate all of what happened. It was too terrible. Also, the Russians leave so much money in Monte that nothing must dissuade them from coming every year."

"It is best," Angelina agreed. "Always the casino, the hotels and the restaurants come first. Monte would not exist without them."

The baron and the grand duke arrived promptly at noon. The grand duke was dressed in white silk and made an impressive appearance, although a most dejected one, whether real or feigned Lydia couldn't tell. He bowed elaborately and kissed the back of her hand.

The baron translated, "The Grand Duke Dmitri, cousin of the czar, wishes to apologize for the misunderstanding of last evening."

"I don't believe *misunderstanding* is quite the word for it," Lydia said. Her manner, though not rude, was precise.

"My dear Lydia, perhaps it is." The baron was conciliatory. "The grand duke has been explaining it to me. First of all, neither he nor any other Russian sent you an invitation—or command—as you called it."

Lydia addressed the baron. "You saw the card."

The baron said, "Please show it to the grand duke."

She took the card from a drawer and handed it to the grand duke. He was unable to read the English words in the card, so the baron translated for him.

"*Nyet!*" the grand duke shouted and his face grew florid with anger as he exploded in Russian.

The baron said, "He says this card did not come from him, or anyone else in his party. It is a forgery, especially the seal on the back of the envelope."

Lydia asked in astonishment, "If that's the truth, why were they expecting me? Why was everything set up to receive me? Not as an honored guest, which I thought I was, but as a demimondaine."

The baron gestured helplessly. "You were sold to them."

"Sold? What does that mean, for heaven's sake?"

"A man told them you were like Madame Otéro, a gypsy dancer who lends her body to any man who will give her a two-carat diamond ring. He said you had an international reputation as the finest . . . well . . . *la grand horizontal* in the world, rivaling this Otéro."

"Good Lord!" Lydia gasped. "Who did that? Who sold me?"

The baron turned to the grand duke and spoke in Russian. The grand duke replied at length, but only one word made sense to Lydia. He had brought into the foreign jumble the name of Martel.

"Armand Martel?" she interrupted the dialogue.

"*Da!*" the Grand Duke said eagerly.

"*Ja,*" the baron said. "He came to the grand duke and negotiated for the finest—*fille de joie*—that money could provide. It was agreed that she would be called for at this hotel at eight last evening."

"Martel!" Lydia looked troubled by the news. "Martel again. Who is he? Why is he doing this to me?"

"I can't say, and I'm sure the grand duke does not know. He asks if he is forgiven and he throws himself at your feet," the baron translated.

Lydia nodded. "He is forgiven. He was tricked just as surely as I was. Tell him so."

As the baron talked the grand duke's face lit up with pleasure. He turned, strode to the door, opened it and two men entered, each carrying one of the biggest bouquets of red roses that Lydia had ever seen.

"With the compliments of the grand duke, and all those who were at the banquet hall last evening," the baron said. "And should you ever come to St. Petersburg at any time, you will be welcomed at the grand duke's palace."

"Heaven forbid," Lydia said piously. "But thank him anyhow."

The grand duke bowed again, kissed her hand half a dozen times, and continued to bow as he backed out of the room. The baron closed the door and skirted the huge bouquets of flowers, which had been placed on the floor because no table in the room could handle them.

"I wanted to slap his face," Lydia said angrily. "He's the one who dumped a handful of gold coins down my bosom. Even if he was making an honest mistake, he's no gentleman. Which brings up Armand Martel, who isn't either. Baron, we've got to find that man. He's a menace."

"Indeed he is," the baron said blandly. "Do you have any suggestions?"

"I wish I did. I want to know who's paying him to do this. I feel certain he's not doing these things to me for his own amusement . . . he represents somebody else. The only one I can think of is Drury, who is perfectly capable of being behind this." She frowned slightly. "On the other hand, he wouldn't enjoy doing something like this unless he did it himself. I know how his mind works. He wouldn't pay anybody; he'd get more pleasure out of it by arranging and carrying out the whole thing."

"I do not know how the gentleman's mind works, fräulein, but what are we going to do with this fortune in roses?"

"I'll have the hotel people take them to the hospital. Oh my, there's a card attached to one of the bouquets."

"Ah, yes, I see it."

The baron knelt beside the bouquet and removed the object. It was not a card, but a small box wrapped in something that glittered brightly in the sun-filled room.

Lydia took the package and turned it over a few times, doubtful as to what it might contain.

"Be careful," the baron cautioned. "That is not plain paper the box is wrapped in."

Lydia studied the wrapping. "What is it?"

"Gold leaf," the baron explained. "They always give their most precious gifts wrapped in that."

"There seems to be no end to their extravagance." Lydia opened the package carefully, handing the wrapping to the baron, who made a ball of it and dropped it into his pocket. As Lydia pressed the metal button on the purple velvet box the lid snapped open and a diamond sent brilliant shafts of light around the room, for the sunlight had struck it squarely.

"A diamond ring!" Lydia exclaimed. "Baron, look at it! It must be worth thousands."

The baron studied it intently. "No doubt. If you do not care to receive this gift, please throw it away while I am in your presence and forgive me if I break my arm reaching for it."

"Shall I keep it?" Lydia asked, mostly to herself. "If I do, I condone all their actions. I don't want to do that. Yet they were deceived, just as I was. There was really no need for the grand duke to come here, apologize, bring enormous bouquets of roses and leave an expensive gift."

"At least you are beginning to understand how they think," the baron said philosophically.

"I'm not sure I do," she mused. "Or perhaps I well know how they think. They were pleased at the thought of entertaining a courtesan last evening. Or she would entertain them. I'm not certain which."

The baron shrugged. "No need for you to waste time figuring out that poser."

"I must have been quite a disappointment to them."

"I'd say a puzzlement. The more reluctant you seemed

to be, the more of a challenge it was to them. Knowing them, I'm sure they thought of it as a game—one new to them.''

"I must send the ring back."

"I suggest you keep it even if you never wear it. In years to come, it will serve as a memento of an evening that gave you an insight to Russian royalty."

"I won't need the ring to do that," Lydia said indignantly.

"Nevertheless, take my advice and keep it. To return it would offend them, particularly since it was given in the nature of an apology. They know of no other way to humble themselves."

"Are you being honest with me?" Lydia asked soberly.

"Completely," the baron said, his tone as sincere as hers.

Lydia took the ring from the box and asked, "How many carats would you say this diamond is?"

The baron held out his hand and Lydia placed the glittering jewel in his palm. He examined the stone closely before he looked up.

"About two carats, fräulein."

"Two carats!" she exlaimed. "What did that gypsy dancer demand?"

"Two carats," the baron said blandly.

Lydia placed the ring back in its velvet nest and snapped the box shut, much perturbed. She was uncertain what to do with it. "I'd have been far happier if the grand duke had brought me news of the whereabouts of Armand Martel. I feel he was the cause of this ghastly incident."

The baron nodded. "Well, we can be sure of one thing. If he handled this business, he's still in the vicinity. We'll just have to keep searching for him. From the description you gave me of him, I'll spot him if he's around. You can keep your eyes open, too. I agree he's a menace and we must do everything possible to ferret him out before he thinks up more mischief that may be even worse for you."

"What could that be?" Lydia asked.

The baron's mouth opened to speak, but shut quickly. It was apparent what he was thinking, so much so that Lydia shuddered.

"Ah." The baron had spotted the gold coins that Lydia had kicked against the wall the night before.

Her features relaxed. "Take them, Baron. I don't want even to look at them."

He smiled his gratitude and scooped them up, dropping them in his pocket, then bowed a farewell to Lydia and left the room. The casino was open by now.

Ten

That afternoon, Lydia did prepare a short article about the arrival of the exuberant Russians. Nothing in it seriously detracted from them—it appeared to be only a story of their outrageous antics, with no mention of the money those antics cost the Russian people.

She folded the article, slipped it in her handbag and left her suite, a fetching picture in a pale blue linen dress bordered at the hem with a wide band of black velvet. The sleeves of her dress were cuffed with lace, which also formed a cravat at the throat. A large yellow straw hat trimmed with flowers completed her costume, the color of this and the dress complementing her blonde beauty and her sapphire blue eyes. Nonetheless, she felt a trace of uneasiness when she started across the lobby, fearful the story of her escapade last night was now known by everyone. She stiffened visibly when she heard her name called. But only momentarily, for she immediately recognized the voice as that of Jeffrey.

She turned, and saw him striding across the lobby, looking quite handsome and nautical in a blue jacket with gold buttons and white flannel trousers. His arms were opened to receive her, and she rushed into them. He held her an instant, studying her face, their parting coolness of weeks ago forgotten.

He said only, "You're enchantingly beautiful," then drew her close to him. Their lips met in a brief kiss, but even so, Lydia felt her breath and heartbeat quicken.

"I missed you, darling," Jeff said.

"And I missed you," Lydia said. "I have absolutely no shame about it, either."

"What's there to be ashamed about?" he asked. "We're in each other's arms. I like it."

"I more than like it. I thought you'd never come back."

He regarded her with astonishment. "I can't believe it's you talking. What about your career?"

"It doesn't seem important at the moment. You do, though you may greatly resent my saying so." She smiled up at him.

"Don't be a fool. They're the most beautiful words you've ever spoken. I like to hear I'm important."

"But you don't want any romantic entanglements," Lydia reminded him. "And I thought you didn't care about me."

"You don't either," he retorted in answer to the first statement. "At least, you didn't." He studied her face carefully. "And as for not caring about you . . . I love you, Lydia."

Her heart thudded painfully as she confessed in turn, "The longer you stayed away, the more I realized how much you mean to me." Her smile was radiant, her eyes soft with love as she spoke. Then she chided him. "You sound like an ardent lover, but your actions are not those of a man who wishes to be with his lady-love. I'm referring to your absences."

"You know I must go away from time to time." Jeff's eyes asked her to understand.

"So you say, though you're most mysterious." She held up a hand as he started to protest. "And please don't give me that ridiculous story about the rock falling into the sea. If you can't be truthful, say nothing. I'll trust you—for the present anyway."

"We're making some real progress," he said, laughing.

"For the moment," she said, giving him an arch look. "But if you continue with these mysterious sudden disappearances. . . ."

Jeff ignored her trailing sentence, and suggested, "Suppose we take a walk, find a quiet, secluded spot where we can talk—and make love."

She grew serious. "First we'll talk. I've a great deal to tell you. A lot happened while you were away."

"I hope it was good."

"It wasn't. I needed you, but I managed. Perhaps it was as well you weren't here. I believe I suddenly grew up."

His brows raised as he studied her sober features. "Let's get out of here. You're the one who's being mysterious now, and I want to hear your story."

They walked along the street in silence, for the time being content with each other's company. When they reached the casino gardens, Jeffrey guided her onto a path and sought out a secluded bench. He removed her straw hat and set it on the bench behind him.

"Before you say a word, I want another kiss."

There wasn't time for her to protest, nor did she want to. She again felt passion stir within her as their lips touched. She was glad Jeff had selected a secluded spot for she was trembling from head to foot. She'd never known the thrill of genuine love, the hungry desire to kiss and be kissed, the need to love and be loved. His hands were moving in a slow, caressing fashion down her back, then back to her shoulders. He broke the embrace to kiss her shoulders and her bosom through the softness of her dress. Then he pressed his head against her breasts.

"Darling, please—not here," Lydia murmured. "I must talk with you. We can make love later."

He moved his head only enough to look up at her. "Do you mean that?" His tone was urgent.

"Yes," she replied.

He straightened reluctantly. "Perhaps I'd better sit a brief distance from you . . . or it won't be later."

"I know."

They both moved so that there was a little space between them. Lydia leaned over Jeffrey, retrieved her straw hat and placed it on the bench between them.

"Before you start to talk," Jeff said, "am I right in

believing you've changed your mind about me?"

"It wasn't a question of changing my mind as much as coming to my senses. I was just too obsessed with my career."

"And you're not now?"

"Not in the same fashion as before," she replied. "As I told you, a lot happened since you last saw me."

Jeff pressed for an answer. "But which comes first, your career or me?"

"You, darling. Always you."

"Start talking," he said earnestly.

Both had their emotions under control now, so it was easy for Lydia to relate her story. "It began with the arrival of a bouquet of flowers, accompanied by a card. It was from Prince Jouhaud, an Algerian prince who came to Monte to gamble. The flowers arrived on the evening that a banquet was being given by him to which I'd been invited. There was also a corsage nestling in the box. I slipped it into the waistband of my gown. When I reached the casino, a young man snatched them and, almost in a frenzy, pulled them apart."

Jeff looked puzzled. "Was he drunk—or mad?"

"Neither. The flowers were carnations."

Jeff's face cleared. "Why would the prince send such flowers, and where did he get them? Carnations aren't allowed in the casino or anywhere on Monte. They're considered bad luck. I'm sure the prince knows that."

"He didn't send them. I have no idea who did."

"Was the invitation to the banquet genuine?"

"Oh, yes. That really was sent by the prince. It was a charming affair. I was seated beside a handsome young man, the prince's equerry. . . or so he identified himself. We conversed throughout dinner—I was determined not to let the earlier unpleasantness I'd been subjected to by the seemingly deranged young man spoil my evening. Anyway, my dinner companion identified himself as Armand Martel. Have you heard of him?"

"Never."

"No one seems to have. Nonetheless, I accepted his word as to his authenticity. I had no reason to disbelieve him. Also, I thought it would be an excellent opportunity to get a story out of him. He had already given vague hints that the prince was not all he seemed to be, but Monsieur Martel would say no more. Later, I sought him out at the casino while the gambling was going on and over champagne, his tongue loosened. At least that's what I thought. The story he told me, made the prince out to be a far from admirable character, a man who had in fact ruined Martel's sister's life, in addition to numerous other sordid actions. I was filled with revulsion by what I heard. So much so, I wrote a biased story about him and sent it to my paper."

"Didn't you check your story?" Jeff asked in open astonishment.

"No," she replied dismally. "Martel seemed utterly sincere, and warned me that it would mean his death if the story's source was revealed. But my not checking almost became my undoing."

"The prince is a gentleman," Jeff said. "I've met him and I know about his private life. He does a lot of good among his people."

She nodded. "So I heard later. As the baron said, my head had gotten too big. He told me that the very day after the evening this happened. I laughed at him."

"Did your paper print the story?" he asked.

"I thought they had because I wrote the story in great detail, showing up the prince for the knave he was supposed to be—at least according to Monsieur Martel—and sent it by cablegram to my paper. Oh—I must mention that Monsieur Martel made me swear I would not reveal his name."

"Have you been fired?" Jeff asked soberly. "If the story was printed, you must have been."

"No, that's the strange part. The paper never received it."

"If you sent a cablegram, they must have received it," Jeff said matter-of-factly.

"They didn't. That's the strangest part. You see, I asked

Angelina, the floor maid at the hotel, to check on Monsieur Martel. She could learn nothing about him except that the prince's entourage included no one by that name. I checked further. Suddenly I realized I was guilty of a terrible breach of ethics when I didn't check the story. I should have known better but, as the baron said, my head had swollen.''

"What happened to the cablegram?'' Jeff asked.

"My editor, Guy Spencer, wrote me asking the same thing. You see, the moment I learned I could well be wrong about the prince, I got the cable operator out of bed and sent my paper a message to kill the story on the prince. They sent a cablegram asking, what story? That's when I knew the cablegram had never been received.''

Jeff said flatly, "I repeat . . . if it was sent, it was received.''

"No, Jeff. The man at the cable office here asked the New York office of the company about it and they said there was no record of it. I believe him when he insists he sent it. Why on earth wouldn't he have done so?''

"I don't know. Did you contact Martel?''

"No one seems to be able to do that. No one has even heard of him except me. At least, not so far. One thing's sure—he doesn't work for the prince. I believe it was also Martel who sent the flowers and corsage.''

"It would seem so,'' Jeff mused.

"I did write an article about the kaiser—at least, he wasn't supposed to have been here, but he was—incognito. And that's how I wrote it. As if he had a double who was an impostor.''

Jeff chuckled. "It couldn't have been a pleasant story, though I'm certain that after your experience with the prince, you were careful.''

"Well, I wrote it before I knew my other story was slanderous. Nevertheless, the kaiser's story was a good one, with photos to belie the statements,'' Lydia replied. "Then I received another invitation—sent by Russian royalty.''

"Good God!'' Jeff exclaimed in disbelief. "I hope you didn't go.''

"I did, against Angelina's advice and dire warnings, which I dismissed lightly."

His features tensed. "What happened?"

"First of all, let me say it was a bona fide invitation. I should say it was a *command* to appear. There was even a royal crest on the envelope. It was horrible, but thanks to Baron Maxfried Hetzler, I escaped."

"Were you harmed?" he asked quickly.

"No, but I was humiliated. They expected a Spanish dancer—one who is paid with a two-carat diamond ring. They thought I was she and that my protestations were a game which was quite new to them."

"My God, Lydia," Jeff exclaimed anxiously, "just what did go on?"

"I was pawed, my gown torn, gold coins dropped down the bodice of my gown. They even brought a bed into the banquet hall. But the baron learned where I was and arrived in time to save me from what would have been a nightmare. Those Russians thought I was a harlot, a famous one, and it was explained to me later that they had paid someone to furnish me. They denied sending any message. The invitation was a fraud. And . . . the grand duke explained that the man who sold my services called himself Armand Martel."

Jeffrey looked angry. "I don't get it. This is a campaign to either blacken your reputation or destroy you. But why? And who?"

"I can only think of Bryant Drury. He's here—in Monte—presumably to write a book. I'm not certain I believe him, though it could be true. He had the nerve to unlock the door to my suite and sit down to wait for me to come home. He knows about the story I wrote concerning the prince. I told him that I thought he was behind it, but he denied having had anything to do with it and claimed he'd been in Cannes and Paris at the time. He might be telling the truth."

"If he had Martel working for him, there'd be no need for him to be here." Jeff spoke thoughtfully. "In fact, he'd have an alibi by being far away.''

"Since I haven't another known enemy in the world, Drury seems the most likely suspect. He's highly capable of doing such things, but I doubt he's the type to delegate something like this. He'd want to be there, arrange it and watch it happen. Besides, I think he'd want a revenge that would be complete. After all, the cable didn't arrive. This is beginning to assume more of the aspects of harassment—I keep wondering what's going to happen next.''

"I'll tell you," Jeff said grimly. "We're going to find Armand Martel.''

Lydia looked dubious. "If hotel servants, croupiers, even Baron Hetzler who knows everybody, haven't been able to uncover any sign of him, he must have another name or a perfect place of concealment. He may have already left Monte, or he's remaining undercover while he plans some other outrage.''

"I'll go to the police. They may be able to help, or at least have access to someone who knows of Martel's whereabouts. However, it's my opinion that Bryant Drury is the one most likely to be behind this," Jeff reasoned.

"I've already had a talk with him and he denies it. He was disagreeable and made no attempt to hide his dislike for me, but he denied making trouble for me. He also denied knowing anyone named Armand Martel. Somehow, much as I hate to admit it, I felt he was telling the truth.''

"You said he made no secret of his dislike for you?" Jeff asked, fingering the straw hat between them.

"That's understandable, since I was responsible for him losing his job. He wanted to get even with a very influential man in New York City. Drury saw his opportunity when he observed the man's wife dining with a young man many years her junior. Drury left immediately to write it up and put it in a sort of international gossip column he wrote from time to time. I went to the ladies' room and met the woman there. Her name was—is—Mrs. Paul Hallett.''

"Oh, yes. Hallett's a financial wizard.''

"Bryant Drury hates him. Anyway, she was antagonistic

toward me at first, then relented. I learned from her that the young man was her brother, and I went directly to my newspaper to try to find Drury. He wasn't at his desk, so I went to the night editor, who was successful in having the story killed before it got into print. It seems Drury had done such things before. This was the final straw. They fired him. So I can understand his bitterness toward me."

"Whom do you blame for not having checked the story on Prince Jouhaud?"

"Myself," Lydia said without a second's hesitation.

"The same holds true of Bryant Drury. He shouldn't blame anyone but himself."

"Thanks, Jeff. I really wanted to help Drury when I returned to the newspaper office that night."

"You did help—both him and the paper."

"He doesn't see it that way. He's convinced I was after his job."

"May I ask a personal question?"

"Of course."

"Were you seeing a lot of him—socially?"

"It was the first and only time he took me out. In truth, he was my idol before that incident happened. He was a big name in the newspaper field."

"He was," Jeff agreed. "I'd say he's in limbo now. That's probably why he's writing a book. If it's a success, he can work his way back up the ladder." He paused, then frowned and added, "What I'd like to know is, why were you with him? Was it business or social?"

"Strictly social. At the beginning of our dinner, he told me he wished to help me with my career. I was overjoyed."

"Go on," Jeff said quietly.

"Perhaps he thought the champagne would allay my standards of morality, but in the course of the meal, he brushed his knee against mine—no accidental gesture—then suggested it would be far easier on me financially if I moved into his apartment, which was a very large one. That was when the bubble burst and I saw Drury for what he is—an amoral opportunist. I suppose I should have left then, but it would have created a scene in the restaurant.''

"Besides," Jeff reasoned, "you might not have saved your paper from a libel suit. To say nothing of Drury. Anyway, I'm glad I don't have him as a rival."

"Heaven forbid," Lydia said, managing a laugh. Jeff had stood up and now offered her his arm. They began to stroll back toward the lighted casino.

"Since we seem to have eliminated the one person you think might have a grudge," he went on, "I suggest we look over your articles. In some of them, you've been quite candid. It's possible you could have antagonized someone who's bent on getting even and doesn't care how it's accomplished. If that's the case, it would be someone important—someone who knows these people, or a great deal about their private lives and can gain access to their social functions. If we don't find any clues in the articles, I suggest we concentrate on this man Martel. We've got to find him, make him talk. If he's guilty, that'll put an end to the trouble. If he isn't, we'll have to keep looking. In the meantime, I suggest you have dinner with me each evening I'm here."

Lydia's features brightened. "That will be exciting. Of course, the baron won't like it. He'll have to fend for himself."

"From what I've heard, he's quite adept at that."

"Speaking of him, he's coming this way."

"He's a dapper-looking fellow. Certainly dresses well," Jeff remarked as they stepped onto the lighted terrace.

"I marvel at how he does it."

"That's no puzzle," Jeff said. "He recommends the best tailor in Cannes, Nice and here in Monte. He's a walking advertisement, and a good one. For that he gets enormous discounts on his wardrobe."

The baron was too close for further discussion. Jeff bowed slightly as he reached them.

Lydia said, "Baron Hetzler, this is Mr. Jeffrey Marcus."

The two men, who knew each other by sight and hearsay only, exchanged greetings, then the baron extended a newspaper he was carrying. "My dear Lydia, you must read this. I am deeply upset to have to show it to you—unless you've already seen it."

"Does it concern me?" Lydia asked, as the baron fell into step with them.

"Very much," he said tersely. "Please read it."

She scanned the page, then found the item which the baron had marked in pencil. She exclaimed aloud, then addressed Jeffrey.

"Please read this. It's from that muckraking newspaper printed in Paris. Why it has such a wide circulation, I don't know."

"You should, my dear," the baron said blandly. "As a newspaper reporter, you certainly know that nothing sells papers as much as a choice bit of scandalous gossip."

Lydia ignored his telling reminder as Jeff read the brief paragraph, included in a gossip column, but well separated from the rest of the material and printed in large, very black type.

Well-known international reporter said to have been involved with the recently arrived archdukes and the grand duke from Russia in an escapade that makes even the usual antics of the Russians look tame. Monte never saw anything quite like it, and if this reporter was looking for a story, she certainly found one. We dare her to print it in full, rather than the anemic version she did submit.

"No name, nothing specific, just innuendoes," Lydia said angrily. "The lowest possible form of newspaper writing."

"The moment you arrived here, you were subject to this," Jeff said. "It goes with your work. If you help one paper increase circulation, you anger all the others. It might even be possible that . . . no . . . no, I don't think any publishers would agree to the sort of thing that's been happening to you."

"Baron," Lydia asked, "have you heard any comments?"

"Only one or two around the newsstand, and they were

in your favor. People who said it was a shame you couldn't conduct your work here without this kind of harassment. I doubt anyone here believes you deserved this."

"I wonder," Jeff mused, "how this story got to Paris so fast."

"I haven't even filed my story yet," Lydia said. "I was on my way to the cable office with it when you . . . distracted me . . . darling."

"I think this was written even before you went to that banquet with the Russians. Which means it was all set up." Jeff's voice was grim.

"It would have been a lie if I didn't go," Lydia said thoughtfully. "But what would they care about that? The whole thing is so vague I couldn't possibly make a case against it. Still, everyone knows whom they meant. Yes, it had to be written before the event took place. We can make certain of that by going to the cable office. Maybe the story was sent by wireless to Paris and if it was, the operator will tell me."

"Let's go see him," Jeff suggested.

"I must ask to be excused," the baron said. "I have an appointment with the manager of the Hermitage where the Russians stay. I hope he will know something about this affair."

"We'll meet you later," Jeff said.

"Perhaps it would be best if we talked about it over the supper table?" the baron asked in hopeful tones.

Before Jeff could demur, Lydia said, "An excellent idea, Baron. At my hotel. It will give you a chance to get better acquainted with Jeff, who also happens to be the man I'm going to marry."

"Ah." The baron gave Jeff a nod of approval. "You convinced Lydia that there is more to life than being a good reporter. You are to be commended, Herr Marcus."

Jeff laughed. "Make it Jeff. I have a feeling we'll be good friends."

"Certainly we think highly of the same young lady. Has she told you all that has happened to her?"

"Yes. I'm concerned about it."

"That makes two of us, Jeff," the baron said. "Lydia spoke highly of you. I only hope you will not need to be away from here so much."

"I wish I could say I wouldn't," Jeff replied, "but I can't. So I want to find out who this Armand Martel is before I leave Monte."

"So do I and I won't waste any more time."

Jeff said, "Thanks, Baron. Lydia and I are going to the cable office now to see if we can find out who sent this article. If, indeed, it was sent from here."

On their way, Jeff said, "The baron won't need to worry about eating tonight."

Lydia's face crimsoned. "He's been so kind to me and so attentive. He saved me from a horrible evening with Russian nobility. I couldn't refuse him."

"You're right," Jeff agreed. "I owe him a debt of gratitude myself, for looking after you so well." He caught Lydia's arm and slipped it around his. "Just remember—you promised me some time with you later."

"I won't forget," she replied and her eyes revealed she would not.

Lydia paused, then added, "Jeff, I gather, from your continued reticence to speak of yourself and your work, I'll continue to be alone here at Monte from time to time?"

"I hope not for too much longer," he said seriously.

"Why must you be so mysterious?" she asked.

"I don't mean to be," he said slowly. "I don't want to be, but I must ask for your trust and understanding."

"You resented it when I said my career must come first. Yet you ask me to be understanding about the fact that *your* work comes first."

"I know it doesn't seem fair and it isn't really," he admitted. "But my work is important."

"And mine isn't," Lydia said coolly.

"Of course it is," he replied quickly. "Darling, let's not quarrel. I don't want anything to spoil our happy reunion."

"Very well," she relented, smiling up at him. "I'm

happy, too. Much too happy to spoil things. I love you, Jeffrey Marcus."

"And I love you, my darling. Now let's go to the cable office and see if we can get any further information."

Minutes later, the operator shook his head. "No such story was filed here, monsieur. I swear it was not. Ah, but I have a cable for you, mademoiselle."

It was from New York and Lydia opened it apprehensively. The cable was brief.

WHAT KIND TROUBLE RUSSIAN ROYALTY INVOLVING YOU?
SLEAZY PAPERS HAVE IT IN A.M. EDITION. CAN WE HELP?

It was signed George Morgan, Lydia's publisher.

"The story must have been cabled to New York from Paris," Lydia exclaimed. "This whole affair was well arranged even if it didn't turn out quite the way they intended. Excuse me, Jeff, while I write an answer to Mr. Morgan and file my story of the incident. I was surely scooped on this one."

She wrote out a brief report, promising a follow-up letter with a complete explanation. The operator was sending it as they left his office. On their return to the hotel they didn't talk much but, hand in hand, Lydia felt safe and happy for the first time in days.

At supper, the baron told them that so far as anyone else on Monaco was concerned, Armand Martel did not exist. The officials at the Hermitage had never heard of him.

"So far as I have been able to find out," the baron went on, "only you, Lydia, have ever seen the man."

"Baron, he was at the banquet given by the prince! I talked to him in the crowded casino, where there were a great many people around. You saw him yourself."

"There are so many strangers in Monte," Jeff said, "that no one is studied very carefully unless he's a famous figure. Lots of people come to Monte, and nobody knows them when they arrive or when they leave."

"I talked to croupiers and barmen," the baron added.

"I described the man as you described him to me, and as I vaguely remember him at the banquet. Nobody remembers him and try as I might, I cannot find out how he managed to get an invitaton to the banquet."

"Or how he came to be assigned a chair next to Lydia," Jeff added. "At least you did see him, Baron, so we can't put him down as a ghost."

The baron looked uncomfortable. "I suppose I saw him, but he made no impression."

"I have a feeling that he's here, probably close by, and knows everything that's going on," Lydia said. "I'm deathly afraid of him and what he's going to do next."

"Whatever it turns out to be," Jeff said. "The moment you recognize some trick aimed at you, let me or the baron know before it progresses too far. If you even suspect anything unusual, let one of us know. You won't be alone, as you were walking into that trap with the Russians."

"I'll do my best," she promised. "The only thing is, how do I recognize it as a trap? I surely suspected nothing when I went to what I believed would be a banquet with Russian royalty. Before I realized I'd got myself in a difficult situation, it was too late."

"Don't look now," the baron said, "Herr Drury just walked in with an attractive girl on his arm. He's seated about four tables behind you, Jeff, and to your left."

Jeff turned around and studied Drury, who was already discussing the menu with his lady friend. He happened to glance up and saw Jeff regarding him. Drury smiled in amusement, nodded to Lydia and then the baron. Neither Lydia nor the baron returned the greeting.

Jeff said, "I've seen his picture in the newspaper and I've seen him around here. He's handsome, a good dresser, very self-assured. Needless to say, I don't like him. Knowing how he treated Lydia is enough to make me biased. But he's brazen."

"Brazen is the perfect word," the baron said stiffly. "I only wish I were a younger man."

Lydia said, "Don't let him upset you. I wish I knew if

he was really writing a book."

"Why should you care?" the baron asked.

"I don't," Lydia said. "It's just that if he weren't, I'd know for a certainty he was here to make things difficult—or at least make a good attempt to do so. He told me he'd get even with me. That's what he was going to do to Mr. Hallett the night he wrote that gossip about Mrs. Hallett."

"Even though he got fired for it, he should be eternally grateful to you that the story was never printed," Jeff said. "You didn't tell me before he swore he'd have his revenge."

"I'm doing my best to be fair," she said. "I don't want to work up a hatred for him as he obviously has done toward me. That's childish."

"Yes," Jeff agreed. "But what's happened to you could have resulted in great danger to yourself."

"Do you know if that man who made trouble for you is still in jail? The one whose picture appeared in the papers resulting in his arrest."

"Osgood Trencher? So far as I know," she replied.

"I'll check on it. We can't leave any avenue of danger to you unexplored.

Lydia said, "Drury claims he's been researching in Paris and Cannes. Do you have to go there?"

"Yes," Jeff admitted, coloring slightly. "I didn't want to mention it just now."

She gave him an understanding smile. "This time you can do me a favor. Please inquire at the libraries and see if he's been there. They have rare books—they make you sign for them and they must be studied in the reading room because they can't be taken out. Perhaps you might find his signature. If so, we'd know he's being honest about writing a book on Monte Carlo. It would be a relief to eliminate him as a suspect for the harassment I've been subjected to."

"You may be assured I'll do it," Jeff said. "I'm as anxious to know what's going on as you. Only then will we be able to put a stop to it. The sooner, the better."

"So long as we have finished eating and you are apparently not going to buy me another brandy, we might as well leave," the baron now suggested.

"Yes," Lydia agreed. "Besides, I must write a letter to my publisher explaining the Russian debacle."

The baron said, "You may be assured, my dear, if you need verification of your story, I will gladly give it."

"Thanks." Lydia bent and kissed his cheek.

"I will even go to Paris and Cannes," he added, pleased by her gesture.

"No, you won't," Jeff said. "I'll do that. I'd like it to be a honeymoon, but that will have to wait a while."

"I had no idea a romance was in the making, but you Americans waste no time. Yet, with such a beautiful girl, how could you want to wait?" the baron chided.

"I don't," Jeff admitted. "But just as Lydia has her career, I have mine."

The baron gave them a disapproving look. "When I was young, love came first."

"It does with us also, Baron," Jeff said. "But there's a difference. We have to work to pay our way."

"Considering I like you so well, I will overlook the inference," the baron said stiffly.

Jeff laughed. "No hard feelings, Baron. Escort Lydia to the lobby. I'll see you both there."

"What are you up to?" Lydia asked in sudden alarm.

The baron took Lydia's arm and urged her to the exit. Jeff was already on his way to Drury's table.

"Come, Lydia," the baron said. "You cannot afford to be mixed up in anything. You have enough explaining to do now to your newspaper. Besides, Jeff doesn't want you here."

She went along reluctantly, knowing the baron was right, but she hated to leave Jeff alone with Drury. She knew the latter could be ugly.

"Come, my dear," the baron consoled. "Jeff can handle himself."

"You're right," she admitted, though her face reflected her uneasiness.

Once in the lobby, she paced back and forth nervously.

The baron calmly puffed a cigar, his usual urbane self. Minutes later, Jeff appeared and Lydia ran to him.

"What did you do?" she asked worriedly.

"I went to Drury's table and told him that if he made any further trouble for you, he'd answer not only to me, but to the police. He denied making any trouble for you."

"Did he sound convincing?" the baron asked.

"Yes, dammit. Otherwise I'd have invited him outside."

"Please, Jeff," Lydia pleaded. "I don't want any trouble. I'm going upstairs now to write to Mr. Morgan and try to explain this gossip item and the one that appeared in the American papers. In a way, I'm glad you believed Drury. I did, too, and though he seems the only one who would want to do me ill, I really feel sorry for him."

"I don't," Jeff said firmly. "Not one damn little bit. But let's forget Drury. I'll escort you upstairs."

"No need for that," she said.

"Oh, yes, there is," he said. "Or don't you remember?"

For an answer, Lydia blushed.

"Good night, Baron," Jeff said.

"Good night, my friend," the baron replied. His face bore a contented smile as he watched them start up the stairs.

Lydia unlocked her door and Jeff followed her inside. He closed it with his foot as he gathered her in his arms. She was as eager for the kiss as his arms closed about her and his lips sought hers.

Then, to her surprise, he released her.

"Why?" she asked in astonishment.

"So you can write your damn letter." He smiled tenderly at her, his eyes slightly mocking. "Good night."

He was out the door and had closed it before she could reply. She leaned against it and pressed her face against the wood panel, as if that would bring her closer to him.

She sighed wistfully as her hand, still holding the key, slipped it into the keyhole and turned the lock. Still weak from the thrill of that embrace, she tossed her evening bag on a chair and walked unsteadily to the desk. She got out a piece of paper, opened the inkwell and dipped the pen in it. She forgot to touch the tip of it to the side of the inkwell and a blot of ink smudged the page. She crumpled it, threw it in the wastebasket and got out another page. She closed her eyes and took a deep breath to steady herself and get her emotions under control.

It took a while, but when she dipped the pen in the inkwell the second time, she remembered to touch the tip to the sides and let the excess ink roll off. She started writing and, to her amazement, her hand was steady and her mind calm.

Yet, thoughts of Jeff never left her. She reveled in the knowledge that he loved her. Had he been playing a game with her, waiting for her to awaken to him, or had their enforced separation made him aware of his love for her? It was that separation that forced her to admit he was far more important than her career. She was deeply moved by the generous and thoughtful gesture he had made, leaving the suite after a good-night kiss so that she could write her letter. She knew that had he stayed, she'd never have denied him.

Eleven

Lydia spent a lot of time composing the explanatory letter to her editor and publisher. However, the next morning, before she could mail it, Angelina's knock sounded on the door. She entered, accompanied by a bellboy carrying a cablegram. After he left, Lydia excused herself and opened it with some anxiety, fearful that something else she was not aware of had been printed about her. Her face brightened with relief when she read it.

"My publisher is coming here, Angelina. Mr. Morgan is sailing today to help me clear up this terrible business. He's arriving next Tuesday. I'll want you to meet him as a representative of what's good about Monte. I hope Jeff will still be here."

"You do not think this gentleman—your—publisher—is coming because he is angry?"

Lydia sobered. "I never thought of that. I hope not. No, I mustn't entertain such a thought."

"I shall pray it is not so," Angelina said. "Will you attend the gala tonight?"

"The Prince of Wales!" Lydia exclaimed. "So much has been happening I forgot about it. Of course I'll go, but what will I wear? Help me pick out something that will do justice to a British prince."

Angelina said, "The ladies vie with one another for elaborate gowns with very daring décolletages. They know the prince has an eye for female charms."

"So I've heard," Lydia said thoughtfully. "There's a very beautiful and simple white satin gown that I haven't worn yet. It has a high décolletage, puffed ruffled sleeves and several rows of narrow ruffles which start at the hem and come halfway up the skirt."

"You are young, mademoiselle, with youthful beauty, true. But, as I told you, the other ladies will be wearing their most elaborate gowns, with very low décolletages."

Lydia gave Angelina a knowing look. "I will be different. Perhaps I won't even be noticed by the prince, but I won't be wearing something that says—you must look at me because my gown is both beautiful and daring."

Angelina nodded. "You are wise, mademoiselle. You will also be the most outstanding young lady there."

"I don't know about that. I do know the idea of going to an affair to vie with the other ladies for the prince's attention doesn't appeal to me."

"They want more than that, mademoiselle," Angelina said. "It is amazing—they are ladies. At least, they are considered such, but they throw themselves at his feet, offering themselves to him. He knows it and takes full advantage of it. Who can blame him?"

"Not me," Lydia said. "Jeff and the baron are meeting me for dinner. I'd better dress."

Lydia met them for their noonday meal in the hotel dining room. Both arose as she approached their table. Jeff had already ordered caviar for an appetizer, and Lydia spread some of it on a biscuit after she was seated.

"I'm not exactly thrilled with caviar," she admitted. "It reminds me of something I'd rather forget. This is all the Russians served at the so-called banquet I was invited to attend."

"I didn't think of that," Jeff apologized.

"Ach, caviar," the baron said softly, "it is not something to apologize for. When I eat it, I love the Russians."

Lydia changed the subject. "Jeff, there's a big affair tonight. A ball, honoring the Prince of Wales. He arrives today and I have no escort."

"Oh yes, you have," he replied archly. "I'll be honored to have you on my arm this evening, mademoiselle."

"And I," the baron added, "will take your other arm, if I may."

"Two handsome men," Lydia declared happily. "I'm charmed and very lucky."

"I am not the handsome one," the baron said, "but my rank permits me to wear a blue ribbon across my chest and so they will bow lower to me than to you, my friend Jeff."

"You're half right about that. They won't even bow to me. I'll be waiting at eight, Lydia, in the lobby."

"You'll have to do better than that, darling. I'm part of a delegation to welcome the prince at the railroad station. About a hundred of the more prominent people have been invited. I have arranged to have you two peasants be part of the reception committee."

Both Jeff and the baron looked pleased. "That should be enjoyable. Will it be full dress?"

"Indeed, yes. His train arrives half an hour before the ball begins. I'd hate to have to dress in thirty minutes. It's a very tight schedule this evening. He wants the ball tonight, and then, after that no further recognition while he amuses himself with the roulette ball and . . . other diversions."

Jeff nodded good-naturedly. "I know what you mean, but see that you're not someone tricked into his suite. Don't forget the Russians, my sweet."

"On that note," she said, "I'll leave you. I'll come down at seven."

Her serenity and gay mood was short-lived. Alone in her suite she began to develop a strange foreboding. There was no reason for it except that she believed this mysterious Armand Martel was ready to strike again. The excitement generated by the prince's visit would be a perfect time to harass her in some embarrassing way. She was still possessed of this uneasiness when Angelina came to help her dress.

"It's silly, I know," Lydia said, "but I can't help feeling that Martel is still here and waiting to cause me further trouble. And I don't even know why."

"I have continued to ask about him," Angelina said. "But no one has any knowledge of him. If he comes and goes, it is with stealth, not in the open."

"That's why I'm frightened. I don't know when he'll pop up. Jeff and the baron can't always be with me and I have a feeling Martel will be aware of the times when I'm alone."

"You might persuade your editor to send you somewhere else," Angelina said. "I would miss you, but if you are in danger, I don't want you here."

"Angelina, I'm staying until I find out what or who is behind this. I won't leave now—or even later if I find the answer. I love Monte. It's almost like home to me now, and despite what has happened, I enjoy my work here. Also, I met Jeffrey Marcus."

Angelina nodded. "Which almost makes it worth what you went through. I am pleased you will stay. Now I must get your bath ready. It is almost three and we have much to do."

A beautiful nosegay of pink rosebuds nestling in lace arrived with a card from Jeff. Angelina examined it carefully and concluded it really did come from him. At the appointed time, she dressed Lydia's hair simply, drawing it up leaving it free of ornament and so that the curly ends brushed her shoulders with artless grace. Around her neck would be only a choker of delicate seed pearls. Then Angelina helped Lydia into her gown and handed her the above-the-elbow-length gloves. After she slipped them on, she held out a small fan of white feathers.

"You must have something in your hand, mademoiselle."

"I shall carry only the nosegay." Lydia picked it up and regarded it lovingly. "Just looking at it makes my heartbeat quicken."

"Ah, yes," Angelina agreed. "Love does something beautiful to us."

"Are you in love?" Lydia switched her glance to the young girl standing opposite her.

"I was. He was killed. I grieved, but now I am over it. So in time, I will love again, but it will never be like before. That only comes once to each of us. You have it now. I am very happy for you."

"Thank you, Angelina," Lydia said. "I hope your new love will come soon."

"So do I while I am still young. I want children. Do you, mademoiselle?"

Lydia exclaimed aloud at the idea. "How strange it is that I never thought of that before. Of course I do. And Angelina, while I am thinking of it, thank you for being here. You've helped me more than you know."

"Perhaps you were too busy making a living for yourself to have time to daydream," Angelina said wisely.

Lydia pressed the nosegay against her heart as she spoke. "I was. Lonely and frightened, though I never admitted it to anyone. Now I'm in love and I feel brave and strong. Or am I talking foolishness?"

"Always remember, mademoiselle, there is nothing foolish about love. You look like a very young girl."

"Despite how I look, I feel like a woman who knows she is loved and who loves in return."

Angelina accompanied Lydia to the door and held it open for her. "Have a happy evening, mademoiselle. I will not worry about you this evening since you will be with your Monsieur Jeff."

"And the baron," Lydia reminded her.

"Of course—the baron." Angelina gave a gentle shrug of her shoulders. "He keeps life interesting around here. Don't you agree?"

"I do, Angelina. Good night."

When she emerged from the lift, Jeff and the baron were there. Jeff made an impressive picture in formal dress, as did the baron, with his blue ribbon across his chest. He looked both proud and dignified, and so regal was his manner that one never noticed his lack of stature. They both complimented Lydia on her appearance and led her out to a row of carriages waiting to take the large party to the railroad station. Lydia held up the nosegay for Jeff to admire and thanked him for it.

"You look radiant," he said, his eyes seeming to drink her in.

"Thank you, darling," she replied. "I must confess though, that inside I'm a little uneasy."

"About Martel?"

"How did you guess?"

"It's natural," Jeff said. "Just remember I'll be at your side. Anyway, I think the prince is in far greater danger than you."

Lydia forgot her own uneasiness. "Good heavens, why?"

"Every time a person of rank or distinction moves about, there's apprehension. The world is full of weird individuals. All important personages have to be protected. It's a sad commentary on human nature, but that's how it is."

They climbed into a landau and soon arrived at the station, where a large group had already gathered, more arriving with each carriage. Lydia, Jeff and the baron casually mingled with the elite of Monte, for they knew most of them. The talk was mainly about the prince, with whispered suggestions as to whom he would favor this time. A few names were mentioned, along with raised eyebrows. Lydia ignored such gossip. The prince was an important, respected and well-liked gentleman and she intended to treat her reports on him in that manner.

It was a balmy evening, though rather dark, for there was no moon over the harbor and few stars in the sky. The chattering ceased temporarily when the sound of an oncoming engine became plain. Then it resumed again, to taper off as the special, finely appointed cars ground to a stop on the rails. The prince's servants and followers left the train first and, finally, the prince himself appeared. He cut a fine figure, though Lydia heard a murmured comment that he was inclined to be a bit stouter than the last time he had visited Monte. She watched as he removed the inevitable cigar from his mouth, raised his derby and shouted a greeting.

Lydia and Jeff moved closer, the baron tagging behind, delayed by a member of the greeting party who elbowed him aside. The lights from the cars cast a dull glow on the crowd, but there was sufficient light for Lydia to see a man furtively slip into the fringes of the crowd. For a second she thought he looked like Martel, though she only had the barest of glimpses.

"What's wrong?" Jeff asked.

"I thought . . . Martel . . . "

Jeff turned quickly, his eyes searching for a sight of any furtive movement. Lydia saw the man emerge again, his features cold and tight with hatred. She grasped Jeff's arm, turning him in the direction of the man. Suddenly Martel, who had apparently crouched down, stood up. Jeff, without hesitation, promptly threw himself upon Lydia and dragged her to the ground as two shots rang out.

Someone screamed in pain. Someone else shouted, "Assassin!" Out of the gloom a dozen men emerged, not of the greeting party. They closed in on the prince and bodily shoved him back into the car. Others began moving through the crowd.

Jeff helped Lydia to her feet and looked around. "The baron's coming this way. I'll be right back."

He pushed his way through the excited crowd, gradually approaching the train. The baron reached Lydia's side.

"What happened? I was in a crush back there. I couldn't see anything."

"Martel," she said breathlessly. "I saw him. Be careful, he may still be close by."

"Martel! After the prince?"

"I don't know, but the way Jeff sent me to the ground, I think he felt Martel was after me. I can't be sure, of course. I have no reason to think he was trying to assassinate the prince, but then I have no reason to think he'd try to shoot me, either."

"There were a large number of plainclothesmen around

the station. Maybe they got him.''

''That would be the best news I've ever heard, but I wouldn't count on it. He was close to the edge of the crowd and probably ran off in the darkness before any kind of search could be organized.''

''If you even catch a glimpse of the man, you had better get down.''

''If I promptly fall to the ground, you'll know I did. No, he wouldn't stay around now. Too risky for him. If he's caught, it will go mighty hard on him and he knows that. Look, Baron,'' Lydia pointed to one of the cars, ''Jeff's coming out of the prince's car. What's he doing in there? I shouldn't think they'd let anybody inside.''

''Jeff has a way with him,'' the baron reasoned. ''I gather he knows his way around.''

Jeff spotted them and came to their side. The crowd was beginning to return to the carriages as Jeff took Lydia's arm and led her to a landau, set apart for him at the place where the others waited. As they neared it, two men standing at the rear of the vehicle moved away, mixing with the few stragglers still evident. Jeff helped her aboard and climbed in beside her. The baron ran around to enter from the other side.

Jeff said, ''A woman was struck by one of the bullets, but she doesn't seem to be badly wounded. A second bullet hit the side of the car.''

''Martel must be insane,'' Lydia said. ''To try and kill the Prince of Wales!''

''Darling, the prince stood near the steps of his car. The woman who was wounded stood a few yards beyond us. The bullet hitting the car penetrated it in a straight line with the wounded woman. A straight line—with you. He had a clear shot at you. That attempt was not aimed at the prince, though it's going to be said that it was. So please say nothing about the truth of this matter. Don't discuss the incident with anyone, or write a word about it. The attempt was on your life. Martel was close. I pulled you down just in time.''

Lydia looked at him in fear and amazement. ''Are you

certain he was aiming at me?''

"I'd say so, from the location of the wounded woman and the bullet hole in the car. He surely wasn't aiming at the prince, for he stood ten feet to the left of where the bullets hit. That was an attempt on your life, my dear. If it succeeded, it would have been said you were an innocent victim in the attempted assassination of the Prince of Wales.''

"I feel faint,'' Lydia said. "I'm frightened, Jeff. I'm beginning to shake.''

His arms enfolded her, and he held her close. "I can't say I blame you, but you're safe now.''

"Brandy is good for that,'' the baron said. He removed a silver flask from an inner pocket and handed it to Lydia. "This always works. Gives me courage. It's false, but after a few nips, I don't know the difference. Please take a drink, Lydia. I'm going to have one, too. I guess I am as frightened as you.''

"The baron's right, Lydia,'' Jeff urged. "Take a few sips. It'll relax you, take away your fear.''

Lydia obeyed, bracing a little as the fiery liquid went down.

"I'll see you to your suite,'' Jeff said.

"You'll do no such thing,'' she said firmly. "We're going to the ball, and what's more, we're going to enjoy every moment of it.''

Jeff studied her carefully. "Are you certain you want to? I know Martel got away. He could try again.''

"I'm not so shaken I'm afraid to go to the ball. I guess the brandy works as well as you claim it does, Baron. Anyway, I feel better and I've lost my fear.''

Jeff thought a moment, then said, "You'll probably be as safe there as anywhere. Your gown is a little soiled, though. Sorry I had to throw you to the ground.''

Lydia kissed his cheek. "Don't apologize for saving my life. As for the gown, it's mute testimony that the prince's arrival was fraught with melodrama. Besides, I'll get a story out of this evening. An important one. And there's something more.''

"I'm not certain I can stand many more surprises," Jeff said.

"The publisher of my newspaper, Mr. George Morgan, is on his way here from New York. I'm not certain how he'll regard this situation, but he's not going to find me locked in my suite because of fear of Martel."

"I love you," Jeff said and planted a kiss on her brow.

"Can you not do better than that?" the baron asked mildly, after having taken another generous swallow of brandy from his flask.

"Yes," Jeff replied, "if you'll only turn your head the other way."

The baron obeyed and Jeff gave Lydia a long, lingering kiss. This time she pushed him away.

"I'll let that do me until the end of the evening," she said tremulously.

The brief journey finished, the baron hopped out and walked around the carriage while Jeff helped Lydia down. She took his arm and squeezed it gently.

"Besides," she whispered before the baron joined them, "why should I be scared? Not with you wearing a gun under your arm, darling. I saw it when you pulled me down to the ground."

"Uh . . . yes," he said, as if he was slightly embarrassed.

"Are you sure you won't get into trouble? I believe there's a law against carrying a gun here."

"I've a police permit," he explained. "Sometimes in my work I have to go into unsavory places. I wore it tonight, just in case. I had the same vague feeling as you did."

"What's the whispering all about?" the baron asked as he joined them. "You look like conspirators."

"We were talking about Martel," Lydia said, "wondering if he might take a chance and come to the ball."

The baron shuddered. "I'll have to refill my flask," he said.

The so-called assassination attempt on the prince was on the tongues of everyone, but nevertheless the dancing had begun at the ballroom of the Metropole. It was, in every respect, the major ball of the season and not even an attempt to kill the prince was going to stop it. Even he was inflexible on that score.

The room was always richly decorated, but for this event, there were added touches, with British flags the main motif. They seemed to be everywhere. There was even a throne set up on a small, raised platform where the prince would sit if he ever wished to during the festivities. He was known to take an active part in any kind of blithesome assembly, and this would be no exception.

An orchestra, hidden behind palms and live orange trees, played popular music. The dancing had already begun and Jeff swept Lydia out onto the floor.

"You dance well," she complimented him.

"With you it's easy. Tell me, did you really see Martel? I mean, did you recognize him? You're certain?"

"I'm certain. You saw him, too."

"I saw the man you indicated. I never saw Martel before."

"I'm sorry. I forgot that. Yes, it was Martel. I saw him twice."

"The police are searching every inch of this place. If he hasn't managed to escape by sea, they'll find him. The roads are blocked and the border heavily patrolled. Yet he could have reached the harbor and got away in a boat waiting there for him."

"Jeff, my darling, I appreciate your trying to reassure me and it helps, but I'll be damned if I'm going to let Martel spoil another evening for us. We can talk about trouble later. Right now let's just pretend there is no Armand Martel."

"A fine idea. I understand there's a lavish banquet later on. I'm certainly ready for it."

"Despite what happened at the depot, everyone's jovial," Lydia said. "It's like a dream. Beautiful ladies, gorgeous gowns, handsome escorts and laughter and gaiety to go with it." She paused and missed a step.

"What is it?" Jeff asked, sensing her change of mood.

"I just thought of that woman who was wounded. Is there any way you could inquire as to her condition? It doesn't seem right for us to be enjoying ourselves."

"I'm sure she wouldn't want you to put on a long face. This is the prince's evening. If you were the one who'd been wounded, would you have wanted the festivities to be canceled?"

"No," Lydia admitted. "Yet I still can't help thinking about her."

"I'm thinking of her, too, and since the baron is eyeing us both, I believe he wants to dance with you. It'll give me an opportunity to check on her. I know you'll also include that in your article."

"You mean you don't mind my writing it?"

"You'd do it anyway," Jeff replied good-naturedly. "Just let it be the prince who was supposed to be the target of the assassin's bullets."

Jeff turned Lydia over to the baron who promptly whisked her onto the dance floor. But his mood was anything but light.

"You look worried, Baron."

"I am. Since that gunman wasn't caught, he might very well be in this ballroom."

"True. But Jeff and I decided we're going to enjoy ourselves. I'm surprised you can't."

"Probably I could if I weren't so concerned about you," he grumbled.

"Baron, if you don't start smiling and dancing with the grace you've always shown, I'm going to leave you in the middle of the floor."

"Oh, all right. I suppose that assassin must be scared, too, and has run off."

"Do you think the prince will ask to dance with me?" Lydia asked the question more to get the baron's mind off what had happened rather than because of any particular longing on her part.

It worked because the baron chuckled. "If he doesn't, he's an idiot. And I assure you, my dear, *that* he is not."

The dance ended just as the prince appeared. The baron and Lydia stepped to the edge of the dance floor where Jeff joined them. All conversation ceased and everyone stood in respectful attention. The prince cut a dashing figure in his Highland kilts, his medals pinned across his chest. He was an imposing man and every eye in the room was on him.

He danced first with Her Serene Highness, the wife of the ruler of Monaco, then with a few other ladies. Lydia stood between Jeff and the baron and was taking mental notes of the dancing partners of the prince. He suddenly looked directly at Lydia, gave her a smile and a brief nod. He returned his dancing partner to the gentleman who accompanied her and came directly over to Lydia. She curtsied, Jeff bowed and the baron made an eloquent bow.

The prince laid a hand on Jeff's shoulder. "It is good to see you again, my friend."

Jeff bowed and said merely, "Your Highness."

The prince moved to Lydia and extended an arm, and she placed her hand on it as they moved onto the dance floor. He said, "You are the loveliest young lady in the room. You have an innocent charm about you."

"Thank you, Your Highness," she replied. "And thank you for not complimenting me on my gown, which is soiled."

"Could it be that happened at the railroad station?"

"It did," she replied smiling. "My escort, whom you seem to know, feared I was in line with the assassin's bullet. I'm pleased you escaped his madness."

"Thank you," the prince replied. "May I compliment you on your choice of escorts?"

"Are you referring to the baron?" Lydia asked.

"The baron?" The prince looked puzzled for a moment, then he chuckled. "Yes, of course. The baron."

He guided her into some intricate steps to which she adapted well. "You are the journalist from America," he said. "The one who . . . " he laughed aloud, "wrote about the kaiser's imposter coming here to lose money at the wheel. It was a marvelous story. I had a jolly good laugh over it. I'm still amused by it."

"Your Highness," she asked, "would you happen to know how the kaiser felt about that story?"

"No, I wouldn't, and if I met him today, I wouldn't dare ask. Willie has a temper."

"I hope I didn't offend him, Your Highness."

"That's easily done, my dear. Those of us who know him enjoyed what you did. However, a word of advice, don't go to Berlin for a few months at least." He chuckled.

"I won't, Your Highness."

He guided her back to where Jeff waited. The baron was already dancing with a rather imperious-looking woman who had been won over by the blue ribbon across his chest.

Lydia curtsied again as the prince sought out other youthful partners. She then glanced at Jeff, who was regarding her speculatively.

"Jealous?" she teased.

"About him? No. No, I wouldn't say so. That dance was a command. It would be childish to resent that."

"And you can't resent the fact that the prince seems to know you. He all but embraced you."

"You have a fertile imagination, my dear. I saw him right after the shooting because I wanted to be sure he had not been hit."

"So after an attempt on his life, as everyone believed, they let you board his car? Jeff . . . please."

"Darling, I told you before, you must trust me."

"I do. That is, to a limited extent. It's just that some of the things you do sorely puzzle me."

Jeff said, "You asked me to inquire about the condition of the woman who was wounded at the station."

"How is she, Jeff?" Lydia asked solicitously.

"The wound isn't serious. She'll recover."

"Thank God," Lydia said.

"As for us," Jeff said, "I admit I haven't been open

with you as regards myself. However, you believe me when I say I love you, don't you?"

"With all my heart."

"Then trust me."

"All right. I won't ask you again what you do or who you really are."

A smile widened Jeff's mouth. "Good. Now let's enjoy the evening. They're beginning to line up for the grand march and, I might add, there's a new French chef brought in for the occasion. His name is Auguste Escoffier and I understand there's none better, so be prepared to indulge yourself."

They joined the grand march as the music began. The prince and Her Serene Highness, the princess of Monaco, led the march, followed by the more important dignitaries, with Lydia and Jeff winding up near the middle. The baron, by dint of his blue ribbon, was well up front.

The dining room, as usual, was decorated to suit the taste of the British prince, with the emphasis on India. The waiters were dressed in uniforms much like those of the Bengal Lancers, with helmets, epaulettes and shiny boots.

The prince made a brief speech, expressing his gratitude for the effort extended to make his welcome outstanding. Then a banquet of many courses began. The food was based on that of India, and was spicy, but the French chef was wise enough not to overdo the condiments.

Oysters under a savory sauce were served first, then a baked fish course, followed by one featuring lamb and finally beef encased in a thick piecrust. The meat was very rare.

"Is it cooked enough for you?" Lydia asked.

Jeff nodded doubtfully. "I think it might respond to a stethoscope, but I'll manage."

Wine in thin glasses changed with each course. Brandy came with the dessert—a hot soufflé laced with orange liqueur. Each course was served and eaten in leisurely fashion so that it took up most of the evening that remained after the dancing. The ball, however, would continue. As coffee was served, a man in a business suit entered the room and looked about. For a moment Lydia thought he was coming over to talk to her, but he bent to whisper in Jeff's ear instead.

Lydia saw Jeff stiffen and his face assume a startled look that quickly turned grim.

"Thanks," he told the newcomer, who promptly left. To obtain permission to enter this banquet hall dressed as he was meant the man was someone of importance, probably someone of authority with an urgent message, Lydia deduced.

Jeff took a sip of coffee before he turned to her. "We're going to leave the room quietly. Something has happened and we're both needed."

They walked very quietly out of the banquet hall, followed by the baron's astonished stare. Since he wasn't asked, he didn't follow. The orchestra was tuning up for the second part of the ball, but Jeff led Lydia directly to the lobby where two men awaited them.

"What is it?" Lydia asked impatiently. "Jeff, please tell me."

"First get in the carriage," he said. "There's one waiting."

They were escorted to the street, and Jeff helped Lydia into the vehicle, which promptly drove off, followed by another containing the two men who had waited for them.

Jeff said, "The news is both good and bad. They just discovered what they think is Armand Martel's body. They are asking you to identify it. Are you up to that, darling?"

"I . . . suppose so. Yes, of course I am. Oh, my God, what next? How did he die?"

"The police are not positive it's Martel, though they're reasonably certain the man answers the description you gave me. He was discovered hanging from the limb of a tree."

"He made me no end of trouble, but to take his own life! He must have been convinced that he could never get out of Monaco."

"First, let's make sure it's Martel. They're waiting for

us in that little park just east of the palace. This may be a bit rough."

"I'll manage," she assured him, though she was wondering if she really could. Jeff took her hand and gripped it tightly.

The carriage turned up a steep street. At the top of it, the driver turned off and drove up to a grove of trees where the light of several lanterns marked the area in which a group of men were waiting.

Jeff helped her down, took her arm and led her to the spot. She saw a length of rope dangling from a high limb. Below it someone had covered the body with a blanket.

Jeff introduced her to a rather stout but powerful-looking man. "This is Inspector Fontaine of the Monaco police. Inspector, I have the honor to present Miss Lydia Bradley."

"An honor, mademoiselle." The inspector lifted his hat and bowed. "I am sorry to put you through this, but it is necessary."

"What are the details?" Jeff asked. "We were told nothing more than to come here at once to identify, if possible, the body of a man described to me by Miss Bradley."

"A couple, perhaps bent on romance, came upon the scene. I am afraid their thoughts of romance faded. The girl fainted, but the man kept his head. The body was not quite cold. We estimate he had been dead for two or three hours . . . very soon after that nasty business at the railroad station. A doctor will tell us better. We cut him down, monsieur. Now, if you please, mademoiselle . . . ."

He led her to the form under the blanket. Jeff grasped her elbow as the blanket was pulled away from the dead man's head and shoulders. Lydia didn't turn away. She asked that a lantern be brought closer. When it was, she straightened up.

"That is the man I knew as Armand Martel. I'm positive."

"*Merci*, mademoiselle."

She glanced up at the high branch. "How did he manage to tie the rope up there?" she asked.

"We are not sure, of course," the inspector said. "But it seems he must have managed to climb up the tree trunk, go out on that branch somehow, tie the rope and then . . . poof!"

"Just a minute," Jeff said. He knelt beside the body, grasped the dead man's head and twisted it rather sharply. Then he arose and covered the body.

"Inspector, if he climbed up to the limb, put the noose around his neck and jumped, the distance would make it certain his neck would have been broken. He dropped through about fifteen feet of space. His neck is not broken. By the color of his face I'd say he strangled to death."

"We must be very certain of that, Monsieur Marcus."

"Maybe we can be. Lydia, I'm going to uncover him completely. You may turn away if you wish."

She nodded, but didn't change her position.

Jeff first examined the dead man's clothing, paying special attention to the fabric at the knees and elbows. Then he reached for one of the lanterns, held it very close to the dead man's hands and examined the fingers intently. He threw the blanket over the body again.

"If he climbed that tree, he had to shimmy up most of the way. The bark would have stained or, at least, dirtied his clothes, or pulled threads in the fabric. His hands would be scratched, there'd be slivers of bark under his nails. I find none of this."

"Murder then?" the inspector asked. "You understand, monsieur, that we did not examine the body and these facts would have been discovered in due time."

"It would be well to search the area around this tree, Inspector. This is not suicide. It's murder."

Jeff led Lydia to the carriage and they were driven back to the brighter and livelier parts of Monte Carlo.

Lydia said, "I don't want to return to the ball. I hope you don't mind."

"I'm sorry you had to be put through that, Lydia." His tone was full of tender concern.

"It was unsettling, but necessary. I'm just glad it's over.

215

Tell me, though, are you connected with the police?'' Her eyes sought his.

"No," he said flatly. "However, the Monaco police know me so I'm able to get about better than most. I assure you, darling, that I don't carry a Monaco police badge."

"I'll take your word for it. Now I'm wondering what kind of a news report I can make of this."

"Not a very comprehensive one," Jeff said. "The police won't be releasing any information for a while. I suggest you treat it with less importance than it deserves. If it turns sensational, you can build it up later on."

"I'll do my best," she said. "I don't want it to sound like a suicide, either. The casino wouldn't like that."

They dismissed the carriage, but instead of entering the hotel, turned down the street in the direction of the harbor.

Jeff said, "I suggest a walk."

"Thanks," Lydia said gratefully. "I don't want to be alone quite yet."

"I don't want you to be."

"Jeff, I realize how hard it is to answer this question, but do you think anyone is going to take up where Martel left off?"

"It's possible. He may have done his work and they got rid of him before he caused complications."

"You said 'they.' Who are 'they'?"

"I haven't the slightest idea, but it seems to me that Martel wasn't murdered for the sport of it. Perhaps he bungled something. In fact, I'd say he bungled the entire Russian affair. Since he had no apparent reason for carrying on this campaign against you, there must be someone behind him—and that may be why he was killed. He knew too much. And the police were looking for him."

"Then I'm in as much—or more—danger than before?"

"I'd consider that a strong possibility. It should make you doubly careful."

"I still ask myself why. I can't think of anyone I've seriously hurt by my writing. Surely not enough to harass me this way. I may have ruffled a few feathers, but that

216

doesn't lead to what have certainly been attempts to destroy me. I still believe Drury has something to do with it, for he's the one person in the world whom I know hates me. And with good reason, from his point of view."

"Be on guard," Jeff warned. "Be doubly cautious not to be alone with him if he should seek you out."

"He hasn't come near me since that first encounter I told you about. Even then, his manner wasn't threatening, though it wasn't friendly either."

"I still consider him a man to be wary of."

"You sound as if you'll soon be leaving again."

"I will. That's why I'm so worried about your safety."

She pointed to a bench that sat a few feet from the walk and had a clear view of the harbor. "Let's sit there. The lights from the yachts give it a fairyland appearance—it takes my mind off danger."

Jeff dusted off the bench with his handkerchief and they sat down. He reached for her hand, removed the glove and kissed each fingertip.

Lydia said, "When will you go?"

"In the morning. I hate to, but it's necessary."

"I know that. Just as I now know your work is important and dangerous."

"Be assured, my love, I'll return as soon as possible."

She rested her head on his shoulder. "Wouldn't it be pleasant if there'd been no Martel, no Drury—just you and me sitting here looking at the stars and the lights blinking on the yachts?"

Jeff kissed her brow. "I suppose I could weigh that against the fact that if there'd been no Drury, you might never have come here and I'd never have known there was a Lydia Bradley in this world. That's a wretched thought."

"And I'd never have known there was a Jeffrey Marcus," she realized. "You're right, my dearest. I'm not going to think I'm in danger. I have a feeling that whoever killed Martel will remain in hiding for awhile. Especially since Martel's body was found so quickly."

"I'd like to say I agree if for no other reason than to give you reassurance," Jeff replied soberly, "but I can't. You could be in danger, and you must be on guard every moment. In fact, the danger might be greater now. These murderers—whoever they are—might have access to the information the police possess. Or know of a way of getting such information."

"How?" Her voice revealed her concern.

"Bribes, my dear," he said. "I hope it isn't possible, but you must guard against any possibility."

"I will," she said quietly. "And hurry back to me, my darling."

He nodded and urged her to her feet. His hands enclosed her waist, turning her toward him. He shifted his position so that he faced her, then drew her close.

"My lovely Lydia," he said quietly before his lips closed on hers. "My lovely, lovely Lydia."

Twelve

Lydia wrote in detail about the attempted assassination of the Prince of Wales by an unknown assailant. It was a story that would immediately grip the reader, for the setting itself was glamorous: the railroad station gaily decorated for the prince's arrival; the ladies and gentlemen in formal dress, their excited chatter and merriment as they waited for the train to pull in; the sudden silence after it did as they took positions facing the exit of the car in which Edward, the Prince of Wales, rode. Then his appearance, followed by shots and the screams of startled onlookers.

Lydia had found it necessary to question the baron about the attempted assassination, for Jeff had forced her to the ground to avoid bullets that he firmly believed had been meant for her. If she hadn't been subjected to prior harassment, she'd have thought it ridiculous that the assassin had meant her to be the target rather than the prince.

Because of the exhausting events of that day, Jeff had parted from her at her hotel door, and he left Monte the following morning. For three more days Lydia's work became routine. She didn't allow herself to dwell on Martel's murder nor that she might still be in danger. Monte Carlo was filled with tourists and she turned her attention to hunting down stories about them.

They came more easily than she had hoped for. One Hungarian duke lost everything in the space of twenty-four hours, and the management graciously provided him with a railroad ticket and sufficient funds to return home. His sad plight made good copy.

A baroness whose husband had, over many years, lost a million or more at the tables, came back to Monte as a widow, with very little money, no recriminations over her husband going broke, and a sincere love for the place. Lydia found a unique story there, especially when the management presented the baroness with a small but lovely villa and placed her on a pension for the rest of her life. She discovered this wasn't the first time the casino had taken care of those who loved Monte Carlo. There were several widows living there who had no means beyond that which the casino cheerfully granted them.

Even the baron was a fine example of that. His rent on his tiny apartment was partially paid by the casino because the baron, in his own inimitable way, lent both glamour and local color to the casino and the hotels. He was a genuine baron, a relation of royalty, and often assigned to devote his time and charm to ladies without escorts.

Monte Carlo, she had long ago learned, was not a place where visitors were systematically parted from their money in a heartless, strictly commercial way. And no one wept when the casino lost heavily to some lucky gambler.

In the time she'd been at Monte she'd acquired an affection for this small piece of land. That was one reason she was apprehensive about the arrival of George Morgan, her publisher. He'd been extremely kind and generous, trusting too, in giving a beginner like her such an important assignment. If he learned of her troubles, he might revoke this post and send her elsewhere. She expressed her concern on this point to the baron as they stood on the railroad platform waiting for the train on which Mr. Morgan was a passenger.

"Why worry," the baron scoffed. "You have done nothing to deserve such treatment. What happened was not of your doing. And as for Monte, there was no necessity for you to write about that murder. The police have not even reported it as murder."

"The story of Martel's death will come out one of these days," Lydia said. "Certainly, my paper will want to know why I didn't reveal what I knew. If I could only tell the story now, I'd have nothing to explain later."

"Why the police don't want it known, I have no idea. But Jeff's concern is my concern and he asked me to look after you. I will not let him down. Do you love him?"

"You know I do," Lydia said emphatically.

"Then you cannot betray him. No matter who is your employer. No matter that you are keeping information from your paper regarding what happened yesterday. I mean, of course, the fact that Martel was murdered after he tried to kill you."

Lydia nodded agreement, touched by the baron's stern manner of speaking. It was evident that he took his responsibility seriously.

"Tell me, my dear, what is this very important publisher like?"

"Other than being important I don't know too much about him. However, he's responsible for my getting this assignment. He'd just returned to the States after a visit to Monte. His sending me here was done on a whim, I believe. Perhaps he never expected I'd be able to handle it. Certainly, I was as green as grass."

The baron eyed her proudly. "You are not green as grass now."

"You deserve much of the credit," Lydia assured him.

"No," he refuted. "If you hadn't had the talent for knowing a story and then searching out the details, and learning all you could about the people involved, the help I gave you would have no meaning. Besides, you write in an entertaining fashion."

"Thank you, Baron."

"I will tell your publisher how hard you have worked since you came here."

"Please don't," Lydia pleaded. "If he thinks I deserve praise, he'll give it."

"Good. In that case you may let him know how I helped

you. A good word spoken for me here and there doesn't hurt.''

Lydia repressed a smile. ''I'll do that. Also, I'll tell him that it was Regina's photographs that were of such help to the articles.''

''And you might add she is a friend,'' he cleared his throat, ''of mine.''

''He will be told everything.''

''Not *everything*,'' the baron protested strongly. ''After all, I am a member of royalty. Regina is a commoner.''

''Of course, Baron. I'll be discreet.''

''Thank you. Regina has sold several pictures of the kaiser for very good prices. And she is careful to print on the back of each photograph that the man is an impostor, but a perfect likeness of the kaiser.''

Lydia changed the subject. ''Mr. Morgan promised, in a letter, to investigate Drury's claim that he was in Monte Carlo to write a book. I hope it's true. Drury is qualified to do a book on almost anything. He's a good writer and he's been just about everywhere.''

''I don't care how brilliant he is, I do not like him and I do not know how you can speak well of him.''

''I don't have to like him to respect his ability as a reporter. He's brilliant. A pity it went to his head.''

''It went to yours, too, my dear,'' the baron reminded her, ''but you came to your senses in time.''

''Thanks to you—and Angelina,'' Lydia replied without rancor. ''I hope I recognize Mr. Morgan. I doubt he'll remember me.''

The baron regarded her comely features and smiled. ''I guarantee he will. I have never seen you so uneasy.''

''I'm worried. He might have come here to tell me my services are no longer needed.''

The baron chuckled. ''If so, he'll take one look at you and reinstate you. Your walking dress is quite fetching. And so are you, so stop worrying.''

The noise of the train's arrival broke off further conversation. Lydia looked about, sure that she scarcely remembered George Morgan. She'd seen him only those few times and that had been almost a year ago. It seemed incredible that the months could pass so quickly.

But she recognized Morgan instantly, a tall, older man with military bearing and a hearty manner. For the second time she was reminded of her father who had believed in her abilities and encouraged her so long ago. For an instant she wished it were he approaching her now, and her eyes moistened. Then Morgan saw her and waved. His features brightened in a smile as he walked with long strides to embrace her, and hold her at arm's length while he regarded her critically.

"As lovely as ever," he exclaimed. "What keeps you looking so well?"

"Monaco," she replied promptly. "It's like having a window on the world. Every type imaginable comes here."

"Your stories are making it sound attractive to the rest of the world. And this gentleman must be the famous baron you write about."

"Baron Maxfried Hetzler," Lydia said with a smile. "He's been of immeasurable help to me."

"How did you guess who I was, sir?" the baron asked curiously.

"It was no guess," Morgan replied. "Lydia described you perfectly in her articles. Even to your regal carriage."

The baron beamed and rewarded Lydia with a grateful smile. He knew well what she'd written, but to have Morgan comment on it raised his already cheerful spirits.

The two men shook hands. Morgan seemed a little older to Lydia, but he was certainly aggressive and forceful. The baron thought so too, from the way he grimaced as his hand was squeezed in a hard handshake.

"I'll be here a day or two only," Morgan said briskly. "Long enough to talk to you and apprise the situation and . . . to lose a couple of thousand gambling. Baron, do you know any systems bound to win?"

"If I did, sir," the baron said, "I'd own half of Monte by now. There is no system, Mr. Morgan, but I might be able to see that you do not lose too much."

"That will be very helpful. Now, Lydia, where can we go to talk? A long talk. I've a great deal to say and you must have ten times as much."

"I will be at the casino this evening, Mr. Morgan," the baron said. "Please excuse me now. I will leave Lydia in your care."

Morgan watched him walk away. "Astute little fellow. I like him. Is he really a baron?"

"Yes, sir, he really is. But not in favor with the emperor of Austria, who is a relative. The baron lives here permanently on a frugal pension. He's a compulsive gambler but with little with which to gamble. However, he knows everybody and at Monte has entrée everywhere."

Mr. Morgan informed Lydia he'd already made arrangements for his baggage to be picked up at the station. They then took a carriage to the Café de Paris, where they were provided with a secluded table. Morgan ordered champagne and a light lunch for himself; Lydia had dined earlier so she settled for a glass of champagne. Morgan lifted his goblet in a toast.

"To you, my dear Lydia, who have been instrumental in further raising the circulation of, and interest in, our newspaper. We consider you highly successful and we're proud of you."

"Thank you. I'm grateful also for your having given me the opportunity—one which is usually given only to reporters with experience."

"As I've already told you, I'm a gambler. With you, I bet on a sure thing. You did well, right from the start. I had a hunch you would."

"That's good news." Lydia sat back in relief. "I want to credit the baron with a great deal of help."

"So you told us in your letters," Mr. Morgan said smiling. "He seems to have taken you under his wing."

"Even more so since the attempt on the life of the Prince of Wales."

"That was a nasty business," Mr. Morgan said.

224

"I already sent an article about it. I was at the station when it happened."

"Not in any danger, I hope," Mr. Morgan said. "I know one woman was wounded."

"Fortunately, she'll recover. I was with the baron and a Mr. Jeffrey Marcus. I don't suppose you're acquainted with him?"

"No, but from the expression on your face, I gather he's more than a casual acquaintance."

"Yes. He's appointed the baron a sort of guardian. Since that business at the railroad station, Jeff doesn't like me to be alone any more than necessary. But I doubt I'm in any danger."

"I hope not. I'd feel responsible if anything happened to you since this assignment was my idea. Oh, another thing. This Armand Martel whom you wrote us about, asking for information concerning him—were you able to locate him?"

"No. But the police did. He was found hanging from a tree."

"I saw nothing in the paper about it," Morgan said, startled.

"So far, the police insist on keeping it quiet. I identified him as the man who gave me the false information on the Arabian prince. Also, as the one who fired the shots at the station. No one knew him. He wasn't seen in public. I seem to have been the only one who knew of his existence."

Morgan's eyes revealed his puzzlement. "I'm not sure I follow you. In fact, I don't know what you're talking about."

"Of course you don't. So I'll tell you, although you may fire me just as you did Bryant Drury after you hear the story."

She went into detail, beginning with finding that Armand Martel was her dinner companion at a banquet given by an Arabian prince. She told how Martel had identified himself as an equerry of the prince and had dropped hints regarding his unsavory character and his cruelty to his subjects. She

225

told of seeking him out later and ferreting out more information regarding the prince. George Morgan listened in silence until she completed the story, including the fact that she had neglected to check on the accuracy of the story regarding the prince. She revealed that not until after she had sent the cablegram regarding him did she learn her facts were not only incorrect but they'd done the prince a grave injustice.

"So Martel was no part of the prince's entourage."

"He was not. Thank God, you never received the cablegram."

Morgan frowned. "I agree, though it's the first time I've known of a cablegram that was sent but not received. It smacks of a conspiracy."

"That's what Jeff—my friend—said. Yet who would wish all this trouble on me?"

"That's easy. Bryant Drury."

"I don't think he'd go to such extremes. Besides, he denied he had anything to do with it."

"You're referring to that business with the Russian aristocracy?"

"There was more. The night I went to the banquet for the Arabian prince, I received a bouquet of flowers, along with a corsage that I tucked into my waist. The corsage was made of carnations.

"What have carnations to do with this?"

"They're not grown here, nor are they allowed in the casino. They're considered bad luck, a gamblers' superstition, of course. But certainly a prince who gambles regularly at Monte would know of that. Obviously, it was done to embarrass me, and it did. I talked to Drury about it and he denied everything, insisting he was here merely for the purpose of writing a book on Monte Carlo."

"He's telling the truth. I checked on him in New York as I wrote you I would. He really is here to write a book on Monte. Your stories about Monte excited the interest of a book publisher and when Drury submitted an outline of what he intended to do, he was given a contract and on the strength of his reputation, a sizable advance. He's sent in several chapters, and the book looks as if it might be a success.''

Lydia smiled in relief. ''I'm glad to hear it. I know it doesn't lessen his animosity toward me and that he's sworn vengeance, but he also swore he was innocent of any conspiracy to harass me. He sounded so convincing I had to believe him. Even Jeff talked with him and came away convinced he was telling the truth.''

''Coming through Paris, I did some more investigating by means of newspaper people I know. Drury has been seen frequently at the big libraries and is digging into the history of the people who began Monte Carlo. He's working at it without question, spending time in the newspaper morgues as well.''

''That's welcome information,'' Lydia said.

''He's a formidable enemy,'' Morgan warned. ''You know that as well as I, but I don't believe his purpose in being here is anything more than the writing of his book.''

''I wrote you and Mr. Spencer about the harassment I've been subjected to and which I first believed could be attributed to Bryant Drury. Since we've eliminated him, my thoughts turn again to Armand Martel. Were you able to uncover any data about him?''

''We had no more success than you. Why has no word been released by the police about his death?''

Lydia gave a little shrug. ''You know the casino wants no publicity regarding any suicides that take place here. Also, the police wish to do further investigating. Don't forget—it was the Prince of Wales who was shot at.''

''What part is Jeff playing in this?''

''I don't know—and that's the truth,'' Lydia said, this time looking Morgan directly in the eyes.

He smiled. ''I know it is. You still have that charm and naivete that were so evident in your first articles. You lost it for a little while, but it's back again. Except for maturing, which is natural and a good sign, you haven't changed. I'm pleased. Now—back to Martel. Was he murdered? I won't violate your confidence. But when the story breaks, I hope you'll be in on it so we can have it first—whatever it's all about."

"Very well, Mr. Morgan. I'll tell you what I know, though I've been sworn to secrecy."

"You can trust me."

Lydia said, "Martel's body was discovered hanging from a tree branch. The police believe it was murder. No one came to claim his body and he's buried in an unmarked grave."

"Why the secrecy?"

"If it was murder, they want the murderer or murderers to think they've been completely deceived. If it turns out to be suicide, the casino will try to keep it very quiet."

"Looks like you'll have a story one of these days."

"I hope it's soon," Lydia replied with a shudder. "I can still see his face."

"You're certain it was the man who gave you the false information about the Arabian prince?" Morgan asked.

"Positive. I sat next to him at the banquet. Later, I saw him at the casino and sipped champagne with him while he gave me the story about the prince."

"Speaking of suicides, the article you wrote debunking the old tale about the secret cemetery for suicides was very good." He paused while the waiter refilled their glasses. "Now—have you any questions?"

"Yes. Something that puzzles me very much. Do you know who could have been responsible for that nasty and untrue gossip that appeared about me—though it was kept anonymous—in that Paris scandal sheet? The one concerning my rendezvous with the Russians."

Morgan said, "I investigated that when I was in Paris. I know the owner of the paper. He informed me they received an anonymous letter—no, it was a wireless. Sent from Cannes. They wondered who could be responsible, but it sounded authentic, so they decided to run part of it. I suspect now the wireless came from this Martel. Raoul will be pleased to know that."

"Raoul?" she asked.

"I forgot to tell you. Raoul Duprez, the owner of the paper, is an old friend of mine. I hadn't seen him in years, but I did stop by at his request when I came through Paris. I'd already cabled him regarding the article. The fact is, he wished to apologize for running it. He didn't know about it until after publication, for he swears he doesn't run anything without full facts behind it. His editor came very close to getting fired. Raoul intends to apologize to you personally in the next day or two."

"Is he coming to Monte?"

"He may already be here. His wife Blanche and his son Claude are with him. He's coming by yacht. A fifteen-hundred-ton yacht. You could sail around the world in it."

"There are so many yachts in the harbor," Lydia said, "representing a great deal of money."

"Raoul lives big. He loves luxury and has been on the verge of bankruptcy more than once, but he always manages to pull out of it. I suppose at present he's very wealthy. He must be. His yacht is worth a fortune."

"He should be interesting," Lydia said. "I'll forgive him for the article. I may even write one about him, with his permission."

Over his coffee, Morgan elaborated on the Duprez family. "Raoul's not a bad fellow. His wife is somewhat haughty, and his son is an eccentric, to put it kindly, but I think you'll like them in spite of it. You can show them around Monte. He hasn't been here in years, and his wife and son have never been here."

"I'll be glad to give them a tour."

"Good. I'll be grateful for it. One more thing. I intend to talk to Drury while I'm here. Do you wish to be present? It may result in some fireworks."

"Over me?" she asked.

"Yes. I want to be very certain that he's not behind these vexations you've been subjected to. I can't think of another soul who'd wish to harm you, or my newspaper, and I have small regard for Mr. Drury. He's aware of it and may resent my talking to him. You may sit in or not, as you choose."

"Since you've assured me he's working on a book, I see no reason to fear him. Yes, Mr. Morgan, I'd like to hear what he has to say."

"Do you know where he usually dines? I want to catch him off guard. Then he'll have no time to set up a story."

"An excellent idea," Lydia agreed.

"And an excellent lunch." Morgan wiped his mouth and placed his napkin on the table. "I'm going to have a brief rest, then do a little gambling. Will the baron really be at the casino?"

"Indeed, yes. In any case, may you have the luck of Mr. Wells who broke the bank."

"That was a great story. We scooped the world on that one, thanks to you. I doubt that kind of luck will ever be repeated. Are you sure he didn't cheat somehow?"

"If he did, he was more clever at it than anyone else. It would take some doing to cheat at roulette, Mr. Morgan."

"I suppose so. Well, one mystery is partially cleared up. The strange cablegram you sent asking us to kill a story concerned the Arabian prince. We never did understand it."

Lydia said, "I'm ashamed of myself for what happened, but it did. You recall Drury tried to publish those few paragraphs on a woman whose husband he hated? He didn't check on the truth of what he wrote. I did and it enabled you to kill his story."

"I remember very well. You were so good at covering his omissions that I decided to send you here."

"Thanks, Mr. Morgan, but I did the same thing."

"I recall the story you sent about the prince and the banquet. There was nothing wrong with it."

"The one I wrote first would have created a monstrous situation. I wrote what Martel told me, and he lied. I still don't know why."

"Ah, yes, the cable. I don't understand it. A cable can't be lost in transit."

"I thought so, too, but the man at the cable office, whom I know quite well by now, swears he sent it. He even inquired at the New York office and they swore no cablegram had been received at that time."

"One or the other is lying," Morgan declared.

"I know. However, I trust this man at the local office. He's reliable, an old employee, and was instructed by the owners of the casino to grant me privileges not allowed to anyone else that I know of. I can't see him as part of any scheme aimed at me. Besides, if he was somehow involved in this strange plot against me, why did he not send a cable that would have gotten me into more trouble than I'd have ever known in my life?"

"I don't understand that one," Morgan admitted. "Although it was to your benefit."

"Would I have been fired if you'd got it and printed it?" Lydia asked.

"The fact is, we didn't receive it so no harm's been done."

"But if you had received it?" Lydia persisted.

"What is the prince's name?"

"Prince Ali Jouhaud."

Morgan's brows raised and his lips pursed as if to whistle softly. "I happen to know he's a most charitable man and a very fair ruler. I'd rather not answer the question about your dismissal."

"Please do."

"Suppose you answer it for me."

"I'd have been fired and deservedly so."

Morgan smiled. "Right. However, I'm sure you'll never make the same mistake again."

"I won't, but I'm not certain I deserve another chance."

"I think you do because you did ask the baron and the hotel maid to check up on Martel. It was just that you filed your story about the prince before you checked the facts on him. You were in a hurry."

"That's what Drury did with Mrs. Hallett."

"Not exactly. He was out to extract vengeance."

"My writing wasn't objective in regard to the prince."

"Nonetheless, I'm convinced you learned your lesson. You wouldn't catch Drury being so honest about his mistake, my dear. You've faced it and owned up to it. So we won't waste more time on that. Tomorrow I'll take you to meet Raoul aboard his yacht. Let's see, I'll be gambling late tonight . . . what about twelve noon? I'm staying at your hotel.''

"I'll meet you in the lobby then.''

"Fine. Now, where does Drury dine?''

"When he's in Monte, he dines here almost every night.''

"Excellent. Meet me in the hotel lobby at seven for supper. By the way, I certainly enjoyed the food I've just eaten.''

"You won't be disappointed tonight,'' Lydia assured him. "If you don't wish to take my word for it, the baron will convince you.''

Mr. Morgan laughed. "I'm sure he will. Just now, I'm more interested in a rest. I enjoy travel, but it wears me out.''

Lydia returned to the hotel, stepped out of her dress and slipped into a negligée. Then she sat down at her desk and wrote an article about Mr. George Morgan's arrival in Monte Carlo for a brief stay, at which time he would visit the editor of a Paris newspaper aboard his yacht. Then she lay down for a short rest, after summoning a bellboy to deliver her story to the cablegram office. To her surprise, she drifted off to sleep and was wakened by Angelina. Lydia sat bolt upright in bed.

"Goodness, what time is it?''

Angelina laughed. "Relax, mademoiselle. It is only five o'clock. Are you dining with your employer tonight? I hope he invited you.''

"I'm to meet him at the Café de Paris at seven.''

"Good. Do you like him?''

"Very much. He's a most forgiving gentleman.''

"You told him of the trouble with the cablegram that did not arrive?''

"Yes,'' Lydia replied. "He doesn't understand that. He forgave me for my carelessness in the story regarding Prince Ali Jouhaud, though he admitted he'd have fired me had it been printed.''

Angelina made a face, then said soothingly, "I will draw a bath for you, mademoiselle, then I will lay out your clothes. What do you wish to wear?"

"Nothing too lavish," Lydia said, "as the evening may not be very pleasant."

"How could it be otherwise when you like Monsieur Morgan?"

"We may see Mr. Drury. He can be most disagreeable."

"I choose the lavender gown for you then. It is modest, but also beautiful."

Lydia bathed leisurely and let Angelina style her hair high in a sophisticated manner.

"The baron looked me up this afternoon," Angelina said.

Lydia regarded Angelina's sober features in the mirror. "Is there something wrong?"

"Not with him. He is worried about you."

"What did he say?"

"He told me about Martel and said I am to watch your suite and let no one in if you are not here. He was most insistent."

"Why did he do that?"

"Don't get angry with him, mademoiselle. He is worried for you. He told me Martel was murdered."

"Good heavens, he shouldn't have done that."

"He swore me to keep it secret. I will tell no one, mademoiselle. I swear it. But I am frightened for you, also. What does it mean?"

"It means that with Martel dead, there's nothing to worry about," Lydia said quietly.

"You say that so I will not worry. The baron said if someone murdered Martel, whoever did it might murder you, also."

"I'm not going to lock myself up in this suite, so stop fretting," Lydia scolded.

"I will pray that the police solve the mystery soon, mademoiselle."

"I hope so, too. I just wish Jeff had more time to be with me."

"I have not yet met this man," Angelina said. "You are

233

in love with him. Is that not so?''

"Very much in love with him. I'll admit I'd feel safer if he were in Monte.''

"Perhaps it would be best if you married him and went away.''

"No, Angelina. I'm not going away. Jeff knows I hope to keep this assignment in Monte.''

"*Oui*, that is good. Now it is time to dress.''

Lydia met Morgan in the lobby promptly at seven. He was in tails, with a gray top hat that he removed as he took her hand and bowed over it.

"How youthfully mature you look, and how beautiful.''

"Thanks to your generosity,'' Lydia said graciously.

"I remember you in the New York office that night we fired Drury. Guy Spencer agreed you would make a good reporter, but he had some doubts you could handle yourself in a place like Monte Carlo.''

Lydia laughed. "He wasn't the only one, Mr. Morgan. I almost called it off once I reached Paris, I was so terrified.''

"That's understandable. Spencer said you were too young and unsophisticated, that you'd have a hard time holding yourself up to the image of the women who came to Monte. You've proven him wrong. I was sure you could make it and I was right.''

"Mr. Morgan, I'm grateful you gave me the opportunity.''

"And you made the best of it. You're an asset to the newspaper.''

"Thank you. Did you rest well?''

"I meant to, but the fever got me so I visited the casino instead of having a nap. I should have napped.''

She laughed. "It happens all the time.''

"I'd like to win for a change. You know, if that man Wells did have a system and you knew what it was, you could become a millionaire in a very brief time. There are a lot of people who still think he knew what he was doing, and that it wasn't all luck.''

"I talked with him. He insisted there was no system. But he shrouded six tables in black after he broke them one by one."

"I can dream," Morgan said wryly.

"That's what keeps Monte going," she laughed.

As they moved into the dining room, Morgan said, "I hope Drury is here. I prefer talking with him in a public place. He established a reputation in New York for being short-tempered."

"It's true," Lydia said. "I know, because I've been on the receiving end of it."

"Come to think of it, I'd rather you weren't with us. The language may become rather strong. No place for a lady. My main idea is to find out if he has been in any way involved in the unpleasantness you've been subjected to."

"I think you'll be convinced he wasn't. I was, after I talked with him. Jeff questioned him also and hated to admit that he had to believe Drury's story held up."

Mr. Morgan pointed out Drury's table to the maitre d', who escorted them there. The rather voluptuous blond girl was the same one Lydia had seen him with before. There was no doubting his astonishment when he saw Morgan, but it was quickly replaced with a look of arrogance as he got to his feet.

"What the hell do you want?" he asked.

"I want to talk with you," Morgan said quietly. "It would be better without the ladies present."

"I'm not leaving," the blonde said defiantly.

Drury looked down at her. "Yes, you are. Stay with her, Lydia."

The blonde regarded Drury indignantly, opened her mouth to speak, then thought better of it. She got to her feet and glared at Lydia before she walked from the room.

Morgan said, "Drury, when you left my paper you handed the cashier a forged cashier's order for a substantial sum. You passed the word around that I was someone you'd never work for again. You did your best to discredit me wherever and whenever you could. I could have had you arrested on that forged order, but you'd likely have made capital of that too."

"I grieve for you," Drury said. He flashed an angry look at Lydia. "I didn't think you'd be a party to this."

"She's not," Morgan said. "This is the first time she heard how you cheated me. Maybe she'd best not hear the rest of it. Will you excuse us, Lydia?"

Lydia nodded and glanced at Drury. "I'll be with your companion."

Drury eyed her coldly, but made no answer. Lydia left them, hoping to find out something of Drury from his companion. She found the girl in the ladies' room, seated at the long table facing the mirrored wall.

"Bryant doesn't like you," she said spitefully, carefully applying lipstick to her full lips.

"I'm aware of that. What's your name?" Lydia asked in neutral tones.

"Madelaine. He's going to marry me when his book is finished."

"Congratulations. Have you known him long?"

"None of your business," she retorted.

"That's true," Lydia said calmly. She sat down in the chair next to Madelaine.

"He's been very good to me. I'm a dancer. I was working at the Folies-Bergère, you know." Madelaine seemed to want to talk, despite her suspicious attitude.

"You have the face and the figure for it, Madelaine. Aren't you working there now?" Lydia asked.

"I was fired."

"Because of Drury?"

"I didn't even know him then."

"I'm sorry. Do you travel with Drury? I mean, do you see him in Cannes and Paris?"

"Of course. I said we are going to be married, didn't I?"

"Is he working hard on his book?" Lydia pressed.

"Sometimes I don't see him for days. All he does is sit in a musty old library reading books. And when he's not doing that, he's writing page after page. I told him he ought to spend more time making me happy. He said he would when the book is finished.''

''Does he ever slip away from you? For days at a time and you don't know where he is or what he's doing?''

''You ask a lot of questions,'' Madelaine said cautiously.

''Just trying to make conversation.''

''I've been with him every day when he's not at his damned libraries.'' She touched a powder puff to her nose and looked straight at Lydia's reflection in the mirror. ''I'm with him every night, too,'' she added defiantly.

''Then I can't see how he could slip away without your knowing it.''

''He never has. He justs works on his book when he's not with me.'' She tried to take the offensive. ''Who's that man who came to see Bryant?''

''Bryant once worked for him.''

''I hope Bryant doesn't make a scene. He gets very mad sometimes. Your gentleman friend better watch out.''

''Shall we go back and see if any blood has been spilled?''

Madelaine looked astonished, then laughed aloud. ''Blood spilled! That's good. In the Café de Paris? Who ever heard of such a thing?''

The only blood they saw on their return was that which suffused Drury's face. Morgan sipped champagne from the glass at Madelaine's side of the table.

''You understand me, Drury,'' he said. ''I can still put you in jail and queer this assignment you have with the book.''

''I understand what kind of a son-of-a-bitch you are, Morgan, and I know you can break me if you want to. But I'm not lying. I'm not making any trouble for Lydia. That's over, though not forgotten.''

''All right,'' Morgan said. ''We'll let it go at that. Just remember, if I hear you are involved in any kind of troublemaking, I'll have you locked up and sent back to New York for trial. I'm not fooling about this, Drury. Someone has been harassing Lydia and you're the only one who has any reason to.''

''I came here to write a book. I told Lydia that when we

first met. Sure, we had arguments, but I didn't lay a hand on her and I never will. I'm not doing anything to make trouble for her and I don't know who is—or why. If I'd known this before, I'd feel sorry for her, but not after tonight. I just don't give a damn what happens to her—or you."

Morgan summoned the headwaiter and asked for a table across the room. Once seated, he lost no time in ordering a bottle of champagne and consulting Lydia on a dish of her choice.

"Are you convinced Drury is working on a book?" Lydia asked.

"Yes," Morgan said. "I told you he had a contract for doing a book on Monte from a New York publisher, so I knew that part of it was legitimate. What I wondered was whether he came here to make trouble for you. Certainly those embarrassments you suffered were done by someone with a grudge."

"With Drury the only person here with a known motive."

"Correct. Yet he swears he has no interest in you. He admits also he dislikes you because of what he insists you did. I reminded him you did him a favor."

Lydia gave Morgan a chagrined look. "Please don't tell me what he said. I know well how he regards me because of that."

"He's pigheaded and dishonest. In fact, I can't think of any good points he has. Perhaps I'm biased, but I don't think so. His attitude toward you proves his pettiness, and his forging a cashier's order proves his dishonesty. Yet somehow, I can't believe him guilty of the vexations you've been subjected to. I wish I could. He may well be and is simply too clever for us."

"Perhaps we won't need to worry more about it," Lydia said, hoping she sounded convincing.

"I hope not," Morgan said. "Yet since it was Martel who gave you that trumped-up story about Prince Ali Jouhaud and he was found murdered—."

"A suicide," Lydia corrected.

"Very well," Morgan replied with a trace of irritation. Just as quickly, his tone became placatory. "Forgive me, Lydia. I shouldn't let Drury upset me, but he's such an obnoxious individual, I can scarcely bear to talk with him."

"I know what you mean," Lydia said. "But I feel only pity for him."

"How could you?" Morgan asked in astonishment.

"He was at the peak of his career—highly respected and very talented—and because he sought revenge, he became careless and destroyed himself."

"You're right, of course, and thinking in a far more adult fashion than I. Suppose we forget him and concentrate on our supper."

"An excellent idea," she agreed. "I'm famished."

They avoided all talk of anything disagreeable throughout the rest of their meal. Lydia questioned him about New York City and Morgan warmed to the subject, narrating a series of anecdotes about politicians, society folks and the latest news of the theater plus the accomplishments and escapades of some of the actors and actresses. Before long, they were both laughing and the tension that had enveloped them had completely disappeared.

"My dear," Morgan said when he took a final sip of coffee, "when I sat down, even the thought of food didn't excite me. You made it a pleasure. It's been an amusing two hours."

"I enjoyed it, too," Lydia said. "I'm sure the baron is already at the casino impatiently awaiting your arrival."

"Before we go, I would like to ask you a question. Did you get any information out of the woman Drury had with him?"

"Only that he's going to marry her," Lydia replied. "I hope she won't be disappointed."

"I don't know how disappointed she'll be," Morgan replied chuckling. "But I'd lay odds he won't. Drury likes variety."

"Oh—she did say he spent most of his time at the library and writing his book. She said she was with him the rest of the time, and every night. That, too, I believe because she was annoyed with the little attention and time he gave her."

"If it's true, it bears out our opinion that he took no part in your harassment."

Lydia said, "Jeff is of the same opinion."

"I'd like to think it was over," Morgan said.

"I pray to heaven it is," Lydia said.

"Well, you won't have time to dwell on it tomorrow. You'll meet Monsieur and Madame Duprez and, I hope, their son. You'll like them."

"I'm looking forward to it," she replied.

"Good. Now let's go to the casino." Morgan's eyes lit up.

Thirteen

In the casino they met the baron, who gave Morgan some expert advice on how to play roulette. Later he claimed it was a great success, because he lost only a few hundred francs, a great improvement over his earlier trip. Then Morgan walked Lydia back to the hotel, but decided to return to the casino to gamble some more.

"I won't be here too long," he explained. "This time my wife's not with me. I don't like people standing over my shoulder and breathing hard when I win, and breathing harder when I lose, along with gentle hints that it's time to quit, even though I know it."

Lydia said, "I may as well warn you I could be guilty of the same thing."

"Just remember," he laughed, "I'm your boss. By the way, when will that young man of yours come back? I'd like to meet him."

"I don't know, Mr. Morgan. He doesn't confide in me."

Lydia used the lift to carry her up the single flight because she was genuinely tired. It had been a long day, though except for the unpleasantness with Drury, a rewarding one. She was satisfied that he was not the threat she had feared he might be. Mr. Morgan was satisfied, too, that Drury really was writing a book. Even Madelaine had confirmed that.

Ever since her encounter with Trencher and, later on, with the appearance of Drury in her suite, Lydia had grown very careful before entering. She made certain no one hid in the corridor as Trencher had done, and when she unlocked the door, she didn't go in immediately but listened and explored the wall with her hand for the light switch, turning it on before she closed the door.

The parlor was empty, and there were no signs of anyone having been in the suite. She removed her evening wrap and carried it into the bedroom. When she turned on the light there, she gasped aloud and felt once again those first elements of fear that could rapidly mount to a state of terror.

Framing the bureau mirror, pinned to the draperies, strewn over the bed were pink carnations. At least three dozens of them. Carnations that were not even grown in Monte Carlo because they symbolized bad luck. To Lydia, they seemed an omen of evil. She realized they'd been placed there to instill fear in her, and they had.

She immediately threw the wrap over her shoulders, left the suite, used the stairs to descend and almost ran back to the casino. She saw Morgan and the baron at one of the tables. Looking about, she saw Drury and his blond companion at another. She made her way through the crowded room to her friends.

Morgan saw her approaching. Her tense features revealed something was wrong and he stopped playing at once. The baron, his attention on the table, hadn't seen her approach. He was startled when Morgan arose abruptly and went over to Lydia, leading her to a quiet corner. He hurried to join them.

"Carnations?" Morgan asked, mystified at the meaning of the mysteriously appearing flowers. He welcomed the baron with some bewilderment. "Lydia has just informed me that she discovered her bedroom awash in pink carnations."

"They are bad luck," the baron said promptly. "The worst kind of luck in Monte."

"I know that now," Morgan said. "Lydia explained it to me. And it's the second time she's been subjected to that indignity."

"It is nothing more than a superstition," the baron said, "but personally I would not care to wear one while I was gambling."

Morgan said, "I'm concerned with its significance in regard to Lydia."

Lydia said, "I suppose it's a way of letting me know that I'm not clear of those who wish to harm me. What else can it mean? I came back here as quickly as I could. I knew Drury was gambling when I left, and had been for some time before that. I wanted to find out if he had left the casino in time to place those carnations in my suite and return without his absence being noticed."

The baron said, "I saw Drury arrive shortly after you two did."

Morgan said, "I saw him, too. I'm sure he didn't leave his table."

"Then Drury can't be responsible," Lydia said. "Not directly anyway. I wanted to be certain of that. Perhaps I assumed too much because I don't trust him."

"Don't be concerned about misjudging him," Morgan said firmly. "He lacks character and he's a cheat. Also, I doubt there's not much he wouldn't do to lay his hands on a respectable sum of cash. Still, I don't see how he could have done that. He was in my line of vision in the dining room, and he was there ahead of us. The baron saw him enter the casino when we did, and I kept my eye on him here."

"I'm convinced of that now," Lydia admitted. "If only I had even a suspicion of who is responsible—and the reason. But I can think of no one who has any reason to torment me."

"I'll walk you back," Morgan offered.

The baron said, "Allow me. After all, I gave Jeff my word I would look after you."

Morgan regarded Lydia with fresh alarm. "I didn't know that."

"I wish the baron hadn't mentioned it," Lydia said with a trace of irritation.

"Since he has, I insist on accompanying you." Morgan took Lydia's arm, but she braced herself and refused to move.

"Lydia, don't be so obstinate," he said.

"If Jeff is that concerned about my safety, he shouldn't have left," she said stubbornly. "I'll not allow either of you to accompany me. It's still early and there are enough people about to hear me scream should there be a need. Thank you anyway. Now please, Mr. Morgan, let go of my arm."

He did so reluctantly. "I'm afraid if I don't, you'll make a scene."

"I would," she said firmly.

"Are you sure you're not feeling sorry for yourself because Jeff isn't here?" Mr. Morgan asked.

"Certainly not," she said indignantly. "It's just that I'm more angry than afraid at the moment. I don't have even a suspicion of who's behind this."

"Lydia," the baron said, "I must protect you. I gave my word."

She gave a negative shake of her head. "My answer is still no. Go back to your gambling. I'll be quite safe. Good night."

"Do you still wish to meet the Duprez family tomorrow?" Mr. Morgan thought to ask.

"Yes. I'll see you at the appointed time."

She turned and walked briskly out of the casino. Once on her way to the hotel, the mental vision of her room brought a return of the fear she'd felt when she viewed it. She realized she'd been both stubborn and reckless in refusing an escort. However, if she was going to remain here, she had to try, as best she could, to learn who was badgering her. Yet how much chance would she have if there was someone lurking in the darkness ready to shoot her? Jeff was certain the bullets fired at the station when the Prince of Wales appeared on the platform had been meant for her. If he was right, wouldn't the murderer strike again? Her footsteps quickened at the thought. By the time she reached the hotel, her brisk walk had turned into a run that would make her a less than perfect target.

Once she entered the hotel, she slowed to a walk and forced herself to think calmly. Was the bravery she had evidenced before Mr. Morgan and the baron false? Some of it was, she knew. However, since Jeff was absent, he must have had enough faith in her ability to handle herself. Either that, or he didn't believe she would be shot at or strangled or clubbed. Someone wanted to instill fear in her. Who or why she didn't know, but she was determined to find out. That decision made, she felt the tension leave her.

In her suite once again, she removed all of the carnations and carried them down to the end of the corridor where there was a servant's waste bin. She deposited them there and shivered just a bit on her way back to the suite. Though she'd always disliked the scent of carnations, she admired their beauty. Now she was coming to hate the flower, even to fear it. Their use as a means of rending her someone was not finished with her yet had turned them into an omen of evil.

The suite was still filled with their spicy fragrance, and opening windows didn't seem to lessen the perfume. She had a difficult time getting to sleep, for the aroma only seemed to intensify when she turned out the light and closed her eyes. It was only an illusion, she knew, but it did upset her.

Angelina professed complete ignorance of the warning next day. "I have hoped this would be ended for you by now," she said. "I saw the flowers in the refuse bin this morning and I asked myself where they came from."

"I'm afraid too much has happened to allow them to stop now. Tell me, are there many keys to these rooms?"

"Yes, mademoiselle. All employees have them. There is a master key that opens all rooms, but individual keys are not hard to obtain. Anyway, I think the locks could be opened easily, even without a key. They are very old-fash-ioned."

"I recall Mr. Drury had no trouble letting himself in. I

shall ask the management to install a chain on the inside so that I can, at least, sleep safely.''

''I will take care of it, mademoiselle. The housekeeper is a woman of understanding. There shall be an installation today.''

''Thank you. It may not keep them out when I'm not in the suite, but it will when I am. I'll feel more secure.''

''It is strange, this business. I hoped that perhaps this man from the United States would have the answer.''

''He's as mystified as I,'' Lydia said.

The morning breakfast table now arrived and, as was their custom, Angelina and Lydia enjoyed coffee and croissants while they discussed Lydia's costume for her visit to the Duprez yacht.

Angelina clapped her hands in delight. ''The yachting costume from Worth, mademoiselle. It is so beautiful. Very light, thin white wool with full skirt, fitted basque—it will look beautiful with your small waist. A short cape ruffled at the neck, and on the head a white straw covered with white lace.''

''Goodness,'' Lydia protested. ''That's very fussy.''

''Very French, mademoiselle,'' Angelina corrected.

''I've seen ladies with trim outfits. A tailormade gown with a sailor hat and reefer. It's neat and simple.''

''And austere.'' Angelina looked shocked that Lydia would prefer anything English to French. ''What is the name of the gentleman who owns the yacht?''

''Monsieur Duprez.''

''French, yes?''

''Yes. He owns the newspaper that published the gossip item concerning my encounter with the amorous Russians.''

''You would not listen to me then, would you?''

Angelina's question demanded an answer.

''Unfortunately, I did not,'' Lydia admitted.

''Then I suggest you listen now. You have this so beautiful yachting costume. From the house of Worth. Nothing is better. Also, it is French. So take Angelina's advice.''

"Very well," Lydia acquiesced with a sigh, admitting defeat.

Once dressed, she had to admit the costume was breathtaking. Morgan's admiring glance as he met her in the lobby was further proof Angelina had been right. He helped Lydia into the landau and sat opposite her, while she opened her white brocade parasol with a wide lace edge giving further protection from the sun and heat of midday. As they neared the waterfront, they could see the crowded beach to the right, and the colorful bathhouses set in a row, resembling Arab tents from which they had been copied, but in more substantial material.

It would not have been difficult for Lydia to pick out the Duprez yacht, for it was among the half dozen really large ones. It was christened *Parisian Nouvelles*.

"I should think they'd be ashamed of themselves, using the name of that awful newspaper on their boat," Lydia commented.

"My dear young lady, they regard their newspaper as an excellent one, although they admit they print scandalous news sometimes. Duprez maintains those stories make a newspaper popular. He's right."

"Then must I forgive them for printing that terrible story about me? My, look at the size of that yacht! They could sail around the world in it."

"They already have," Morgan assured her. "Claude is quite a sailor, but beware of him. He's a noted lothario as well."

"I doubt I need worry. You know I don't flirt. Besides, I work for you. I'm curious about this family and rather anxious to meet them, in the hope of getting a story."

Morgan chuckled. "I wish you luck."

When the landau stopped at the entrance to the marina, they were scarcely out of the carriage before a young man in white duck trousers, a blue jacket and a yachting cap came running along the dock to greet them.

He was, Lydia noticed, a tall, well-built man, golden

brown from the sun, with thick, curly hair so blond it must have been bleached by the sunlight. He didn't check his approach until he had a startled Lydia in his arms. He danced her around the dock with a charming grin upon his face.

"Beautiful," he said. "Lovely . . . adorable . . . I have yet to see anyone lovelier. M'sieur Morgan, you have done me the favor of my life bringing her to me."

Lydia finally managed to free herself of his embrace. She stepped away from him, breathless and still in a state of astonishment.

"M'sieur," Lydia finally managed, "what in the world . . . ?"

He bowed dramatically. "It is you, mademoiselle. Yes, you who make me act this way. I am overwhelmed by your beauty, your poise, and now your voice. Very sultry. It has set my whole being afire."

"This," Morgan said with a sigh, "is Claude Duprez. Monsieur Duprez, Mademoiselle Lydia Bradley."

"Monsieur Duprez," she said, "I think you're quite mad."

"Of course I am. Who would not be upon meeting a dream like you? Mademoiselle Lydia . . . yes, Lydia is such . you . . . a beautiful name. I am going to marry you."

Morgan said, "Don't be alarmed, Lydia. He's harmless. He always acts this way."

"No . . . not always, M'sieur Morgan. Only when I have met the girl of my life. Let me see . . . yes, your eyes are blue and I adore blue eyes. Lovely blonde hair, fair skin . . . everything about you . . . ."

"If you don't mind," Morgan said, "we'd like to go aboard and meet your parents."

"But of course. I will escort Mademoiselle Lydia. You may walk along, Monsieur Morgan, but before us for you older than we. Mademoiselle, you and I shall never grow old. We shall always be young and in love."

"I don't suppose it's of any use to tell you I'm not in

love with you, M'sieur Duprez."

"No use at all, mademoiselle. The fact remains, I am in love with you. Therefore you will fall in love with me. It is only a matter of time."

"You're the most absurd young man I've ever met," Lydia said, still astonished.

Aboard ship Raoul and Blanche Duprez awaited them. He was a tall, slim man of about fifty, perhaps a few years more than that, still a quite handsome man with hair graying only at the temples and the firm, square chin of a man who brooked no nonsense. Blanche, on the other hand, was an attractive matron, growing a bit thick around the waistline, but with a face still young and the smile of a woman who enjoyed life.

"So this is the famous Mademoiselle Lydia," Raoul Duprez said. "I am charmed, mademoiselle. You exceed by far the stories I have heard about your beauty and, no doubt, your brains. We're honored to have you aboard."

Blanche Duprez embraced her and kissed her on both cheeks as was the French custom. "We are both ashamed of ourselves that the newspaper would print that awful story about you and the Russians."

"You're forgiven," Lydia said. "But may I ask how you received the news so quickly that it was in your morning edition?"

"It was an anonymous wireless to our man in Nice, and he relayed it at once. It came from Cannes."

"Don't you always cover Monte?" Morgan asked.

"Oh no," Raoul replied. "Monte has been enjoying its present popularity but a short time—four or five years now—and we have paid little attention to it until it grew even more famous when that little man from England broke the bank. Mademoiselle, that was a story of great magnitude and reported splendidly. Congratulations."

Claude whispered aside to Lydia. "You can talk business later. Right now I wish to convince you that I am going to marry you. That cannot be done in public, unless you wish to have everyone see me grow humble and begin begging."

"Pay him no attention, mademoiselle," Blanche Duprez said with a tolerant smile, seeing Lydia's bewildered expression. "Claude often talks nonsense when a lovely girl appears."

"Ah, but this time I am in love," Claude said vehemently. "But of course, if being in love makes a man talk nonsense, then I am talking nonsense. I like it. Are you going to disappoint me, Lydia?"

"I'm afraid I am," she replied. "I wish to know your father and mother better."

"Then she may begin to understand *you*," Morgan chuckled. "Leave us, Claude, unless you're business inclined. We're newspaper folk and there's much to talk about."

"Come below," Raoul invited. "We'll have coffee and champagne. Please join us, Mademoiselle Bradley."

"Thank you, I will," Lydia said happily. She'd been relaxed when she arrived. Now Claude's foolishness added to the merriment of the day.

Below meant a cabin as big as her parlor and paneled with ebony, set off with ivory-framed paintings, white furniture and a white wool carpet. Chairs were large, soft and very comfortable. On an ebony table were glasses, coffee service in gleaming silver, a tray of canapés and little sandwiches of cucumber and watercress. A cabin boy in white poured coffee and champagne and then quietly withdrew.

"I'll show you around the boat later," Claude promised her. He'd stopped much of his foolishness, but he rarely took his eyes off Lydia to her embarrassment. He seemed no more than an outrageous clown, yet his eyes had grown serious since he'd ceased his antics.

"We considered sending a man permanently to Monte," Raoul said, "but we have no one enterprising enough to take on this young lady and who would outdo the best we could offer. So we abandoned the idea."

"I sent her here on a hunch," Morgan said. "Just one of those spur-of-the-moment ideas. It's paid off far better than I expected and I'll admit I expected a great deal."

Blanche Duprez said, "That's high praise, but well warranted, I'm sure."

"Mr. Morgan knows my gratitude is boundless," Lydia said.

"So is mine for what you've accomplished," he replied.

For an hour or more the conversation concerned itself with newspapers and publishing. Raoul and Blanche were both almost apologetic at the type of publication they ran, but it was a moneymaker, and they could hardly change policy now. When Morgan commented they'd hardly want to, they agreed. They talked about the Paris edition of the New York *Times*, a fairly new innovation that seemed to be catching on.

Claude left them and returned from time to time; finally he stood in the center of the cabin and announced that he was taking Lydia on a tour of the yacht and that was all there was to it. She acquiesced with a smile.

On deck, he showed her the wheelhouse and then led her below to the engine room, for this was more than a sailing vessel. "She can do well for speed," he said, "and we can easily sail around the world. We shall do so on our honeymoon."

Lydia thought it was about time to put an end to his nonsense. "Claude, you may as well know that I'm already engaged to be married, to a man I love very much."

"You will toss him aside once you get to know me better, because you will discover with him it was infatuation." He sounded quite serious. "Now come and I shall show you the galley. We can cook almost anything aboard. There is a crew of three good men. After the galley I'll show you the staterooms. I don't think you will find a boat with beds any more comfortable than ours."

"Just don't talk about my falling in love with you," she said. "I won't. I love Jeffrey Marcus."

"Never heard of him."

"That isn't surprising. You're a gentleman of leisure. He has to work for a living, just as I do."

"What does he do?"

The question caught Lydia by surprise and though her mouth opened, no words came.

"Don't you know?" he asked soberly. "Are you certain

251

you can trust him? Don't forget, Monte is filled with people who come here under false pretenses.''

"He isn't here under false pretenses. He's a geologist."

He looked puzzled. "He works on Monte as a geologist?''

"I didn't say he worked here."

"Oh—he's on a holiday.''

"Yes," she answered quickly, hoping to avoid further questioning. Once again, she realized how little she knew of Jeff's work and even less of his mysterious absences.

Claude said, "That's different. Because it is difficult to see how Monte would have need of a geologist."

"I know," Lydia said flatly. "I've been here long enough to know that about Monte."

Claude regarded her with admiration. "You have spirit, mademoiselle. I like that in a woman. Especially one who has caught my fancy."

He turned quickly and brought her to a stop along the deck. "But, Lydia, I swear I do love you. A man can fall in love on the spot, at the first sight of the girl he always knew existed somewhere. Love does not have to grow like a flower. It can bloom at once, all of a sudden. With me it did."

"Please," she implored him. "I'll have to leave the yacht if you keep this up."

"As you wish," he said amiably enough. "But I am not finished. I am not abandoning my project of getting you to fall in love with me."

He did stop what Lydia termed his nonsense and conducted her on a thorough tour of the ship. She was impressed, for in her opinion, it was a miniature ocean liner, as she saw it, complete with everything a great ship should have. The cabins, four of them, were luxuriously appointed and were furnished with beds, not bunks. The galley could seat perhaps a dozen comfortably, and there was a central room for social gatherings done in wood paneling, with silk draperies and a thick carpet underfoot.

Back on deck, Lydia found Morgan ready to leave.

"Claude gave me a most interesting tour of this elegant craft," she said.

"I trust my son did not make a nuisance of himself," Blanche said.

"We came to an agreement," Lydia smiled. "He was very thoughtful and kind."

"Yes," Claude said, "but she actually made me stop telling her I'm in love with her when I really am. I swear it."

"Claude," Raoul cautioned. "It is not polite to talk of love to a girl you have just met. Especially when she's not in love with you."

"Wait and see. I'll win her over. I promise you have met your daughter-in-law to be. There is no help for it. I cannot be denied."

"He sounds as if he means it," Morgan said during the ride back to the hotel. "I warned you he was eccentric."

"He certainly is."

"I want to meet Jeff if possible. Should he return before I leave, will you arrange a meeting?"

"I'll be delighted. You'll understand why I fell in love with him."

"You must have," Morgan said with a grin. "Claude surely pressured you enough. Of course you're aware the Duprez family have a great deal of money. At least they did have. There have been some financial problems for the newspaper, but I think they've been overcome. At any rate, their wealth hasn't been confined to the publishing business alone. That's only one phase of Raoul's interests. He's a sharp business man and he can be mighty ruthless when the circumstances call for it. I don't think his son fits the mold of his father too well, but then, why should he if all he wants is a life of pleasure?"

Lydia said, "Raoul Duprez is such an intelligent man, I'm surprised he'd permit his editor to run a story based on anonymous information. I'm referring to the item concerning my encounter with the Russians."

"He did say it was verified by one of his men in Cannes."

"Then his man must have been a very poor reporter, or a careless one, for the whole weird affair was easily verified. He could even have come to me for an interview."

"Come now, Lydia, you know that's not the best way to conduct such a paper. You could have told him a cock-and-bull yarn."

"True," she admitted. "I suppose it's no longer of any consequence since it's ancient history now. My present task is to uncover the identity of the man who was behind Armand Martel. Those carnations last evening terrified me. However, I've calmed down, though obviously someone still bears me a grudge."

"I wish there was something I could do. If anything similar happens, it might be best if you left Monte. I'd hate to have you go, but your own safety is far more important than the newspaper."

"Whoever it is could just as easily follow me wherever I went," she reasoned. "It could be someone who bears me a grudge because of an article I wrote."

"I hope not. Your articles are featured now and drawing a great deal of acclaim. I'll leave the decision of remaining here or being assigned elsewhere up to you."

"I'll stay," she said immediately. "Another thought occurred to me. It might well be that someone is creating these harassments with the idea of getting me away from here. That sounds far-fetched, but then, nothing that's been done to me makes sense."

Fourteen

In the morning a gigantic bouquet of flowers arrived for Lydia, with Claude Duprez's name on the card. In mid-afternoon a large, expensive bottle of French perfume was brought by messenger. That evening, just before Lydia left for the casino, another package was delivered, containing an exquisite pearl necklace.

"Truly," Angelina said, "this man must be in love with you, mademoiselle."

"He's a spoiled, self-centered, idiotic young man who spends his life doing nothing. I believe he makes a fool of himself over every girl he meets."

"And gives her a garden of flowers, perfume only a handful of people could afford and now, this necklace. It is worth a fortune. I know, for I have seen some like it while waiting on the wealthy ladies who come to Monte."

"I can't very well send the flowers back, but the perfume and necklace will be returned. Claude is getting out of hand. This has to stop," Lydia said indignantly.

She made a package of the perfume and the necklace and sent it to the yacht by messenger, while Angelina looked on, not exactly in approval of this.

"If he is such a fool, to give you these presents," she reasoned, "you should keep them, if only to teach him a lesson. To show him that it is no matter to you what he does, or how many expensive gifts he sends, you will not fall in love with him. He will stop, then. How can anyone afford to keep sending gifts such as these?''

''The trouble is, he can keep sending them and he will. Even if I have to go to his parents, I'm going to put a stop to it. It's absurd.''

''I wish I had a man chasing me who is as absurd,'' Angelina said with a wistful sigh.

''I'm afraid he's going to make a nuisance of himself, not only in private, but in public. He is, I must admit, handsome, but totally lacking in responsibility. Certainly, he's devoid of any restraint. I doubt his parents ever interfered with what he wished to do. I don't dislike him—I don't believe anyone could—but his behavior is both irritating and embarrassing. He simply shrugged off the information that I love another man!''

''What will happen if they meet?'' Angelina asked.

''I don't know. Jeff is a tolerant man, but how could anyone disregard the way Claude acts? And Claude would think nothing of telling Jeff he and not Jeff is going to marry me. With all the trouble I've been having, I don't need a foolish, irresponsible man around.''

''Perhaps,'' Angelina said thoughtfully, ''it might be best to let him take you about. M'sieur Jeff isn't here enough to protect you well. The baron can't cope with an attack on you . . . he is too old and not a fighting man. But Monsieur Claude—he would be able to defend you.''

''Angelina, you sound as if you're in collusion with him.''

''Mademoiselle, I swear . . .'' Angelina cried out in dismay.

''Of course, I didn't mean that. And you might be right, but I don't believe I can stand very much of Claude. He's overwhelming. If I give him an inch, he'll assume I'm weakening. The only thing I can do is hope he'll lose interest. I wish Jeff would come back.''

So far as Lydia knew, an ordinary night at the restaurant and the casino lay ahead of her. She would tour the likely places where famous people might be, take her mental notes as usual and derive a story out of them, somehow. But as she crossed the lobby on her way to the casino, she saw Drury seated in an obscure corner, smoking a cigar and reading a newspaper. He didn't see her, for he never took his eyes off the paper. Lydia hesitated. Drury had nothing to do with the dangerous situation that had enveloped her, she was now sure. She'd even accused him of it and he'd convinced her she was wrong. Her determination to fight back when she was assailed in any way was always present, but there was also a spirit of fair play. When she was wrong, she felt the necessity to admit it. On the spur of the moment, she walked slowly toward Drury, who looked up as she neared him. She saw no friendliness in his eyes, nor did he stand when she addressed him.

"May I sit down?" she asked. "I wish to talk with you."

"It's a public place," he said. He resumed reading the newspaper, taking long puffs on his cigar, letting the smoke curl about him like a cloud.

"Some time back, I accused you of being responsible for the trouble and embarrassments I've had here."

"I haven't forgotten. I even enjoyed knowing something had happened to anger you."

"Certainly you weren't concerned about my accusations," she admitted.

He lowered the paper and looked up at her. "No reason for me to be since I didn't know what you were talking about. Though I can understand your blaming me since I did make a threat to get even with you if ever the opportunity should arise."

"I believe you even said you'd see that it did arise," Lydia said.

"True. But I think time has healed the wound." He paused and smiled cynically. "Perhaps I did get even with you, though not in the way you think."

"What do you mean?"

"I read your articles on Monte Carlo. They gave me the idea of approaching a publisher about doing a book on the place, its history and so forth."

"That's really why I'm here," Lydia said sincerely.

"I know you really are writing a book. When you first came, I didn't believe you when you told me that was your reason for coming to Monte. I felt you made up the story to account for your presence. I owe you a bit of an apology. You're less of a liar than I thought."

"What convinced you?" he asked with a mocking look.

"Just change the *what* to *who*."

He nodded. "Apparently you had Morgan check up on me. I haven't been a reporter for nothing all these years. A good reporter goes to work at once, using every means and every angle possible to gain information."

"You're right, Drury. Mr. Morgan checked with the publishers and discovered you have been commissioned to do a book on Monte Carlo."

"As for Morgan, I respect his ability as a publisher but I still don't like him, though I suppose I deserved to be fired. And it's true, I forged a draft to get extra money out of the cashier to get back at Morgan. As for you, maybe the scales are balanced since I'm writing a hell of a good book on Monte Carlo. Yes," he added with emphasis, "I *am* writing a book."

Lydia couldn't help but smile. "Madelaine further convinced me. I'm sure she'll be happy when it's completed."

He chuckled. "She's registered at this hotel, while I live elsewhere. She's been sadly neglected and I don't blame her for sulking. Between the time I spend at the libraries and the hours writing the book, the only attention I give her is when we eat. At the gambling tables—and I find time for that since it's a form of relaxation—my attention is on the game."

"So long as she's with you, I believe she's willing to overlook the rest of it."

"I hope so," he replied. "I'm going to marry her."

"So she said," Lydia replied noncommittally.

He eyed her speculatively. "But you don't believe it."

"No," Lydia replied promptly. "You haven't changed that much."

"Sorry to contradict you, but I have. If you stay around here, I'll see that you get an invitation to the wedding."

"If I do, be assured I'll attend—and extend my congratulations."

He sobered. "I have a feeling you're laughing at me."

"No. I just don't believe you'd allow yourself to be tied down."

"Time will tell." He spoke without rancor.

"I just wanted you to know I never felt the slightest animosity toward you," Lydia said. "Nor do I now. Good luck with the book."

"Thanks." He got to his feet when Lydia stood up, his manner a contrast to what it had been when she approached him. "Just don't expect me to dedicate it to you."

She left him, knowing he still disliked her and aware she distrusted him as much as ever as she made her way to the casino where she intended to dine. She knew the baron would be somewhere about, awaiting her. He'd be impatient and famished, as always. It was a mercy he hadn't turned into a butterball. Certainly he had a ravenous appetite. The thought was as amusing as the ridiculous antics of Claude Duprez. At the time, she hadn't found him funny, but in retrospect, he was.

She discovered the baron at one of the tables, watching the play with a disconsolate expression. He'd either lost all he had, or he was envious of those with enough money to play. He brightened when he saw her.

"I looked for you all day," he said. "Were you around the gardens or in the casino?"

"I was busy meeting people."

"I haven't seen Mr. Morgan about, either."

"We were meeting the same people. No doubt he'll be here tonight. I believe he's going home in the next day or two."

"I shall be sorry to see him depart. He's a fine loser, a fine man. Whom did you meet?"

Lydia smiled. "I wondered how long you could contain yourself. We were aboard the Duprez yacht."

"The big one? The biggest in the harbor?" His eyes widened.

"That would be it, Baron."

"The Duprezes do not come here often. I have heard of them, perhaps seen them, but we are not so well acquainted as to even bow."

"I'll introduce you," she promised. "Now, may I have your company at supper?"

"I thought you'd never ask. The casino has a great menu this evening. I have already studied it and smacked my lips over the beef. Tournedos tonight—tasty and tender."

She took his arm. "Has anyone of exceptional importance been here today?"

"No kings or grand dukes or even a kaiser. Things have been very quiet. No one has broken the bank, not even a table. They have put the black shrouds in mothballs." He studied her serene features. "You look quite relaxed."

She didn't reply until after they were seated. "I made up with Bryant Drury this evening. I suspected him of all sorts of things and I've been wrong. He really does have a contract to write a book on Monte, and he's been working hard at it."

"He has been gambling a good bit of the time, too. Would that be research?"

"What do you mean by gambling a great deal?"

"Every afternoon and evening he's here. Now that you say he is working on his book, is it possible that he considers gambling as something necessary for his book?"

"It's possible. How does he seem to be doing?" Lydia asked.

"Loses a little here, wins a little there. I think he comes out about even, but he does play big now and then. I saw him bet a thousand on the black this afternoon. It came up red, of course. I have watched him at *chemin-de-fer* and I am sure he memorizes the cards. He plays a sure game and wins, but of course not as he might win at roulette. Perhaps he memorizes something to do with the ivory ball and the wheel as well."

"Is it possible to win by memorizing anything about roulette?"

"No. You can take notes all day, all year, about where

the little ball falls, and your figures would be worthless. No one can control the wheel. Anyone who wins at roulette wins honestly. The management of the casino long ago offered a reward of one million francs to anyone who could come up with a system that can beat the wheel. Nobody has collected.''

"And you . . . how have you been doing, Baron?''

"There is no need to ask. I never win. Or if I do, I lose it the next minute. I am a poor gambler, but it is in my blood to gamble. I cannot help it.''

"I'll supply you with a hundred francs for the evening,'' she said.

"*Merci*. My tongue has been hanging out to make a bet. If I am lucky, I will buy supper tomorrow night.''

"And if you lose?''

"You may buy it. Have you heard from Jeff?''

"No. He doesn't write. Apparently, he moves about so fast he doesn't have the time. He did say he wouldn't be gone long.''

"What he needs is to become afraid he might lose you.''

Lydia looked up with a start from the menu as a man entered the casino restaurant, then replied to the baron, "He knows I love him too much. I might say I'll have no trouble in bringing a rival to his attention. Don't look now but Claude Duprez just came in. He's at one of the tables, and he's bound to see me. He may even stand on a chair and announce to everyone in the casino that he intends to marry me. If he does, I shall throw something at him.''

"Is there something the matter with him that he acts this way? He comes of a fine family—very rich.''

"If he keeps on sending me the kind of gifts I received today, the family isn't going to be rich very long. I already received an expensive bouquet of roses, a bottle of costly perfume and a pearl necklace.''

"He is serious, then.''

"I doubt it's his nature to be serious about anything. At any rate, I sent the perfume and the necklace back, which I'm sure I'll hear about when he sees me—and perhaps the casino will also hear about it. He's impulsive, clownish, and embarrasses me no end.''

The baron stroked his side-whiskers, and said, ''You have influence in the casino. You could have him . . . well . . . ejected, to be polite about it.''

''I doubt it. They're an important family, with a powerful newspaper.''

''Then suggest that they politely hint he is not to annoy you further.''

''That would only make him worse. I wish to heaven that Jeff would come back. That would convince Claude I'm not interested.''

''Well, dear Lydia,'' the baron said, indicating a man across the room, ''you won't have to wonder what he'll do because I think he's seen you, if that is Claude Duprez, and in all my life I never saw a face light up as his just did. I think he *is* truly in love with you.''

''Oh dear,'' Lydia sighed. ''He's carrying the box the necklace came in and he probably has the perfume in his back pocket. Stay with me, please. We must avoid a scene.''

Claude crossed the room with long strides, seized her hand and kissed the back of it. He straightened and glanced at the baron.

''This is Baron Hetzler,'' Lydia said. ''Baron, Claude Duprez.''

''Is he the man you intend to marry?'' Claude asked, his manner so courteous Lydia could not take offense.

''I told you his name was Jeffrey Marcus,'' she replied coolly.

Claude's smile was apologetic. ''So you did. I was hoping to meet him.''

The baron said, ''Monsieur Marcus is on a holiday.''

Claude switched his attention to Lydia. ''I thought you told me Monsieur Marcus came *here* to holiday.''

The baron's face flamed, knowing he'd committed a faux pas.

''Monsieur Duprez . . . .'' Lydia began.

''Claude, please,'' he begged, ''since I wish to call you Lydia.''

"Very well," she acquiesced. "Claude, I have something of importance to discuss with you. As you know, I returned the expensive gifts you sent me except for the flowers. I'll accept no gifts of any kind from you. And please refrain from sending me any more, including flowers."

"My only intent was to assure you that I am serious when I express my affection for you," he said earnestly. "I hold you in the highest regard. I revere you. Please believe that."

"I'm flattered, Claude," she replied quietly. "But, as you know, it is in bad taste to send such gifts to a lady unless you are betrothed to her. My love belongs to Jeff Marcus. And he loves me. I would be most appreciative if you would not force your attentions on me."

"I meant no disrespect," he said earnestly. "The gifts were a mere token of my . . . ."

"Please," Lydia said sternly. "You know my feelings on the matter. I don't wish to discuss it further."

"Then please accept my apology. As I said, I meant no harm, but I understand. You are a young lady of high moral character. That is evident, and I respect you for it. I would like us to be friends. Please, Lydia. At least, grant me that."

Since his behavior was beyond reproach, she could do no less than acquiesce. "Very well, Claude. I believe all you said. However, you must assure me you will respect my request that you send me no more gifts. None whatsoever."

He bowed his head slightly. "But now I have one request to make. Will you please show me about? I am not familiar with this casino."

She felt it would be ungracious to refuse. "All right, after the baron and I dine, although Baron Hetzler would be a better guide."

"But not as beautiful. However, he may accompany us."

"I said—after we dine."

"I'll await you outside," Claude said. "I have no appetite for food since I met you."

He left the room and Lydia sat back with a discouraged

sigh. "Now you understand. Although I must say he behaved much better than I expected."

"He is very determined. You have a problem," the baron agreed. "I'm sorry I said the wrong thing."

Lydia flashed him a smile of forgiveness. "You couldn't have known I told him Jeff came here for a holiday."

"Just what does Jeff do?"

"I haven't the faintest idea." She felt in this case there was no need to be evasive since she didn't know.

"I see," the baron said blandly.

"I wish I did," she replied with a sigh. "Now let's eat slowly. Once we join Claude Duprez, the serenity of the evening will be at an end."

Twice, while they ate, the baron saw Claude come to the entrance of the dining room and regard them. He made no mention of it to Lydia, for he well knew she had not exaggerated the behavior of the young Duprez.

When they could delay no longer, they went to the gambling room where Claude awaited them. The baron led them to a somewhat uncrowded table, and Claude produced an ample bundle of French money, carelessly dropping a large note on the black. The ball clicked its way into the black and Claude's money was doubled. He gathered it up and presented it to the baron, who was too stunned to refuse it even if he'd been so inclined. Claude lost twice, hit eighteen and then raked in another large stack of counters, which he also turned over to the baron. This went on for several minutes, until Lydia tired of the game and deliberately walked away. The baron stayed at the table watching the bet Claude had made before hurrying after Lydia. The play lost and the baron hesitated. He was now supplied with ample funds and was alternately torn between trying to help Lydia and using Claude's money to try and make more. He for once ignored his gambling instinct and trotted toward where Lydia had been stopped by Claude. The baron had an idea that giving him all those winnings was Claude's way of getting rid of him.

Claude was once again trying to impress Lydia with the

fact that he was serious regarding her. "Please, Lydia, at least give me a chance to win your favor. I beg of you, *ma chérie!*"

His voice grew louder as he pressed his case and he was beginning to draw attention. Lydia felt her cheeks begin to flame.

"Monsieur Duprez," she said. "I will agree to anything if you will only stop this insanity. You are creating a disturbance."

"I'm sorry." His voice lowered and his manner became instantly contrite. "I know I behave like a buffoon on occasion. It is usually when something pleases or excites me. I cannot seem to control myself. It isn't that I desire to create a disturbance or to embarrass you, Lydia. I swear it."

"I don't wish to be rude, but I haven't sought out your company and you can't seem to control your emotions when you're with me. I don't like your behavior."

"I understand. I am too impetuous, perhaps too French."

"Whatever it is," Lydia replied, "I don't like it."

"Do you dislike me?" he asked, his voice so soft she could scarcely hear him.

"I'm trying hard not to," she said, softening her statement with a smile.

His smile was apologetic. "I certainly did all the wrong things trying to impress you, didn't I?"

She nodded. "I'm sorry to have to agree."

"Will you give me another chance? I mean I would like the opportunity to show you I won't force my attentions on you. If nothing else, at least I would like to earn your friendship."

"That's not asking too much," she replied. "Just don't forget for an instant that there can be nothing between the two of us but friendship."

"Thank you, Mademoiselle Lydia." He bowed from the waist, but made no attempt to kiss her hand. "Now, may I escort you through the salons to the foyer?"

"You may," she replied quietly, "because I'm returning

to my hotel. As you know, I work for a New York newspaper. I have an article to write and finish in time for the morning cable.''

''Then please allow me to escort you back to your hotel,'' he urged.

Lydia eyed him reflectively. ''You may, though the baron will also accompany us.''

The baron, who had been standing to one side, now moved closer and addressed Claude. ''Are you certain, monsieur, you wish me to keep your winnings? Or do you wish them back?''

Claude smiled down at the baron. ''They're yours. Why don't you return to the table and double them?''

''I would like to—but first I must escort Lydia back to her hotel. I am her official escort until Jeff returns from his holiday.''

''You're very lucky,'' Claude said. ''I would like to meet this Jeff Marcus so that if he had to go on holiday again, he might appoint me Lydia's official escort. But for now, the baron and I will both escort you back to your hotel.''

The baron looked back longingly at the gaming tables as the trio made their way to the exit. To Lydia's surprise, once outside, Claude turned the talk to the beauty of Monte Carlo . . He spoke of the pleasant surprise he had as he'd strolled the streets, noting their cleanliness. The baron informed him that they were swept and washed every morning. Lydia, relieved that the talk had turned away from her, asked if he'd noted that the tall palms that graced the boulevards had been trimmed so that their branches looked like feathery ostrich plumes.

The talk was light and impersonal and the walk so pleasant that Lydia was almost sorry it ended. Claude excused himself at the entrance, stating he would allow the baron to escort her to her suite. He bowed so graciously and his manner was so gentlemanly that, to her astonishment, Lydia extended her hand. He took it, raised it to his lips and immediately released it.

''Good night, Claude,'' she said, giving him a friendly

smile. "I really enjoyed our brief promenade."

"Good night, Lydia," he replied. "I hope I may see you again soon."

"I'm sure our paths will cross," she said. "Come along, Baron."

He did so, waving a farewell to Claude as he followed Lydia into the lobby. He walked her to the lift.

"I can't believe he is the same Claude Duprez I met on his parents' yacht," she said. "His behavior was exemplary."

"He knew you would tolerate no nonsense."

"Yes," she agreed. "I'm of the opinion one must be stern with him."

"I doubt he'll give you any more trouble."

Lydia looked dubious. "I'd like to believe that, but I still haven't forgotten my first meeting with him, or the expensive gifts he sent. I was offended."

The counters in the baron's hand were burning his palm and making it hard for him to concentrate on Lydia's uneasiness. "And yet he is a hard man to dislike, Lydia. It is his enthusiasm that gets in the way of wanting him around. One thing, he does not care who knows he's in love with you."

"I care, because I'm not in love with him. Baron, I know what you want. Once the lift comes, go back and lose what Claude gave you. I will say that he is a generous man and I don't think him unkind, but I wish he'd get aboard that yacht and sail to Bombay."

The baron lifted his gray silk hat in the lobby, said good night and made a hasty exit. Lydia then entered the lift and, upstairs, took the usual precautions before entering her suite.

Once there, she changed into a silk robe and sat down at her desk to compose an article she had in mind. First she had to calm herself. To her surprise, in a short time she was laughing at the memory of the baron's astonishment when Claude handed him counters. The baron was right. Claude was a hard man to dislike.

The writing wouldn't come. She finally gave up and thought about Jeff, reminding herself how different he was from Claude. How she wished he would knock on the door or send up a boy from the lobby to summon her. She was lonely, an attitude she never believed could happen to anyone in Monte Carlo, especially someone with as many friends as she had gained. But it was Jeff whom she prized. She resented the way he had to leave, without explanation, and without her knowing when he'd return. It was his work, of course, whatever his work really was. She no longer believed any of his story about being an engineer assigned to study conditions in Monaco. If it was true, he would have talked more about it, and stayed in town longer because, after all, he couldn't inspect the mountain from Cannes or Paris, could he?

Yet she trusted him. If he misrepresented what he really was doing in Monaco, there was substantial and important reason for that. She realized now that he appeared to exert considerable authority, and that he handled himself like a man well able to take command of any situation.

She also began wondering how much longer those who sought to harm her would remain quiet. Except for Claude, it had been tranquil for too long a time. She had a strong hunch they hadn't given up. They were only biding their time and would strike at her again as soon as they were ready.

She even toyed with Morgan's offer to send her elsewhere. It was an attractive offer under the circumstances, but Lydia was determined to learn who was behind the harassment she'd been subjected to.

When she finally went to bed and extinguished the bedlight, she half expected to hear Claude banging on the door, insisting in a loud voice that he was in love with her.

Fifteen

When Lydia emerged from the lift the next morning, she was surprised to find Drury standing directly before it. He smiled, bowed and removed his hat.

"Good morning," he said amiably. "I'm waiting for Madelaine."

"Good morning," Lydia returned the greeting. She was about to continue on, but Drury touched her arm.

"I saw what was going on in the casino last night . . . I'm talking about Claude Duprez. You apparently caught his fancy. Does your friend Marcus know about him?"

Lydia's face flamed angrily. "No. But he will."

"He should." Drury spoke with feigned concern. "Certainly the baron couldn't handle him. But then, his parents can't control him, either. Spoiled and too much money. He's also very persuasive, I hear, so I suggest you be on guard."

Lydia wondered why he bothered to warn her. "I can handle him, Mr. Drury. No need for you to concern yourself."

"I have no intention of becoming involved, Miss Bradley." He mocked her formal tone. "By the way, just what does your Mr. Marcus do?"

"He's a geologist and he's trying to determine the stability of the mountain. There seems to be some indication it might slip . . . something of that nature."

Drury's smile was disbelieving. "This rocky point slipping into the sea? I never heard of any danger of that and I've asked a thousand questions about Monaco for my book. Maybe I should investigate it. Might make an extra chapter.

Would Jeff Marcus talk to me, do you think? We did have something of a rough session. Perhaps if you interceded.''

"I'm sure you could research it," Lydia said crisply.

"I will. Historical books could do with a bit of humor. Remember what I said about Claude Duprez. He can be very bothersome."

"I told you, Mr. Drury, I can handle Duprez."

He'd succeeded in angering her, which was undoubtedly what he'd set out to do. Before she made a fool of herself by losing her temper, Lydia turned abruptly and left the hotel, his mocking gaze following her. She walked swiftly down to the cable office with the brief dispatch. She was out of breath by the time she reached it and, despite the balmy breeze, bathed in perspiration. She got a grip on herself and slowed her steps. The day was beautiful and the sky blue and cloudless. She decided to stroll down to the beach rather than return to the hotel. She'd rarely gone there, and had found no time to indulge in swimming. At this time of morning the beach was mostly empty, a fine place to enjoy the warm sunlight and the sea-drenched air.

Halfway along the walk she realized her mistake. Coming toward her with loping steps and a big grin on his face was Claude Duprez. There was no doubting who the object of his attention was. She couldn't retreat or run, so she took a long, slow breath and continued her leisurely pace until he faced her at close range. At least she had her temper under control.

"I was about to begin searching for you, Lydia," he told her.

"I would really like to be alone," she said frankly. "I have a headache."

"I'm sorry. You were so kind to me last night. I hope I'm not the cause of your headache."

"You're not."

"I'd like to believe that," he said, turning to walk in the same direction as Lydia.

"It's the truth."

"I hope so. I also hope you don't dislike me."

"I'm sure few people would dislike you if you'd stop behaving like an idiot," Lydia smiled.

"You're right. I don't know what gets into me. Well, in your case I do. I know you won't take me seriously when I say I love you, but . . . ."

"Claude!" she warned sharply.

"Let me finish, please. I know also that you're in love with someone else and I can't do anything about that. I wish to heaven you were not engaged, but seeing that you are, I promise to stop what you call my nonsense, even though I don't consider it nonsense to tell a girl you're in love with her."

"Let's not discuss it further," she said. "I'll forget what you just said, and to make sure you don't say it again, I won't see you and you're not to call on me or send me gifts. Should we meet, I'll be friendly and your behavior must be decorous. If you send me a gift, simple or lavish, I shall return it. Those are my conditions."

He nodded slowly, his face morose. "I accept them. I know the depth of emotion I feel for you is hopeless, but I'll never cease loving you, even if I never see you again. I say this only to let you know that I am sincere. That over with, my parents would like you to call on them, right now, if you have the time. My father wishes you to interview him for a story on how Monte treats the owner of a great newspaper. The sort of thing that will make him and Monte look well in the eyes of the world."

Lydia had been searching for a story, and this idea seemed to be a good one. "I'll be delighted to see your parents and interview your father," she said graciously. "I had hoped he would allow me to do an article about him. Will you be present?"

"I'd like to be, but I'll behave." He raised his right hand. "My word on it."

She allowed him to take her arm and, nearing the yacht, she admired it once again. "It must be exciting to be able to just lift anchor and go wherever you please."

"Not half as much fun as you think, not after you've been everywhere. It becomes a bore. Don't mention that to my father. Owning this yacht has been the dream of his life."

A crewman stood on deck watching them as Claude led

271

her across the deck and down to the cabins below. He knocked on one door. Lydia heard no answer, but he opened it, took a firmer grip on her arm and led her into the cabin. There was no one to receive them.

He closed the door, turned the key and put it in his pocket. "Sit down, Lydia."

Her face flushed angrily. "I insist on knowing if I'm going to see your parents."

"Not now. Maybe later. I want to talk to you, calmly and, I hope, effectively."

"You brought me here on a ruse. Open that door and let me out of here!"

"In due time, my sweet Lydia . . . in due time." He sat down opposite her in one of the big leather chairs. "It won't hurt you to listen to me."

"I know what you're going to say, Claude. It's not only a waste of time, but you're making me very angry."

"I will risk it," he said. "I won't let you off this boat until you listen to me, and with an open mind."

"I'm tired of listening to your foolishness—you act like a deranged man. I don't like being tricked into coming here, either. You made up that story of your father wishing me to interview him."

"I could think of no other way to get you here. Anyway, they'll be back this evening. You'll see them, but for now I intend to make you listen to reason. I am not crazy. I am not drunk. I have something to say and you will listen. If you wish to get out of here, you will listen."

"What will you do, keep me a prisoner on this boat?" Lydia tried reasoning with him. "Claude, be sensible. I'll be missed. Someone will think of you, recall your antics of last evening and suspect you may have a hand in my disappearance. The baron can't fail to think that you might be responsible. This is virtually a kidnapping, and you're going to be in very serious trouble."

"If they catch me. Even so, they'll be considerate, knowing how much I'm in love with you. The French always sympathize with the jilted one in a crime of amour. Also, my father has a powerful newspaper. Monte wants favorable

272

publicity. Our paper is important . . . it can give Monte that.''

"I can't force my way out of here, but I can disregard anything you say," Lydia retorted.

"Is it not possible for a young woman to shut herself off from the world for days at a time?"

"Days? What are you talking about?"

"I'll begin talking in a moment. If you do not listen, if you refuse to make comments, even nasty ones, I shall see to it that we weigh anchor and sail. To anywhere, just so long as nobody can reach us. Are you now convinced that I insist on making my speech?"

She didn't reply and looked away from him. He laughed, not loudly or mirthfully, but as if he was mocking her.

"Lydia, I have a great deal of money. Father will leave me more, along with a successful newspaper. I promise that I shall hand you the ownership of the newspaper to do with as you will. That's one small inducement. Of course, you'll have to marry me first. Are you listening?"

She made no response, didn't even look his way. He shrugged.

"Take all the time you want. Eventually you will see my side. I can offer you every opportunity. I'm not rough or cruel. Actually, I'm kind and quite gentle. I've been well-educated, I have a brilliant future to which I've paid no heed whatsoever because I had no reason to. You will give me that reason. In a year's time, I'll make us one of the most important and sought-after couples in Monte, Paris, London or anywhere else."

Inwardly, Lydia was beginning to grow frightened. This smiling man, young and handsome, might really be deranged. He might grow violent if he encountered too much frustration. Still, she couldn't bring herself to accommodate him by listening and arguing. He'd never see her side, anyway. He seemed really obsessed with the idea of marrying her, absurd as this was, and nothing was going to stop him, not even the fact that she loved someone else. His behavior was that of a petulant child or of a lunatic.

"I haven't much more to say," he went on. "Now it is

your turn. If you don't speak, you will go on a long voyage with me. Do you understand? I promise not to harm you. I will not even touch you until you acquiesce. But that you must do even if it takes a journey twice around the world."

She made no reply and refused to look at him even though she was listening. More and more she was convinced she was dealing with a madman, a quiet sort of madman, but likely as dangerous as one given to violence.

"My love for you is not the love of an immature boy," he said. "It is honest, genuine adult love. Now I humbly ask you to marry me. You will agree or I shall get this ship underway."

She was concerned, worried and at a loss as to what to do. If she tried to answer him, it would be only to reject his wild idea. This would cause only more problems. He would continue his pleadings, this time on a yacht that was sailing somewhere . . . or nowhere.

He waited a moment, then exploded fiercely. "Damn you! You refuse to believe me, but I warned you, Lydia. I'm not fooling. In one minute I'm going on deck, and I'll order this ship be made ready to sail. Do you understand me?"

She sat immobile, silent, her head still averted so she wouldn't have to look at him. There was nothing else she could do unless she gave him the answer he was insisting on. She reasoned that when she was missed and the yacht known to have sailed, no one would have to guess where she might be. Not after the way Claude had acted at the casino. But she had to take some sort of action. The way to do that was to make certain everyone in Monaco knew he was pursuing her in a way that could only be termed molestation. If he was arrested, he might begin to see reason.

Claude cursed again, arose, took the key from his pocket, and unlocked the door, while watching her every moment so she had no opportunity to rush past him. Then he stepped out, closed the door and the key turned in the lock.

Lydia stood up. First, she made sure the door was really locked. Then she walked to the porthole, which was closed.

If it happened to face the dock she might be able to attract the attention of someone, a passerby or a worker. She discovered that the porthole was sealed and therefore impossible to open; Claude had apparently carefully planned this beforehand. If he hadn't encountered her on her stroll, he would have sought her out and brought her here, using the interview as a reason.

She wondered if the crew would respond to his order to sail, or if they'd recognize what he was trying to do and set her free even against his orders. If they obeyed his command, they would be as guilty of kidnapping as he. They might realize this, and she could persuade them to free her. But they might also believe she went willingly for a *rendezvous d'amour.*

Ten minutes went by. Then she heard some kind of engine start up, followed by the creaking of the winch that raised the anchor. Claude was going through with his crazy scheme! She pounded on the door with her fists and called out, but no one came, nothing happened. Soon now they'd start the engine and the yacht would sail. She'd be powerless in his hands from then on. It was possible he might keep his promise not to touch her, but she couldn't be certain of that. If he tried to take her, there'd be no one to stop him. She fought tears of frustration and sat down, trembling with fear.

She heard the key turn in the lock and she braced herself for whatever Claude had in mind. But it was a seaman, a member of the crew who opened the door and silently beckoned to her, at the same time indicating with his straightened forefinger pressed against his lips that she must be quiet.

"He's in the engine room," he said softly. "The man is crazy, mademoiselle. Get off this boat as quickly as you can, but please . . . don't tell anyone I let you escape."

"Thank you," she whispered. "Thank you very much."

"Wait for a few seconds," the stocky Frenchman said. "Give me a chance to get on deck. I'll signal if it's clear."

"Yes," she said with great relief. "Yes, I'll wait."

He disappeared. She began to count, her heart beating quickly. It would take him perhaps two minutes to reach

275

the deck, another to orient himself so he could watch for anybody who might see her leave. She tiptoed along the corridor, and had almost reached the companionway when she thought she heard footsteps on deck, coming her way.

She promptly tried the door of a cabin beside her. It was unlocked and she darted inside, closing the door and putting her ear against the panels to determine if anyone was down here. If it turned out to be Claude and he found her gone, she was defeated. But she heard no footsteps, no further sound. She paused another moment to get her breath back and when she turned away from her listening post at the door she saw that this cabin contained several bulging burlap bags, one of which had been torn partially open.

Curiosity, even in the face of this danger, caused her to bend down and examine the contents of the torn bag. She was looking at a brand-new, highly polished roulette wheel. By sense of feel she determined that the other burlap sacks, five of them, also contained roulette wheels. But there was no time to wonder what they were doing aboard. She left the room and cautiously made her way to the deck, where the same seaman signaled all was clear. In a blind panic she crossed the deck, left the boat, and once she reached the dock, kept running.

She didn't stop until she was so winded she couldn't go on. On one of the garden benches she collapsed, almost gasping for breath. Her knees were shaking—partly from the effort of running so fast and partly from the remnants of the fear that still gripped her. Lydia told herself between gasps that she must reward that seaman somehow, without Claude or his parents knowing about it. She was convinced now that Claude was a maniac, a man unresponsive to reasoning and perhaps even savage when the mood was upon him. With some of her strength regained, she made her way back to the hotel. The terror of her latest encounter with Claude was slowly being replaced with an overwhelming longing to feel Jeff's arms around her while she told him what had happened.

The baron wouldn't be able to help. Mr. Morgan would only get angry and go to the yacht where Claude might harm him. She doubted Monsieur and Madame Duprez were even aboard. Would they be shocked if they learned what their son had tried to do? She wondered if perhaps he'd done it before.

But for the kindness of that seaman, she'd be sailing now, and utterly at the mercy of Claude. When he discovered she was gone, it wouldn't be beyond him to look for her again, even to using force to get her back on the yacht. She shuddered at the thought of it.

Nevertheless, she couldn't stay shut up in her suite. She must go about her business in the face of whatever difficulties Claude might present. If he tried to carry her off bodily, she meant to scream and fight him all the way. After an hour's rest, she changed her dress for an afternoon walk to the casino. Surely she was safe enough in daylight with people about. She was bound to find the baron there, and he could offer some sort of protection, if only to add his shouts to hers if Claude returned with renewed intent to kidnap her.

She found the baron watching a table at which Bryant Drury was playing. He seemed to be having some luck from the array of counters on the table before him. When the baron saw her, he promptly left the table to greet her.

"Is something wrong?" he asked, seeing the anxiety on her face.

"Indeed it is. Have you seen Claude?"

"No, not since last evening."

"The man is mad. He locked me in a cabin on his yacht and threatened to sail off with me if I didn't agree that I loved him. He's totally gone, mentally I mean. Stay with me, Baron. From now on I shall go nowhere without you or Mr. Morgan. If only Jeff would come back! I don't want to be alone again, because there's no telling what Claude will do."

"My, you are upset. You should go to the police." The baron took her arm and sat her down on a bench along the wall.

"I can't do that. Maybe I should, but I can't bring myself to let this become public. Partly for the sake of his parents, who, I'm sure, are fine people, but mostly for me. This could even be another way of tormenting me, except that it's been done openly and can't be the work of whoever arranged the banquet or the encounter with the Russians. I can't see Claude being mixed up in the murder of Martel, either. But he's certainly added to the humiliation I've been subjected to."

"Has Mr. Morgan left?"

"No. At least, I don't think he'd go without telling me," Lydia said.

"He stayed very late last night, gambling. He won a few thousand up to the time I left. Perhaps he's just sleeping. I know it's afternoon, but a whole evening of gambling wears on one."

"We'll know soon enough. Take me to dinner, please. I'm not very hungry even though I haven't eaten since breakfast."

"I am famished, as usual. I must tell you, however, Mr. Drury is doing quite well. If his luck keeps on, he'll walk away much richer than when he started to gamble."

"I don't want to talk to him, either, Baron. All I wish to do is pass the time until Mr. Morgan shows up. I'll have to tell him what happened. Perhaps he'll have some sort of a solution—I know I haven't. I'm at a complete loss as to how to handle Claude."

They were leaving the casino when the baron seized her arm and brought her to an abrupt stop. He pointed at a blond man down the street.

"There—the madman Claude. He is going back to the yacht."

"We'll stay here until there's no chance of his seeing me. I don't want another encounter with him, not today."

"Why did you go on the yacht with him, Lydia?"

"I went for a stroll and met him. He apparently was on his way to seek me out with a trumped-up story that his father wished me to do an article about him. Since the Duprez newspaper is important and Monsieur Duprez well known, I was flattered. And you know I'm always after a story."

"He appealed to your vanity," the baron reasoned.

She nodded, coloring slightly. "Anyway, his parents were nowhere in sight when he brought me aboard."

"That alone should have made you suspicious."

"It didn't, because he told me they were below. I followed him without the slightest hesitancy."

"So if any of the crew were watching, they would immediately draw the conclusion that you had a prearranged rendezvous with him."

"I suppose so." Lydia decided not to mention the seaman who had arranged her escape from the yacht. The baron might inadvertently let the story slip, and the seaman might lose his job or—with Claude—be physically harmed.

"In that case, it would be useless for you to go to the police. If they questioned the crew, they would state they saw you board the yacht willingly in the company of Claude, whose behavior was gentlemanly if not gallant."

"Surely the crew must know what he's like!"

"They might very well know, but remember, their jobs would be at stake. Some American ladies come here and behave in a very bold manner."

"I'm sure there are European ladies who do the same," Lydia said testily.

"Of a certainty. However, this argument is getting us nowhere, and I am hungry."

"You're always hungry," Lydia said, scolding him mildly. "I talk about my honor almost being compromised and you talk about your stomach."

"At my age, my dear, that's just as important as your honor."

She laughed. "If Jeff knew that, he wouldn't have left me in your care."

"I wonder why he did," the baron mused, giving her a reproving glance, "when you go hither, thither and yon without me."

"I'm not a child," she retorted.

"I don't think a child could have as many escapades as you. Not even a soldier of fortune!"

"They're not of my doing," she reminded him.

"The one this morning was owing to your trusting a man you yourself termed a maniac."

"He swore he would respect my wish not to be further annoyed by him."

"And you foolishly believed him."

"I told you my story. I won't say more." Lydia's voice was stubborn.

"Just the same, you were reckless to set foot on that yacht."

"Also, just the same—it was kidnapping. Claude locked me in the cabin. Luckily, I managed to get out and escape."

"Yes, if you were locked in it certainly was kidnapping. But since you escaped and you're safe, I agree—we won't discuss it further. We're on the verge of a quarrel. You're a stubborn young lady and a courageous one."

"I was terrified," she exclaimed indignantly. Then, for no reason, she burst into laughter. The baron regarded her with amazement, then joined her, and the tension broke.

"Will it be the Café de Paris?" he asked, wiping the tears from his eyes.

"Yes." She slipped her arm around his and as they resumed their walk, she glanced down at the docks. Claude was almost at the yacht.

Once they were seated, she breathed a sigh of relief. "I think I'd enjoy a glass of champagne."

"So would I," the baron agreed. He raised a hand to signal the wine steward and gave the order.

"Oh dear, what now?" Lydia saw the headwaiter approach the table, holding a small package.

"It was left for you, mademoiselle."

"Thank you," she said, somewhat mystified. She removed the coarse outer wrapper, revealing a purple, velvet-covered oval box. There was no card. She thought of Jeff and wondered if it might be from him as she opened the box carefully. Nestling in a bed of satin were large emeralds set in a chain of gold. In the center was a card on which was written, "I love you. Claude."

"Damn him!" she exploded. "Won't he ever leave me alone?"

Sixteen

George Morgan had not awakened until well after noon and this only because there was a sharp knock on the door of his hotel room. He slipped into a robe, walked barefoot to the door and looked with a puzzled expression at the man who stood before him, smiling slightly.

"Mr. Morgan?" he asked. "Mr. George Morgan?"

"Yes. Do I know you, sir?"

"No. My name is Jeffrey Marcus. Perhaps Lydia has mentioned me to you."

"Jeff," Morgan exclaimed and reached out for Jeff's hand. "Come in. Please, come in. I've been anxious to meet you. You have no idea how much."

"I just got back. I came to see you at once, hoping you hadn't left Monaco."

"I intended to leave this afternoon, but I overslept. I was gambling until all hours."

"I trust you've been lucky, sir?"

"Middling. Look here, I haven't even brushed my teeth yet. Would you be kind enough to ask that breakfast be sent up. For two. Or would you favor the restaurant?"

"I prefer the privacy of your suite, if you don't mind."

"Not at all. I think it might be best, what with the things we have to talk about."

"Indeed," Jeff said grimly.

"Have you seen Lydia?"

"No. I wanted to talk with you first. It's extremely important."

"I'll be ready quickly. Takes me only a few minutes to shave. You do the ordering," Morgan said as he disappeared into the bathroom.

Jeff went to the row of buttons on the wall beside the door and pushed the one for room service. The waiter came a minute later and Jeff ordered, then sat down to wait for his host. Morgan entered the parlor just as the waiter arrived with the breakfast table.

"You didn't tell me what you wanted," Jeff said. "Nor even if you preferred dinner, so I used my own judgment and ordered breakfast. I skipped mine, also."

He poured coffee while Morgan served the eggs, sausages and potatoes. There were also hot rolls and marmalade. Morgan looked across the table and asked, "Who starts first?"

Jeff smiled. "I think I might. I don't know what Lydia has told you about me."

"She's in love with you and she thinks you're a very mysterious gentleman," Morgan said succinctly.

"As for the latter, I don't wonder. I have to leave her often and unexpectedly. Also, I told her a weak story about my being a geologist interested in making certain the Alps aren't going to slide into the sea and take Monte Carlo with them. I should have known better. She was too clever to accept that."

"What are you doing, then?" Morgan asked. "Or are you at liberty to tell me?"

"With the provision you keep it a strict secret. Oh, yes, I also have permission to tell Lydia now and, perhaps, the baron. He's been of great help to her—and to me. I'm a member of Interpol."

Morgan's hand paused with a forkful of food halfway to his mouth. "International Police?"

"Yes. We're a fairly new organization covering worldwide crime. We heard, through a number of sources, some reliable but most of them very unreliable, that there was something afoot concerned with Monte Carlo. I was sent here to see what I could find."

"And did you find anything?"

282

"Nothing. Not even anything unusual . . . until some-one began harassing Lydia."

"She told me about it, and she's naturally extremely worried. Is she in real danger, do you think?"

"I don't know. I've found it impossible to reconcile what's been happening to her with any crime designed to break loose in Monte. Frankly, this is the hardest case I've been assigned to. The trouble is, whoever happens to be back of all this, is very suspicious of everyone who has any connection with Lydia. I know for a fact that they checked on me, back as far as my college in Massachusetts."

"Did they discover who you are?"

"I doubt it. You see, I really am a graduate geologist. I thought I'd make it my career, but I found it boring after a while and when an offer came to join Interpol, I jumped at it. Of course my association with Interpol is strictly secret. If they check further, they'll discover papers indi-cating a geologist was needed here. I'm safe, I think, but Lydia is not, and that's where the problem lies. I can't figure out why they've chosen her for a target."

"Target? Was there an attempt on her life?"

"I believe so. Has she told you the complete story?"

"More than she intended, too. I wheedled it out of her." He grinned. "I'm a newspaper man myself, you know. But she made no mention of being a target."

"First they tried minor things to embarrass her. Then it grew worse. They tricked her into writing a story about a very fine man, an Arabian prince. The information she was given would have resulted in more trouble than she could handle if it was ever printed."

"It would also have got her fired. She told me about the cable she sent that never got through. Can you explain it?"

Jeff laughed softly. "The man in charge of the cable office is one of us. We find such people of tremendous value. He consulted me and then destroyed the cable. Both he and I swore up and down to Lydia that it was a great mystery. I know it has driven Lydia half out of her mind trying to figure out what happened, but I haven't been able to tell her about it. Not yet. Not even the fact that we had an Interpol man in a room on the floor of her hotel to keep an eye on her. A good thing we did. I was checking some things with him when that Trencher crook waylaid Lydia in her suite. Her scream brought us to her aid, though she'd already frightened Trencher enough by the racket she made so that he ran from the suite straight into my arms. We had alerted the police to keep an eye on the hotel, too, and their man was right on the spot within moments.

"Is the Interpol fellow still here?" Morgan looked concerned.

"Like me, he's had to move back and forth to Cannes and Paris, but he'll be a part of this operation so long as we feel Lydia is in danger."

"It's that serious?"

"We believe it is."

"Was the affair with the Russians also set up?"

"Cleverly. They fomented that trouble through a man who went by the name of Martel. He somehow bribed someone to be assigned a seat next to Lydia at the Arabian prince's banquet. He must have been a very convincing man, because Lydia believed everything he said. He also arranged to sell Lydia to the Russians and, finally, at a railroad station reception for the Prince of Wales, in a pretended assassination attempt he fired two shots at Lydia. She saw Martel before he fired, pointed him out to me and we were able to avoid the bullets. Now, if he had succeeded in killing her, it would have looked for all the world like an attempt on the life of the British prince, with Lydia the unfortunate victim of a man with a poor aim."

"They must be a dangerous group, whoever they are."

"I'm not certain the bullets were meant to kill. They missed by too wide a margin, but Lydia was terrified and I don't mind telling you it gave me quite a scare."

"That's understandable. I know Martel is now dead."

"His death was made to appear as if he had hung himself, but actually we know he was murdered. By whom we've not the faintest idea. As for Martel, there was nothing on his person. Not a tailor's label, not a laundry mark. We don't even know who he really is or where he stayed in

Monte. Certainly not at any hotel or villa. We've exhausted every means of trying to identify him. Because we have no leads, tracing his movements has been almost impossible.

"Lydia has no idea what's going on, or why. Neither have I, even though I've wracked my brains to find some sort of reason. I did suspect Drury. You know about him, of course."

"Oh yes, I know all about him. I fired him."

"Lydia told me in detail about that. I warned him to stay away from her."

Morgan said, "She suspected him at first because he swore to get even with her, but now she swears he's not involved. We checked him through our newspaper and discovered he's telling the truth when he says he's here to write a book on Monte. I even confirmed it through the publisher."

Jeff smiled. "I know you did. We've investigated him back to his day of birth. He's a soldier-of-fortune type. A very good journalist."

"Good, but not trustworthy."

"We discovered that, too. Perhaps the powers behind these attempts and this plotting hoped Drury would be blamed. No matter what his character might be, there's absolutely nothing to tie him with . . . what shall I say? A gang? Or a single ruthless individual? I don't know."

"When will you tell her about yourself, Jeff?"

"When I went down to order breakfast, I sent a man to the Café de Paris where she's dining with the baron. At the end of their meal she'll be told that you wish to see her immediately in your suite. She should arrive shortly."

Morgan smiled. "At which time you'll take her into your confidence."

"Yes. I've permission to do so, finally. We can protect her better if she knows we're around to help. Also, she'll feel safer. She's been through enough."

"I'm glad to hear you say that. I was afraid you had neglected her. Certainly you weren't around when she needed you."

"True. I'm sorry to say my superiors insisted on using

her as a decoy, no matter how much I protested. They deliberately let her be vulnerable in the hope the trouble-makers would reveal themselves in some way. That's why I made sure we had a man in her hotel to protect her—though I must say, she still had some close calls. Too close. Since the decoy didn't work, I have a feeling that they're as clever as they are deadly."

Morgan frowned. "I'm not sure I want Lydia to be a part of this—even knowingly."

"She'll be well-guarded henceforward—even more than she knows. I think if you put it to her, she'd refuse to leave Monte."

"I suppose you're right; she told me already she wants to stay. She has lots of spirit, despite what she's been through."

"We have a hunch that whatever is going to happen here will take place soon."

"What about the baron? Do you completely trust him?"

"Yes. Don't you?" Jeff asked cautiously.

"I don't know. He seems perfectly harmless, perhaps too much so. I know he's given Lydia valuable information, and helped her enormously when she first arrived here. But that too, could be to maintain contact with her and allay any suspicion she might have about him."

"I doubt that, though anything is possible since we have no idea who's behind what is to take place or even what it is they want. As for the baron, his movements have been carefully monitored. He has a modest apartment, plus a mistress who sees to his needs and who's an excellent pho-tographer. I believe you received several pictures which she took—one of which enabled England to catch a criminal."

"Of course. I forgot that. I still don't think we should eliminate the idea of revenge against her," Morgan rea-soned. "After all, it could be that someone found one or more of her articles offensive."

Jeff dismissed that argument. "We checked everything she's written and eliminated the individuals she's written about from our list of suspects."

"I'm glad you don't think it's the baron," Morgan said

reflectively. "I like the little fellow. I suppose what made me suspicious of him was the fact that he has such a weakness for gambling despite his rotten luck. Compulsive gamblers are easy to bribe or threaten. Will you have a cigar?"

"No, thank you. Light up if you wish."

"Goes well with coffee," Morgan said. He leaned back to enjoy his smoke. "What's next? What do you intend to do?"

Jeff gestured helplessly. "Wait. That's all we can do. Wait and hope that the next time some outrageous stunt is pulled to frighten Lydia, we can find a clue. It's a sad thing to say, but I'm stumped. So is the whole organization. We know something is brewing and it has to be big, but why it concerns Lydia we've no idea. And neither has she."

"Then you're right back where you started from."

"Unfortunately, Mr. Morgan. We're a fine organization, but we have no crystal ball. We need a clue or evidence of some sort."

Morgan drew on the cigar. "I admit I'm well comforted to know the Interpol is aware that there's something amiss. For Lydia's sake."

"I only wish we knew what." Jeff drew out his watch and snapped it open. "Lydia and the baron should be here any minute."

A moment later a light tap sounded on the door. Jeff got up and opened it.

Lydia stood there, too stunned with surprise for a few moments to say anything. Then, with a cry of joy, she ran into Jeff's outstretched arms. Morgan smiled and tactfully turned to tap his cigar over an ashtray. He liked Jeff and seeing Lydia's joy at sight of him was further reassurance that she'd be looked after.

She said, "Jeff! How I've missed you. I'm pleased and relieved that you're here at last . . . and annoyed that you never stay."

"Stop talking and let me kiss you," he said.

The kiss was long and fervent and they clung to each other while Morgan stared thoughtfully at the ceiling. Afterward, they held the embrace without saying a word. For the first time in days Lydia felt free of fear and safe from danger.

Jeff broke the embrace finally, but his hands gripped her arms lightly as he studied her face and her eyes, soft with love for him.

"I can tell you this, my darling," he said, "I won't be going away again."

"Oh, Jeff! That sounds too good to be true. But I hope so—especially after what happened today."

"What happened today?" he asked with concern.

"Before I tell you, I'd like further assurance you meant what you said—about not going away."

Mr. Morgan stood up. The movement startled her, since she'd not even been aware of his presence.

"I didn't mean to frighten you, Lydia," Morgan said, "but I'm sure with Jeff's arm around you, you'll relax quickly. I'm pleased Jeff is here. And I'm sure after he's talked with you, you'll be convinced he won't be absent again."

"That's good news, but I'd like to hear it from Jeff," she said stubbornly.

Jeff led her to a small sofa and they sat down side by side, his arm around her shoulders. Her face beamed with happiness, but her eyes still questioned his, asking for reassurance.

"As you know," he said, "I've been called away at odd times without giving you an explanation. Now I can, for I've received permission from my superiors who believe it's time for you to be told the whole story."

"Good," Lydia said with a sigh of relief. "I'm tired of mysteries."

"There's mystery involved," Jeff said, "and part of it concerns you. First though, I'll enlighten you about me. I'm a member of Interpol."

"Interpol!" she exclaimed. "You mean the International Police?"

"That's correct," Jeff said. "I belong to their network."

"Just what are the duties of Interpol?" she asked curiously, trying to take in this startling revelation.

"We're an investigative unit, darling. We leave the arresting to the police."

"What does that have to do with me?"

"Let me start at the beginning. We've known for some time that a plot is hatching to commit some crime in Monte Carlo. The most likely place would be the casino, since it would be a perfect target for thieves. However, so far we haven't found the slightest clue of what's planned or who's doing the planning."

"How do I fit into it?" Lydia asked, perplexed.

"We don't know. What we suspect strongly is that they want you out of the way."

"You mean they want to murder me?" Lydia cried out in dismay.

"I doubt that," Jeff said. "Such a thing would bring on an investigation. After all, you're here representing an important New York City newspaper."

"I'm thoroughly confused," Lydia said. "Please explain."

"We've had you watched for some time now; we even installed an Interpol man on your hotel floor," Jeff said, "for that purpose. I was visiting him when the incident with Trencher happened. That's how I was able to get to you so quickly." Jeff continued as understanding dawned in Lydia's eyes. "You see, we believe that for some reason they want you to leave Monte Carlo, and the harassment and embarrassments you've been subjected to following the incident with Trencher were part of this. We don't believe Martel was hired to kill you, however, for the reason I stated earlier—you work for an important newspaper."

"But had that article you thought you'd cabled—the one concerning that Arabian prince—got into the paper," Morgan broke in, "I'd have had no recourse other than to fire you as I did Drury. You'd have had no reason to stay in Monte."

Lydia nodded slowly. "I see." I would have left, just as they may have planned.

Jeff confessed, "About that missing cablegram. I was responsible for its not being sent."

Lydia's eyes widened. "You! The last person on earth. . . ." Then she smiled. "I forgive you." You saved my job.

"Now," Jeff said, "tell us what happened to you today."

"Nothing concerning what you just told me," she said.

"I still want to know," Jeff said.

"I went for a walk and was lured onto a yacht where I was locked in a cabin and told I wouldn't be released until I consented to marry the man responsible for my kidnapping."

"Good God!" Morgan leaned forward. "You must mean that pup Claude Duprez."

"That's exactly who I mean, Mr. Morgan."

"Tell us more," Jeff urged.

"Claude Duprez maintains he's so deeply in love with me that I must marry him. It doesn't matter what I do or say. I told him I love you, Jeff, I've called him insane, but nothing makes any difference. He has given me very expensive gifts, which I've returned except for the most recent of them. Here . . . look at this. It's his way of apologizing for what he did this morning."

Jeff examined the emeralds. "These are worth a fortune. Our training in Interpol includes judging the value of gems. I should say this was worth about twenty thousand American dollars."

"I'd like to throw this in his face," Lydia added. "I know that's not ladylike, but he has me at my wit's end. He's embarrassed me, followed me, argued with me in public, all this even though I told him how hopeless his cause is. He thinks money can buy anything, or money can let him get away with anything, like this foolish thing he did today. I was so mortified and so frightened I think I aged a few years. The man is impossible!"

"Now give me the facts. Exactly what happened?" Jeff asked grimly.

"I'd like to know how you got away from that idiot," Morgan added.

"I had help," Lydia said. "But let me start at the beginning. I decided to go for a stroll down to the docks this

290

morning. The day was ideal and the walk would relax me. Only when I reached the water did I realize I'd made a foolish mistake. Claude Duprez was coming toward me, a welcoming smile on his face. My first impulse was to run, but I knew he'd catch up to me, so I decided to attempt to reason with him. To my amazement, there was no need. The first thing he did was apologize for his behavior. Then he swore I'd never have occasion to be offended with him again. He said he knew he'd been wrong, he knew I loved another man and his manner would henceforth be respectful of my wishes.''

"And you believed him.'' Mr. Morgan's features evidenced his chagrin.

"Yes. He really seemed sincere and there was something else. He told me his father wished me to interview him for an article for my paper. Naturally, I was delighted. He said that his parents would like to welcome me to the yacht and the interview could be done at once. Again, I believed him and went on board willingly.''

"Were you seen?'' Jeff asked.

"Only by members of the crew.''

"Who would believe you were a willing guest of Duprez,'' he reasoned.

"Yes. Claude brought me below, telling me his parents were waiting there. Once I entered the cabin and looked around to see it empty, I knew it was a ruse. Before I could escape, he locked the door and put the key in his pocket. Then he started the foolishness again, stating he was going to marry me and would hold me prisoner until I consented. If I refused, or waited too long, he would order the yacht put to sea. Of course, I refused. I didn't dare speak to him or look at him. He unlocked the door and before I could get to it, he was out of the cabin and had me locked in.''

"Did he manhandle you?'' Jeff asked angrily.

"He didn't come near me. He never has attempted anything rough. He simply stated before he left that he was going to order the yacht put to sea. I knew then his parents weren't even on board, or he could never have gotten away with such a thing.''

"How did you escape?" Jeff asked.

"One of the crew opened the cabin door and told me he would get me off the ship. He said Claude was crazy. That was the word he used to describe Claude's behavior."

"I agree," Morgan said. "Though I attributed it more to eccentricity."

"Mr. Morgan," Jeff asked, "do you know if that yacht is used for any purpose other than pleasure?"

"You mean any of the Duprez business ventures?" Morgan replied.

"Yes."

"I couldn't answer that," Morgan said.

"It's certainly a large ship," Lydia mused. "Do you suppose they plan to use it as a gambling ship?"

Jeff's brows raised at the question. "Why do you ask that?"

"Because after I left the cabin where Claude had imprisoned me, I thought I heard someone coming down the companionway, or about to, so I let myself into another cabin. While I was there, I saw several burlap-wrapped objects, one of which had been torn open. It contained a roulette wheel."

Jeff frowned. "A roulette wheel? Darling . . . are you sure it wasn't some miniature wheel used in private games?"

"It was full size. I've certainly seen enough of them to know that. Also the other bundles contained more wheels. I didn't actually see these, but it wasn't hard to identify them by size and shape . . . I felt all of them to be sure. There were five or six roulette wheels in that cabin."

Jeff glanced at Morgan. "That's interesting."

"I agree, though I suppose there's no law against carrying roulette wheels about?"

"No, but there has to be a reason." Jeff looked thoughtful.

"Jeff," Lydia asked, "do you think the Duprez family are up to something?"

"I can't answer that any more than your question about who has been tormenting you. Perhaps there's no connection whatsoever, but I'm going to be mighty sure of that. This fresh angle bears careful investigation."

"What kind of investigation?" Lydia asked.

Jeff regarded her speculatively. "Do you think you could get me aboard that yacht?"

"No," she said firmly. "Unless you want me to tell Claude I forgive him and I've reconsidered his proposal."

"You're right, of course," Jeff said. "Could you sketch a drawing to include the location of the cabin that contained the roulette wheels?"

"What's on your mind?" Morgan asked.

"I'd want to do a little checking," he replied.

"I'll go with you," Lydia said impulsively.

"No, you won't," Jeff replied. "You've been through enough."

"It's because of what I've been through that I'm as anxious as you to find out just how I'm involved, and what the role of the Duprez family is."

"It's too dangerous," Jeff said.

"Please, Jeff," Lydia said quietly. "I have a right to go. Besides, I'm a reporter. I'm sure Mr. Morgan would agree that the paper could use a good story if there is some big crime planned."

"You're right, Lydia," Morgan said. "But I don't want you risking your life to get it."

"Jeff will be with me, and he carries a gun. Now I know why. No more arguing. I'm going."

"You say you saw only three crew members," Jeff said, obviously relenting. "It's just possible two of them may be allowed shore leave and only one will be left on guard. That's customary with this type of crew. Lydia, you know where the roulette wheels are, you know the layout of the ship. With you along, I could do what has to be done in three or four minutes."

Seventeen

Jeff gave Lydia a nod of approval when she stepped from the elevator. He had suggested she dress simply—no frills, furbelows or jewelry—so she chose a pongee dress with plain lines, devoid of trimming. They ate a hasty supper and went directly to the casino. On entering, they saw the baron wandering about, his usually alert features devoid of expression. However, the moment he saw them, he brightened.

Jeff spoke first. "Anything unusual tonight, Baron?"

"It is very quiet," he reported. "Nobody winning much, nobody losing much, including me."

"Has Claude Duprez been around?" Lydia asked.

"Not yet, though I have been watching for him. But Drury is here with the girl he claims is his good luck. He has been playing more heavily of late, but nothing to attract any great attention."

"How has he been doing?" Jeff asked.

"About even. He picks certain numbers and keeps playing them. Lots of players do. They win on one thing and play it all night, thinking it's lucky. There is no such thing as a system, involved or simple."

Jeff led Lydia and the baron into the adjoining café where they secured a table. Jeff ordered drinks.

Lydia said, "Baron, Jeff and I have every faith in your integrity, so you're going to be taken into our confidence. You must in no way let this information go beyond you."

"There'll be the devil to pay if you do," Jeff added.

The baron was so impressed he put down his brandy

inhaler before he took his first sip. "You may be assured that I never violate a confidence," he stated. "Especially where it concerns Lydia. And now you, Jeff."

"Good! Because I want you to know that I'm an officer in the organization known as Interpol."

"So that's it!" the baron exclaimed. "I knew you were part of some official group. You are not, then, a geologist?"

"Indeed I am," Jeff declared. "I'm a graduate of one of the best schools in the United States. At present, I'm just not working at that profession."

The baron addressed Lydia, his smile amused. "So he fooled you."

Jeff said, "I warned her she'd have to trust me."

"You know I do, darling," Lydia said. "Now tell the baron what our plans are."

"Lydia," Jeff explained, "discovered something aboard the Duprez yacht that must be investigated. Claude's parents are at Nice—I verified this—and I'm sure Claude will be at the casino this evening. He's going to be . . . detained. Never mind how. But as soon as this happens, Lydia and I are going to try and slip aboard the yacht. While we're doing this, I want you to keep your eyes open. If Claude happens to be released quickly, we want to know it. If you see him, hurry down to the beach and station yourself in the first bathhouse. It's the closest to the yacht mooring. You'll find a lantern there. Light it, step outside and swing it back and forth. We'll be watching for any sign of it. Can you do that?"

"It seems well within my mental capacity to handle it, Jeff," the baron said dryly.

"Good. And from here on, watch every newcomer who perhaps doesn't quite fit the picture of someone who comes to Monte. I can't explain it, but there may be a number of strangers who might act furtively, or ask too many questions. I'd like to know if you've seen them before. Take note if they've dressed well, their approximate age, a description of their faces, any moles or scars and so on."

"You might enlist the help of Regina." Lydia turned to Jeff with an explanation. "She's the baron's friend, and an excellent photographer with cameras you've not seen the likes of. One fits into the palm of her hand and takes fine pictures. She took the ones of that English embezzler and the kaiser for me.''

Jeff brightened. "I remember. That could be very useful. I'll pay for any pictures she takes of such people.''

"She will be with me,'' the baron assured them. "May I ask what is going on?''

"I can't answer that because I don't know,'' Jeff said. "Whatever it is has to be something of great importance, a crime that may involve many people. Perhaps a holdup of the casino, which would be far more profitable than holding up a bank. We're just not certain what's in the wind.''

"But the Duprez family! *Mon Dieu!* Are you accusing them of being criminals?''

"So far we've made no accusation against anyone. But aboard that yacht are half a dozen roulette wheels, Baron. That's what Lydia discovered. I cannot for the life of me guess what they are intended for, but you can't tell me carrying about six roulette wheels is just catering to some hobby.''

The baron drew a sharp breath at the significance of what he had just been told. "Roulette wheels on the yacht? Could they be crooked? Could they be substituted . . . but no. That is not possible. There is no way. The casino has security officers always. There has never been the slightest trouble. No cheating, no stealing, no—whatever those wheels are meant for, it is not at Monte.''

"They must be crooked. Otherwise why should they be here?'' Lydia argued.

"I agree,'' Jeff said. "We're on to something, I just wish we knew what. Let's go back now.'' He opened the case of his watch. "Yes . . . we haven't much time. If Claude is in the casino, it will begin soon. We'll have to move quickly.''

The baron had been so excited he'd forgotten to finish his brandy, which he did now in one big gulp. They returned to the casino. Claude was there, moving about as if he was looking for someone. He spotted Lydia, waved frantically and hurried toward her, elbowing people aside rudely in his determination to reach her before she got away.

"I have looked for you all evening," he exclaimed emotionally. "Lydia, forgive me! Please forgive me. I cannot apologize strongly enough. I had been drinking. I was unable to think. I . . ." he glanced at Jeff. "Who is this?"

Lydia regarded Claude coolly as she spoke. "His name is Jeffrey Marcus. He's the man I'm going to marry."

"Indeed not!" Claude said emphatically. "No offense to you, Monsieur Marcus. It is I who will marry Lydia. My life depends on it, for without her I shall find life not worth living."

Jeff said, "If you force your attentions on her again, sir, you may reach the same conclusion. I know what happened and I've taken steps to protect her against any future escapades like the one you inflicted upon her. I would strongly advise you not to tamper with Monte Carlo law, which can be very severe. Do you understand, Mr. Duprez?"

"The law does not affect me," Claude declared disdainfully. "You will learn that to your sorrow, Monsieur Marcus. Lydia, I beg of you, consider me before you commit yourself to this man. You know what I can do for you. You know that I am in love with you to such an extent that I do foolish things. You alone can save me from myself."

"I'm going to marry Jeff," Lydia said firmly. "The only feeling I have for you is one of contempt. I can't believe you would even speak to me after what you did today."

The baron said, "Monsieur Duprez, you come of a family held in high esteem. Why do you make such a fool of yourself?"

"I am not going to lose Lydia, old man. Call it madness if you like, but I'll stop at nothing to get her. Please understand me, Lydia. I mean it." His tone was threatening.

Before anyone could respond, two husky men came directly toward them and lined themselves on either side of Claude. He looked at them with considerable annoyance.

"What do you want?" he demanded. "I don't know either of you."

"Monsieur Duprez," one man said, "you will please come with us. The commissioner of police wishes to discuss an important matter with you."

"You must be mad," Claude declared.

The pair grasped his arms tightly. "You will come with us, monsieur, or we shall take you. It would not be well to create a fuss in here."

Claude faced Lydia in disbelief. "Is this of your doing? Have you made a complaint against me?"

She made no reply. The men tugged at Claude and he surrendered, but with style. He shook himself free of them, made an elaborate bow before Lydia and stalked off with the pair following at his heels.

"I do not think Claude will ever forgive you," the baron said. "To him this is humiliating, and of a certainty he has enough influence to force his release very soon."

Jeff said, "We expect that. But he'll be questioned at police headquarters long enough for us to get aboard the yacht. Our main worry now is the crew. There's no way we can determine if the yacht is guarded by one man or three. We'll have to take our chances."

The baron said, "I will leave at once for police headquarters, so I will know when Claude is released."

"You know what to do?" Jeff asked.

"I'll do my best. I hope there'll be no need for me to flash that lantern."

Lydia said, "So do we."

"Come, Lydia," Jeff's arm enclosed her waist. "This has to be done at once."

As the baron left to take up a position close by police headquarters to watch for Claude's release, Jeff and Lydia walked swiftly down to the beach, skirted the water's edge and reached the dock without letting themselves be seen as they approached the yacht.

The harbor was quiet. No one strolled the dock; everyone with a yacht in the harbor was either at the casino, in one of the hotel dining rooms, or attending a performance at the theater adjoining the casino.

Jeff spoke in a whisper. "I'll go aboard first and take a

look around. If all's well, I'll signal. Come aboard as quickly as possible. From then on, we'll have to take our chances with the crew.''

"I have a feeling that when Claude is released, he'll come directly back to the yacht," Lydia whispered.

"I'm sure of it. If he's involved in some kind of scheme to rob or defraud the casino, he'll suspect from now on that someone has tumbled to him. What we have to hope for is the baron's alertness.''

"The porthole in the cabin where the wheels are faces the beach. The bathhouse there is the one from which the baron can signal, right?''

"Now I realize why you insisted on knowing that. Be careful, darling.''

He nodded, bent down, kissed her briefly and moved quietly toward the yacht. She saw him board it, then disappear probably to explore the deck first. When he reappeared, he beckoned to her to join him. Lydia paused as soon as she was on deck to remove her shoes, for the hard heels were bound to make noise. Clutching these, she followed Jeff to the companionway. He peered down the ladder.

"You know where the cabin is," he said. "We want to go directly there. If we prowl about, we may stumble on a cabin where the crew may be asleep, or passing the time some other way. That would be catastrophic.''

She nodded and followed him as he descended the companionway; they stopped at the bottom and listened. Then Lydia moved on directly to the cabin where she had seen the roulette wheels. She stepped aside so Jeff could try the door. It was locked. From his pocket he took a slim instrument that he used with the skill of a burglar. Soon he swung the door open and they both slipped inside, Lydia closing the door behind them noiselessly. It was pitch dark in the cabin until she opened the porthole to let some light filter in. Jeff lit a match while Lydia watched out the porthole. She was able to make out the beach and the bathhouse from which the baron would signal an alarm in the event that Claude was released.

"There's nothing here," Jeff whispered. "Are you sure this is the cabin?"

"I'm positive," she replied.

"Well, the wheels are gone. Maybe they anticipated something might happen. There are aspects to this I don't like. But we can't search the whole yacht and risk being discovered. They wouldn't leave the ship unguarded if they're up to something. We'd better get out of here as quickly as we can."

"There's no signal." Lydia spoke from her position at the porthole. "Evidently they didn't let Claude go."

"They're instructed to hold him until we get there if they can. Close the porthole. We're getting out."

She obeyed and moved to Jeff's side. He opened the cabin door, then shut it quickly and silently.

"Someone's coming," he whispered. "I think whoever it is must be on some kind of patrol. Get behind the door and don't move."

As Jeff finished talking, the doorknob rattled. They remembered it was supposed to be locked. When it opened, whoever was on the inspection tour was instantly alerted. He threw the door wide. Jeff was flat against the wall just inside the cabin door, and Lydia was pressed behind the door itself.

Jeff said, in an accented voice, " 'Allo!'

The crewman turned in Jeff's direction, straight into the upswing of his fist. It hit the crewman's jaw with a jolt that sent him staggering. Before he could recover, Jeff hit him again, this time with a well-aimed punch meant to knock him out. He caught the crewman as he fell and eased his unconscious body to the floor, then bent over the man, searched him, removed his watch and his wallet, and wrenched a thick ring from one finger.

With Lydia close behind him, they left the cabin and headed for the deck. As they reached it, the crewman, who turned out to be tougher than Jeff realized, regained consciousness and shouted in alarm.

On deck they heard running steps at the starboard side. Jeff seized Lydia's wrist and pulled her to the port side where they were out of sight, but only for a moment. A third man seemed to have appeared, from the shouted orders that were being given.

"No help for it," Jeff said. "Jump!"

She knew what he meant. She leaped over the rail into the warm sea without hesitation, quickly followed by Jeff. In the water he immediately swam toward her, motioning her to stay close to the yacht and to follow him.

Swimming silently, he led her close to the dock, depending on the darkness to conceal them. They could hear shouts on the yacht and lights skimmed the water. By now, Jeff and Lydia were already swimming well away from the yacht toward the edge of the beach.

They scrambled ashore, dripping wet. She looked at Jeff and he returned the stare. Suddenly, the situation and their appearance struck them as humorous and they both burst into smothered laughter. He quickly enveloped her in a moist hug while they indulged in a hasty kiss.

"Here is what to do," he said, serious again. "Go back to your suite and change. If you have a dress that looks like the one you're wearing, put it on. Dry your hair as best you can. Then take a carriage and meet me in front of police headquarters. The quicker you do this, the better."

"Yes, Jeff . . . twenty minutes. Thank heaven the hotel is close by."

They fled in the direction of their respective hotels. Lydia walked boldly into the lobby, her head high, despite her sodden and bedraggled condition. She received a few surprised stares, and one dowager raised her lorgnette to survey her from head to toe. She suppressed the smile that tugged at her lips and continued to move swiftly on stockinged feet. She'd dropped her shoes in the water when she jumped overboard.

She used the stairway, let herself into the suite and went at once to the bedroom. There she removed her clothes and employed heavy towels to dry herself and her hair. This done to reasonable satisfaction, she attended to her hair first, coiling it at the nape of her neck to conceal the fact that it was only partially dry. She had an identical dress of the same beige color as the pongee, except that it was made of lace. A woman might notice the difference, she reasoned, but a man probably wouldn't.

After depositing her wet clothes in the bathtub, she hurried downstairs and luckily found a carriage at the door. Five minutes later she stepped out of the carriage in front of the ornate City Hall, where the police maintained their headquarters.

Jeff and the baron quickly materialized out of the gloom, Jeff in an identical outfit to the one he had worn earlier. He moved her toward the lighted windows of the building.

"You don't even look as if you changed," he marveled. Then, more crisply, "The baron tells me Claude is still inside. He mustn't know, though he may guess, that we were on his yacht. Oh yes . . . thank you, Baron, for your help. One more favor. Take this wallet and the rest—it's the loot I took off the man I knocked down. I did it so they'll think it was just the work of some footpad; there have been incidents along the yacht harbor before. The watch you'd better keep hidden, and the ring as well, but you can say you found the wallet in a few days, and wish to return it to its owner." Jeff handed these to him, along with a hundred-franc note.

The baron accepted the articles and stowed them in his pockets, smiling his gratitude for the hundred francs before he moved briskly in the direction of the casino. He never tarried if he had the funds to gamble with.

"You know what to do," Jeff said, turning to Lydia. "Just carry it off in a calm way. I'll say little, if anything."

"I'm ready," she said. "Thank heaven we had a little time before facing him. My heart is still pounding from our escape from the yacht."

They were promptly escorted to the office of the inspector in charge. Claude was seated in the room, his legs crossed, his attitude as languid as if he were aboard the sundeck of his yacht. He came to his feet as Lydia entered.

"Lydia, I didn't think you would do this to me," he exclaimed. "I never believed you could be as cruel as this. I know what I did to you was wrong, but to have it end this way . . . in the office of a policeman . . . ."

The inspector spoke from behind his desk. "I have lectured him, mademoiselle, and informed him that what he did was a kidnapping. If you insist I shall have him locked up and tried for this crime. Still, you must understand that he comes of a fine family, a most influential one. And he swears what he did was inspired by—well—amour. He has informed me that he asked you to marry him on several occasions and he took this means of trying to make you change your mind and accept him. An unconventional way, yes, but still, a man in love . . . ."

"And that," Lydia said, "cannot be construed as a crime, m'sieur. True, I was angry and rightfully so, because of what he did. I was frightened, too, because he acted in a threatening manner. However, I was not physically harmed. I made this complaint against him because I'm afraid he may try the same thing and next time head out to sea with me aboard as a prisoner."

"Then what you wish, mademoiselle, is for Monsieur Duprez to be warned that if he does this again, or annoys you in any way, we shall arrest him at once. You agree to a warning only?"

"Yes, M'sieur Inspector. As you say, he is not a vicious criminal. I suppose I should be rather pleased that he feels so strongly toward me that he would take such foolish steps. However, I know what being in love is like." She glanced at Jeff and smiled. "It does things to the mind sometimes. I would ask that he be released under the provision that he will not annoy me again."

"M'sieur," the inspector glared at Claude, "you have heard mademoiselle. She is being very generous. You will give me your word that you will not bother Mademoiselle Bradley again."

Claude gathered up his hat and gloves from the inspector's desk. He stepped before Lydia. "I thank you for not pressing charges and I give you my word I will not force my attentions on you again. However, I am sorely disappointed in you, for I had much to offer. One day you will realize that." He regarded Jeff with disdain. "I should

303

challenge you to a duel, but I must think of my parents.''

He growled something under his breath and left, banging the door behind him. Jeff shook hands with the inspector.

"Thank you for your cooperation," he said. "Miss Bradley and I are pleased with the way it was handled.''

"Did you learn anything, Monsieur Marcus?" the inspector asked.

"Unfortunately, we did not. There will be a report of a burglar aboard the Duprez yacht shortly, and you will be told he attacked and robbed one member of the crew. Please don't look for this robber too diligently. The man's wallet will be 'found' in due course, but not the thief.''

"I am sure he will *never* be found, m'sieur. Yet please be good enough to inform us of anything out of the ordinary, any suspicion you may have of further trouble.''

"At once," Jeff promised. "I'll probably need all the help I can get. *Bon soir*, Inspector.''

Lydia took his hand for a moment, and added her appreciation. Then she and Jeff walked out and continued on along the deserted streets in the direction of the casino.

"All we can hope for now is that they don't call off whatever they planned," Jeff said.

"Wouldn't it be best if they did?" Lydia asked.

"I don't think so. They'd only postpone whatever they have in mind and that could be worse for us. So far, things have worked out well. You made a complaint, the police picked Claude up and while he was held, we conducted a search of the yacht, even though an unsuccessful one.''

"Which also included a swim in the ocean." She smiled up at him as she linked her hand under his arm and moved closer to him.

"I'm very proud of the way you behaved when things went badly for us," Jeff said.

Lydia laughed. "There wasn't time to be frightened. Besides, with you, I wasn't afraid. I'll confess, though, that once in my room, I felt thoroughly frightened.''

"Still afraid?" His tone revealed his concern.

"Yes, but I think it's because we don't know what's about to happen—or even if something is.''

"Be assured something is. I know my superiors believe that. They've ordered me to remain here until whatever crime is to occur is carried out. Are you sure you saw roulette wheels on the yacht?"

"I swear I wasn't mistaken," Lydia replied.

"I believe you, but there wasn't a sign of them when we went there, which means one of two things. Either they suspected you might have seen the wheels, or they needed them ashore and their plans are ready to hatch. If only there was some way we could find out. Then we could be ready for whatever they're up to."

"Do you suppose Claude was part of the scheme? Making a nuisance of himself by proclaiming his love for me, taking me on the yacht and threatening to take me out to sea unless I'd promise to marry him. It was blatant foolishness, but shattering, too. I was angry and frightened at the same time."

"Naturally," Jeff said. "I suspect the idea was to frighten you so that you'd leave Monte."

"Then you think Claude is mixed up in whatever is about to happen?"

"I don't know. He and his parents may be, in some way. Or they may even be the ringleaders."

"Or they might be completely innocent," Lydia pointed out.

"They might be." Jeff sounded dubious. "But let's not forget the roulette wheel you saw. And you believed there were several in that cabin."

"Yes," Lydia said solemnly. A sudden thought worried her. "I hope they don't suspect you're connected with Interpol."

"I doubt they have any idea of that," Jeff assured her, "though they may suspect something is getting in their way. That's why I'm of the opinion that whatever plan is afoot, it's going to be carried out quickly."

"How quickly?" Lydia asked.

"I wish I could answer that," he replied, a trace of discouragement in his voice.

"Will there be danger?" Her hand on his arm tightened.

"There's always danger in dealing with a situation like this. I'm sure the type of people behind it play for keeps. However, now my concern is that they'll get away with it before we can stop them. Remember, their preparations have been carried out with a great deal of cleverness. No amateur arranged for Martel to be seated next to you at that banquet. The episode with the Russians could have been a disaster for you. If they'd succeeded, you would surely have been fired from the paper and have had to leave Monte. That's what they've been after all the time—to be rid of you. And I don't know why. If we knew it, we'd be well along to stopping them."

"Jeff, I came here because of Mr. Morgan's spur-of-the-moment decision to send me. I'd never heard of Monte Carlo before. In New York, I had no enemies. In fact, I knew few people. Except of course, Bryant Drury. And I didn't know him well until the evening he took me out."

"We've investigated him down to his footprints," Jeff said, "and came up with nothing. If he's involved, it's certainly in such a clever way we can't find it. Also, what reason would he have to get rid of you? Other than revenge . . .and that concerns only himself."

Lydia said, "We both know he's writing a book, so he has a legitimate reason for being in Monte. And we have proof that he's been working at it."

"We won't quite rule him out, however," Jeff said.

"Jeff," she looked about the now well-lighted street, "we're going past the casino . . . ."

"We'll go there later. Right now I've something of greater importance to discuss and it's best done in private."

"More trouble?" Lydia asked in dismay.

"Relax, my love. It's something that's been on my mind for some time. Ever since I met you, in fact. We'll find a bench somewhere in the gardens. It's a balmy night—even for a swim."

His arm enclosed her waist while they sought out an empty, secluded bench.

Once seated, he took from his pocket a small jewelry box, opened the lid and took out a ring. "I'd like to make our engagement official,'' he said quietly.

She held out her left hand for him to place the ring on her finger. "It's beautiful," she said. "Thank you, darling.''

"It doesn't compare with Claude's emeralds—" he said with a smile.

"Say no more," she broke in. "Put the ring on my finger, then kiss me.''

He obeyed on both counts, smothering her face with kisses, lingering long on her lips. She slipped free of his arms, breathless and radiant with happiness.

"Darling, much as I hate to say it, I must go to the casino. There might be a story there and my paper expects me to submit copy regularly.''

"I'll take you there, but first I want to ask you a question. Will you marry me?''

"As soon as possible," she said rapturously.

"I'd like it sooner than that," he said. "But I want this mystery cleared up first.''

"So do I," she replied.

"I'd like something else, also.'' He caressed her lips with his.

"Yes?''

"Let me take you back to your suite tonight," he whispered.

"Darling, I promised you that long ago, didn't I?'' Lydia's eyes softened with love and desire.

"Let's leave now," he said hoarsely.

She held back. "Jeff, I must go to the casino first.''

"That damned casino!''

Lydia forced a firmness into her voice. "Jeff, I must.''

"Very well," he said with a sigh. "On the way I'll tell you something else, if I can clear my head enough to talk lucidly.''

"What's it about?''

"You . . . me . . . our future. I've made certain preparations to go back to my true profession—geology.''

"I thought you gave it up to join Interpol.''

"I did. As I once told you, geology seemed boring, but

you must remember that I was very young when I made that decision. Now that I'm practically a married man," he grinned, "I see the fallacy of that. There's really nowhere to go in the service. A geologist is needed here, I found out. There's much to be done along this beautiful coastline, and I'll be placed in charge of a considerable department if I take the job. Which I already have. However," he added soberly, "there's always the chance I'll be sent elsewhere."

"Wherever you are, I want to be by your side."

He looked surprised. "Despite your career?"

"Once you place a wedding ring on my finger, you'll be my career."

"Darling," he said, "that's wonderful, but you're clever at ferreting out stories and you write good copy. I don't want you to throw that aside."

"If I can ferret out stories, as you say," she replied calmly, "and Mr. Morgan is still interested in my services, I'll find stories wherever you're sent."

"I know you will, Lydia. I'm betting on it just as Mr. Morgan once bet on you—for which I'll always be grateful. We'll have to invite him to the wedding."

She kissed him and held him to her, but this time it was he who gently disengaged her.

"Since we must, let's go see what's happening in the casino," he said. "Perhaps Claude came back, or there there may be strangers about who might be acting unlike the usual gamblers who come here and lose their money."

They walked hand in hand to the casino. The baron, his face flushed with excitement, hurried up to them. "I have won a thousand francs already. A thousand . . . with that hundred-franc note you gave me. A thousand, mind you!"

"Baron," Lydia said, "you should go at once to Regina and hand her that entire sum of money right now. Without even passing another roulette table. Out the door with you! You may return, but *not* with the money."

"I don't know if I can . . . go all the way . . . without turning back."

"You must," she insisted.

"I could try," he said hopefully, with a wistful glance

at the busy tables.

"Before you leave," Jeff said, "did Claude come back here?"

"No, and I have watched. Monsieur Drury has been playing heavily. He insists that girl remain right at his side for he claims she is very lucky. And he has won—quite a sum, though I think he is giving it all back about now. I will return, very soon. I will keep out fifty francs. I can lose that and keep my reputation intact, if you do not mind."

"Run along," Lydia said. "Do as I say. Make me proud of you."

"It will not be easy, Lydia. Don't blame me too much if I fail, but I'll try."

"What next?" Jeff asked, after the baron left.

"What do you suggest?" she asked, her smile teasing.

"Are you serious?" he asked.

"Yes," she replied. "And fast growing impatient."

Once inside the suite, Jeff turned the key in the lock, swept Lydia into his arms and carried her into the bedroom. He placed her gently on the bed and undressed her. When his hands fumbled with her garments, she helped. Strangely, she felt not the slightest trace of embarrassment.

Jeff removed his clothes, got into bed beside her and saw the light still on in the parlor. He muttered an oath and went to put it out. The one in the bedroom he left lit.

"I want to look at you," he said when he returned. "You're so beautiful, Lydia. From now until the moment I truly possess you and afterward, I never want to take my eyes off you."

He gathered her close, his arms stroking, fondling, caressing her while he covered her body with slow, sensual kisses that grew more and more urgent. Lydia's passion quickly rose to meet his and when he settled her on her back, she was eager to receive him. After the first moment of pain, she responded to his maleness and their passion soared until it reached fulfillment. Afterward, they lay quietly a few moments, then spoke the language of lovers the world over.

Eighteen

When Lydia wakened the next morning, memory came flooding back. She turned, her arms already extending to embrace Jeff. When she discovered him gone, a note pinned to the pillow quickly ended her dismay. She slipped it free and read,

> Dearest Lydia,
>
> Forgive my having to leave you but I couldn't bear to waken you. I'll see you later today. I must report to my superiors and check to see if there are any new developments.
> Last night will stay with me for the rest of my life. And you, also, I hope. From now on, may our separations be brief.
>
> > All my love,
> > Jeff

She kissed the note, placed it in a drawer among her handkerchiefs and went to draw her bath. She was completely dressed before an apologetic Angelina entered, along with a waiter carrying a large tray. He set it down and left.

"I am so sorry, mademoiselle. An impossible dowager kept me waiting on her. I could not please her. Finally she told me to get out . . . ." She broke off and her eyes studied Lydia's face carefully. "How beautiful you look this morning."

Color flooded Lydia's face. "Thank you, Angelina.

Look.'' She extended her left hand, revealing the ring.

"A diamond ring!" Angelina exclaimed. "It is not the one given you by the Russians."

"No," Lydia replied. "Can't you guess where I got it?"

"You are engaged," Angelina exclaimed happily. "It is true at last. When will you marry?"

"As soon as we find out who's responsible for making all that trouble for me."

Angelina sobered. "That means you will leave Monte."

"No. Jeff and I agreed that we'll remain here until his work takes us elsewhere."

"May that not be for years."

"Excuse me a moment, Angelina." Lydia went to the bedroom where she took the ring given her by the Russians from her bureau drawer. She opened the box and studied it as she walked back to the parlor.

"There is a difference," she acknowledged.

"True, mademoiselle." Angelina studied the large stone that sent shafts of light about the room when the sun's rays touched it. "It is priceless."

"To me, Jeff's is priceless because it was given with love."

"I understand and I agree."

Lydia reached for Angelina's hand and placed the box in it. "I don't want the Russians' ring. It's yours."

"Mademoiselle!" Angelina said in awe. "This cannot be. You are surely joking."

"Take it. I don't want it. It reminds me of something I'd rather forget. Jeff's ring reminds me of something I will never forget. That ring now belongs to you."

Angelina took the diamond from the box, slipped it on her finger and glanced at Lydia. "It is far too much. Such things are not for me. I would be afraid to wear it."

"Then sell it. I wish only to be rid of the thing."

"With what this would sell for, it might even allow me to retire," Angelina said softly. "But you could sell it."

"No. It's yours."

Angelina embraced Lydia and offered no more argument.

But she removed the ring from her finger, placed it in its satin nest and slipped it into her bosom. She set a place for Lydia on the small table in the center of the room, cautioning her to eat her breakfast.

"Can't you at least have coffee?" Lydia asked.

"Not this morning, mademoiselle. Please forgive me. I will be back later to straighten your suite. Since it is late, I brought you a large breakfast."

"Thank you. I'm famished."

Lydia ate the fruit, ham, eggs, rolls and marmalade and drank three cups of coffee. She had just finished when Angelina returned, bearing an envelope.

"It came by messenger, mademoiselle."

"Is there a return adress on it?" Lydia asked.

Angelina turned the envelope over. "It is from Madame Blanche Duprez."

"I expected something like this. Claude's mother must have heard what happened. Please open it and read it to me."

Angelina read the brief note.

My dear Mademoiselle Bradley,

I humbly beg that you call on me and my husband at our yacht as soon as possible to accept our sincere regrets for the foolishness of our son.

Sincerely,
Blanche Duprez

"Will you go?" Angelina asked.

"Oh yes, if for no other reason than to try and persuade them to see that their son stays away from me."

"What will you wear?"

"The shirtwaist and skirt I have on."

"You look so British, mademoiselle," Angelina protested gently.

Lydia smiled at her disapproval. "I like the costume. It's neat, feminine and practical."

312

Later, as she stepped aboard the yacht, the seaman who had allowed her to slip off the ship after freeing her from the cabin in which Claude had imprisoned her, gravely saluted her without any show of expression or recognition. She hoped he hadn't been the man Jeff had fought with on her second expedition to the yacht. She didn't think he was, for his face revealed no trace of a bruise.

Madame Duprez, wearing a yachting costume, hurried along the deck to meet her. She embraced Lydia, then led her along to the lounge, a glass enclosed cabin placed well forward on the yacht.

"My son is too impressionable," she said. "He falls madly in love with attractive girls, but never before was he so demonstrative, mademoiselle. Thank you for not pressing charges."

"So, he told you."

"Yes." Madame Duprez sighed.

"Believe me, madame," Lydia said, "I am not complimented by the fact that he seems to have paid more attention to me. What he did was unforgivable. I have informed him that I do not wish to be with him again."

"And rightly so, mademoiselle. We have warned him, too. But that is not the reason why we have asked you to honor us with a visit. My husband and I wish to humbly apologize."

"There is no need for you to apologize for your son's behavior. But it's gracious of you. I do hope he's not aboard."

"We sent him to Cannes on an errand. We trust he will be gone for some time."

Raoul Duprez entered and bowed and kissed the back of her hand. "I can only add my own apology, mademoiselle," he said. "I wish there was something we could do to offset the indignities and embarrassments that our son inflicted upon you. I can assure you he is going to be punished for this in some way. Neither I, nor Madame Duprez, will tolerate such lunatic behavior, even from our son."

"I hope not," Lydia said. "But please tell your son that should he engage in further mischief, I shall be compelled to take more severe action than merely a reprimand by the police.''

"He has already been warned," Raoul Duprez said. "If he refuses to heed this and makes the slightest trouble for you, please have the police place him under arrest and brought to justice. Madame Duprez and I pride ourselves on our own deportment and we deplore the excesses of our son.''

"We spoiled him long ago," Blanche declared. "Now we are paying for that. Will you be good enough to stay for tea, mademoiselle?''

"I'm afraid not," Lydia replied. "I have copy to write and people to see, but I do thank you and I appreciate your graciousness.''

"We are the appreciative ones," Raoul said. He escorted her out of the lounge and along the deck where he bowed, kissed her hand again and murmured his thanks for her coming.

Lydia left feeling far from certain that they'd be able to keep their promise to compel Claude not to interfere with her again. She believed him to be much too willful to be restrained by anyone, even his parents.

Jeff, seated on one of the garden benches overlooking the harbor, stood up and started down to meet Lydia the moment he caught sight of her. She saw him almost at the same time and began to run toward him. When they met, she threw herself into his arms. They kissed again and again and, in between kisses, murmured words of love.

Finally, he held her away from him and spoke in a voice unsteady with emotion. "Did you get my note?''

"Yes, my darling. I'd have been desolate if you hadn't written, letting me know you didn't just walk out on me.''

"No chance of that," he said tenderly.

"How did you know I was on the Duprez yacht?''

"When you weren't in your suite, I checked with the maid Angelina and introduced myself. She seemed to know all about me.''

"Not all." Lydia said archly. "She doesn't know you're an officer in Interpol. Or that you spent the night with me.''

"Sorry?" he questioned. "About last night?"

"Oh darling, how can you ask? Despite the tension all around us, none of it is touching me this morning. It's not hard to guess why."

"I'm delighted to hear I have such healing powers," he joked. Then, more seriously, "Angelina told me you went to the Duprez yacht."

"Did you think I'd been kidnapped again?"

"I'd be aboard by now if I did. Truthfully, I knew they sent Claude away. What did they wish to do, apologize?"

"They did so, and very courteously. What do you think of them, darling?"

"I don't know. Duprez has been a respected citizen of Paris for many years."

"Mr. Morgan says he runs his paper in a manner that is way behind the times. That's why he began to print gossip. It got him a higher circulation, but it's vicious. However, he has a most extravagant life-style."

"We know about that, too. Did they say anything about clearing out of Monte?"

"No. Do they intend to leave?"

"I've no idea. I thought that what happened—Claude's run-in with the police—might encourage them to clear out."

"They may intend to, for all I know. But there was nothing said or done to hint they would sail," Lydia assured him.

"We'll keep an eye on them. Now, there's something else. It may be important or not. It may be connected with the strange things that happened to you, then again, it may have no bearing at all. The casino manager will explain, and he has a favor to ask of you."

"What is it?" she asked with a fresh note of worry.

"The facts should come from him. For your information, he knows who I really am and he has been working with me for some time. I doubt this latest episode presents any danger to you, so don't worry about it. I'll see you to the casino."

Jeff escorted her to the manager, whose sober face brightened at her appearance.

"Mademoiselle Bradley, my sincere thanks for your promptness. Please," he motioned in the direction of a closed door, "my office for seclusion."

Mystified, she entered his office where he closed the door to insure privacy. She was waved toward a soft leather chair that faced an enormous antique desk.

"Mademoiselle," he began when he was seated behind his desk, "we have cooperated over the months you have been here. You know that we regard you with the greatest esteem and trust you with secrets we would tell no one else."

"Thank you, monsieur," she said. "I promise if this is also a secret, I won't divulge it to anyone."

"*Merci*. That is what we ask and, of course, you're entitled to an explanation. There is a chance you might hear of this from someone else, so that's why I wish to tell you first. We have discovered a well-established system of cheating at the casino."

"On the part of patrons, monsieur?" Lydia asked, shocked by his words.

"But no. That would have been even more serious. We have discovered that a few of our security guards have been rifling money, and two of our croupiers have been managing to steal a few counters even though we do not allow them to have pockets in their trousers. They put handkerchiefs up their shirtsleeves and have created a device where they can actually conceal counters in these very handkerchiefs. It's most annoying. We are, therefore, discharging these men and all the security people and replacing them with men from a Parisian agency that specializes in providing honest guards. It will be as if they are our private police, with some of them even in uniform."

"A wise precaution, monsieur, but what has this to do with me?"

"We ask, very earnestly and humbly, that you do not write any articles or stories about this unfortunate matter. It will not enhance the honesty the casino wishes to portray to everyone. It may, in fact, create some doubts about our professional integrity. In short, it may harm the casino."

Lydia nodded. "I can see that. In my opinion it will do little good to have the honesty of the casino tarnished in any way. The casino is not doing the cheating . . . the casino is the victim. You have my word that what you have just told me I did not hear. Nothing will be written about it and I won't mention this to anyone."

"*Merci*, mademoiselle. You have always been an asset to Monte and now you have proven this more than ever. Nothing must touch the good reputation of the casino, for we bend over backwards to employ only honest methods."

Lydia arose. "Thank you for warning me. If I'd heard this elsewhere, I might have been tempted to use it, but now there is no chance of that. I can only congratulate you on the integrity of the casino."

"*Bonjour*, mademoiselle. You have our thanks."

She joined Jeff, who was seated in one of the large, plush chairs outside the gambling arena. She sat down beside him.

"You know what he told me, no doubt," she began.

"Yes, and I want to talk to you about it. There's something here that doesn't smell quite right. Oh, there've been cheating croupiers and dealers before, but their methods were crude and they were promptly fired, then blackballed in every gambling house in Europe. This seems different. There were not only a few cheats among the croupiers and dealers, but the security guards were apparently in league with them. They found ways to take a little off the top of a table's winnings when they were counted, or even while transporting them to the counting rooms."

"Jeff, are you implying that this may be part of the scheme that's put me in danger?"

"It's possible. Another cause for worry . . . the cheating was discovered after an anonymous tip."

"But how in the world could I have interfered with their plans? And is that operation so big that I somehow became important to it? I was not under the impression it was that huge."

"It's no penny ante operation, darling. It seems to have

been well organized. That's what bothers me. It was as if these people were *paid* to cheat and even to let themselves be exposed as such. Now, there's no proof of that, but it's an idea of mine.''

''You don't think those guards were gotten rid of so new ones could be hired?'' she asked slowly.

''It could be exactly that.''

''Jeff, from what I was told by the manager, the new guards come from an esteemed company that furnished guards to all sorts of places.''

''I know. The reputation of the guard agency is fine, but are the guards fine? And agencies can change owners. I know what you're thinking—that maybe enough guards could be assigned here to actually take over the casino and rob not only the counting room, but every patron.''

''Good Lord, what an operation that would be!''

''If it came off, I agree you'd have a story that would shock the world, especially the gambling world. But no, I don't see that as the reason for all this. In the first place, how would it involve you? And, believe me, it's certainly included you up to now.''

''I couldn't stop them or expose them,'' Lydia agreed. ''There's no reason why such a plot would make it necessary for me to be sent away, or even to be injured or killed.''

''There's one thing more that perhaps you were not told. They're changing all of the roulette wheels . . . bringing in brand new ones.''

Lydia sat erect in excitement. ''The wheels I saw on the yacht! They could be somehow made to cheat the casino. They're the ones that will be installed.''

''Little doubt of it. That certainly brings in the Duprez family. Claude and his parents must be in on the maneuver, for one could not be doing this without the other knowing of it. Besides, this scheme is so delicate and big that it would take a large number of people to carry it out. The owners of the casino think it's a scheme to hold them up and the patrons as well. I don't agree. But that doesn't mean I'm right.''

Lydia spoke reflectively. "We have cheating croupiers and guards; mysterious roulette wheels turning up on the Duprez yacht; new guards coming in to replace the old ones, some of whom have been found stealing counters. Each fact is puzzling, and surely there is the potential for something big."

"I still believe the secret to it is locked up in those attempts to frighten you away from Monte. When the kidnapping didn't cause you to flee, my greatest concern became for your safety."

"Are you inferring they wouldn't hesitate to kill me?"

"I don't know how far they'll go to carry out their plans, so I won't take any risks where you're concerned."

"Do you think the Duprez family is mixed up in it?"

"It would seem so, though other than the roulette wheels that you saw, we have no proof. And that, of itself, is no evidence they're about to commit a crime."

"Did you learn anything further about Martel?"

"Nothing," Jeff admitted, disgust edging his voice. "It's apparent he was murdered because he either failed in his mission or knew too much and tried to squeeze more money out of them. Again, it's supposition."

"Have you told the police everything?"

"Except for the roulette wheels, they know almost as much as we do."

"Shouldn't they know about them?"

"Possibly. However, the Duprez family is important and powerful. We can't make accusations or innuendoes on mere suspicion. Besides, someone on the police force might be involved. I'm not saying anyone is, but we can't take the chance. The guests and staff of the casino are being watched to see if there are any known criminals moving about either openly or in some sort of disguise. Since we know a little more than the police, we're also watching the Duprez family and Bryant Drury."

"And the baron?" Lydia asked.

"The baron is not high on the list of suspects," Jeff replied, "but neither has he been entirely cleared."

"I hope you're wrong," she said with a sigh.

"Personally, so do I," he admitted. "I've liked him from the moment I met him. I in no way believe he's involved. But I can't take him off the list just on good feeling alone. He's been here so long, but he loves gambling and he is a sponger."

"But he does it with such charm," Lydia said, pleading his cause.

Jeff looked unmoved. "My superiors would simply say he's had lots of practice."

Lydia grew serious again. "Just what do you think is going to happen?"

"I can only surmise they'll install the crooked wheels somehow."

"It seems like an impossible undertaking."

"Nothing is impossible, my darling," Jeff said patiently. "Those people have put a lot of thought and time into whatever it is they're about to do. Obviously, they expect big rewards for their labors."

"Then you don't think their plans concern a holdup of the casino?"

"They'd never get away with it. Monaco is situated in a bad area for anyone running from the police. The roads out of here are so few and really only one main one can be used for carriages, making it an easy one to block. The only other escape is by water or the Alps. And as a geologist, let me tell you, nobody is going to scale those mountains carrying a sack of gold coins or even a large satchel of paper money. There'd be no easy way to get their loot out. That's what worries me most. They must know of some way of escape. And somehow, to me, you're involved. You have to be a danger to them or they wouldn't have gone to such pains to get you out of here."

Lydia forced a smile. "Perhaps if I knew more about how I'm a threat to them, I'd have left long ago."

"That's understandable. From tonight on, we must be prepared for anything. Beginning with supper, I want to be with you every minute. If I'm called away, the baron must be close by."

"But he's a suspect!"

320

"Officially, yes, he's on the list. Still, we've checked him closely and he certainly has no criminal record. He's merely a confirmed moocher, as you well know, and an eccentric of sorts. Besides, he likes you, and I believe we can trust him. I wouldn't let him near you otherwise. He's able not so much to protect you, but to give an alarm by making a commotion."

"What about after hours," she asked, "when the casino is closed?"

"You don't think I'd leave you alone in your suite, do you?" he asked seriously. "I said I wanted to protect you."

She smiled in memory. "No thought of fear entered my mind last night."

"It wouldn't speak well of me if it did," he replied. His eyes held hers.

"Jeff, darling, please don't look at me like that," she said, coloring.

"All you need do is look away," he replied, the merest trace of a smile touching his lips.

"I don't want to, so I'll talk about something."

"What do you want to talk about?" he said tenderly.

"No one but us. However, since that's not a safe subject in public, I'd like to ask if you've given Bryant Drury a clean slate."

"No," Jeff replied firmly. "Why do you ask?"

"He's the only person who knew me before I came to Monte. Yet I can't think of any connection he'd have with Raoul Duprez or his family."

"We've thought of that, too, and we've checked. His only contact with that family, so far as we could learn, was as a reporter."

Lydia frowned. "How could Drury be of help to them or to whoever is behind this?"

"I wish I could answer that. That's the absolute hell of it, not being able to find the answers to any part of this puzzle. Tonight we'll watch the gambling tables closely. And we'll especially watch Drury. We'll remain until after the casino closes for the night, and be on hand when the

321

wheels are changed. Also, we'll go down to the railroad station and watch the new guards come in. They're due at about nine this evening.''

''Thanks for letting me be a part of this, Jeff.''

''There are two reasons for it. First, I want you with me constantly, as I already told you. Second, as a reporter, when this case is solved, and it damn well better be soon, you'll have a story that you'll be able to tell from every angle.''

''For me that will be an exciting tale. For you, it would be better if you could prevent whatever is going to happen.''

''That's what we've been trying to do, but so far without success. We can't prevent something from happening, when we don't know what the caper is.''

''Then I suggest we take a stroll in the gardens to take our minds off this unpleasantness.''

''Your suite would be more private,'' Jeff said softly, his tone suggestive.

''There are too many people around and Angelina might come in. She and I have become quite good friends.''

''Your door does have a lock,'' Jeff reminded her. ''I used it last night.''

''And you may use it again tonight,'' Lydia said, smiling up at him. ''Until then, you must exercise restraint.''

''It won't be easy,'' he replied, his smile caressing her face. ''But I'll expect my patience to be rewarded.''

''Be assured it will,'' Lydia promised. ''Now let's find a secluded bench where we can make plans for our future.''

Nineteen

At supper in the casino dining room Jeff explained the baron's absence at the table. "He's keeping an eye on the gambling and the woman who takes pictures—what's her name?"

"Regina LeFond," Lydia replied.

"She's with him now, and has brought along her camera to use if necessary."

"Then you believe whatever is going to happen will take place tonight?"

"The new guards are coming. If among them are individuals who have been sent here to take part in the action, they'll have to move quickly before they can be identified. Also, the new wheels are being installed by the manufacturer right after the casino closes for the night. It's likely that they'll make their move almost immediately."

"Is it possible that these new wheels have been tampered with?" Lydia asked.

"Anything is possible, but the casino has bought wheels from this manufacturer for years. We'll examine them, of course, but even if we find they have been tampered with, we won't do anything until after the thieves expose what their plans are. And, I hope, forever explain the mystery of your involvement."

"I surely hope it's over soon. I'm finding it difficult to concentrate on my work."

"I can understand that, but when it's over, you'll probably have the biggest story since that Englishman broke the bank right after you first arrived.''

Lydia reluctantly finished the dessert of cake, custard and an orange liqueur, a specialty of the newest chef from Paris. Jeff finished his cognac and they left the café to enter the casino, where there seemed to be a great deal going on.

The baron came immediately to greet them. ''Mr. Drury is playing heavily,'' he said. ''Enough to keep a crowd of people at his side.''

''How is he doing?'' Lydia asked.

''Not badly, but he isn't breaking any tables, I can tell you. I would say he loses about as much as he wins, but everyone thinks he is playing a system and, I must say, that seems to be true. He has this blond girl at his side and she takes notes of the numbers that fail and those that win.''

''That's been tried thousands of times,'' Jeff said. ''It doesn't work. Even the casino management is not worried about it. Roulette is a game of chance. There's nothing mathematical about it.''

''Then I wonder why Drury is doing it?'' Lydia mused.

''I don't know,'' Jeff said. ''Maybe he does believe in it. Or maybe he's making some kind of a grandstand play. All we can do is wait and watch.''

Lydia said, ''Thanks, Baron, for bringing Regina and her camera.''

''I thought if anything happened, it would not hurt to have a picture,'' the baron said.

''It's a good idea,'' Jeff said. ''Come to think of it, the new guard detail is due to arrive in the next half hour. I'd like Regina to try to get some pictures of the men, if she can.''

''I'll ask her to go with me. Shall we leave at once?''

''It would be best. Give her a chance to see where the light is most ideal for her camera. Lydia and I will follow soon after you leave.''

The baron hurried over to intercept Regina, and Jeff and Lydia walked over to the table where Drury was playing. While they watched he lost a thousand francs. He left that table, with the girl at his side, and moved to another. Lydia was not surprised to see that his helper was Madelaine. This time he won, but not a great deal. Certainly not enough to offset what he had just lost. The girl dutifully entered the numbers.

"I don't understand it," Jeff said. "It isn't very apparent, but I think he has a certain plan because of the way he plays."

"You said no system works," Lydia observed.

"They don't. That's what makes this so interesting. I have no answer to it, but he does seem to be playing with some sort of pattern he's figured out. To me, it looks as if he's playing to an audience, attracting as much attention to himself as possible. And the entries in the notebook made by his blonde companion are the cause of all that interest."

"I wonder why," Lydia said softly. "I've never known him to do anything without a reason."

"Maybe before the evening is over he'll give himself away. Right now, we'd best get down to the depot. I want to see these new guards before they go on duty."

"Do you think they could all be dishonest?"

"I doubt that, but if a few of them are, it would mean something of importance. That is, if I could recognize them. Chances are I won't be able to, but I can't pass up this opportunity. Regina may get some pictures and they might help."

Jeff called a landau for the trip to the depot. Once there, they waited in the vehicle for the train to pull in. If the baron and Regina were there, they were keeping out of sight, which was just as well if Regina hoped to take pictures.

There were two dozen new guards, about half in rather gaudy uniforms, but still in keeping with the dignity of the casino. All were muscular, tall and lean. Those in uniform made an impressive appearance, while those in plain clothes could easily pass as visitors. A uniformed man, with epaulettes to designate added authority, seemed to be in command. As he lined the men up on the platform, Regina ambled by. The men stood just below the lighted train windows, so there was sufficient light, Lydia thought as she watched the little scenario Regina had planned. Regina, she had learned long ago, knew her business.

The men standing for inspection were now dismissed. As they broke ranks and began walking toward the casino, Jeff told their driver to take them to the casino also.

"I didn't recognize any freebooters," he told Lydia. "That agency providing the men is a good one, but it's been infiltrated before and I have little doubt this group is no exception."

"What can they do?" Lydia asked. "How can they be effective if all of them are not dishonest?"

"If there are dishonest men among them, they'll know exactly what to do. More and more I begin to realize this is a big operation. They handed out money for Martel, including bribes, so he could get a seat at the banquet. The mysterious roulette wheels are costly and not easy to come by. And now this group, which may or may not include people about to help cheat the casino. Besides that, every one of their actions have been so well handled and concealed that even Interpol with its influence and experience has not been able to come up with anything to help."

Soon after their return to the casino, the uniformed guards appeared; no doubt the ones not in uniform were circulating. The baron appeared, approached Lydia and Jeff, greeting them casually. He kept his voice low as he spoke.

"Regina is sure she has some good pictures. She is home now getting them ready so you can see them tonight." Jeff continued the charade, smiling easily. "Good. That may be the biggest help yet. I'll send whatever she has to our main office where they have files on all known criminals. Some of these guards may be recognized."

"How has Drury been doing?" the baron asked.

"We haven't been near the tables since we came back," Lydia explained. "I've seen him moving about, so he must still be playing."

"I will circulate, too, and see what is happening," the baron promised.

Drury, it turned out, was not playing as heavily, but the

blonde girl was still openly making notes and always remained close by Drury. Some of the crowd had wearied of watching him play since he was not doing anything spectacular. Shortly after midnight he stopped and left the casino. The main excitement was dying away by now. Half the players had departed, some to celebrate at the costly cafés, some to try and forget their losses in much needed sleep. It was always like this at Monte.

When the casino finally closed, Lydia and Jeff were allowed to stay. The changing of the wheels began at a fast pace. Removing a cylinder from its base set in the table was not a long or difficult operation. As each wheel was installed, Jeff and casino officials moved in with spirit levels to make certain there was no tilt to the wheel or the table. The installation was being done by experts, so a rigid check of the wheels was a simple task. Not one proved to be in any way carelessly installed.

Next they went around to each table again, this time throwing the ivory balls and watching the simulated play. There seemed to be no defects. Jeff, using calipers, measured each ivory ball for perfect roundness and size. Not one proved deficient.

"It seems," Jeff said, "that we were mistaken, gentlemen. I can't see how anyone can cheat with these wheels."

"It is a great relief," Monsieur LeGrand said. "But we have been doing business with this manufacturing firm for many years. They have our trust."

"Did you know the ownership changed hands about six months ago?" Jeff asked.

LeGrand expressed surprise. "No one informed me of this. I have been dealing with the same people."

"Not many important employees were let go," Jeff explained. "At any rate, we've found nothing to call them to account for."

Lydia said, "And I'm ready for bed, darling. It's been a long day."

"And night," Jeff conceded. "I'll see you to your hotel."

They were allowed to leave through a door that had been

kept locked during the installation of the wheels. Lydia, in the cool night air, found that some of her sleepiness had left and wanted to walk to the hotel. They strolled slowly along the deserted streets, not saying much at first.

Lydia finally glanced up at Jeff's somber face. "I have the impression that you weren't satisfied with the wheels."

"You're mighty observant," he said.

"Yet you checked every wheel. The casino is satisfied they're ready to be played."

"And they likely are, but . . . there are a couple of ways to cheat that aren't in plain sight, or can even be discovered by looking very closely."

"Why didn't you mention this to the officials?" she asked.

"I could be wrong. Besides, if those new wheels are to be used to cheat with, I think it better to let them alone. Allow the cheaters to move in, and then spoil their plans. At least we'll know who they are."

Lydia nodded agreement. They reached the hotel, found the lobby deserted except for a bellboy who was fast asleep and a desk clerk who was also dozing.

Jeff said, "We'll wait here for the baron. He's gone to see if Regina has finished developing and printing the pictures."

They sat on a sofa facing the door.

"All I hope," Jeff said fervently, "is that this business will soon be over with and settled for good. I'm leaving the service right after that. I have my eye on a secluded villa for sale at a reasonable price. It has a lovely room you may use as an office, and another study for me and my kind of work. I'm accepting nothing that takes me away from you again. There's been too much of that already."

He was just about to kiss her when a subtle, polite cough distracted them. The baron stood before them in an obvious state of excitement.

"Regina!" he said. "It is a terrible thing . . . ."

Jeff came to his feet quickly. "What is it? What happened?"

"The police say someone entered her apartment and

robbed her. They struck her so hard she is at the hospital, badly injured. A neighbor heard her moaning and called for help.''

"It was no robbery,'' Lydia exclaimed.

"I agree,'' the baron said. "I have been in her apartment. It looks as if it has been well looted. Yet the camera she was using is very valuable, and that was left on the floor with all the film exposed. Any thief would have taken it.''

Jeff said, "I'm going to the hospital. Baron, you stay close by Lydia.''

"The three of us will go to the hospital,'' Lydia said, her anxiety mixed with anger. "The cowards! To attack a helpless woman. Someone must have seen her take the pictures.''

"We should have taken precautions,'' Jeff said bitterly.

"They must be about to carry out their operation,'' Lydia said.

They wakened a sleeping carriage driver and were taken to the Monaco hospital. At the desk they were, at first, refused permission to visit Regina or even to ask any questions about her. Jeff produced an identification which changed the behavior of the hospital authorities very abruptly. The three were then taken to the second floor where Regina's room was located.

Her face was swollen, one eye blackened, there were cuts around her mouth and she was barely able to talk. Evidently they had throttled her as well.

"She will recover,'' a doctor told them. The baron knelt beside the bed and gently stroked Regina's hand. "She was brutally attacked, however. It's a wonder she wasn't killed.''

"Is it safe to let her speak to us?'' Lydia asked.

"Oh, yes, but you'll have to listen hard. Her vocal cords are badly swollen from either a choking grip or a blow on the throat.''

With a tender expression, Lydia bent over Regina, who looked up at her with eyes still haunted by the terror of what she had undergone.

"Can you tell us what happened?" Lydia asked. "If it doesn't hurt you to speak."

"I don't know," Regina whispered in a hoarse voice. "I entered my apartment and . . . was struck on the head by someone I didn't even see. When I woke up, I was in the hospital."

"They were after the pictures you took," Jeff said. "And I'm afraid they got them."

Regina tried to sit up, but Lydia gently restrained her. She was in a high state of excitement. Jeff had to bend down and place his ear close to her lips to understand what she was saying.

"I put . . . new film in my camera before I returned home. It was blank. The film I took . . . my handbag . . . have you found it?" she managed to ask.

Lydia stepped quickly to the bureau on which lay Regina's handbag. She opened it, examined the contents more carefully and looked up in consternation.

"Regina, there is no film in your handbag."

"Keys," Regina managed. "There are keys . . . ."

Lydia extracted the set of keys and held them up, still puzzled.

Regina's voice seemed to gain some strength out of sheer determination. "I thought I saw light in my window . . . when I returned. It went out. I was afraid. I stopped in the lobby and put the film in my mail box. The key . . . is there."

Jeff said, "Regina, you're a wonder."

"Not such a wonder," she said with an attempt at a smile. "I was foolish to go into my apartment. But I wasn't sure . . . the light . . . I could have imagined it. I don't know . . . one makes mistakes . . . ."

"Regina," Lydia bent down and kissed her swollen cheek very lightly, "what you did was nothing short of wonderful."

Jeff touched her hand as it lay on the covers and promised, "Regina, I'll have the film developed and printed. You just be quiet and get better soon. Your doctor and hospital bills will be paid. If what you did helps to identify the people behind this scheme—whatever it may be—you'll be granted a substantial reward.''

Regina nodded and closed her eyes. The terror had left them, but she was still suffering from pain and the shock brought on by the attack. She needed rest.

''I'll stay here,'' the baron said. ''I'm not going to leave her until she is much better and I feel she is safe.''

''We'll have the police state it was just a robbery,'' Jeff said. ''Let them think they got away with it. Come along, Lydia. It'll be dawn soon and tomorrow we may both need our wits about us.''

Lydia nodded, bent down and kissed Regina again. She touched her cheek to the baron's and then followed Jeff out of the room. Outside, the carriage was waiting for them.

Lydia said angrily, ''That was a terrible thing they did to Regina.''

''But she outsmarted them. They must have been satisfied that the film in the camera was the roll that had been exposed. You must remember, the cameras Regina used are unusual, and the kind of thugs sent to her apartment wouldn't know anything about them except to expose any film they discovered.''

The carriage paused at Regina's apartment house. Jeff stepped out of it and paused to look about carefully. There seemed to be no one watching, so he opened the mailbox, found the film and hurried back,then gave the driver the name of Lydia's hotel.

''I won't leave you alone until we discover who and what is behind this. I'll sleep on the sofa since you must be exhausted. The devil with tradition.''

''Thank you, darling. I am upset and more than a little afraid. Will the pictures help, do you think?''

''I've little doubt about that. I'll send them to Cannes by special messenger and in twenty-four hours, we'll know. They may help once this is finished with or if those responsible manage to slip away, at least we'll have some kind of a lead. I'm very grateful to Regina, as my superiors will be, also.''

Lydia went to sleep immediately, but Jeff was not so fortunate. His long frame didn't fit the sofa and after twisting and turning, he got up, moved softly into the bedroom and slipped in beside her. She moved into his arms and he gathered her close, holding her tenderly, his lips touching her cheek. His closeness wakened her and her arms went around him. Her lips sought his and their desire, as on the night before, mounted. She received him eagerly and, when their passion was spent, went to sleep still in his arms.

The next morning, he awakened her, speaking her name softly. "Sorry, darling, but I'm not leaving you here. Time to get up. I've already bathed so the bathroom is yours. I'll order breakfast."

She gave him a hasty kiss and slipped from his arms with a mischievous laugh when he tried to make more of it. She bathed hastily and chose a simple skirt and blouse. It was easy to move about in, and she sensed their day would be busy. She thought of Regina and the baron, who had spent the night with her. His anguished face, when he saw her swollen and distorted features, was evidence she was firmly entrenched in his affections. Much more than a passing fancy. Lyida knew that Regina cared about him, but she hadn't been certain how the baron regarded Regina. After last night, there was no question of it.

Angelina was in the parlor when Lydia entered it. She refused to join Jeff and Lydia for breakfast, sensing that they really desired to be alone together.

They wasted no time eating and then took a carriage directly to the hospital. It was late morning, and the baron, red-eyed from lack of sleep, signaled for them not to speak when they entered the room. Regina was sound asleep. He led them down the corridor to a small conference room.

"She is doing splendidly," he reported. "There are no broken bones, only all those lumps. If I ever find the men who did this . . . ." He shrugged and made a gesture of despair. "What can I do? Run for the police? I am too old and too small to look for personal revenge, but I swear I shall see that those responsible are punished somehow."

Jeff said, "You, and Regina, too—have one consolation.

332

The crooks didn't get what they were after. I'm sure the pictures are going to help. I've sent them to Cannes by special messenger."

"When?" Lydia asked in surprise.

"I took care of it when I went down to order our breakfast," he replied.

"What can we do now?" she asked. "We've no idea what they will do, nor even when."

"At least we can guess where. They'll be at the casino, perhaps this afternoon, maybe not until tonight. Baron, you've done more than your part. Stay with Regina, just in case these devils return after realizing they didn't succeed in robbing her of what they wanted."

"Tell her we wish her a quick recovery," Lydia said.

"She'll be pleased you came," he told them, managing a smile.

Lydia and Jeff left the hospital and were driven to the beach. It was almost midday and there were only a few bathers swimming in the water. They strolled along the beach until it became too warm, and then returned to the casino where it was cooler and quite comfortable in the lounge.

Their presence was reported to casino officials, who came to assure them that the casino was peaceful and that nothing out of the ordinary had happened. It wasn't until dinner time that Lydia became aware of a rising excitement at the gaming tables. She and Jeff made their way to where a crowd was assembled, growing larger every moment.

"It's Drury," Jeff said. "I didn't even see him come in. He must have been here before we arrived."

"He must be winning," Lydia said. "The way the crowd acts, it seems the word has gone out, too, because people are streaming into the casino."

Jeff and Lydia gently forced their way through the crowd around one table, until they were close enough to watch. Drury had his back to them, so he was not aware of their presence. Not that it would have made much difference, for he was winning large sums and making very substantial

333

bets, right up to the table limit.

From time to time he would lean over to Madelaine, the blond girl, and consult the notes she had previously made. Then he would bet heavily. The croupier signaled someone and an official appeared promptly. Drury made another large bet, won it, and a black shroud was brought to signify he had broken his first table.

Drury gave a shout of exultation and promptly moved to another table. The crowd surged after him.

"Jeff, what's going on?" Lydia asked, startled by what had occurred.

"He's certainly running a winning streak."

"He keeps referring to the notes the girl is holding."

"I've noticed. Either he has developed a system or he wants to give the impression he has. I don't know which."

"Can he be cheating in any way?"

"Not in any way we can detect now. But if he keeps winning all day and night, if he breaks the bank as that Englishman did, then what these crooks are after is well on the way to being accomplished. Drury can win a million American dollars if this keeps on. If it's crooked, be assured he won't stop."

"Shall we do nothing except observe?" Lydia asked.

"For now, that's all. We have to see this through. Once Drury is finished we can move, but not until then. We mustn't give away our suspicions."

Lydia looked bewildered. "You don't mean we're to cheer should he break the second table."

"That's exactly what I mean," Jeff replied calmly.

"I'll do my best, but it'll be an awfully hollow cheer."

Twenty

By suppertime Drury had cleaned out another table, so two were now shrouded. That evening the restaurants did very little business. Word had gone out and every visitor to Monte crowded the casino. The heat became stifling, even though all means of ventilation were utilized, with doors and windows opened wide. The cool Mediterranean breezes had little effect on this sweltering crowd.

Drury was on his third table and doing well. He did lose and often a very large amount, but his winnings nevertheless kept mounting. No one had a really accurate idea of how much he had won.

Jeff and Lydia managed to get close enough to Drury at the third table to find it possible to glance at the notebook the girl held, the one that Drury kept consulting. It seemed to consist of columns of figures.

Drury, sweating profusely, looked up as the croupier tossed the ivory ball and his eyes met Lydia's. He broke into an expansive smile.

"I'm going to make some big news for you, Lydia. Biggest since the time that cockney broke the whole bank. I'm going to break it, too."

She managed to return the smile. "I wish you luck. I'll get a fine story out of it."

"Believe me, you will. I've got a feeling. What do you think, Mr. Marcus?"

"It was done once before," Jeff replied amiably enough.

"I suppose it can be done again, but you're still a long way off."

Drury winked, reached out and patted the book in the hands of the blonde. "Keep watching. I say I'll do it and I will. Cheer me on, Lydia. This will make a bigger story than the other one. Author writing a book on Monte learns how to break the bank. Be sure to include that. I only wish I was back in the reporting business so I could write the story."

Someone mentioned the fact that he'd won again. He turned his attention to the table and raked in the counters. He flashed another smile at Lydia before turning back to make another bet.

"What do you think, Jeff?" Lydia asked as they left the crowd around the table and strolled casually about.

"He has no system. The entries in that notebook are fakes. There is no system and nobody can make me believe there is."

"Therefore," she stated with certainty, "Drury is winning dishonestly."

"Either that, or he's having a run of luck just as the other bank breaker had. The difference is, the Englishman didn't claim he had a system. He swore it was only luck."

"I know, he told me. What if Drury does break the bank?"

"If he breaks the bank, he won't be allowed to leave Monte until those wheels are gone over by men more expert than anyone in the casino. They're coming from Nice."

"The wheels were inspected," she argued.

"True, and rather well, too, but there is always a chance that we didn't look quite far enough. By tomorrow we'll know, because it looks as if Drury intends to gamble steadily until he does break the bank."

They wandered out of the building and into the warm sunlight, continuing on along the garden paths.

"What about the roulette wheels I discovered aboard the Duprez yacht?"

"All in good time," he said with a smile. "I can't explain

them now, but the answer is coming and soon. What we must do now is wait and see how Drury makes out. He's betting heavier than anyone I've seen play roulette for such a long period of time. Certain facts are beginning to take shape in my mind, but not with enough substance to discuss yet."

"If Drury wins it all, what will he do then? Just leave as quickly as possible? After he's cleared, of course."

"Of course, but not until the casino is positive he didn't cheat."

"Do you know what I've been thinking? It may be so impossible that it's crazy, but we have evidence that the men brought as new guards cannot all be honest,or no attack would have been made on Regina. So, if there are dishonest people among them, perhaps they will see to it that Drury escapes before the wheels can be examined again."

"It's an idea. Well worth thinking about, but if they try it, there's going to be a miniature war. The Monaco police are already alerted. Interpol has men covering the exits, too. Whatever this is, it happens to be very big time and has to be crushed before someone else gets the same idea, polishes it a little better and tries again. It has to be exposed as much as possible. I realize now that's where you fit into this whole thing. You can do it in your newspaper and in papers all over the world."

"Jeff, do you think that's why they tried to frighten me away? Even tried to kill me?"

"Possibly. We're operating on theory, but that's going to change to fact in just a few hours. I suggest we rest a bit, dress for the evening and have supper."

"I'd like that. Do you think we dare leave?"

"He can't possibly break the whole bank until late tonight at the earliest. Nothing is going to happen until then."

With the help of a greatly excited Angelina, Lydia changed into an evening gown, a simple one in case she might have to move quickly in which case an excess of material would be an encumbrance. She also wore little jewelry, only her engagement ring and a gold bracelet.

337

She found two husky men waiting in the corridor when she left her room. She was startled at first, but they smiled reassuringly and one of them presented evidence that they were from Interpol. Jeff hadn't failed in his promise to keep her guarded.

She found him in the lobby, the baron with him. He, too, was in evening clothes with his blue ribbon stretched across his ample chest. He had apparently rested, for his eyes were clear and his cheeks once again had color. Lydia kissed Jeff warmly and touched her lips to the baron's cheek.

"How is Regina?" she asked.

"She is recovering and much of the pain has eased. They will keep her in bed for two or three more days, but there is no permanent damage."

"Thank heaven for that. Have you heard how Drury is doing?"

"He's going to break the bank around midnight if his luck holds. You never saw so many people in the casino. Jeff, do you think he's winning honestly?" the baron asked.

"No. Do you?"

"I have no opinion. I only wish it was I who had already shrouded three tables and was on my way to kill the fourth."

"Well, when he breaks the bank, we'll be there to watch," Lydia said. "Right now I think supper is as important."

They dined, for a change, at the Hermitage, though Lydia was soon sorry she made the suggestion for the Russians, in their white uniforms, had abandoned the casino to dine there. She was met with a succession of salutes, clicked heels and much kissing of her hand. It was their way of apologizing, but she was still seething over what had happened and though she was polite, her manner was formal.

"They're irresponsible," she commented once they were seated, "and live only for today."

"They may not have many more," Jeff said. "We in Interpol have picked up information that there's great dissatisfaction in Russia and there is bound to be trouble.

However, tonight you may have a problem more trouble-some. Claude is back.''

"Oh, Lord!" she exclaimed. "I couldn't cope with him tonight.''

"I doubt he'll bother you. He's bound to watch the play in the casino.''

"I meant to tell you," the baron said, "Drury has insisted on being paid off as he shrouds each table. He wants only gold and he sends it for safekeeping to the vault in his hotel.''

"Something to keep in mind," Jeff said.

They touched on more theories as they enjoyed their meal, but they didn't dally when it was over, and made their way directly to the casino. They had trouble getting in, so congested was the entranceway, and resorted to using a side door that admitted only officials. They had no trouble there.

Inside, the casino was packed with excited people. Drury was still enjoying his winning streak and, if it kept up, he would soon break the bank. Each time he won, cheers arose from the onlookers. The noise from the excitement made it almost impossible to keep track of his winnings.

The manager, Monsieur LeGrand, and Jeff conferred for a few minutes. After he left, Jeff said, "Everyone's waiting to see what's going to happen when he kills the last table. There may be a near riot, so it's best if we just stand aside. Five minutes after the play ends, the shroud on each table will be lifted, and the best experts in Europe will converge on the tables to examine them.''

"Will Drury be held until that's completed?" Lydia asked.

"Yes, but he won't know it unless he tries to leave." Jeff looked at his watch. "It shouldn't be long now. You can tell by the sudden tenseness of the crowd that Drury must be very close to his goal.''

They waited in a small room off the lobby from which they could watch what was going on without being subjected to the press of the crowd. Darkness had settled in long ago.

339

There would be few people on the streets; everyone was in the casino to watch the second breaking of the bank.

The baron, stifling under his hard collar, excused himself and went outside for some cool air. He wasn't gone very long when he came back, looking puzzled.

"I think you should have a look, Jeff," he said. "There's a funny reddish glow in the sky at the end of the long dock. Way out. It may be a fire, but it's so far away I can't be sure."

"A fire!" Jeff exclaimed in sudden awareness. "That's it!"

One of the guards now rushed in announcing the fire at the top of his voice. "All the yachts are burning! Everything is on fire. It's terrible . . . terrible . . . the harbor is a mass of flames."

The man in charge of security climbed on a chair and waved his arms while he shouted for attention.

"I saw the fire. It must have been started by someone because all the yachts are burning. The casino may be next. Everyone is to leave at once . . . no exceptions. This building will go up like a torch. Leave quietly. Don't rush to the doors. Move quickly, but don't panic. Everyone out."

There were a few brief scuffles at the doors but the guards straightened them out. The casino was almost empty, except for the guards, when Jeff and Lydia made their exit. Behind them the doors were slammed shut by the security people. The crowd was already hurrying down to the harbor for a better view of the flames, or, by a few, in a vain attempt to salvage something from their yachts. An impossibility, for the roaring blaze had jumped from ship to ship. They were moored closely together, and the spread of the flames was awesomely fast.

People were shouting for the fire department to be called. Some just stood there and wept as their lovely yachts became hidden behind the smoke and the fire. Some cursed bitterly about security precautions being so lax.

"Oh, Jeff," Lydia said. "It's awful. It's the worst fire I've ever seen."

Brilliantly white yachts grew black from the advancing flames and then an entire ship became a ball of fire in seconds. There was considerable fuel aboard some of them and this began to explode and add to the flames. The horse-drawn fire vehicles could be heard as they approached, but they'd be able to do nothing, and the shying horses would only add to the confusion. The fire had already spread too far for that.

The whole harbor was alight and masts had now begun to crash. Lydia heard desperate shouts from one group who were afraid there were people on board their yacht, though that proved to be false. Anyone on the ships had left at the first sign of fire, it was found. There would be no casualties.

The fire department pulled up, hoses were unrolled, pumps started, but all that could be done was attempt to save at least part of the docks. These were now burning furiously, making it impossible to even approach the burning ships.

Lydia, caught up in the excitement, and with the instincts of a good reporter, ran down the slope to the waterfront. Jeff slowed her down by seizing her arm.

"There's nothing we can do," he said. "The fire department likely isn't equipped to handle a catastrophe like this. A few million dollars in yachts is going up in flame and smoke."

"All of them seem to be on fire. If only Regina were here with her camera! But how could those fires start at the same time? They couldn't have spread this fast."

Jeff suddenly pointed out, "The Duprez yacht is not involved and won't be, for it's moored far enough away from the others that the flames won't reach it. Any sparks will be put out by the crew."

"Are the fires part of the scheme?" she asked suddenly, turning to Jeff.

"We'll very soon know. But until the fires are out, there's not much we can do. Where's the baron?"

Lydia looked around. "I don't know."

"Probably gone down for a closer look. We might as

well get closer too. It's not often you can see millions going up in smoke."

The fire department, a meager one, arrived and enlisted the help of as many men as it could. The fires began to go out an hour later, but not entirely owing to the work of the firefighters. Most stopped because there wasn't anything left to burn. In torch light, the devastation was complete. There'd been two or three hundred lovely yachts in the harbor at sundown. By sunrise more than half were gone. Only those anchored farther out and those along the strip where the Duprez yacht was tied up seemed to have come through without even a scorch mark.

"Time to go back," Jeff said after a glance at his watch. "Now it's our turn. Stay close to me and keep your eyes open."

When Jeff and Lydia entered the casino, it was still well-lighted, but except for several rather suspicious guards the entire building was cleared of people. Soon they'd begin drifting back. The croupiers would be first, and then the gambling would resume, even indulged in by those who had lost their yachts. Nothing stopped the gambling for very long. Only the magnitude of the disaster of the burning yachts had made them leave the tables.

Jeff spoke to one of the uniformed guards. "Please close and lock all doors. No one other than casino officials is to be allowed in."

"And who is giving such orders?" one of the guards asked with more than a touch of belligerence.

Jeff produced his credentials, a gold badge and an identification card with his photo on it. The guard apologized meekly and ordered the others to obey.

Presently the casino officials joined Jeff and Lydia and with them came the experts on roulette wheels. They went to work, using instruments strange to Lydia. Magnifying glasses were put to use. The guards stood aside. Outside, the gamblers were clamoring to be allowed in. A full hour went by.

Jeff spoke to Monsieur LeGrand. "What happened to Drury?"

"He went out to see the fires also, but first he sent the rest of his winnings to his hotel."

"He didn't break the bank then?" Lydia asked.

"Not yet. But he came very close."

"How much did he win?" Jeff asked.

"We don't know exactly, but it's in the neighborhood of several million francs."

"More than the Englishman won?"

"Much more, and without breaking the bank. We employ higher stakes these days and keep more money on hand."

"Did he insist on payment in gold only?"

"Yes. He said it was easier to change later. He's right, of course. Especially if he intends to take his winnings elsewhere."

The experts joined them. The discussion lasted half an hour and at the end of it one fact was very plain. The roulette wheels were not dishonest. There was absolutely nothing about them to indicate they'd been tampered with.

"And now, M'sieur Marcus," LeGrand asked, "what shall we do? It seems to me there is nothing. Monsieur Drury has won honestly."

"Drury never did anything honestly," Lydia spoke up. "I know him too well. I don't know how he accomplished this, but I doubt very much he won all that money by sheer luck."

"But how do we prove he did not?" LeGrand asked.

"Right now we can't," Jeff said. "Perhaps with daylight, we'll find something. I think you can open the doors now. Even to Drury, if he wants to keep on until the bank is broken."

With the dismissal of the experts and the opening of the casino doors, the bedlam began again. The small hours of the night made no difference. Suddenly the baron joined the small group.

"Where have you been?" Lydia asked. "We missed you."

"I think I must talk to you, Jeff. Where there are no ears close by, except Lydia's and M'sieur LeGrand's."

"This way," Jeff said. He linked one hand under Lydia's arm and the other under LeGrand's. In the private office of the manager, the baron placed Regina's small camera on a table.

"I took this from Regina's apartment before it could be stolen. I also put fresh film in it. Tonight, when the fires sent everyone outside, I didn't go. I concealed myself behind those thick, gold-colored draperies in the casino."

"And you saw what?" Jeff asked eagerly.

"When the building was almost cleared of people, the guards pushed the rest out and closed the doors. Locked them too, except for one rear door through which other guards carried in burlap sacks containing roulette wheels. Everything was ready, special tools were put to use and in an unbelievably short space of time, the roulette wheels were exchanged."

"You have pictures of it?" Jeff asked.

"I don't know. The light was poor, but I did my best. However, I am a witness to what went on."

"Thank you," Jeff said. He glanced at LeGrand. "I would suggest a large pension for the baron. He risked his life to get the evidence we needed."

"There will be no objections," LeGrand said while the baron beamed. "But would you please explain to me what is going on?"

"Of course. The Duprez yacht sailed into the harbor with new, perfectly sound roulette wheels. They were brought into the casino while everyone was drawn to the waterfront watching the fires—which were purposely set, I'm afraid, to get everyone away from the casino. Those who did not leave were forced out by the guards. Incidentally, some of them must be linked to the thieves who set up this entire operation. Now, before Drury leaves with the fortune he cheated you of, the wheels would again be examined and found intact. Drury could then claim he won honestly and you could not refute that claim."

"But we examined those he played on," LeGrand insisted.

"Not as thoroughly as we might have."

"But those dishonest wheels are now gone," LeGrand protested.

"We have to find them," Jeff said. "With daylight we'll begin looking. They may be on the Duprez yacht, but I'd look elsewhere first. Lydia and I will take care of it right after dawn. Baron, you stay here and guard that film. In fact, give it to Monsieur LeGrand to be placed in his safe. Then wait until we come back."

When Jeff and Lydia ventured out into the first light of dawn, everything seemed unreal. Under the coral-streaked sky the harbor was a desolate-looking place. The air was filled with the smell of burned wood. A few people were standing along the far end of the dock, looking forlornly at the remains of their once-beautiful boats, and wondering when the blackened hulls would cool off enough to allow them to go aboard and determine what, if anything, was left.

The Duprez yacht was still a gleaming white, beautiful craft showing no damage. A few small boats further out were apparently not anchored. They were likely those of sightseers from somewhere along the coast.

"We're after the wheels they removed from the casino," Jeff reminded Lydia.

"Would they be on the yacht? Would they take such a chance?"

"It's time," Jeff said, "to take direct action. Under my authority I am going to order Raoul Duprez not to leave the harbor and I'm sending men aboard to search the ship. Then I'm going to leave while they regard me as some sort of idiot who gives them such a chance to be rid of any evidence. Like the wheels, for instance."

"Jeff, if they're desperate enough they may not let us off the yacht."

"Who said anything about you going with me? Remember how we asked the baron to hide in that bathhouse and watch while we boarded the yacht? That's what I want you to do right now, while I go aboard. If the wheels are aboard, and I think they must be, because none of them are aware we know as much as we do—we've solved the case.''

"I'll watch. I won't take my eyes off the yacht. But what if it sails?''

Jeff smiled. "It won't get far. Meet me in the lobby of your hotel.''

"Jeff, don't take too many chances. After the preparations they made and the money they must have spent, they'll be desperate. And don't forget—they must be responsible for the murder of Martel, which makes it all the more important that they get away.''

"I'm afraid we'll never prove the Martel killing unless one of them confesses. I admit, though, that it adds to the seriousness of this crime. I'll give you time to reach the bathhouse. Don't let them see you. Keep an eye out. If you think they've spotted you, walk along the beach and then go back to the casino and do nothing. Promise?''

"I'll do exactly as you say. I'm more worried about you than about myself. Good luck!''

By taking a roundabout route and skirting the row of bathhouses along the beach, Lydia was sure she had reached the last bathhouse without being detected by anyone aboard the yacht. She left the door ajar and discovered she had a full view of the yacht from a distance that enabled her to see everything that went on.

She watched Jeff walk briskly along the dock. Before he boarded the yacht, a crewman blocked his way. Jeff talked to him and presently Claude appeared. There seemed to be some sort of an argument until Claude's father joined them and then the situation grew calmer.

Lydia's anxiety grew as she saw the other crewmen appear and for a moment she worried that Jeff was going to be attacked. But nothing happened. Presently Jeff walked off the yacht and strode quickly along the path to the casino. Now Lydia grew even more watchful, never taking her eyes off the yacht.

Immediately after Jeff reached the casino, no doubt observed by those on the yacht, a small boat was lowered.

There were two men in it. They rowed out a distance of about a quarter of a mile and one of them began dumping large articles into the harbor.

Lydia needed no more. She slipped out of the bathhouse, moved along the same route she'd adopted in coming here and made her way to the casino where Jeff waited, watching the yacht with binoculars from one of the casino windows.

"They rowed out and threw the wheels into the water," she reported. "I'm sure it must have been the wheels."

"That's what I counted on. They took the wheels to the yacht because they had no idea they were suspected. And there's more than the crooked wheels on that ship. We've learned that Drury claimed he was sending his winnings in gold to his hotel vault. What he sent there were sacks containing coins, but they weren't gold. The winnings are likely on the yacht, so that if Drury got into trouble, the gold was safe. We're close to the end of it now."

"How did the Duprez men act when you ordered them not to sail?"

"Oh, they were highly indignant. Claude was a bit more than that. He threatened to kill me if I ever tried to board the yacht again. Raoul, of course, was far more suave. Madame Duprez stayed below."

"Do you think they'll try to sail?"

"Quite likely. Can you recall the approximate spot where they dumped the wheels? If that's what it was."

"I think so."

"We'll find a rowboat and go out there later. Right now we both need rest. Has it occurred to you that we've been up all night?"

"It's beginning to," Lydia admitted wearily. "Please don't do anything rash, darling."

"Well, if I do, we'll do it together," he said with a grin. "This is just about over, I think. Drury will be detained and Duprez won't dare sail. Interpol has men here, and the Monaco police are well alerted. If we find the wheels, it will be over."

"Do you think the harassment I suffered was just to get me out of Monaco?"

347

"I'm sure of it. Including your kidnapping by Claude and your release by one of his crew. It's because you knew Drury. While he covered his association with the Duprez family very well, you would be suspicious of him if he broke the bank. As a journalist, you'd have done something about it, and so they were afraid of you. They couldn't just kill you because the repercussions would have ruined their plans. However, if they made you leave, by the time you caught on to what was going on, they'd have their gold and have faded away."

"To think that people like Raoul and Blanche Duprez could be involved in something like this! Claude, yes. He's unstable, but his father and mother . . . ."

"They prospered with their paper when they first turned it into a scandal sheet. From the profits of that, they acquired other interests. Then the paper started to slip and after that their other businesses fell into dire straits through bad management. They were able to keep their financial reverses quiet, but they needed a large amount of money. This was the way they planned to get it. When that Englishman broke the bank, Raoul Duprez must have based his scheme on that. Trouble is, the Englishman really was lucky. Duprez had to manufacture his so-called luck."

They walked back to the hotel, discussing the various developments.

"We'll soon have word about the pictures Regina took. They'll likely show some of the new guards have criminal records. Maybe the baron's pictures will help, also. I'm not sure about those—they were taken in bad light, but we can hope."

"They must have spent a great deal of money planning this," Lydia observed.

"I'm sure they bought into the small firm that has always manufactured the roulette wheels for Monte. They must also control the agency that supplies the guards. Still, the profits would be tremendous, as we very well know. Drury depended on his reputation as a famous journalist now engaged in writing a book. He would claim to have learned the secret of beating the system and, with his fake figures

348

in that little book Madelaine carried, he might have made everyone believe he did find the answer.''

Back in Lydia's suite, though they shared the bed, they slept out of sheer fatigue. Lydia awakened first. It was mid-afternoon and Angelina's day off, so she selected a perfectly plain dress. By the time she was ready, Jeff had awakened. In a short time he was ready.

They walked down to the beach where a rowboat was tied up at the end of the dock. Jeff looked keenly at the Duprez yacht. There was no one in sight.

''We'll be taking a chance, you know. When I ordered them not to sail and warned I'd be back with a warrant and men to search the yacht, they had to get rid of those wheels in a hurry. The only way to do that was to dump them overboard. So, as I say, there may be some danger.''

''I'm going with you, Jeff. I know the spot where they dumped the wheels.''

He nodded. ''I'll be right back. My men have left a bathing suit in the bathhouse.''

She hugged him and some of the tension left her. He emerged minutes later, wearing a dark blue bathing suit, but he also carried a holstered, long-barreled pistol over his shoulder, which he placed inside the rowboat. He helped her into the little boat, manned the oars and began to row.

''Keep an eye on the yacht. Maybe they won't see us, but if they do and anyone appears on deck, I'd like to know it.''

She guided him to the spot. It was no more than a fifteen-minute row. ''It's around here,'' she said. ''Is this too deep for diving?''

''I don't think so, if I can spot the wheels. If I don't and the whole bottom has to be searched, I'll bring in profes-sional divers, but they wouldn't get here for several days and I don't want to wait. All I have to do is see roulette wheels on the bottom of the ocean.''

Lydia, never taking her eyes off the water, gave a small cry of excitement. ''Jeff . . . look there! Just below the surface. It's one of the burlap sacks in which the wheels were kept. I'm sure that's what it is."

Jeff said, "Keep the yacht under observation. I'll only be two or three minutes. Can't hold my breath any longer than that. Wish me luck, darling."

He let himself roll overside, swam out where the burlap sack floated, swam back and handed it to Lydia. He gave her a confident smile and disappeared. She was watching the yacht. Jeff's plan was bold and dangerous, but she recognized the necessity for it. Duprez must not be allowed to sail and Drury must not leave Monaco. But to prevent either event from happening, some solid evidence was needed and that was what Jeff now sought.

He surfaced once, took a long breath and went down again. Lydia turned her eyes toward the yacht. There were three men standing at the rail, looking her way. One of them raised binoculars and she knew they had been recognized.

When Jeff surfaced, she called out a warning to him. He swam to the boat and she grasped his hand and helped him aboard. Something struck the side of the rowboat.

"Get down!" Jeff said quickly. "They're shooting . . . ."

She heard the whistle of another bullet. Jeff knelt in the boat, holding the long-barreled gun with both hands to aim better. Lydia heard him fire twice. She looked up and saw the man on deck stagger backward. Another man picked up the rifle the wounded man had dropped. He held it high over his head, then threw it into the sea and raised both arms in a token of surrender. She recognized Raoul Duprez.

Police and Interpol agents, who had been alerted to follow Jeff's search through binoculars, now boarded the yacht.

When Lydia and Jeff reached shore, the Commissioner of Police was waiting for them. "We should have moved faster," he admitted. "We didn't think they'd resort to this kind of violence."

"Whom did I hit?" Jeff asked.

"Claude. He's badly wounded, but we think he'll live. He's already been taken to the hospital under guard. We have arrested Drury, Monsieur Duprez and his crew. Now

I would like an explanation of this whole affair, if you please.''

A carriage was waiting and they rode to police headquarters. There Jeff dictated his side of the story to a man who would later transcribe it. Jeff was then told a few details he didn't know.

''The girl with Drury has confessed that it was all a hoax, this system for breaking the bank,'' the police commissioner explained. ''And soon we shall have the wheels that were thrown overboard. No doubt they will reveal the real method Drury used in breaking the bank.''

''I suspect,'' Jeff said, ''that you'll find the partitions dividing each number will vary in height. Each wheel would be different, but Drury would know which of the partitions would accept the ball more often than any of the others. It's done by exquisite work that involves lowering one side of certain partitions. Only an expert could do it, but I'm sure that's what you'll find. Any ordinary examination of the wheel wouldn't show up these defects, but naturally those crooked wheels couldn't be left for a more thorough examination. Hence the fires, set to draw everyone away. The guards then called in the men, probably the Duprez crew members, who changed the wheels. The crooked ones were removed, the honest ones replacing them. If Drury was then accused of cheating, you'd never prove it by the new wheels.''

''Then it is about over.'' The commissioner turned and smiled at Lydia. ''Mademoiselle, I give you permission to make use of this information the moment we have retrieved the crooked wheels from the sea.''

''It will be a better story than the one about the Englishman who was only lucky,'' Jeff predicted.

Lydia had listened without comment, thoroughly intrigued by the facts as they were revealed to her. ''I'm already thinking about how to begin it,'' she said. ''Jeff, may I be excused now? If anything else comes up, please let me know. After all, I am a reporter and what a story this is!''

A week later, Jeff lifted Lydia into his arms and carried her across the threshold of their new villa. He put her down and she moved about exploring the rooms, exclaiming over them, approving the furniture that had come with the purchase of the place. A large bouquet sat on a table in the center of the parlor, sent with the congratulations of Guy Spencer and George Morgan, along with a bonus suitable for both a bride and the story she had submitted, which was an exclusive one appearing only in the Morgan newspaper. There had also been pictures, taken by the baron under Regina's supervision. Those he had taken in the casino proved worthless, because conditions were not right for the film, but what he had witnessed made up a great part of the prosecution of the criminals. Finally, Mr. Morgan had assigned Lydia as a roving reporter, making it easy for her to accompany Jeff if he had to change locations.

Angelina, without Lydia's knowledge, had taken over the cleaning of the villa; it was spotless.

"I've been happy before, but not like this," Lydia told Jeff.

"I know," Jeff said with a smile. "You've written a marvelous story about the whole thing, you've been assigned to Monte for as long as I'm assigned here. The trouble and danger are past. Yes, you have every reason to be happy."

"You're being very silly, did you know that? What's a story, a bonus and an assignment? What's a beautiful villa? Add all those together and it amounts to little, compared to my having you as a husband. Or had you forgotten that?"

He reached for her, lifted her in his arms and kissed her passionately. He had not forgotten.